What It Takes to Get to Vegas

Also by Yxta Maya Murray
Locas

Grove Press
New York

What It Takes to Get to Vegas

YXTA MAYA MURRAY

Published simultaneously in Canada
Printed in the United States of America

FIRST EDITION

Library of Congress Cataloging-in-Publication Data

Murray, Yxta Maya.
    What it takes to get to Vegas / Yxta Maya Murray.
       p.   cm.
    ISBN 0-8021-1642-6
      1. Mexican Americans—California—Los Angeles—Fiction.
  I. Title.
    PS3563.U832W48 1999
813'.54—dc21   98-50766
                                                      CIP

Design by Laura Hammond Hough

Grove Press
841 Broadway
New York, NY 10003

99 00 01 02   10 9 8 7 6 5 4 3 2 1

What It Takes to Get to Vegas

The Fake Saint

*W*e could hear them doing it down the hall. Us and the rest of the world, it turns out, because it was a hot spring night with weather so thick that everyone in East L.A. had left their windows wide open to catch a breeze that might blow in and cut through the molasses air. The house was colored with after-midnight shadows and creeping moonlight, but Mama and Mr. Hernandez were busy whooping and praying as the springs bucked and sang under their bodies, while church-going neighborhood women laid stiff as twigs in their clean clean beds and tried to stuff a pillow inside each ear.

"I know what that is," my sister Dolores said. It was May 1986, and she was eleven then, and I'd just turned thirteen. "I know what they're doing."

I hitched up on my elbows to hear better. Mama was laughing. "No you don't. You're a liar."

"I am not." Dolores's head was under her pillow.

"Liar."

"I do too know." She peeked from under the pillow and shrieked. "They're making sex!"

I looked out the bedroom window. There was the neighborhood pretending to sleep, the black houses like humped giants, the naked trees reaching up the same as praying padres. The red sundown was hid now, nothing left up there but blue moonglow.

Mama's laugh floated into the street, making one of the houses finally flick on its electric eyes.

Señora Montoya, done up in sponge curlers, swung open her front door and threw a witch-shaped shadow on her front porch.

"Putana! Hey, Zapata la putana! Cut out your fucking so we can get some sleep!"

Her yelling made the other mujeres who'd been staring at their ceilings brave enough to switch on their lights and join in on the complaining. Pretty soon we had a row of those cat-eyed monsters staring right at us.

"Lola Zapata! Shut the hell up!"

And Mama, like to answer them, quieted her laughs down into low chuckles, then pitched a wild Siamese howl that must have perked up the ears of every tom for miles around.

*M*ama always was braver and louder in the nighttime, especially when she had her hands on a man. The next morning, after Mr. Hernandez had gone home to his wife, she sat at the kitchen table in a red poly-silk robe that matched her manicure and smoked her second Marlboro Light sort of moody and quiet, like a Mexican Bette Davis but without the bitchy one-liners. She was a beautiful woman. Dark, with good skin and high bones and a mouth that could go without lipstick, but not much of a talker at that hour. I ate my Lucky Charms and Dolores had her Raisin Bran out of the plastic blue bowls we'd bought at our next-door neighbor's garage sale, and we might as well have tried to figure out Mama's thoughts from the smoke signals she was making as expect her to string more than ten words together. Still, even if we threw her simple questions she was too grouchy to give us the answers we wanted: when we asked her right then to take us shoe-shopping over on César Chávez Avenue, she just shook her head no.

"You know I hate that place," she said, then lit up a third cig.

Dolores looked at her. "But my sneakers are busted."

"And I need sandals for summer," I said.

"No."

"Please, okay?"

"Please, Mama?"

"No."

It took us two hours of whining to get her out the door, but as soon as we hit the streets I was happy. Back then I usually liked our town and could sometimes fool myself into thinking I fit in it; I liked walking through it, looking at it, thinking on how far it stretched and what was hid in its four corners.

My piece of east was this big: wide and deep enough to fit a mess of hoboes, boxers, nine-to-fivers, nutso church ladies, trigger-happy con men, knock-kneed Catholic-schoolers, and a handful of sexy-walking women in a space about twenty-five miles back to front. Up on top is our old street, Fisher, a nice stretch of fixer-uppers decorated with dead lawns and chained-up dogs, and to the west there's Eastern Ave where the homeless tip back Bird in the shadow of the 710 Freeway. Down south there's the number streets where the super-low-renters squeeze five or six into kitchenette studios, and then turning to the east is Divine Drive, the richest block in town, where you'll find the church ladies who stay busy barking at their maids and polishing their silverplate.

Some of the biggest action, though, was where we were walking to right then. After Mama got dressed, her, me, and Dolores headed down three blocks until we hit Chávez Ave, which is a straight black line that cuts all the way through the town like the Nile or the Styx, full of beggars and sinners dipping into the waters. César E. Chávez Avenue is that road that's named after el King César with the grapes and the marches. In L.A., there's this funny thing with naming the streets, everybody's got to see their hero up there on a sign like it means something. There's that big stretch of Martin Luther King Avenue by downtown, the Sun Mun Way in Chinatown, even the Anglos got MacArthur Place out in Oxnard. And when the Mexicans made a big enough stink we earned ourselves César Chávez Avenue running from Dodger Stadium all the way down to Monterey Park. Orale, the day they changed it from Brooklyn to Chávez, you'd think that we'd had a Second Coming or something, I remember how there was the biggest parade with the balloons and the beautiful mariachis and the neighborhood people standing out on the corners smiling, but walking there now alongside my silent mama, my sister with her flapping sneakers, and about a hundred neighbors, I knew that the street wasn't special because it got haunted by César's ghost. The place was great because it moved, with these slow-footed viejas gliding back and forth down the sidewalk, a purse snatcher streaking through the crowd followed by three thugs and a cussing churchie, and a couple sweet young things in spikes swaying past the display window showing the leopard prints that were all the rage that season.

Chávez *was* the place for shopping: Anything you needed you could get on the Avenue. Feeling religious? Here on the corner of Arizona was the santos shop run by that spooky Señora Gallegos who'd read your palm for free. Hungry? Right next store was Rudy's Super where you could get the city's cheapest frozen chicken, and across the street Sancho's coffee shop sold two-dollar chocolate malts. Fashionwise, farther down you'd find Carlita's Fashions for sexy-girl dresses and Diamond Jeweler's for your two-carat cubics, but since we needed sneakers and sandals we went to Payless Shoes, where you could get half off on Reeboks and my favorite jelly sandals.

"You coming in?" Mama said, holding open the door.

I went straight for the new arrivals and sniffed at the tangy plastic shoes. Dolores was already by the sportwears. She wound up spending close to an hour trying on all the size-five sneakers until she settled on some white Vans. I picked out a jelly sandal in violet. Even Mama bought this wild pair of five-inch heels in fuchsia which the love-struck shoeman sold to her at an 80 percent discount. She was laughing when she teetered out of there, and was trying out the kind of Mae West walk that a woman can only work on that height heel, when we passed by a couple of Divine Drive churchies wearing the same poodle hairdos and eye-blinding diamonds.

"Ay, look out," one of them said when they saw Mama, "here comes the home wrecker."

That was the Widow Muñoz, a triple-chinned busybody who got the money for her pre-owned-Halston habit from her lawyer husband's estate. I guess she used to be a skinny looker with a lot of legs but by this time she'd turned into a retired matriarch who liked to dress up in name brands and run around judging and nagging everybody to death. The more dangerous poodle was the other one, her best and closest friend in the world as well as her next-door neighbor, Señora Hernandez, who we all called La Rica Hernandez, she had so much money. La Rica was a redheaded, Dior-outlet-wearing Evita Peron wanna-be, not to mention Mama's boyfriend's wife and the unofficial mayor of East L.A. Every big decision went through this woman first—not just where to hold the church bake sales or how many turkeys each family should donate to the homeless come Christmastime, but even what to do about the wayward wife with the gambling problem (she'd cut up all of Lucy Campos's credit cards with her kitchen scissors), or how to punish a borracho ex-husband who'd stopped making his child support payments (her and six friends had gone over to old George Medina's house and carried out all his stereo equipment and his two TVs). I knew La Rica had plans for Mama, too, who hadn't just bedded down her man but didn't care who on this green earth knew about it, either, so I was relieved when she only slowed in front of us, huddled up with her crony, sucked on her teeth, and said: "Get back, putana."

"Nah, you get back, you old bulldog," Mama said.

And then those two made a big show of staring at us sideways and stepping around us like we stank.

Still, relieved or not, I did wish then that I hadn't made us come out there. Of course, I didn't feel like I fit in now, and neither did Dolores, who was pretending not to notice and was staring weird at the display window showing metallic loafers. But what was worse was watching Mama try to walk away from those churchies as though she was a fine señora, and like she didn't hear the Widow Muñoz saying bitch under her breath, because it was a real trick to step ladylike in those new fuchsia shoes. Just as she was trying to walk off without switching her behind, her heel caught in a sidewalk crack, and then there was a god-awful moment when she had to flap her arms around her head, lift up one foot, and balance on the other like a tightrope walker, just so she wouldn't go crashing to the ground. When the churchies finally passed us by she took off those shoes and slipped on her old cheapies, and didn't say one word the rest of the way home.

*M*ama learned that balancing act from all the times she'd got knocked flat on her behind, but when she'd first come out to L.A. from Calexico she could get tripped up pretty easy.

A few hours after we'd run into the churchies she took out some old pictures that she stored in a shoebox and looked at the one a stranger took of her when she'd been here for just two days. She did that sometimes when she got in a funk: sit on the living room floor with a scotch and spread out the snapshots on the carpet and make me and Dolores look at them with her. We didn't mind, though. We liked it.

"Here it is," she said, picking the picture up. She was on her stomach, barefoot, flipping through the old black-and-whites and Kodachromes. "Now don't you think I could have been a Bond Girl? Couldn't you see this honey kissing Sean Connery?"

"Who's Sean Connery?" Dolores asked.

"Sean Connery was a Scottish guy who played Double-Oh-Seven," Mama said.

We just looked at her. She stared some more at the picture.

"But I don't remember ever seeing a Mexican Bond Girl," she said.

I reached out my hand. "Let me see it."

It was my favorite picture of her, and still is, but it took me until I was a grown woman myself to puzzle out the story behind her pretty face. It's a washed-color three-by-four glossy with a white border that's dirtied up with little-girl thumbprints from all the times me and Dolores took it out to look at our red-lipped Mama standing in front of a pagoda and grinning.

She really was something. Just looking at her bubble hairdo and Peter Pan collar you could see that the girl was green. It makes you wonder: How'd a chica like that get on a Greyhound with just sixty bucks, then drive to a town where she didn't even have one tía or abuelito to call?

Well, who knows. And I guess who cares when you got a face like that? What she saw in the mirror must have asked her, Why not you, Miss Thing? Go on and take your shot in the big city, where any pretty sucker can make it, if she lives through it. City's where they got con artists in leather-interior Caddys passing for film-studio money men, and studio men hid up in their high-rises screwing the cherries they promise starring parts to. Not that Mama ever got to set foot in one of the high-rises, although she did wind up seeing her fair share of cowhide backseats. But back then she believed in it, the hands and feet pressed in concrete, the ice-cream counters where you're sure to be discovered while sipping a soda. And so there she was froze in 1967, fresh from the border town and posing outside Mann's Chinese wearing her best Barbarella bouffant and Rita Moreno smile, looking so fine you barely noticed that homemade skirt cut like a lamp shade, the clunker church-sale shoes, the Naugahyde handbag ugly as a dead dog. That takes some talent, too, because those off-the-bus Calexico clothes she was wearing must have stuck out sore in Hollywood. But Mama had what it took for Technicolor, I'd say. She had star quality.

That's what she was going to be. A movie star. Could have been one, too, in another life. She had the knockout body, the husky cigarette voice. Even yard-sale clothes hung neat and tidy off her curves, and she walked slow and swivel-hipped, like she was made of money. She'd learned how to move from watching old black-and-white movies, copied the strut-your-stuff from Grable and Crawford, the slinky-cat from la Superloca Lana Turner, the make-them-cry from Monroe, but she was born with that face pretty enough to make other ladies mad. Same as me. I loved it when people told me I was just like her; I'd run to the mirror and smile at my lashy eyes, black hair, big wide mouth. But when I got older and a little bit smarter, I saw how they didn't mean it as no compliment. Good looks and a trip to Hollywood didn't bring my mama any luck. Didn't get her name on any marquees. Just gave her high hopes and a bad reputation.

Neighborhood folks forever been saying Mama's a putana and even the God-fearing church ladies forget their love-thy-neighbor where she's concerned, but she wasn't nothing but a stripper for a couple years. Before she came to the city she'd been stuck in Calexico, California, the border armpit where all they've got is some cowboy bars, a third-run movie theater, and a fill-'er-up gas station for the blondie surfers passing through on their way to Mazatlán, and it's the kind of two-bit place where Mexican girls work a couple years behind a counter before they squeeze out a six-pack of niños and get old too damn fast. Not my mama, though. After she'd spent her early years feeding up on B-movie dreams she ditched her folks and hopped that Greyhound all the way to Sunset and Vine, looking out for Eastwood and Brando and waiting to get discovered by a big shot director while strolling down the street in her hand-sewn dress.

And why not? Lightning had struck brown girls before. Bet you never knew Rita Hayworth was a hot dish of Spanish rice and beans, and then there's old Dorothy L'Amour, dressed up in that sarong and as dark skinned as an Aztec. It didn't hit Mama, though, and the Boulevard gets dark and lonely if you don't get picked up by that producer right away. She got hungry, then scared, and instead of heading back home she broke down like most pretty and proud things do. Started dancing at the Cathouse, this downtown stripper club, and that's where she finally got famous for a while.

They called her the Spanish Fly and fools from all over L.A. paid good money to drink watered-down whiskeys and feed her G-string full of dollar bills. She met lots of men that way, had her pick of deep-pocket gangsters who wintered in Palm Springs and boozer CEOs with money to burn. But she wasn't a hustler, at least in the love department. She didn't choose the one who could set her up nice, with minks and penthouses, a

convertible and a checking account. Mama wound up falling hard
for this love-and-leave road boy, a California Mexican trucker
named Eddie D who came by the Cathouse once a month with
roses and poems and a busy way in bed. The man was as fertile
as a field, and seemed marriage-minded. He bought her a powder-
blue suit and kissed her in front of a preacher before he knocked
her up with us, but then one night he said he was taking a haul
of eggs down to Barstow in his eighteen-wheeler and that he'd
be right back in the morning. She never saw him again.

"Mr. Romance," she said now, in our living room. She
was still rustling through the shoebox and she'd picked up his
picture. Mr. Romance was what she always called him. Her voice
when she said it makes you think of burned-black Valentines
and Don Juan devils with slippery hips and toothpaste smiles,
but you wouldn't know he was a playboy just to look at him. The
man was, to put it plain, ugly. The picture she held up showed
a guy with a crop of black curls and a face that was kind of
crooked in the nose and jaw; he looked like an old boxer who'd
took too many hits.

She was quiet for a minute, tapping her ash into a sau-
cer. "Wonder where Mr. Romance is now, eh? Probably drunk.
Or dead, maybe. I bet he died in that damn truck of his."

I took the picture from her and looked at my dad's busted
mug. I knew Mama was wrong but I kept my mouth shut. I was
sure Eddie D was still trucking through the dust bowl. I knew
this because I'd once seen him alive, right on our doorstep, but
I'd never told her or Dolores nothing about it.

It'd happened the year before. He'd come by the house
after school, dressed up in a red tie and black pants and carrying
cellophane-wrapped flowers, but I'd seen that picture of him so
many times I knew who he was right away.

"Your mama home?" he'd said, then stepped back to give me the once-over. "Jesus, little Rita. Just like her. You should be proud you look so much like your mama. What about your sister, eh? Dolores? And Lola? Lola girl, you in here? Surprise, surprise. It's your old lover man come back for a visit, baby. Sweeping you off your *feet*."

The dusk was coming in through the door, but Mama had still been at work. She'd lost her Spanish Fly moves when she birthed Dolores, and had been short-order cooking at Denny's ever since. I knew she'd bust a vein if she came home and found the man who'd put her behind that stove standing on her steps like a salesman and asking nosy questions. And I didn't like him much myself, either. He was peeking past me into the house, seeing the rat-colored rug, the flower wallpaper losing its stick, and when he stepped up close to get a better view I saw how his suit was patched and he was starting to sweat. So no way. Even at my age I could tell he was a con man, and I wasn't going to let him weasel in here and try to razzle-dazzle Mama and Dolores with his slick talk and his rayon tie and his supermarket roses. Before he could push his way through I opened up the screen, leaned over, and spit on his suede shoes, which were pinhole wing tips with rubber soles.

"Go away," I hissed, wiping my mouth. "Get out of here. We all hate you." And then I shut the door on his wide eyes, bolted up the locks, and sung the theme song to the telenovela *Maria de Nadie* until I heard him shuffling away.

"Shoot," Mama said now. "He sure was a charmer, though." I could tell she was feeling a little bit of the scotch because of how hard she concentrated on the picture, and then how she stared steady and not blinking at my sister. I put the picture back in the box. I was glad I'd never told her. In that whole year he'd never come back, which was proof that he wasn't nothing but a wolf in bargain clothes, anyways. And we had enough of those fools running around already, didn't we? Hoosh, our place was a halfway house for every dog in town who had an itch. That's why I kept my meeting Eddie D a secret. We didn't need another no-good jitterbugging in the bedroom and eating every damn thing in sight.

Since Eddie D had split on Mama, she'd shacked up with every kind of hombre there is to try and forget him. We'd never know who'd show up in the kitchen at seven in the morning, dressed in his boxers and rattling through the fridge, looking for the coffee, coughing after his first cigarette. Could be the grocer, the mailman. The janitor from across the street. Only Mr. Hernandez, who worked in a bank, was more regular than most—every few months like clockwork. She never let him or anybody else stick around for long, though. When a few weeks had passed she'd get bored and snappy, start humming show tunes, and then buy a new pair of high heels. After that it wasn't too long before she'd shoved the poor bastard out the front door, got dressed, and set out to the Pink Lady, where she liked to get smooth-talked by the barflies. Those nights she would usually come back with a stranger, and Dolores and me would wake up to the sound of her stumbling drunk in the dark.

But you didn't need no Ph.D. to know why Mama and her men never worked out. All you had to do was look at her right now, leaning her elbow up on the coffee table and staring at Dolores. She couldn't really forget her first love, even after a hundred one-night stands. Not with my sister around, looking like she does.

Mama scooted over to her and cupped Dolores's chin in her hand.

"Aw honey," she said. "You're so pretty, just like your daddy."

Dolores shook her head. "I'm not pretty."

Mama was right in one way, though. Dolores was short and thick and crooked with a heap of curly hair, and sitting there, surrounded by those old pictures and watching her and Mama sprawled out on the rug and smiling at each other, I thought again about that flimflam man who'd stood on our porch and tried to hustle his way into the house. It was true—my sister was a copy of him: She'd been a chip off the old blockhead ever since she was born.

But only on the outside.

*T*here was once a miracle in our neighborhood. It happened a few months after our trip to Payless for summer shoes. A sharp-dressed stranger named Mr. Quiñones had moved a couple blocks down from us three months before, and by the fourth or fifth day we'd had him figured for a check-washer or a drug dealer because he didn't seem to do anything for a living besides sit on his front porch in zoot-suit pants and an undershirt and toss back beers. He seemed harmless enough, though. Quiet. Pretty much kept to himself.

But that Saturday morning we all woke up breathless to the sound of that Mr. Quiñones hollering out the rosary, and when we looked out our window we saw him running down the street barefoot with the whites of his eyes showing and his bathrobe flapping wild behind him.

"HAIL MARY FULL OF GRACE," he's yelling.

Afterwards we heard what happened. Mr. Quiñones, never mind the porch beers, called himself a religious man. He told anybody who'd listen he took a plaster Mary with him everywhere he went, so as to do his prayers. But that morning, when he'd gone to kneel, confess, and kiss the cross, he'd looked up and instead of staring into Her all-forgiving but chalk-dry face, he saw how She was crying real living tears.

Well, all us had to go and check that out, of course. It isn't every day you hear about a miracle north of the border.

So we went. On Sunday Mama pulled out her finest black head lace and made me and Dolores wear our blue dresses and white tights, but we didn't get one block down before we were already standing in line. Every mujer, niño, and even a number of dragged-along men from the neighborhood had skipped church to see the sign and bring an offering. There was old Widow Lopez with the dead arm that curled like a bird claw, and next to her was the half-deaf Widow Perez. Farther up, I saw the neighborhood crazy Panchita Sanchez wearing a bath-robe and chain-smoking Lucky Strikes, and Lupe Salinas the beautician with the red beehive. And up in front the huge-butted Divine Drive ladies—La Rica Hernandez, the Widow Muñoz, and their friend Señora Miranda—were busy flashing their quar-ter-pound cubics and smacking at their giggling, hiccuping hijas so they'd hush.

We all marched up slow, past the sinking houses and winking cats curled up on the driveways. Past the chain-link fences that had split in half and rusted gold-red. When we got closer I saw Mr. Quiñones standing in front of his open door waving so folks would go inside, and there were viejas spilling out that same door waving their hankies to the sky and bawling and hollering like TV Baptists. Then it was our turn. We got one minute each. Mama wanted to go in alone and when she came out she was whooping into her black lace the same as the viejas. Next it was me and Dolores, and we went in together, holding hands, to get blessed by la Virgen.

I'd never seen nothing like Her before.

She was three feet tall and standing in a back corner of the messy kitchen, all white and gold and flickering shadow, with Her eyes closed, Her head bent, Her stone-pale hands stretching up. The shades were down and She was circled by glowing candles, so it looked like She was swimming in sun-colored water. She was surrounded by a truckload of presents, too: gold- and pink-wrapped boxes done up with satin ribbon, fruitcakes, bottles of tequila, jars of red jam, a dish of cold tamales, and, most of all, money. There were lots of fives and tens stuck between Her white fingers, but some of the rich churchies had left crisp fifties and even hundreds spread out at Her feet, anybody could guess who. Me and Dolores just had one dollar each. I reached up to give Her mine and that's when I felt it, what we'd come for. Mary's hard cold face was leaking warm water and it spilled on my skin.

"Dolores! She's crying!"

I squatted down, trying to remember my Hail Marys, but my heart was beating triple time from the hand of God reaching into this little kitchen and all I could remember were the words to "Feliz Navidad." If He could make plaster of paris cry, what else would He do? Turn me from flesh and blood into salt? I was whooping now myself the same as Mama, the same as the viejas, and trembling all over with the holy fever and religion. Dolores was calm, though. She held on to her dollar and stepped up to la Virgen, pressing her face close to Her face like she was trying to breathe in Her living breath or hear the Word whispered from Her mouth, but then she turned to me and started saying something that didn't make sense.

"What?"

"It's fake. Look at these holes in the eyes where the water's coming out."

I stayed where I was, blinking in the glowing dark. Dolores was fussing around now, digging under the presents, poking behind the Mary. Then she stooped down and snooped under towels thrown on the floor, and saw how they weren't dumped there careless, but on purpose, because they were hiding a green snake that was crawling under the back door.

She picked it up. It was a garden hose, hooked up under the hollow Mary and pumping the miracle tears from a backyard faucet.

Mr. Quiñones started calling to us. "Okay, girls, let's get a move on in there."

Dolores covered up the hose again quick, then looked at me with jumping eyebrows.

"We've got to tell somebody," I whispered. "*You* got to tell them."

She reached up to snag my dollar from between Mary's fingers. "Yeah, I'll tell Mama."

But when we went back outside she put the dollars in her pocket and watched the believers carrying on like a holy circus full of sister freaks speaking in tongues and shuddering with the faith. The Divine Drive ladies fell all over each other with the weepy hugging and scripture quoting, even while their hijas bit their nails and their husbands stuffed their hands in their pockets and shot looks at each other. The viejas had lost their heads, too, because Widow Perez started yelling I CAN HEAR YOU at the Widow Lopez, who stretched out her claw and hollered that she was healed. Even two clear thinkers like Lupe and our mama were shaking like grass while Panchita Sanchez smoked furious, grabbed hold of Mr. Quiñones, and sang out "What a Friend We Have in Jesus."

Then Mama looked up at us and smiled beautiful. She held her hands out and we ran to her, hiding our faces in her skirt.

"Did you see it?" she asked. I held my breath.

Dolores sucked on her lip for a minute, then nodded her head and shut her eyes. I closed my eyes too and smelled Mama's warm skin, and then both of us listened to the sound of Mr. Quiñones calling out to the new crowd of suckers lining up, Come in, come in, come on in.

*L*ater I asked her, "Why didn't you say nothing?"

We were in the front yard, watering the lawn. Dolores put her thumb over the hose mouth and sprayed a rainbow over the grass.

She shrugged. "I don't know." She kept watering while I ran in and out the rainbow. She did all the grass and the gold-brown hedges and even sprinkled the neighbor's dirt lawn. Then she turned off the water and stood there with her toes turning in and looked at me. "Because they'd be sad?" she said.

I nodded. "Yeah, they would have been sad you told them."

But they found out anyways. The next week one of the husbands got up the nerve to tell their wife that the whole thing was a phony, and so La Rica Hernandez and her army of Divine Drive ladies went and busted up the house with broom handles and baseball bats and ran Mr. Quiñones out of town.

He still made out pretty good, though. Later we put our minds to it and figured he must have robbed the neighborhood of more than two thousand dollars, not counting the dollar of mine that Dolores had been smart enough to snatch back from that Virgin's cold, stiff, thieving fingers.

Cigarettes

*S*sssst, girl! Check out these missies just hanging out on the curb as la-dee-da as can be, twirling their Dippity-Doo curls around their fingers, laughing behind their hands, showing off their look-alike flower print dresses and high-shine Mary Janes and them new glitter socks that cost two dollars extra. Why don't you go on over there and give one of those fools a nice hard kick? Go and pull the tail on one of them donkeys, hermana! I dare you, eh? I'll give you a dollar.

I was saying something like this to Dolores while we waited on Chávez for the school bus to take us to our first day of class. I was starting the tenth grade but I was more in the mood to set the school on fire. To our left, the neighborhood boys were busy boxing each other, like Jose Mendoza, a kid from over on Fifth Street, and Pedro Paredes, a runt with a nearly blind eye that he'd messed up while trying to make a bomb the year before. To our right was a clump of in-crowd chicas who stood by the curb, whispering into each other's ears and trying to make eyes at the scufflers. From the bench where we were sitting we could just see the backs of these chicas' heads, which were mostly done up in complicated hairdos—French braids strung through with ribbon, long crimped waves, ponytails tied with glass-balled elastic bands or clipped with shiny barrettes, except for Gloria Sanchez's, whose plain loose hair told you that she didn't have a mama who fussed over her in the morning with a can of Aqua Net and drugstore accessories.

The reason why I was muttering to Dolores on that bench instead of flirting on the curb was because none of those girls would so much as give us one word, ever since Veronica Hernandez, La Rica Hernandez's only pup, had spread the news she'd heard at the dinner table, which was that Lola Zapata and her two daughters were a family of man-stealing, VD-carrying trash. That is, none of those blue-blooded prudes with their silver first-communion crosses and their four-dollar socks would say boo to us except for Gloria, the only popular girl in school who'd stoop down low enough to pitch us a hello sometimes, like she did right then.

She turned around and grinned when she saw us. "Hello, Rita; hello, Dolores."

"Hey, Gloria," I said.

"How's it going?"

Dolores tugged on a piece of hair. "Okay."

Gloria turned back around and started laughing at Jose, who was thumping on his chest and saying to Pedro, Go ahead, man, take a shot at me, fool, take your best shot.

Gloria was a weird sort of bird. She was a number street girl who had to be happy with Goodwills and Salvation Armys the same as us, so she wasn't official uppercrust. She had another bad strike against her, too, which was that her mama was Panchita Sanchez, the neighborhood crazy. Panchita Sanchez was a nicotine junkie and a nympho. Not exactly a loose woman, like Mama; she was more of a looneytune who just didn't have enough sense to keep her mouth shut, or her legs, either. Panchita liked to wander the streets wearing nothing but a bathrobe and a wild pile of hair, and flirt weird with any man she saw by hooking her arm round his arm then promising him a blow job or worse for the price of a packet of Lucky Strikes. Usually the dudes laughed and brushed her off their elbows, but since Panchita was still on the good side of thirty and nice-looking, with Chinese eyes and brown beanstalk legs peeking raunchy out of that bathrobe, lots of times the men—hardworking eight-to-eight men, Sunday church men, family men—took one look at her cinnamon knees and dirty feet and that pink tongue slipping over her lips, and hightailed it to the drugstore.

You can just imagine her reputation. Las mujeres couldn't say her name without screaming, and when the men were out walking with their families and saw her weaving down the street their faces would turn the color of fresh liver. Most of them wanted to see her dead and buried, or at least behind bars, so every couple months a wife called the cops and Panchita wound up in the boobyhatch again, where she'd try to fuck nurses and doctors and janitors for those famous cigarettes, and Gloria and her abuela would always go downtown and beg the pencilpushers to set her free one last time.

It was a miracle that all that shame didn't stick on Gloria, the poor thing. That's what everybody called her. Poor ugly good-hearted Gloria. She didn't seem to have any of her mama in her, either the pretty or the bad. The girl was skinny as a crane and with the same hooked beak for a nose. She'd been born with knees that stuck out bony instead of peeking out cute from under the hem of her dress, and flat pancake feet that would never fit inside stylish shoes when we got older—the platforms, the spike heels, the sexy cap-toed slingbacks—but belonged in rubber-soled ortho sneakershoes with white laces.

Still, Gloria was smart. She must have looked at the rich churchies with their fourteen-karat-gold St. Sebastian medals hanging off their throats and her own mama smoking those hard-earned cigs and figured out that her best shot at making good in this town was becoming a Bible thumper, and so she went and did it, she hatched herself out a brand-new egg. Did the padre need help at the soup kitchen? There she'd be, wearing a hair net and spooning out slop. Baby need a sitter? She'd do it for free, and teach the little bastard both fingerpainting and how to say his ABCs in one afternoon. Pretty soon the padre took notice of her, and then, of course, so did the Divine Drive churchies, and they started pressing her on to their hijas, the same in-crowd chicas who hated us so bad. And you had to give her credit, because Gloria knew how to play that game too. She took on their supervirgin act and did it even better than them. She never teased a boy, never mind let one touch or kiss her. She walked with the same knock-kneed stride as those candy-asses, too, and even agreed with every tiny-brained thing they said— except when it came to me and Dolores, because, I guess, we all came from the same side of the fence.

So now she was powwowing with that Veronica Hernandez and Frida Muñoz, a ninth-grader who'd smiled tight-lipped ever since I'd cracked her front tooth for calling Dolores a wetback, but when the richies started sneaking us looks and giggling, Gloria shook her head and said shut up loud enough for us to hear.

Dolores was sitting next to me on the bench, hunching inside her clothes.

"What do you think they're talking about?" she asked.

There was a hole in my sock. I bent down and pinched it closed. "Shoot. They're talking about us, what else?"

That's when the bad thing happened. I was so fixed on hiding my sockhole from those girls that I didn't hear how a hush had spread over the bus stop until a shadow fell on my foot. I thought it was Jose or Pedro trying to show me their muscles but when I looked up I wasn't staring at a pug nose. I was looking into the sick, sharp-boned face of Carlos "the Bull" Guerrero, an ex–Golden Gloves champ and onetime pro contender who'd had his heyday in the early sixties, when he'd won an undercard match in Las Vegas, which, as everybody knows, is la crème de la crème in terms of boxing locales, I think even better than the Garden or Atlantic City because from what I've seen in magazines it's got more of the pizzazz—classier hotels, hoochier showgirls, meaner mobsters, and jackpots just busting out from slot machines everywhere you look. Anyway, boxing is big, see, in East L.A., and with those credentials alone Carlos the Bull was still sort of a hero around these parts, even though a whole lot had changed for him since the sixties. In other words, he wasn't doing so good, because from all the hits he'd took to the head he'd lost like a hundred points on his I.Q. and besides that he'd took to drink and chasing jailbait girls, and what that meant is that when any of the mamas saw him wandering around in his twelve-year-old suits they'd grab their daughters' hands and run right home, except there were no mamas around right then and there he was standing right in front of me.

"Go away," Dolores said. "You get out of here!"

But he wasn't looking at her, he was eyeballing *me* something strange. And the Bull, he would have been handsome except for the booze; he looked a little like Elvis after he'd been dead a couple days. His eyes were sleepy, with lashes as long as a girl's, and he stared down and smiled. I stared back hypnotized until I remembered everybody else. Jose and Pedro had stopped boxing and were looking at us sideways. Veronica and Frida had dropped their jaws and Gloria was raising her eyebrows, and I liked it. Maybe this guy was a has-been, but he was still a fighter and famous enough to shut those girls up.

"Hi," I said.

"Hi." His grin got wider. Everybody was still watching. He started to dig under his coat and took out a cracked pack of cigarettes, tapped a long white one out, and held it elegant between two fingers. "You got a light?"

I said no and a laugh came bubbling out of me, but I kept my eyes fixed on his. My legs were jumping all by themselves. My shoes were tapping on the ground. Carlos the Bull took a puff off the cigarette even though it wasn't lit and winked at me.

"You smoke, baby?"

"Sometimes," I lied. I shrugged my shoulders casual but my knees were still jittering.

I heard Dolores clicking her teeth inside her head. "No you don't." She bit her thumb. "She don't smoke," she said to him.

But he didn't care. He leaned over, close, closer, then close enough to touch, always smiling. The smell of him was a bad secret I didn't want to know, skunky and private, nasty not-washed naked, and it made my eyes water. But I stayed put, even when he reached out his hand and gave me the cigarette, the one he'd put in his own mouth. "Well then here, beautiful," he said, and he sounded smooth as a television lover.

I took it. The tip was wet. The chicas were whispering again. He took his hand then and put it on my knee and squeezed, making sex sparks shoot up my thigh and my eyes water more so that I was crying. Dolores was yelling Stop it now and trying to pull off his hand but it had got glued there, and Gloria was yelling something too but her girlfriends held her back by the elbows, and the boys ran up and pulled on his coat, while I'm looking back at the Bull's happy weird face and feeling his hand there where it shouldn't be.

The bus came then and I guess I got saved by the driver, Mike Dominguez, who'd been a no-talent lightweight five years back but was still strong enough to warn off a fifty-year-old ex-contender. Mike did it respectful, because of who the Bull used to be, by tapping him on the shoulder and telling him it was time to go. The Bull's mouth wobbled, but he didn't take his hand off my knee and Mike had to shove him away. He didn't get scared, though; he stood in the street with his hand still cupped from my thigh.

We piled into the bus, all stomping shoes and swishing hair. Mike barked Sit down at us. The boys were going on about how far the Bull had fallen since his 1961 Vegas win, but the chicas were making mouths at me. I didn't mind them. My thigh was tingling. I turned around to look out the rear windshield and saw him still standing at the stop, watching us drive off. He saw me watching him, too, because right before we turned the corner, he waved, and then for some reason, I waved back.

"What are you doing?" Dolores asked. She reached up and twisted the skin on my arm.

I turned back around and looked straight into the pop-eyed faces of those girls. Gloria asked me if I was okay, but the other two had squinty red mugs on and I could tell they were wishing me a pretty piece of evil. Veronica was bugging at one thing in particular, which was the cigarette I still held in between two fingers like Carlos the Bull had showed me.

"Slut," she said. It was the first time anybody ever called me that.

"Shut up," Dolores started yelling.

Frida bobbed her head up and down. "It's true!"

"I said shut up!"

"She's a slut and you're an ugly face. Fatso!"

Mike hollered Settle down at us over his speaker, Pedro jumped out of his seat and yelled Bitch fight! and Dolores was crying and trying to catch her breath, but the commotion didn't quit until Gloria stood up in her seat and said, in a quiet voice, "Stop it." And because she was the soup kitchen girl and the part-time saint who taught the babies the alphabets and could charm not just a priest but their own water-walking mamas, Veronica and Frida did just that.

Dolores's shoulders were shaking. I wanted to cry then, too, because Gloria stood up for me. But I knew I couldn't in that company.

It hurt the other two not to say anything. Gloria sat down and Frida started sucking on her hand. I could see Veronica trying to cuss at me using ESP. But I didn't gloat. I didn't give them a taste of what they'd just been rubbing my nose in. I sat back in my seat with my feet still tapping uncontrollable on the floor, feeling sexy, sick, and thankful while I watched the neighborhood rushing past. I was still holding that cigarette and I put it in my pocket, kept peeking over at Gloria, and in the next five minutes my heart flipped over. I was hoping hard that her and me would get to be friends now; all of a sudden I was like in love with her. I planned on how I could do her hair, and how me and Dolores could eat lunch with her, instead of always grubbing alone. I imagined how the three of us could be kind of a club, how I could steal her away from the other girls. I didn't tell Dolores my plans, though, because she'd gave herself a bad case of the hiccups. So I fingered that cig in my pocket, leaned on my sister's jerking shoulder, and smiled out the bus window until we got to school.

*T*wo weeks after Gloria stood up in her bus seat for me I was looking at lipsticks in a shop on Chávez called Carnival Liquors. Carnival was owned by a dude named Mr. Dennis, a holdout Anglo with Einstein hair and horse-sized dentures who bragged about being an Eastelayer since the 1930s. Mr. Dennis liked to tell his regulars about how every kind of junkie and gangster had tried to rob him upwards of sixty times in all those years, but that they'd never got lucky because of the trusty old 12-gauge he kept hid under the counter, only a couple of inches from his trigger finger.

I don't know if I believed all his tall tales—oh for sixty would be some kind of record. I did see that 12-gauge once, though. One day some neighborhood tuffs came swashbuckling into the store, knocking over the candy cart and stuffing bottles under their jackets, and Mr. Dennis took out his shotgun and started polishing it with a rag as slow and easy as could be. He even whistled! A mournful tune, the kind you'd expect to hear off the lips of a cowboy. And wouldn't you know it but those pirates put all the booze back and picked up the candy and scrammed out the door before he could finish his song?

I just loved old Carnival. Besides the shotgun sideshow, you could get anything you wanted there at Mr. Dennis's sky-rocket prices. Talk about a liquor store, the man carried everything from barrel-aged Daniel's to bubbly Cold Duck to a quart of screw-top Thunderbird for three-fifty that was popular with economy borrachos. More than that, though, he stocked real kid candy like chewy green-apple tarties and chocolate peanut clusters, plus blue Tampax boxes for girl emergencies, brown-wrapped nudie magazines, hot dogs turning under heat lamps, Cover Girl and Maybelline cosmetics, and one whole row that had nothing else but cigarettes—filter, nonfilter, menthol, low-tar, superskinnies, fat Paraguayan cigars, even nicotine patches for the quitters.

It's those cigarettes that burned me a trail of trouble, although I'd gone in to Carnival that day to buy some makeup. Mama didn't like me wearing any at that age, but I was already painting up plenty, with foundation, eyeliner, blush, and a quarter can of extrahold hair spray a day, and while I stood in the store choosing between a Jungle Red and Frosty Peach lipstick, I saw Gloria scuttling around the cig row stuffing something square under her ragwool sweater, then walking too fast out the front door. Old Mr. Dennis looked up once from his black-and-white Toshiba on the counter but when he saw who it was he went back to his baseball game because he knew as good as anybody else that Gloria was la niña you let watch the shop, not somebody you'd ever chase after calling Thief!

But I knew what I'd seen, the corners poking under that sweater, the ugly shoes skidding outside. I'd been keeping tabs on Gloria these days, following her around at lunch, passing her notes in math, trying to sit next to her on the bus, and even if she hadn't let me be her best friend yet, I'd learned plenty about her, like how, basically, she was Miss Perfect. She never swore so far as I could see and tutored the Special Needs sometimes after school; this sneaky business just didn't seem like her. I figured I'd tag along and find out what she was doing, and then maybe ask her to my house for dinner this Sunday. So I put the lipstick down and ran out too, to the sidewalk, down the alley, and to the blacktopped parking lot behind the store.

It's funny how one head can hold two faces, even three, all rolled up under the skin just waiting for the right minute to unfold like a flower. It's those kinds of secret faces that I saw blooming on Gloria right then. She was standing by a Buick ripping off the top of the pack of them family-brand cigs and when she lit one up and took a drag, she threw her head back loose and easy and smiled while she breathed in fire, then blew out black clouds French style from her nose. Now, was this the same supervirgin who'd stood up in her bus seat just for me? The same tenth-grader I'd just saw creeping around the store like a crab? Nah, Gloria had cut out her Saint Teresa act for just a second and now she was mama's little girl, a chica who wanted the hot taste of Lucky Strikes so bad she'd risk Mr. Dennis's 12-gauge just to get it. Gloria's whole self was different, how she banged out her hip and tilted her chin so you could see her long stretch of swan neck, but it was that wet-lipped smile of hers that stopped me short—her regular tight mouth was gone and the sexy grin she had on looked like it belonged to the ten-dollar women I'd sometimes seen laughing dirty on downtown corners.

Gloria must have felt me there because she turned around and that's when I saw her third face come rippling over her skullbones. I could tell then that she wasn't going to come over to Sunday dinner or even come running to my rescue anymore. She kept smoking that cigarette she was holding slutty between two fingers, and shot me a pair of knife eyes sharp enough to slit my throat. We stood there staring at each other but I was the first one to say uncle because this wasn't no gradeschool girl I was looking at, this wasn't even Eve busy splitting the appleskin with her sharp teeth; instead, I was looking at the apple itself, red and shiny and rotten around the core, the same one that hadn't fallen too far from the family tree.

She finished her cig and stubbed it dead with her shoe, the whole time just looking at me like that. I didn't dare speak up. What was there to say? I'd caught her red-handed, and somehow it seemed like she'd caught me too, gone and snatched me in the trap of her evil eye. There wasn't nothing for me to do, either, but maybe join in the fun. So I dragged my heel on the ground, shrugged, then backtracked down the alley to the sidewalk, and ran home to go digging for my own bad-girl secret, the one I'd kept hid in my underwear drawer.

* * *

$\mathcal{D}$olores would never understand this, but I'd kept that wet-tipped cig ever since Carlos the Bull had handed it to me at the bus stop and I got called slut for the first time. That day when I'd come home I'd stuffed it in my top drawer, and by this time it was a dirty thing buried under my panties. Still, I took it out and sniffed the stale tobacco, fiddled with the yellow filter. Then I went into the kitchen and looked around for some matches.

Strange taste, I know. I could have sneaked any cig I wanted, since mama always had menthols around and sometimes her Don Juans would leave almost-empty packs of Camels by the bed stand or singles half smashed in the ashtray. But this particular smoke was different. It promised me that there were wild woods hid in the heart of the city—that all of a sudden you could open the door on a black magic jungle where a hand-squeeze would shoot lightning into your skin. I mean, I'd just seen a piece of that wilderness in the parking lot, hadn't I? And I'd been struck dumb by what it could do, turn a knock-kneed pigeon into a swan, or a snake.

I thought it could turn me into something special, too.

So I took out the cigarette. I snagged a match from the kitchen and struck it, watched the blue flame dance till it turned red. I smoked. But not like other greenhorns do, with the choking and the coughing. I breathed easy from the first puff. I eased my head back and blew out a long white curl. Twirled the cig between my fingers, banged out my hip, tried saying "How you doing, baby?" in a husky voice. I waited for that black magic to make me into a monster with skin that glowed gold heat, who could start a brush fire with her laugh. But I was just a teenager smoking a cigarette and talking to myself in the kitchen. I was still just the same me. There was the cereal box I'd left out on the table. There were the dirty dishes in the sink. There wasn't nothing wild about it. Nothing electric zapped through me. Nothing happened.

And then, it did.

I heard the sizzle before I felt the heat and I wondered if a hungry heart could make such a noise. But then I felt the killing hot flicker over my face the same time I breathed in the dead-animal smell of my charred hair, the sprayed tips catching a spark from the red end of my cig. Too late for the faucet by then, though. Too late for anything but hollering. I think I was screaming, I don't know. The hair burned quick and the flames raced from the ends down to my blouse and up to my scalp while I thumped my fists over my head and clawed helpless at the hot net. Dolores ran in shouting something, but my mind was dark and I tried to crawl out the door away from the fire till she grabbed me, threw a pitcherful of Kool-Aid on my face, snuffed out my head with dishtowels and yelled at me to stop moving.

I did stop then. I lay there on the linoleum. I was blind. Or was that the towels? The pain was sitting on my head and then it got lighter and easier and started going away until I couldn't feel nothing at all, not even my face. But I was awake for a long time on that floor hearing the shoes stamp around me and the thin leaping sound of shouting mujeres. I had a bad flying feeling, I couldn't feel the floor anymore, or my feet, and I am cold, and maybe I was already almost dead and floating out the window, except then Dolores slipped her hand into mine and anchored me there while men came rushing into the kitchen.

Those paramedics wanted to wrap things around my arms and roll me onto a stretcher and they told Dolores to move. But I knew that strong, small hand of hers holding me down was keeping me alive. So I didn't listen to them. I squeezed her hand and it must have hurt but she didn't pull away, and those docs had to do their business of wrapping me and sticking me and lifting me by working around my sister, because no matter how many times they all told me she had to leave, there was no way I'd let her go.

I was in the hospital twelve weeks before they took off the bandages. It was a fright being blind like that, trying to figure things out from the way that they sound or taste or feel. I heard the nurses ripping paper open and flicking buttons and the hishing of their shoes on the ground. There was Mama and Dolores whispering and crying when they thought I was asleep. And they fed me milk and soft stuff and sometimes, when I was lucky, soda. The thing I remember most, though, was Dolores, who spent her weekends and dinnertimes with me. "Hey, you up?" she'd say. "You all right? Listen to this," then she'd tell me the worst knock-knock joke you ever heard. I still didn't want to let go of her. Her hand wasn't like an anchor anymore, but more like one of those sheet ropes folks throw out the windows of burning buildings, then use to scramble to the sidewalk. I held on to her and waited to touch down. It was such a time, though, smelling my sour skin in all that dark, wondering what I'd be like. Scarred ugly as a prune? Nose twisted like a mushroom? But I'd swear Dolores could hear me thinking out loud because right when the nightmares hit she'd start telling me stories about Calexico, so I'd stop heartaching about my face and see the red dirt town Mama'd come from, picture her swirly-top hairdo when she'd stepped off the bus.

Dolores was there, too, the morning the doc took off my wraps. I heard her walk to the far side of the room, and he put his hand on my shoulder and gave it a light squeeze.

"Now, I don't want you to get your hopes up," he said. He smelled like soap. "The healing process is complicated and can take a long time."

I didn't know what he meant by that. I just said, "Okay."

I felt him bend over me and heard his breath, and then clipping. He snipped off the bandages and the light came through pale at first, then glowing gold, then blind white. I blinked and waited while the snowstorm whirled around and popped black flashbulbs. Mama was crying and saying it was a miracle and the doctor started chuckling a little bit and said Good news. I was healing perfect, except for the moon-shaped scars behind my ears, but that's not the first thing I saw. I was busy blinking into the light while the black got bigger and changed colors and then slowly turned into Dolores. She was watching me by the door and wiping her red face with the back of her hand.

Folks are always going on about blood being thick but I know now that blood doesn't always got to mean the best love. Loving your best means picking somebody, and that day I went and chose Dolores, know what I'm saying? Somewhere that fire must still have been flickering because it burned her name right on me. So I didn't look in the mirror right away. Instead, I just let my eyes settle on my sister, and felt my heart flip over again, but this time for real.

"It's okay to look," she said after a minute.

I picked up the mirror, and watched while it reflected the white fluorescents, and the white wall with a blue painting of a boat. It was too bright and I saw spots again. But then I raised the mirror back up, held my breath, and when the clouds finally cleared I saw my face. Dolores was right. I couldn't cry like her, because of the infection, but I was so happy to see me raw-skinned, not scarred, just tender and red, almost like a baby right after it's been born.

It's funny thinking about how many omens I saw and heard on that day. There was Dolores by the door, of course, and the sight of my own new face. The one I didn't catch, though, was what the doc had told me, which was "don't get your hopes up." Months after I got out of that hospital, and was standing in front of another sign, this one scrawled on a wall, I thought back to what that doc had said and figured he must have been part scientist, but also part psychic.

Because I did get my hopes up in ways that I shouldn't have. I was in that hospital for nearly three months, and it gave me too much thinking time. From April to June of '88 I was helpless, bed-bound, and blinking at the light, but inside my head I made plans. I thought there wasn't nothing could stop a girl who'd shed her skin like a snake. I was going to be a totally different person now. There wouldn't be any more sitting in the back of the class making cracks, or putting on too much makeup, or getting into fights and breaking girls' teeth. I was going to join clubs and get a job and maybe study some more and try and dress better, and I'd even smile at folks and say hi to the girls in my class instead of moping on the bus stop. So I ate them mashed peas. I let the nurses put their needles in me. Then I went home and watched my hair grow back slow, saw the brown color cover up my wet pink cheeks, and tried to wait patient until I could get started with my life.

The first day I went back out in the world I was excited. I bought a long brown wig and new dress for it, something with a round collar and a pleat skirt so everybody could see how careful I'd ironed it. I was set on changing my name too, from Rita to Marisela, which had more of the sophistication. So then me and Dolores went walking out on Chávez on a beautiful Saturday to go window-shopping, but more important, to show off my brand-new self. There was Cha Cha Rodriguez and Connie Martinez, two girls in my class, and I smiled at them but Connie must have had the PMS because she gave me the finger and kept walking. Then I waved at the Widow Muñoz and tried to shrug it off when she gave me the evil eye. There was Señora Campos too, but she crossed the street as soon as she saw us, and Señora Mirande probably had hot flashes because she hissed when we crossed paths. There were the in-crowd chicas on the corner, too, and Veronica laughed right in my face and Gloria stared at me intense and strange. In other words, I was too dumb to notice that most of those women would have liked to stone me to death, until we passed by Carnival Liquors and a crowd of boys and Dolores grabbed my arm.

"Aw, nah, I can't believe this!" she said.

"What?"

I looked in between the heads of a couple gawkers and saw the graffiti scrawled on the side of Carnival in perfect printed letters. It was pretty simple. It said:

RITA ZAPATA HAS HAD SEX WITH THESE GUYS: Jose Mendoza, Pedro Paredes, Chuco Morales, Victor Mendoza, Tommy Saenz, Felipe Peña, Freddie Romero, Lucky Díaz . . .

The list went on and had the names of all the boys I knew from school. Later we'd find out that the gossip was even worse than that, and you know that these girls must have been starved-hungry for real good, real dirty gossip if they believed that pack of lies. Because how could a shiny-headed thing like I was have done a speck of trouble? For months I hadn't been doing nothing but sucking applesauce through a straw! But nobody worried about the details, and there were the most scandalous stories going around, like how that last week I'd been spotted screwing not one hombre but two in the supermarket parking lot, plus only three days ago I'd tried to get inside Mr. Mirande's pants, and of course everybody had heard how in general I was kinky and freaky and could never say no to an open zipper.

All this talk, mind you, was way before any of that mess was true, but while I stood there on Chávez in my Sandra Dee dress and looked past the winking, grinning fools crowding around me to the scowling mujeres, I thought about that warning the doc had gave me the day he took my wraps off. That's when I figured I'd been a fool to think that I could just choose the brand-new me I'd be and change my name and that'd be it. A thing like that takes timing and hard work, and it turns out that somebody had beat me to it—that is, she'd already gone to the trouble of doing the choosing for me, and the naming too. Although we never found out for sure who'd done the graffiti and spread all those rumors I never needed no confirmation, because right then, as I turned around and finally spotted her still staring at me and not smiling, I knew for sure that the hardworking girl who'd beat me to my own future was none other than the chica with the secret Lucky Strikes habit, la one and only Gloria Sanchez.

The Girls With the Most Gold

*B*y summer of the next year I was sixteen years old and had turned from a red-scalped, wig-wearing ugly Sandra Dee duck into a sexy daredevil-dressing woman. In the space of twelve months I'd grown a full head of hair and a wicked sense of style, worse than most of the working girls you'll see on the street corners. Did I wear thong undies? Only if I had to, to keep from being arrested. See-thru shirts? I had a dozen and painted my nipples with red lipstick so they'd show up pretty. The coolest thing about being a hoochie was the clothes, I'd say, but I wasn't just fooling around. I had my reasons for dressing so scandalous.

For one thing, maybe I could have fought my new reputation, but really it just seemed too hard. It was the same as when they first renamed Brooklyn Boulevard into César E. Chávez Avenue—that new street sign had a life all its own. In the next few weeks you could see the change, more kids milling around the sidewalks, more folks shopping, more cars with Chicano-pride bumper stickers cruising up and down the road. It was like that with me, too. After Gloria scrawled that graffiti on Carnival Liquors, people treated me different. Men were nicer, and las mujeres didn't want to have nothing to do with me. And what was I going to do? Beg after those bitches? Fight the men off with my fists? So I tried on that brand-new name Gloria gave me and found it fit me pretty good, after all.

But being easy without an agenda doesn't get you that far, and I didn't start to really work it till I ran into my role model. Folks around here like to say that I got my nature from my mama, but they're only half right. I got my heavy-lidded eyes and this switchy way of walking from her, but I got my style and my life mission from the best bad girl you ever saw. That'd be Cherry Salazar.

Damn, just saying her name's like setting another fire.

The first time I saw Cherry Salazar up close was in the spring of '89, a few months after my head healed. I was wearing a plaid-print minidress I'd made myself and stumbling down Chávez Ave in my Dr. Scholl's until I came up on Carlita's Fashions, the little place where you could get spangle dresses and silky-touch underwear and semiprecious jewelries. Well, that devil girl came swinging out the door clutching a giant-sized shopping bag and wearing a white mink even though the sun's out, and stopped me cold. Those diamonds in her ears must have been worth ten thousand. Her chignon was baby blond all the way to the roots. When she swished by me her fur swung open and I caught her sky-blue shrink-fits, the V neck showing off two inches of cleavage, her skirt cut so high it must have been criminal, and then that skirt hitched even higher when she slammed into me and went tumbling to the ground, dropping the bag and sending boxes everywhere.

"Shit," she said, then looked up.

Nobody had to tell me who this was. Cherry was famous. I'd heard plenty of gossip about her in the produce section at Rudy's Super. This was the girl who'd hit bingo.

We've got one really rich man in this town, name's Ruben Lopez. He's an ex-fighter born and raised in East L.A. who made it to the Vegas Bigs for one whole year back in the seventies. He didn't waste his good name like Carlos the Bull, though. For a while after Vegas he made a killing playing tough guys on Mexican TV and when he lost his looks he spent a couple years bodyguarding Sinatra for big bucks. Since 1985 he'd owned the best boxing gym in L.A., and made his living training local boys. With his beer gut and tomato nose Ruben was no Valentino, but because of his full pockets he could have any woman he wanted, and he'd had just about every sweet-faced linda over seventeen in the neighborhood. But he'd never stuck with a woman for more than a few high-flying months, and you could always tell when it was over from how the ladies would walk around pale and cussing after they got dumped.

That is, he'd never stuck with nobody until he met Cherry. Cherry, man. She just must of been the shit. They'd been together almost a year by the time she tripped over me in front of Carlita's Fashions, but nobody knew her story. She wasn't from around here. Eagle Rock, I think. Or Echo Park. She was the kind that kept to herself. She never stopped by the other chicas' houses for coffee and rum cake or to sneak a quick cig. Had her hair done on the other side of town in this Frenchified beauty shop where they charge a hundred just to give you a wash and cut, half that for a 'do. And because Ruben's so rich you'd never see her pushing her cart at the super or hauling white shirts and boxers to the Fluff & Fold. So you'd only catch a glimpse of her sometimes, sitting next to Ruben in the front pew at Mass dressed in clingy white silk and smart satin spikes, or stopped at a red light in her Cadillac convertible, checking out her lipstick in the rearview.

Every honest woman in town just loved to hate Cherry Salazar. Some said she'd learned how to walk swaybacked from turning tricks on Sunset Boulevard. Others gossiped about how she'd do anything for the old man, like play with dildos and even do the beastialisms and the S&Ms. But I think I know why she won old Ruben. It's because of how she dressed so sexy. Besides that fur of hers, which she'd wear whenever the temp dropped under eighty, she had a hundred paint-on dresses and jumpsuits that didn't leave nothing to the imagination except for the real color of her hair, and I'd bet she had a closetful of those stilettos sharp enough to stab a man dead.

But I'll tell you. Stilettos are sexy, but they sure aren't made much for walking. Which is why I guess she was hands and knees on the ground right then.

"Oh, I'm sorry!" I yelled. Cherry was saying, "Well goddammit that is *just* all I need today," and I bent down to help her. Spread over the sidewalk there was every single size of box I could think of—long flat ones, fat short ones, round ones, square ones, each one tied with gold bows. I put them all back in the big bag, shaking them so I could hear what was inside. Except one, that is. There was one smaller than my hand. Cherry started getting up and sniffed at the mud stain on her mink, and I put my fingers around that box and stuffed it up my sweater sleeve.

"All right," she said. "No damage done." Then she did something I never forgot: Cherry laughed at herself. "Oh hoosh, girl, you see me flying? Damn!" She slapped her leg. Her mascara smeared on her cheeks. She shook her head so the curls came twanging out the bobby pins. I couldn't believe it. Even though her hands were dirty from the ground and her mink was stained maybe for good she thought it was funny. And that's when I learned what I'd never heard said out loud in this neighborhood ever: Rich or not, slutty or not, Cherry Salazar was nice.

But I still didn't give her back that box.

When I got home I undid the bow and inside was a pin, made of pure rhinestone and shaped like a star. I put it in the same place I'd hid Carlos the Bull's cigarette so it would wink at me when I got dressed in the morning. I showed it to Dolores but wouldn't let her wear it, and I didn't wear it either, it was so precious. I priced it once at Carlita's Fashions: two hundred and sixty-two dollars not counting the tax. But I bet Cherry never missed it. A couple Franklins to her would have been like nada. And besides, it was worth way more to me than two hundred sixty-two. Every time I saw the pin I thought about how some-day I'd be rich and pretty enough to laugh off the mud on my mink, my ruined fifty-dollar hairdo.

That star was the first nice anything I ever had in my drawers. Not the last, though. Later came the leopard-skin hot pants and blouses like bikini tops. But even after I got all my fancies I never got over my first piece of pretty glitz, stole from the source. Out of every nice thing I ever had, and mind you, once there was even a real two-carat diamond glinting on this hand, I still think that rhinestone star was always my number one favorite.

After I ran into Cherry Salazar, I spent the next couple months teaching myself how to copy her style, and finally nailed it that summer. One afternoon I was slipping into a black spandex dress the size of a Band-Aid, and when I looked into the mirror I saw a wife's worst nightmare come to life. Wha-bam! Check out this bootie banging out, honey, and I didn't belong around no hungry babies because I'd squeezed inside a B-cup bra so there was three inches of cleavage spilling over. I grinned at my foot-long hair extensions, my Jungle Red mouth. It was perfect. I was all set for manhunting. So I stepped into my mama's fuchsia spikes and set out to Rabbit Street, on the other side of the neighborhood, which is where the best boxers in town fight for gambling money. Making my way down Chávez I walked very slow, sexy, and careful, and only stumbled once.

Because I was getting there in one piece. This wasn't a spectator sport for me. Cherry Salazar was my inspiration, and I'd decided to set my sights on snagging a fighter, like she'd snagged Ruben Lopez. What I'm saying is, I was set on hooking up with a boxer, and not just any old streetfighter: I'm talking a champ.

And really, it should have been obvious to me from the first.

I mean, look around! Who are the girls with the most gold? Boxers' wives, of course. Beyond getting to bed down men made of one hundred percent pure muscle, they also get bodyguards and three-story houses and bouncing babies and fox fur coats and four-star cruises and winters in Hawaii. Take for example Alba Chávez, Paulette Holyfield, Margarita Duran, Deanna Dempsey, Amy Camacho—why they're just chicas with hard-luck stories and long legs who struck pay dirt when they snagged a marriage license! You won't ever see them, except maybe to catch a quick close-up of their shiny faces in a pay-per-view fight, but all of them are rich as Midas.

So it was settled.

Natural enough choice, too, considering this town. East L.A.'s crawling with could-be or would-have-been fighters. Every ski-capped tuff banging on the corner and every rail-thin kid scrapping in the schoolyard wants to be a boxer, not to mention all the nine-to-fivers sitting at their desks and the out-of-work uncles swigging stuff out of paper bags. None of them is worth spending a word on, though, because they've got no future. But I knew where to find the real deal.

Two places. The first is Ruben's Superbox at the far end of Chávez. At Ruben's you've got tiger-eyed comers swinging in and out the door all day long. Except Mr. Ruben wouldn't allow ladies in there, so it didn't do me much good. A better place to scope out the talent was Rabbit Street, which didn't have no rabbits and wasn't even a real road, but was where you could find those same contenders slugging it out for gamblers' cash on almost any afternoon.

Rabbit Street's a dead-end alley off Sixth that still smells of old wine and hobo pee, and on the ground there's dirt and liquor store trash and green broke glass from fights that went wrong, when boxers bent the rules and tried to slice each other with the sharp jags of smashed bottles. The walls are colored dark with spray-paint bubble letters spelling out gang sets, and by the time I was starting to dress right you couldn't see the wall barely under all that mess. But if you looked close under the last few years of tagging wars, you would have found a blood-brown spot at the back, a boy-sized stain, from when Rabbit Camacho got hit by the police three years back.

Rabbit Camacho was a good boy. I remember seeing him walk his sister to school once; he'd held on to her hand and looked both ways before they crossed the street. But all that seemed to change when he got in with the Fifth Streeters, who back then weren't nothing but a pack of penny gangsters who stayed busy strong-arming little old ladies and selling nickel bags of coke. After they jumped him in he turned into a fast-footed pickpocket and purse snatcher, not to mention a meth freak, and the night he ran from the LAPD old Rabbit Street got its name. A flatfoot tried to pat him down on the street outside the liquor store, and as soon as he put a hand on our little man, something broke clear off in Rabbit's poor fried head. Instead of standing still and spreading, he ran with those speedy feet down the alley and when he turned around and pulled out his knife, the cop shot him dead in self-defense.

The neighborhood men thought serious about having a riot. I remember the screaming in the streets and slashed tires, smashed shopglass, a couple torched cars spitting sparks and black smoke, but nobody fanned the fire high enough and so it just burned out. No good folks came close to Rabbit Street after that, though. The church ladies wouldn't walk by without crossing themselves and the kids stopped riding their bikes on that part of the road because the dark stain on the wall was too sad to stand. Sooner or later, the gangsters painted it up and the homeless were sleeping there at night, and then Ruben's Superbox boys moved in and started easy-money fighting in front of the cold hard brick of the haunted dead end.

That's where I went to go find a man. Dressed up that day in my black Band-Aid dress and Mama's fuchsia spikes, I strolled past Chávez and turned down Eighth, and found all the kangaroo boys crowded around the mouth of Rabbit Street punching up fists stuffed full of money and cheering on two string beans. I moseyed closer, cleared my throat, and waited for my perfume to drift. It took a minute, two, tops. Then the boys stopped cheering and turned around, and twenty-five smiles flashed bright at me.

"Hi," two of them said, at the same time.

I smiled, said hi back. It was quiet now except for the slapping sound of knucklebones on muscle, huffing breath. I shifted my hip sexy, said "How you all doing, babies?" in the voice I'd practiced, and it worked. The grins got bigger and the shoes started shuffling while one of the string beans fell on the ground. A pigeon-chested welterweight came up and tried to pull me away from the rest. But I didn't let him. I stayed put, looked at each dude careful, and took my time giving them the up and down. I knew I had my pick.

*M*y first time wasn't too much later—it happened on July 24, 1989, with a slugger named Eddie Martinez, but you never called Martinez by his first name. Martinez was old. Twenty-nine. He used to really be something around here; he was Ruben's number one lightweight back in the mid-eighties because of his uppercut and steel jaw. His claim to fame was fighting Julio César Chávez once at Caesar's Palace, where I guess an uppercut and tough mug don't count for much because we all saw Martinez's gut get pummeled into pudding by Chávez's superman hands and his nose get broke in half when he landed on the canvas, right there on the national TV.

But still, not so bad for a local boy. Martinez came home waving his loser's purse, a whole fifty gees, and used it to buy a Trans Am done up in purple custom and white racing stripes and man but did he race that badass all over the place, gunning the engine. It was a downhill slide for him from there on out, though, first losing to a couple no-names in undercard fights, and then word got out he was taking falls for two grand apiece down in Palm Springs. And still, Martinez just kept lording it over the other boys. Nobody else but him, Ruben, and Carlos the Bull had got in with the bigs, and he was always going on about his glory days and his V-6 engine and his comeback and so he seemed like pretty hot stuff to us.

Or at least he seemed hot to me back when I was sixteen.

I must be my mama's daughter because I'm a backseat girl just like her. I was too scared to go to his apartment so Martinez drove me up to Mulholland, to see the view, he said. And that

Trans Am, it *was* a dream. Besides the leather interior and zero-to-sixty engine, it had a pink fuzzy dash, smoked windows, and a sound system so fine the big bass rattled my bones and thumped inside my belly like a second heart. "Mambo Lover" was playing, I remember, and the beat went so deep it made my teeth chatter.

But there was Martinez in the backseat, looking at me. He was wearing enough Polo cologne for four men and his muscles were working hard to come busting out of that T-shirt.

"Come here," he said. He was patting the seat.

I shook my head. "I want to see the lights. Here, let's look at these lights."

He said he wanted to look at something else, then pulled me back there, smiling. From the backseat you could still see the lights, but I didn't care about them anymore. As soon as I felt the tough bumps under his T-shirt I wanted to do it right away; my legs were shaking and I was already yelling before the ballplayer even had second base in sight. I liked his hands there. I wanted them to split me, I wanted the gold teeth of his zipper to bite my thigh. He was saying, "Okay now, slow down," and I tried not to buck but my hips were jerking by themselves until I got him splayed on the seat and saddled up, and after it stopped hurting I laughed and kept going. Because there it was, that lightning I'd felt before at the bus stop, and not just lightning, but music too, the bumping beat of the bass inside me so it was a thunderstorm, it was a dance hall party, it was a room full of satin-dressed ladies waltzing across the floor while right outside black trees whipped against the wind and the ocean-dark sky flashed white and electric.

But I guess Martinez didn't feel the same way. He was sort of squashed under me and his face was wet.

"Oh, Jesus," he said, squinting up at me. "I told you to wait."

* * *

*M*e and Martinez didn't wind up lasting too long. After a month he took up with a number street chica named Carlita and ditched me over the phone. I didn't mind so much. I'd caught on by then that his pro days were over and plus he was always telling me to slow down. Besides, there were plenty others.

For the next two years I stayed busy turning Gloria's graffiti into one of those kinds of self-fulfilling prophecies. There was Chuco Morales, a cruiserweight headhunter with the genius left hook. Tommy Saenz, the flyweight with a B-plus uppercut. Largo Ortiz with the solid right jab and the asthma. Lucky Díaz the bleeder. Felipe Peña the druggie. Freddie Romero the egg head. Pedro Paredes with the bad eye.

Once they buckled their belts back up I could see how every single one had been a mistake. They cost me plenty, those boys. I caught the gonorrhea from Marco and Felipe stole all my money, and my reputation got so hot las neighborhood mujeres couldn't look at me without crossing themselves. But I couldn't quit them men even so. I couldn't get enough of that first-love feeling. The first hand-hold, his fingers stroking my lifeline. The first kiss snuck secret in the dark. I couldn't help myself. I'd go weak the first time I'd spy a birthmark under the shirt, or saw a hid scar. No matter how many I'd had, I could never get over that feeling of touching a brand-new man.

*T*wo years later I was old enough to have sex under the law, but the neighborhood boys had been calling me the Queen of the Streetfighters for a long time by then. Dolores, though, was going to turn seventeen soon and wasn't real ripe yet. Like where I'd grown long curling hair and C cups her nose had stayed crooked and her baby fat had stuck on her stubborn. We all said she'd just bloom late but in the meantime she sewed her own clothes. This one afternoon she sat at the kitchen table, stitching up a Butterick Chubbies–pattern dress made of baby-blue cotton with matching blue lace on the hem and collar.

"That's pretty," I said. "What's it for?"

Dolores looked up at me, then looked back down. I saw how she had eyeliner on and mascara. "I met a boy I like. I want him to see me wearing something nice."

"So that's who that hoochie-mama eye makeup's for. You met a boy!" I laughed and slapped the table.

"I don't want to talk about it too much right now."

"Who is it? Is it Francisco?" Francisco was a blue-eyed kid who lived down the street, worked in a body shop. "Is it somebody I know?"

Dolores put her dress down. "Yeah, well he's one of the guys from Rabbit Street, so I figured you might have already, you know, dated him. But he hasn't asked me out yet and I like him a lot and so I don't want to know if you and him did anything because then maybe I won't anymore."

"Oh my God. Who is it? Oh no, okay. It's Pedro, right?"

Like I said, I'd gone out with Pedro Paredes. Until last year I'd only ever thought of him as the half-blind seventy-five-pound troublemaker from high school, but then I took notice of him again. He never would be a boxer because of that eye, but he loved the sport more than anybody, and hung around Ruben's Superbox and Rabbit Street all the time just to see boys fight and tell them what was wrong with their defense or footwork. He had a talent for meddling, sure—but he also had a knack for watching and listening. He gave up on boxing once he figured out that his natural talent was politics, both big and little. He watched the news every night, read like three papers, and was the one who settled boys' squabbles, and so by the time he'd turned nineteen he'd become the combination Rabbit Street sheriff, sportscaster, bookie, and official pain in the ass too, because he was always going on about grapes and trying to teach us about the United Farm Workers, those Brown Berets, and come November, he'd start yelling at everybody to vote.

So I liked Pedro, enough to go out with him twice, but half the time I hadn't known what the hell he was talking about and I didn't like hearing about how everything on my dinner plate was the product of a brown man's blood and sweat, and anyway, he'd never be a boxer, so it didn't work out. But as I was sitting there looking at Dolores wearing mascara and sewing up her dress, it hit me how those two were perfect for each other because they were both sidelines types and had a lot going on in the brains department.

I gave her a pinch. "Come on! Is it Pedro? You know, I hope it's him because you two would go good together."

Dolores slapped me off and still wouldn't tell me. She colored up pretty high, though, and so I figured I was more or less on the mark. I told her it better not be those losers Felipe or Marco or even Chuco, come to think of it, because he had kind of a temper when he got drunk, but that she had my blessing to go and bump nasties with Pedro anytime she liked, and in fact, she should put down that Virgin Mary dress and get one of them sure things I had hanging in my closet, those hiphuggers made out of pink satin, or the black lace bikini top, whatever she wanted, so long as she went and slipped on something that'd make the boy's eyes pop right out.

She just laughed and said shut up.

Dolores was so busy getting ready for her big romance that I didn't tell her that I had a boyfriend-catching scheme of my own. Around four o'clock the next day I was walking back down to Rabbit Street carrying a bottle of Spumante. I usually went down there two or three times a week, just to check out the scene and try to pick up who was winning, but today was different. Lately I'd realized that my master plan of snagging a champion had gone by the wayside, because I'd spent the last two years bouncing from one man to the other and earning that Queen of the Streetfighters nickname. And now, believe this, I was alone every Saturday night. I'd speed-dial dudes' numbers all day and leave ten messages on their answering machines, but nobody would call me back. I knew why, too. Nobody had to write it up on the wall, okay? They all thought I was trash.

So my big dreams were going down the drain but it sure had been easy to get sidetracked. For the longest time, all those fools couldn't get enough of me, could they? Nah, I was the one they'd wanted so bad; it was me they'd all been so crazy about. Time was, I'd walk up to Rabbit Street and the dusk would bright up with their grins and they'd all be sticking their fingers in their collars to cool down the hot blood that started pumping soon as they heard my heels clicking on the concrete. The fights would turn vicious when I'd show up, too, there'd be red coloring up one slugger's knuckles because the other forgot his defense when he smelled my cologne, and the rest of them would be reaching their hands out to manhandle me while they asked me to dinner, to a movie, or told me about two tickets they had to a game, and how they wondered if I'd come.

But then they went and changed their minds about me. The day came when I'd walk by and the only dudes who'd bounce up and down were the pipsqueaks just going into the eighth grade. Almost every single one of the real contenders had already touched my pink parts and then moved on, and when I showed up on Rabbit Street they'd either give me the cold shoulder or slap each other some skin and start laughing filthy.

Almost every one, but not all of them. I wasn't finished yet. There was one boxer left. Just one I hadn't messed around with.

That was Jose Mendoza.

*J*ose Mendoza and me had always gone to school together; he was one of the punks who used to box by the bus stop. He'd grown up now, though, into a welterweight with the darkest eyes I'd ever seen and a gentle way of flirting. Whereas the other boys had been shoving each other out of the way to get a chance to tease and touch me, he always hung back behind them, staring at me then looking down at the ground and kicking at the dirt.

You would have expected something different from him, too, because of his family tree. Jose came from two well-known bloodlines—the Hernandez and Mendoza tribes. His long-gone papa was Memo Mendoza, from the famous Mendoza clan of robber-baron badasses out of Compton, who died back in '82 when he stuck up a 7-Eleven and got shot by a cashier. Jose's mama was Patrice Hernandez, the bad-seed sister of Mr. Hernandez, the same man who was La Rica's husband and my own mama's boyfriend. Except for her last name, Patrice wasn't nothing like her brother; she was an old chola with a taste for tattooed bikers and all-night needle parties. And like it or not, she'd kept up with the Mendoza tradition by birthing not just Jose, but his look-alike brother Victoriano, aka Victor, who became a coke dealer with a hundred aliases and the devil's temper. Victor was the king of the Fifth Streeters, a gang with only fifteen members back then, but more than that, he was the most dangerous man in the neighborhood. Word had it he'd once killed a customer over five dollars.

Jose wasn't anything like his family, though. He was a high-fiving, shoulder-punching boy full of jokes and brags till he got close to a girl. He was friends with everybody because he kept his word, paid his lost bets quick, and was a good, fair fighter. But it was something else drew me to him besides all that. The thing I first noticed about Jose Mendoza was his van.

I remember the day he got it. He'd come gunning up the street blowing a horn that played "La Cucaracha" and grinned at us through the tinted windshield and a pair of fuzzy dice swinging from the rearview.

"Hey, you pendejos!" he yelled through the rolled-down window. "Why don't you all check out a real man's ride?"

We all crowded up, hooting back at him. It was a beauty. This was a used Ford Econoline eight-seater cherried out with a V-8, captain's chairs, and enough chrome to make you go blind. What made me look twice, though, was the paint job, which must have cost five hundred at least. The sides were painted with pictures of two different mujeres. On one side there was a mestiza princess wearing two inches of leather and feathers and stretching out sexy, her beautiful eyes staring sorrowful at the sky. The other side had a wild banshee all done up in blue and black, her dark flying hair like a storm cloud, her red mouth screaming, and one sharp-clawed hand reaching out.

I knew these ladies. Everybody around here does. When we were little our mamas would thrill or chill us with their stories before bedtime, when we'd listen wide-eyed, saying Tell me more! or hiding our heads under the covers. They're our fairy tale women.

Did you ever hear about the two brown girls who loved their men? One loved him nice, the other one wicked. There's the princess, whose pretty dead face you'll usually see painted on black velvet, always stuffed in her minibikini and wearing her Indian feathers. She's an Aztec blueblood who fell in love with an ordinary man. Royalty couldn't marry regular people, though, and so her lover went off to war to prove himself to the king. The princess was patient and waited on the top of a mountain for him to come back home, braving the rain and the hot sun, until one day a snake bit her and she died. When her lover came home from the war he asked the gods to take pity on them, and heaven turned them into two mountains so they could sleep together side by side forever.

Everybody loves that story because the waiting woman's so good and pure, but I like the other girl better—she's not such a chump. This one with the black hair and red claws is one man-eating witch. We call her the crying woman, but all her tears don't make her gentle. She's a jealous darkheart, with red hell running through her veins instead of blood. The story goes that after she found out her husband was cheating on her, she led her babies to the river, kissed their heads, and then drowned them just for spite. Then she jumped in herself, swam to the bottom, and turned into a ghost, and now she haunts riverbeds at night, howling like a hard wind and scaring men who pass by.

Instead of black widows, or cobras, or the Mexican flag, these were the two ladies Jose'd had painted on his van. I figured that might mean he knew something about double-hearted women like me so when he stepped down out of the van I went up to him and smiled. He didn't smile back but his eyes glowed and then he reached out and pulled off a loose string from my shirt, very gentle, so it wouldn't snag.

"You're so beautiful just looking at you hurts," he said.

Now, I'd heard a hundred lines by that time and this wasn't no line. He didn't pinch me or make a joke about my ass and for a second, I couldn't breathe. I was doing the tango up around the clouds. But then Marco came up to paw me and for some reason I started laughing and flipping my hair, which broke the spell. Jose dropped the string, then shadowboxed with Pedro, who was his tightest friend, and wouldn't look back or butt in. In the end I left with Marco and wound up getting that nasty case of the clap.

Standing around Rabbit Street right now with my bottle of Spumante, I saw the sun blush and felt hopeful. I knew I couldn't make the same mistake with Jose again. I wanted to hop inside his van and drive off into the sunset. Which is why when I'd heard a few days before that he was going to fight Martinez at 4–2 odds, I'd got an idea. Win or lose, he'd need somebody to celebrate or mope around with, and so I'd gone down there dressed up extraspecial and carrying that bubbly in a paper bag.

The crowd was already packed when I'd showed up. Pedro, dressed in fatigue pants and a United Farm Workers T-shirt, saw me and waved. As usual, he was the moneyman, taking bets and grabbing cash. The rest of the boys were busy mad-dogging each other and head-butting, backslapping, yelling out numbers. Everybody had come. Marco, Freddie Romero, Chuco, hopped-up Felipe. Even Victor, duded out in black leathers and red bandannas, was here to gamble on his little brother.

"Hey now, it's the freak!" he said when he saw me squeezing through the crowd. (Just once, in the bathroom at Chuco's birthday party the year before. Afterwards, I'd wrote down my number in felt-tip pen on his naked belly, but he'd never called.) "What you doing round here, muchacha?"

I shrugged his arm off. "I'm here to see the fight."

"Aw, girl! I think you really came here looking for me." Victor showed his white teeth, snuck a finger under my shirt, and tried to tickle me.

"Shut up, okay? Come on, stop it."

But he'd already stopped looking at me because the fight was starting. Martinez and Jose swaggered into the alley wearing their white tanks and baggies, streaks of sunlight gleaming off their slicked heads. Jose cocked his fists and weaved around, but Martinez didn't go in for the gentleman's style, he went for the inside right away, first swinging to the belt then moving uptown until he hit bull's-eye and drew blood.

Pedro shook a fist in the air. "Get on the inside!"

Everybody was yelling. I had to keep jumping up so I could see better because the gamblers were shoving in front and punching the air like they were fighting themselves. It was hot there in that alley with those sweating crazies screaming around me but I was just as loca as them. Jose had blood dripping down his cheek and he shot body blows to the plexus and it was working—Martinez was bent over and trying to hide in a clinch— and all I could make out was my man's red neck and his elbows while I screamed his name. At the same time, another chica started screaming his name, too, so we sounded like those shrieking groupies at Julio Iglesias concerts who throw their panties and hotel keys up on the stage.

I turned to look to see who it was and couldn't believe it. The other chica was Dolores, all decked out in that baby-blue Butterick Chubbies dress.

I pushed over, grabbed her arm. "What are you doing here?"

"There he is!" she says, pointing at the alleyway. She looked different. Her hair'd been teased into a bush and she'd put my Red Desire lip gloss on, and you could see two inches of cleavage peeking out her V neck. "He's the one I was telling you about. We're going out on a date!"

"Which one?" I asked. Oh, I felt sick. I looked over at Pedro, who was yelling something about left jabs, but I already knew it wasn't him.

The fight was almost over by now; I could hear somebody wheezing in the alleyway. Through the shadows and the shifting heads I could just barely spy Jose working a roundhouse under Martinez's ribs, and he must have hit blackjack right then because everybody hollered HO! at the same time and I couldn't see nothing at all but brown shiny backs and greased ducktails until Jose slipped out of the crowd, red-skinned, laughing, both his hands stuffed full of dollars, and came right for Dolores and called her name.

They didn't even say good-bye to me. They walked straight to the van holding hands and he opened her door. Jose looked back once, twisted his face up, then got in on his side, and when they drove off there was only the moon-pale bruja staring at me as she flew down the block with her black-and-blue hair streaming.

I was still gripping my Spumante. I was dressed up for nothing. But it didn't hit me that Jose'd been my last chance until Victor came up and put his hand on my shoulder.

"Guess that's one boy you won't be able to sink your claws into, huh, Rita?" he said.

I was feeling lower than a grave, and still, when I peered up at Victor I couldn't help thinking how he looked just like his brother. Both of them had those Hernandez eyes, eyes so shimmering dark they make you feel like you're dreaming. I knew why Dolores wanted Jose, and was starting to get a good idea why Mama was so in love with their uncle, Mr. Hernandez. But I didn't want in with Victor. Even if he was handsome he was into the drugs and guns and he didn't have the heart of his brother, and so there, that was it. I was finished. No boxers. No nobody. I handed him my Spumante, took off my shoes, and walked home alone.

The Lucky Pesos

Seven seasons after I watched the bruja fly down the street at the speed limit, I found myself in the hushed, candlelit church staring at a padre spinning Old Testament tales. We were in the early days of '93 now and the closest I'd been to Mass in seven years was that brush with the fake saint because we were usually too tired or too tied up with a man to get up that early. This particular Sunday was different, though, because we had a religion emergency on our hands: Me, Mama, and Dolores had hauled ourselves out of the house to come and pay our respects to the newly dead.

At five o' clock that morning we'd got word that Chita Feliz Zapata, my abuela, had died in Calexico of a bad heart three days before. Me and Dolores never met her, but we'd heard plenty of stories. Chita had been a wild, loose brunette with great legs and a bad cowboy habit: She'd had three steers and six heifers named after her, got proposed to by a cattle rancher, even been crowned a rodeo queen. But Chita wasn't cut out for westerns. Not one of them men had stuck around; more bowlegs had walked out of her front door than she could count.

Mama had walked out on her too, back when she was sixteen and had stars in her eyes. She took the news hard, now.

Locked herself up in the bathroom for two hours and all we could hear was her slapping the tiles with her hands. After she finally came out she said she wanted to light a candle for Chita even though we weren't communicated. So we got dressed for it, found the black lace in the back of the closet and put on our crosses, and then each of us spritzed on a little cologne.

When we got to the Mission, Mass had already started. There was the padre with his white-and-gold robes, glittering in the candlelight and incense smoke. There were the rows and rows of black and red hats, bald husband heads, pigtails tied in ribbon, twitchy cowlicks. The padre was telling the story of Abraham and Isaac.

"God's test to Abraham," the padre said, "it was terrible, unimaginable. Because God is unimaginable. God ordered Abraham to kill the son he loved more than his own life. Without telling his wife, Sarah, without asking any wise men, or even second-guessing his own blind, deaf, and dumb faith, Abraham put his son under his knife. And only when God saw that Abraham could be blind, that his servant could be deaf and dumb, did He have mercy. God let Isaac live, and He gave Abraham His grace. Think of the sacrifice! Could any of us have trusted God so much? Could any of us have passed the test? But that is the heart we must have! We must have a dumb heart! We must have a blind heart! We must be able to call black white and white black if God tells us it is so. And so I ask you: Can you do this? Can you trust God in this way?"

The padre pointed to all of the churchies and they nodded their heads and said amen. When he was done with that he took out the gold cup and the white wafers. He poured the wine and broke the bread, kissed his cross, and then waited for the church ladies to turn into cannibals. I remembered this part from Sunday school. This was the magic minute where the crackers turned to white bone dust between your teeth, and the wine became blood right on your tongue, and after you'd had heaven for dinner you could slip off yesterday like an old robe.

Even though I wasn't a real Catholic, I wanted to do that. All of a sudden, I wanted a taste so bad. Right there I decided I'd go and accept Communion.

But then, they wouldn't let me.

Later I heard people saying they smelled us before they saw us because evil stinks in the house of God and will always make itself known, but that didn't have nothing to do with it. A little White Shoulders cologne never killed nobody! Still, soon as we got inside the door I could hear them all sniffing and whispering and see them pulling on their noses, and then, one by one, they turned around.

They were giving Mama an evil eye so hot you'd think Mary Magdalene had just come in wearing pasties and started treating the padre to a lap dance. And there was Mama's boyfriend, old Mr. Hernandez, in the front pew. If I didn't know better, from the look on his face I'd have said he *had* gone dumb and blind like the padre had told him to. But worse than that was the voodoo look on his wife, La Rica Hernandez, who, very careful, took her hand and put them over the eyes of her hija Veronica, as if seeing me and Mama and Dolores would turn them all into salt.

Then she stood up.

"Get out! Get out! Get out!" she yelled. "Putana!"

The padre jumped and crushed the crackers to pieces. Mr. Hernandez slid so low in his seat he disappeared from view. The rest of the churchies hissed and showed their teeth, except for the couple of viejas too old to be jealous who gave us pity looks instead.

I was shaking in my shoes. I didn't want to mess with La Rica. Really, she was more powerful than the President. I knew she could snap her fingers and all these women would rush us and try to stamp Satan out of our bones.

It was Dolores who stood up to her.

"We're not going anywhere." My sister's voice boomed through the church. "Our abuela died and we're here to pay our respects. Right, Mama?"

But Mama didn't answer. When we turned around she was staring at the empty air floating in front of her.

"Mama?" Mama said.

Dolores and me looked at each other. Then Dolores tapped Mama on the shoulder. "Isn't that right?" she said again.

Mama's teeth started clicking and she slapped her hands over her eyes. "Mama!"

"What the hell's going on?" I said.

And that's when the churchies rose up against us. The wives of the husbands Mama had tumbled started screeching for Jesus to save them, so that them same husbands gripped their heads and yelled shut up, which made the babies scream and the little niñas cry and the chicos sweating in their Sunday suits laugh and the padre run around flapping his robes like a chicken at dinnertime, while La Rica Hernandez stood up straight in the middle of the aisle, all flower-print fabric and cone-shaped triple-D cups and hellfire eyes, and pointed at the door.

Mama didn't even notice she was shivering and bawling so hard, but I could see it was no use. If we so much as made a move for the holy candles those locas would nail us up on crosses and call it celebrating Christmas. We knew we were beat. So we did what La Rica told us to. We got Mama by the elbows and dragged her out of that place.

*B*ack at home, it was hours before she'd say anything. She sat at the kitchen table lockjawed for a long time. We tiptoed around and gave her tea, worried at each other with our eyes. But when she finally talked she didn't blither, she sounded almost normal. It was her words that were crazy.

"I saw your abuela in there," she said after she'd took a sip of cold tea. "I saw Chita's ghost right there in front of me. Andale, hijas! You understanding what I'm saying? I just got a vision. She didn't look dead or nothing like that. So I didn't know at first; what was she doing here? How'd she get all the way here? I was confused. But then I figured it out because she didn't look like I remembered. She was young, Jesus, and she was so beautiful. She was wearing a poncho and those kind of cowboy boots and she was just waving good-bye, smiling and laughing. You imagine? And all these years I been feeling so bad because I never went back home? But she comes back to tell me it's okay and she forgives me for being a bad daughter. It breaks my heart, knowing she loves me so much after I never got down there to visit, after promising and promising. Ay, my head's all upside down. Just look. See how I'm all shaking?"

Mama was crying again. She held her hands up so we could see how they jittered. Me and Dolores grabbed them and rubbed the fingers, but we stayed quiet.

"You don't believe me, eh? Well, believe it."

"We believe you, Mama," Dolores said.

"No you do not. Dios mío, the way I raised you makes me shamed. Didn't I never tell you about dead people? Listen, because this is a true fact: Ghosts can only haunt you when they got business to finish with you. All the other stories about spirits haunting strangers is just a lie. Ghosts only come back when they want to forgive you, or punish you for all the sins you did to them. Which is why she came back to me, see, to forgive me."

We were still holding on to her hands and staring at her.

"Well don't look at me like I'm crazy!" Mama yelled at us. Then the phone started ringing.

"I got it!" I said, but Dolores was already up and running down the hall.

Mama sat there squeezing her hands together. She was thinking of saying something, but I didn't want to know what. I didn't like that look in her eye. So I asked her if she wanted more tea but when I tried to get up she pushed me back down.

"Do you know why I left Calexico?" she said. She hunched closer to me, tapped her nail on the table. "You want to know why I ran away from your abuela and never went back?"

I tried to tell her I didn't but she just railroaded over me.

"Fine, I will tell you now, quick, before your sister comes back in here. I left Calexico because for three generations our family had nothing but heartache in that place: me, your abuela, her sisters, their mama, her sisters. Every single one of us liked the men too much. You think I never heard the word whore before? I heard it plenty. Your abuela Chita, she was the big romance queen of our town. Ooh-la-la, she was took to all the parties and the dances and this man gave her this diamond and this other man he flies her to Cabo San Lucas and everything. But what did it get her? Nothing—worse than nothing. The bad reputation, broke heart, empty bank account, fffft. And she was just like every other Zapata woman, all of them sex maniacs who couldn't pop out nothing but more sex maniac girls, and none of them could ever but ever hold on to a good man. Mama said we'd been cursed with loneliness, but I didn't believe them stories. Those were old wives' tales! But I still knew there was something bad.

"See? This is why I ran away. I said, That's not going to happen to me. I will go to Hollywood and whatever. So that's what I did, I ran away. And everything that's happened in my life, I always figured it was just your regular bad luck, nothing special. I picked the wrong man? Okay, I'll go find another. I moved to the wrong town full of these bitches who want to kill me? Maybe someday I'll move. I always had an explanation for everything. But today when I saw your abuela's ghost, I knew different. My eyes are open now. What they said was right. We were cursed. I am cursed. And I couldn't escape because curses travel."

Mama pointed one finger at me and her hot, pretty eyes burned into mine. She was scaring me. Together those eyes and that finger told me what she was just about to say. In one second she was going to tell me, And Rita, linda, you're cursed too.

But that's when Dolores came back in.

When I saw her face, I knew she had bad news from the telephone. Now usually, a Mexican woman's not going to invite that news into the house. She'd rather beat it with a broom or scare it off with a healthy dose of holy water. Not me, though. I wanted to let it in, to hear it spoke out loud. I wanted Dolores to say anything to fill up the quiet, just so Mama couldn't fix her loneliness curse on me.

I ran to my sister. I put my arms around her and asked her what happened.

"Jose's been arrested for armed robbery," she bawled, loud enough to shut Mama's mouth. "He's down in County. And he needs me to get him two thousand dollars so he can get out on bail."

The two thousand dollars Jose needed from Dolores was the 10 percent we'd have to hand over to the bondsman, because Jose's judge had set twenty thousand for bail. Twenty gees! Like he was Al Capone! It'd be hard enough just scraping up the two grand. But I sprung into action right away, if only to get away from Mama's ghost stories. I rushed to the silverware drawer and pulled out the hundred and fifty we'd stashed there for emergencies. "It's a start!" I said, but Dolores sat down and kept crying. I grabbed her hand and pulled her into the living room, dumped out my purse onto the rug. Among the four lipsticks, two eyeliners, cotton balls, Wrigley's wrappers, bus tokens, and tampons there was thirty-three dollars.

I had us grab up all the emergency money hid in the house, which didn't turn out to be much. We teased two hundred and thirteen bucks from the mattress, the shoebox in the back of the closet, and the cold cream jar under the sink, while Mama sat at the kitchen table holding her head. Then I had another idea, which was to take up a collection. We went door-to-door. On the number streets the women stared at us through their screens, but when we said Jose's name and told them he was a victim of mistaken identity they opened their doors, fished out bills from their purses, and told us about the times he'd walked them home in the dark, lent them end-of-the-month money, or picked their front door lock when they'd lost the key, and so of course, of course, anything to help. We got close to five hundred that way, a thick roll of tens and twenties that made a nice sound when you flipped it with your thumb.

The fighters gave us the rest, all of them digging rabbit ears out of their pockets and writing over their Friday checks. Pedro handed over the most, a cool four hundred in cash that he'd hid in a shoebox. He'd been saving up for a Bel Air Cruiser, he said, and it was no problem, because him and Jose were the best of best man friends. They'd been tight since years back, when they were just twelve years old and together had took down the town psycho, Za Za Medina. Za Za was a sixteen-year-old glue freak who liked to shoot dogs and torch cats, and one day he made the bad move of doing some sex abuse on Veronica, who was Jose's cousin and Pedro's fifth-grade girlfriend. Before the grown-ups could get ahold of Za Za, Jose and Pedro had beat him to pieces with their baseball bats, and afterward Za Za's mother shipped him off to Jalisco to live with his abuelita.

But Za Za Medina wasn't the only reason why Pedro gave us that money. It was because of the politics. After the Rodney King riots died down in '92, he just started getting more and more Malcolm X every day. He didn't just kick around Rabbit Street talking about grapes and telling folks to vote now. He'd become Mr. Back to Aztlan. He hated the Man, la migra, brown-baiters, race-traitors, English-Only, school busing, and he told me and Dolores he'd give us that money meant for a cherry cruiser because he worried sick anytime a Chicano brother got caught in the claws of gringo justice.

"That shit is racial, man!" he said, handing the four hundred over. "Jose's no more a criminal than I am white. But do they care? Do they check it out? No, they just go and pick up the first Mexican they see because, well hell, if he didn't do this, then he must of done something else, right? Jumped the border, sold drugs, or beat up his woman, and even if he didn't do nothing at all he is bound for the hothouse anyhow because let me tell you this, ladies: Round here, brown is the color of bad. They just can't wait to see every one of us locked up behind bars because not only did they kill our kings and cheat us out of our land, but they are so greedy they want our freedom, too."

Oh, he went on. He kept bellyaching all that afternoon and he kept on with it the next day when he drove us to Chongo's Bail Bonds so Dolores could put down the two thousand, and then down to County so we could bail out Jose.

As soon as the concrete block building came into view he was at it again.

"You see that place?" Pedro said. "It is full of brown men, *brown men*, baby, who could be out supporting their families and living a respectful life. That's what they take away from us! Our life and our respect. And you know why they do it? They do it because it makes them feel good. It makes them feel strong. Why you think it takes a thing like a locked-up hermano to make a white man feel like a man?"

Dolores had cried till three in the morning. She had a face like a blowfish. So it surprised me when she turned to him and said, "Pedro, we got some dangerous customers in our town, killers and junkies. What about them? I say those boys do belong in jail."

"You call a man the devil long enough and he'll start living up to that name, girl! Besides, anytime an hermano gives us a real problem, it's the neighborhood who should handle it. Like how me and Jose handled that Za Za Medina."

"Hoosh! That's a bunch of macho baloney, Pedro."

"You don't believe me? Well tell me about this then. If Uncle Sam's so righteous, why do we got to come down here and bail out your innocent man?"

Dolores didn't have an answer for that one. I didn't say anything either. I don't go much in for the politics. But I did hope that Pedro was right about Jose being innocent, and as it turned out he was, thanks to God. What we'd told the number street chicas was true: Jose *had* been a victim of mistaken identity, just not in the way that we'd thought.

Inside the jail it was a confusion. The police lady behind the counter didn't have Jose's name in her files and so she sent us to a desk and then we had to wait in a line, and then go to this office and wait for an hour, and that's when we found out that the charges had been dropped and he'd been set free and was right this minute waiting for us in the release and receive area, which is where folks can pick up their acquitted or bailed-out jailbirds.

When we got there we found Jose sitting on a bench. It was clear enough he'd been through the wringer: He had a bad shiner and some scratches. But he still smiled when he saw us.

Dolores started crying again. She hugged his head and bawled into his hair. "What's wrong with your eye?"

"Aw, I wouldn't let them bring me in without a little fight." Jose was trying to swagger it off.

Pedro papped him on the arm. "So, man. You're off the hook? We can get out of here?"

"Oh, yeah. They cleared me hours ago." Jose told us what happened. Three nights before there'd been a liquor store stickup. A dopehead had put his gun between the cashier's eyes then told him to get on his knees and beg for his life. He'd clicked the trigger, the cashier'd said, or so the police had told Jose when they hauled him in. And after he'd clicked the trigger that dopehead yelled BOOM! so loud the cashier thought doomsday was here and he was dead. Except he wasn't dead. The dopehead made do with shooting at the video camera, which caught both the whizzing bullet and his ebony-eyed face in black and white, and when the police looked in the mug book they found the right man but the wrong name. That is, they'd found Victor Mendoza, who'd used Jose's name as an alias. Jose'd been locked up for thirty-eight hours before they finally figured out the mistake.

By this time, of course, Victor was disappeared. He was on the loose. And who knew what name he was using today?

"Victor's got a million akas," Jose said. We were in the car now. Him and Dolores were smashed together in the backseat and I was in the front next to Pedro. "But I told him. I said, 'Man, don't you use my name. I don't want in with that mess.' And here I am getting thrown in the clink. Did I tell you that they pulled their guns on me? One of them was aiming right at my head and he was screaming! I thought it was lights-out time."

I heard some thumping. It was Jose's leg banging up and down.

"Hey Pedro," he went on, too loud. "You don't think they caught him, do you? He's not too much for handcuffs. He could get hurt or something."

"I hope they catch him," Dolores said. "I hope they catch him and beat the hell out of him."

"What'd you say that for? That's my brother you're talking about, so shut up!"

It got quiet then. You could hear them shuffling apart. We kept driving. I felt the vinyl seat vibrating under my legs. Pedro raised his eyebrows at me and I looked out the window. We passed trees. We passed Eastern Ave, and the number streets. I rattled the door handle. Then we turned onto Chávez and pulled up in front of Chongo's Bail Bonds again, which was dark inside and had a dead neon sign.

"I will not SHUT UP," Dolores said, getting out of the car and slamming the door. Her and Pedro went into Chongo's to go get our money back.

So it was just Jose and me.

His leg started thumping some more and I sat there listening to it thwacking. After a minute it slowed down, then stopped. I could feel Jose staring at the back of my head and my bare shoulders.

I turned around. He looked at my mouth.

"I don't think the police caught him, Jose," I said. "We would have heard right away."

He gripped his knees. "You think?" Now he was staring at his hands on his knees. I saw red welts around his wrists and thought about touching them.

Except by this time Dolores and Pedro had already come back. Dolores was holding a rubber-banded roll of money now, but when she sat down on the far side of the seat she started staring at Jose with eyes big as manholes, and I remembered when I was fifteen and she was the first thing I saw after my bandages came off. I put my hands back in my lap.

We drove for six blocks and nobody said a word. I played the radio and tapped my nails on the dash to drumbeats.

"Pedro. Did you think there was something weird going on with Chongo?" Dolores said. We were coming up on Jose's house.

"Yeah, he was weird. The shop looked closed. And he sure was in a hell of a hurry to get us out of there. But I'd heard he was in trouble. Martinez told me he'd took bribes from one of his bail jumpers and now the heat was all over his ass."

"Why didn't you tell me that before I gave him all our money?"

"Man, I don't know. Chongo's always been a good guy. And there, you got your money back."

"Uh-huh. That's great—he's a good guy. You stupid!"

"I gave you four hundred dollars!"

"Please, just don't say another word. Be real, real quiet. You are giving me a headache."

"Well, I did give you four hundred dollars," Pedro said.

As soon as we got in Jose's house Dolores put the money on the coffee table and said something about making lunch. In a minute she was banging all the pots and pans around in the kitchen. Pedro stood in the middle of the living room whistling and bouncing on his heels and then wandered off to the bathroom.

Jose sat down on one side of the sofa. I sat down on the other side and started peeling up the fake oak finish on his coffee table. There was a live power line between us but I made like it wasn't there, which was easier than you'd expect because of all the banging of pots in the kitchen and the soft sound of my sister cussing. I fiddled with the money roll, which was a bunch of hundreds clumped tight under the rubber band, and said something about all the high-heeled shoes a body could buy with this loot. But Jose wasn't listening. He was shipwrecked. He leaned on his knees and stared blind at his feet.

"I'm worried about Victor," he said. "He'll do something stupid they catch up with him. He'd love to take a shot at one of them police."

I stayed quiet. Everybody knew how Rabbit Street got its name. To think we'd be seeing Victor Avenue sprayed up on another alleyway soon wasn't no stretch of the imagination. I leaned over and patted him on the shoulder, sort of whapping him so he wouldn't get confused about my meaning, which is why it caught me by surprise when he slipped off the sofa and started hugging my legs.

I looked down at his hair, which was so black it shaded into sapphire, and I could smell his cinnamon skin. I will admit that at that minute I thought on touching the blue in his hair or tasting the spice on his neck, but when I looked up I saw Dolores standing in the doorway, and she had on a funeral face so sad I wondered if one of us was dead.

That's when Pedro came back into the room, too, and stopped short. "What's going on?"

Jose sat back, and I stood up. I hadn't done anything wrong but I raised my hands up like a caught criminal.

"Nothing," Jose said. "Nothing. I fucked up. Dolores?"

He went over to her but she just stared at him. Pedro dug the toe of his boot into the shag carpet and shook his head. I had to get out of there, because all of a sudden I felt like one of those poker freaks you'll see at Saturday night neighborhood games, the kind of dude who loses his last dollar then hangs around the play table to cluck his tongue at another man's full house and jingle the keys inside his own empty pocket while everybody tells him Go home.

I patted my hair and pulled down my shirt. I stood up and started walking. By this time, Jose had his hands on her and he was saying I love you and I was only five steps from the door when I went and turned thief. I couldn't help myself. I wanted something. I bent down and grabbed that roll of hundreds from the coffee table and I slammed through the screen door and rushed down the street thinking how I had enough money to buy a used Cadillac, or a pure white mink, or that lifetime supply of high heels.

I thought that at least Pedro would come chasing after me, but nobody did. I don't think they knew what I was doing. Still, as soon as I caught my breath the tingling went away and I felt the guilt. I knew I should turn around and give them the money back, but what was I going to say? Just kidding? I thought about Dolores standing in the doorway, Jose on the floor with his bruises, Pedro driving us to Chongo's Bail Bonds, and by the time I'd got two blocks, I couldn't turn back. It already felt too late.

When I got home I just wanted to see the money spread out. I sat down on the edge of the bed and looked at the green roll for a while, and felt tired. But here I was anyway, I might as well look at it. I undid the rubber band and the money sprung open, and that's when I saw I wasn't the real thief. Chongo was. Only the first bill in the roll was a hundred, and the second was a five, and the rest were faded Mexican pesos that'd been folded tight. We'd later find out that Chongo had closed up his bail bond shop for good and run off to Arizona with his customers' cash.

There were a lot of pesos there, thousands' worth. But in this town they wouldn't even buy you a cup of coffee. They couldn't get you one cigarette. Just because they can't buy you nothing in a store, though, doesn't mean they're worthless.

Fact is, you could say those pesos bought me luck. I had dug down to the bottom of the barrel and come up empty-handed. I knew I was a joke. By then I could have danced naked on Chávez for a full day and still gone home alone. But after I stole the money things seemed to turn around.

See, it was the next day I met Billy.

Billy

During long snowy winters when the frost kills the grass and berries, and the worms and yellow-eyed flowers and blue-gilled fish are covered in the white deep and diamond ice, forest animals suffer something terrible. I know this from watching the specials on grizzly bears that they show on the public TV.

Grizzly bears got persistence. They hide in dead-dark lairs, dreaming of blood and honey, but they don't sleep all season. I have seen them on Channel 6, starving so bad that their cocoa fur hangs ugly from their bones, sniffing the air so their black gums show, while they search for food between storms, digging at the snow and scratching at the fish under the freeze, until the first thaw finally comes and they find red berries poking up from a crack in the ice.

My own spring was a long time coming. I was a nobody here now, and so lonely. But the freeze that almost killed me wasn't the hard shine on a river, it was the cold that would creep into these hombres' eyes when they saw me coming. They'd all sure had enough of me by that time, but I'd still keep coming back to Rabbit Street so I could watch those beautiful boys weave and jab between the rays of sunlight and beat on each other until there was a victor. Plus, besides the good boxing, I just couldn't help but hope that some of them would get interested in me again.

And then Billy showed, the day after I spread out those paper pesos all over my bed. That next afternoon I went to Rabbit Street wearing a low-cut number made out of sheer polka-dot chiffon, but instead of getting my regular menu of catcalls, none of the fifteen studs that had smashed together between the close brick walls looked my way, they were so hypnotized by the business going on in the alley.

Slipping between them, I knew why. The first thing I caught was a pair of fists cutting into Chuco's sinking middle, and then I took in the rest. This was a stranger with Indian eyes and muscles that glinted like beat copper under the sun, and man, but was he a natural. Chuco, now, he was no slouch. Chuco was the number one power puncher at Ruben's Superbox, and for years there'd been talk that he was going to turn pro soon. All those rumors had done him good, too. Plenty of times I'd caught him strutting down the boulevard with his cap set way back on his head, and he'd be high-fiving his friends and making eyes at the señoritas while viejos stuck their heads out of shops and yelled out to him, "When's your next fight, hijo? I got my money on you!" This was the reason he'd been my second choice after Martinez, when I'd had sex with him in my mama's bed and then got my heart broke three weeks later when he dumped me for Cha Cha Rodriguez, that number street chica who stuck to him like white on rice until he dumped her, too, in under a month.

But as I looked into Rabbit Street I knew that man was gone now: the strutter, the heartbreaker. The only dude in the world was this stranger cutting him careful as a surgeon. Chuco tried to hunker down but the stranger fancy-danced around him, throwing left hooks into his mug. He was a headhunter. Here was a stick to the left eyeball, and there was a hook to the side of the skull. The gamblers gawked stupid and shouted out chingados on account of their money was sure to be running on the loser. But even when they were all hissing and booing I think I heard a little bit of gasping, too, because this new man was a magician, and we watched amazed while his Houdini hands unlocked the mysteries of Chuco's bones and cracked open the seal of his skin.

It was almost over now. Chuco tottered clumsy on his heels and punched empty air. His left eye was opened up; his lip was split. The stranger clocked him with an uppercut to the jaw and grinned when Chuco hit the ground knees first. Anybody could see there wasn't need for a ten count, and the money started changing hands right away.

"Pay up, ladies!" Pedro yelled out. It looked like he was the only gambler who'd bet on the money. Jose, Felipe, Freddie, Tommy, and Lucky were scooching uncomfortable in their shoes.

Jose crouched down and put his hand on Chuco's shoulder. "I think he hit him too hard," he said.

"Yeah," Felipe said. "Man looks like he needs a hospital."

The stranger grinned at him. "He looks good to me."

"What you say?" Pedro said. "That's fucked up."

"Fools, you can't hit too hard in boxing," Tommy chimed in. "That's the point."

"Man, I lost all my money, man!" Lucky said.

"What you mean he looks good?" Jose yelled. "Lookit him! He looks like shit!"

"Oh, look who's talking, pendejo," Chuco mumbled from the ground.

"Damn! You got a punch," Tommy said. "What's your name?"

The stranger waited for a second before answering. Then he said, "Billy Navarro."

"Where you from?"

"Cuernavaca."

"Where's that?" Freddie asked.

Pedro slapped him. "Shut up! He's from the homeland, cabron."

"Hey, no, man!" Tommy said. "I mean, what gym you boxing at? You boxing at Ruben's?"

But the stranger had already slipped out the crowd and was making his way down Eighth Street. I didn't need to think too hard about it. I ran after him, even with those boys hollering names at me and calling him a friendly motherfucker. When I caught up to him I touched him on the back and he turned around, eyebrows raised. He was handsome as them heartthrob Mexican actors who play doomed rookies on prime-time police shows, but the thing I noticed most was the C-shaped scar he had carved into his forehead; it was pure white, and deep. I reached up and traced the curve with my thumb.

He grabbed my hand, stepped back.

I wouldn't be scared off. I am bold, and what's more, I got persistence. I laced my fingers in his.

"Hello, Billy Navarro," I said.

I could tell he was different from the others in the first few minutes. He was like me, he didn't waste time. He looked down at me holding his hand and then looked back up and smiled.

"Oh, just check out this little girl. Damn muchachita, who dresses you in the morning?"

I laughed and wiggled a little for him. "Like what you see?"

"Honey, you know I do. You are working it!" He started rubbing my palm with his thumb. "It don't look like you belong in this place. You from here?"

"Born and raised."

He lifted up my hand and then twirled me around so as to get a better view. "Well maybe you're born here but you ain't been raised like the rest of these folks, I can tell that right off."

I didn't know if I liked that. "What's that mean?"

"That means, my baby girl, that you are a one hundred percent genuine beautiful mujer. Ow, chiquita! You so hot you're burning me alive, I can't take it. Why you standing there looking so good? You trying to hurt me or something? You must think it's fun showing off them beautiful legs and excuse me, those chichis too, just to torture these poor pendejos you got around here. But I'm sure they're telling you that here all the time, eh? You got a husband, right? Or you at least got like a hundred men asking you to marry you every day? But hey. You know what? I bet you turn all these nobodies down, don't you? All I got to do is take one look at you and I say to myself, Now, this girl is meant for something bigger and better than this place, am I right?"

Ay, was he a smooth one. I was laughing and gripping on to his hand. But I tried to be smooth, too. "Yeah, you know it. I'm meant for better than this neighborhood."

He stopped and stared at me for a second when I said that. He was still smiling, but the smile was sort of frozen on his face.

"What?" I said.

He shook his head, then smiled wider. "Ah! Just thinking, señorita. You just remind me of somebody. Yeah, I could tell right off. You're a real heartbreaker, huh? A real mankiller.

A woman like you is going to have plans for moving up in the world. You don't have time for no losers."

"That's right."

Billy leaned closer to me then. "Well, chulita, I got to say then that you got your work cut out for you. I been in this town only a week, and I can already tell from how bad these boys fight that they all got real teeny tamales. So I'll tell you what—wait, what's your name?"

"Rita Zapata."

He kissed my hand and shook his winnings at me. "Okay, Rita Zapata. What you say that you and me go out on the town tomorrow night? I'll show you a time so good you'll tattoo my name on your ass!"

"Oh really now?" I raised my eyebrows, but I didn't need no convincing. He could have had me on a platter by then if he wanted. But desperate isn't pretty, so I looked down at my manicure.

"Well, shoot," I said after a few seconds. "Why not?" I told him where I lived, and then asked him to pick me up at eight. "You looking lonely. I'll take pity on you."

It was getting dark now. The sky was the color of smoke. You could hear the sound of rush-hour traffic from the freeway. Billy said he'd walk me home right then, but I said no. I made him give me my hand back because I knew what would happen if he did walk me home: ten minutes of sex in my bed before Dolores came home or maybe a quickie in the bathroom. Then he wouldn't call again. So I told him I had to go meet my sister on Chávez, and that I'd see him tomorrow, and then I walked home alone. It took some strength too, but I knew it couldn't be a wham-bam with him right away, not in the first ten seconds anyhow. I wasn't going to screw this one up.

*   *   *

"*W*here'd you get that scar?" I asked. I was tracing the white moon with my finger and this time he let me. We were in his car, parked in my lucky spot on Mulholland. This was where our whole date was. With any other man I would have been so mad, but with Billy, all I can say is thank God we didn't see a tattoo parlor that night because I would have had that boy's name printed right on my behind, I had such a good time.

He'd brought a picnic basket with chicken and salad and beers and tequila. We'd just been doing shots, and after his second one he sprinkled my collarbone with salt and sucked it before he tossed down his third and bit on the lime. I'd had three myself. I wasn't drunk, but I was happy. Maybe I was a little drunk. I kept biting on my lips and couldn't feel anything. But right now I was touching his face and asking him questions.

He tipped his chin back and looked up. "What, that thing? I don't know. I fell down." He started rubbing his face. He rubbed his forehead with his fist.

I leaned over and kissed it. "Poor baby."

We looked out the windshield. The city lights in the valley glowed red and yellow like a dying campfire. Our breath made white clouds on the windows.

Billy had another shot without the salt, then he started talking again.

"Well there is a story about this scar."

I took his hand and kissed it. "Tell me."

"It's kind of a scary story. It's kind of bad. But it's got a happy ending."

"I want to hear it."

"Okay. So I got this scar about five years ago at home, when I was seventeen."

"Wait, where's home again? Where you from?"

"Huh? Oh, uh—Cuernavaca."

"How'd you learn to speak English so good?"

"I been coming here my whole life with my family, working the seasons and selling oranges. I picked it up easy. Plus I been here permanent for five years. But anyways, let me tell you this."

"Okay, sorry."

"All right. There was this guy in our town named Pancho, like Pancho Villa. I called him that 'cause he had this nasty tough-guy face. Pancho's the one who called me Billy, because see, Billy's not my real name. My real name's Guillermo. But Pancho was a fan of the American cowboy movies and one day he started calling me Billy, after Billy the Kid, and it stuck. So here I am today, Billy Navarro.

"Pancho and me were like best friends since forever. Really tight. He was smart. But man, he had like a screw loose. I mean, he had problems. Of course, at the beginning, when him and me just met, I didn't know that. He was just a good old guy, but then one day he met this girl named Angelina.

"Angelina was a girl in our town. She was something. Really beautiful, and young. Younger than you. She was seventeen."

"What," I said, "did you date her or something?"

"No, nah. I didn't. But listen. So Angelina was beautiful and Pancho Villa fell in love with her one day when we were out together on the street and she passes by. It was love at first sight for Pancho! He couldn't forget her. He laid in bed all night thinking about her. Then one day he writes her a love poem, and then another, and another, and pretty soon she's got more beautiful love poems than she knows what to do with, and she falls in love with him back. Or that's what she said. Maybe she just felt sorry for him. I mean he was an old, ugly man. A nobody! What you might call a loser. But anyway, she said that she did love him and that she would marry him, and for Pancho Villa, this was the best day of his life. So he gives her a ring and they set a date and we all get ready for the wedding.

"But things didn't work out. Angelina was just like a kid. Being just seventeen, she was still growing up. And one day she wakes up and she thinks, I don't want to marry this old, ugly guy. Why I'm going to marry him? No way. He'll keep me in this stupid small town and that's just no good. Because Angelina, she wanted to see the world, she wanted to do things. She wanted to come here—I mean here, to L.A.—and be a singer and all that. And so being with Pancho Villa was going to keep her down. So right before the wedding she tells him, 'Forget it, we're through.' Like that. She breaks up with him, and she starts going out with this other guy, who had a little bit more money and was more of a somebody, and that's when we all found out that Pancho Villa was totally crazy. What I'm saying is, he couldn't take the rejection. Because one day he bought a gun, and then he started following her everywhere."

"Oh my God!"

"I know, can you believe it? It was terrible. He would follow her to the stores, and to the movies, to her friend's house, crying and waving that gun around. Everybody tried to talk to him. *I* tried to talk to him. I said, 'Pancho! You got to stop this! Somebody will get hurt!' But he wouldn't listen. And then one morning, I remember, I heard somebody yelling outside, because Pancho was walking down the street with his gun and saying how he was going to kill them both, Angelina and her new boyfriend. And when I went out there and saw him, I knew he would do it, because of his face. He didn't look like himself no more. He had the eyes of a monster. And he didn't hear a word I said. He kept walking down the street, crying and holding out his gun. So I went inside and got my gun, just in case."

"What'd your parents say? Didn't your dad tell you to get back in the house?"

"Well, they're dead. It's okay, don't look like that, they've been dead a long time. Anyways, when Pancho finally got to Angelina's house, he stood in front of her door and started screaming at her to come out. And she did! She came out and tried to talk to him too, and everybody was out there yelling, but he pointed his gun at her heart, and he told her he loved her, and I knew he would do it."

Billy stopped talking then and looked at me. I was gripping on to my thighs.

"Well, what happened?"

"It was something. I sat there with my gun and I was looking at them and I didn't know what to do at first—kill my best friend Pancho Villa or let this girl Angelina die? I tried to get the gun away from Pancho but he hit me with a rock, which is how I got this scar. And then I saw there was no choice. So I took my gun, and I pointed it at my friend, and I shot him dead in the heart just to save her. I remember he looked at me once before he died, like he understood. Almost like he was glad that I'd done it. But I couldn't forgive myself. It was the worst thing that ever happened in my life."

I stared at Billy, and touched him on the arm.

"I'm so sorry," I said. "That's so terrible." I thought he would cry, but he seemed all right. He drank another shot. We were quiet for a while, looking at the lights. We drank a whole lot. I had two more tequilas, but now I didn't feel so drunk. I sat there holding his hand and resting my feet on the dash and waited.

After a while he said: "But you know, the story kind of has a happy ending, because of Angelina."

"What happened to her?"

"She wound up doing really good. She had real spirit. She left that new boyfriend, and wound up getting her green card and coming here to sing. I heard she might be making a record and that she married this rich guy and is happy."

"Have you seen her? Have you talked to her?"

"Oh, no. Not with everything that happened. She doesn't want to be reminded of all that. I don't bother her."

Then Billy looked over at me again and smiled and rubbed my collarbone some more. "But you know, this is the thing, is that when I saw you, you reminded me of her right away."

"Of Angelina?"

"Oh yeah, mamacita. You're beautiful like her, and more than that I could tell that you want better than what you got. You got plans, right? Like I said, I can tell it. You got dreams and everything?"

I felt quick hot tears coming when he said that. "Yes I do."

"And you want to be a somebody. You want to make yourself better, and different, huh?"

I couldn't look at him. I don't know, him saying those things made my throat close up. People don't usually think that when they see a girl like me. When I couldn't talk he went on.

"Well, you know, baby, I kind of feel like that too. Come on, don't cry. I do, I feel like that. After that thing happened with Angelina, I had to get out of that place. I had to start over, and so I did. That's why I'm here. I've been busy starting over for five years. You know where I been?"

Billy leaned me back, started undoing my shirt, and I stopped sniffling.

"After I left Cuernavaca, I hitched to Arizona." He showed me by drawing a line from my jaw to my collarbone.

On my chest he traced the road he'd hitched from Palm Springs to Phoenix, where he'd worked construction until he had to leave town because he'd beat a man half dead in a bar fight. My left nipple was Phoenix. My belly button was Albuquerque, where he'd been too, busing tables and money-boxing. He'd got all the way to New York and by the time he started kissing my Empire State Building, I was ready to marry him and have sixteen of his babies. Damn but did that Billy know his way around a woman. He tasted my throat and bit my rib bones, and his finger was in my mouth while he nibbled at the soft skin under my arms, and halleluljah! My lips couldn't stop smiling because no man had took his time with me in years, and there it was, now, one leg was out the window and he'd just found the sweet spot and the fat lady was just about to start singing, but then he looked up.

"*Linda*, if you want me to show you how I got to the Bronx then I'm gonna have to take you home."

I was sort of sitting on my head. The whole Valley must have heard me. I reached around and tried to turn the car key in the ignition.

"Oh God," I said. "Hurry the hell up, then."

There is a red sunset outside the bedroom window and it's swallowing a silver jet plane with gold glinting off its wings, but he doesn't see it. He is down there with his hands on me and his eyes closed and when his chin tips back I close my eyes too.

When I'm in bed I move like water.

They can talk about hot tamales all they want but I like it. I like the white sheets buckling under my knees and the rough beard scraping my jawbone. I like that it's me who makes him wait while the firecrackers light one by one under my ribs, and

I like going slow, slow as a girl eating the first ripe plum of the season in tiny bites to make it last. Is it time? Is it ripe? His finger reaches for the trigger but it is me who says now and if I want to I can stop and look outside and watch the hummingbirds or smile at the rose-petal sky, but I don't want to.

I want to dive down. Cheek on the cool sheet, nipples rubbing cotton, and my bones creak and settle under his shoulders while he strokes like a swimmer and breathes rough and moaning. My hipbones flutter up and down like bird wings and there's saltwater on my skin, and that's when the hot thing reaches up and squeezes. If I could I would make it last longer so I could turn around and see his red mouth moving and his eyes open and say Tell me you love me and taste his tongue but then the earthquake comes and it is now, it's right now, it's here, and then when it passes and I get my breath back I look out the window. At first there's nothing, just dark blue air and gold streetlamp light washing down. Then the gold turns into an arm and a neck, and the blue is hair tumbling over a shoulder, and that's when I see a beautiful woman moving in the window, sort of ghostly and floating, but she isn't a spirit. She is me. It's my own reflection. And I am smiling.

*L*ater, in the morning, Billy got out of bed and went out of the house. I thought he'd left without even telling me goodbye.

But then he came back with orange juice and champagne and things in a paper bag and a couple Dixie cups.

"When I was in Arizona I bused tables for a few weeks at this hotel, and the most beautiful women always ordered this at breakfast." He opened up the orange juice and popped the champagne and poured it into the Dixie cups.

I sat up. "Let me help! I'll help you with that."

"No, sit back. I'm doing this for you." He handed me a Dixie cup and told me to drink it and it was delicious. It was better than plain champagne and so perfect and glamorous for the morning time.

"See?" He laughed. "Now you're like one of those beautiful rich women drinking the mimosas in the hotel. You look great all naked in nothing but the sheet."

"What are these?"

"Mimosas."

I drank my mimosa, which sounded like a French word, and felt like I was at the Ritz. Then he took some pan dulce and napkins out of the paper bag. The bread was still warm and smelled like butter. While we ate and drank we held hands and then once he brought up my hand and kissed each one of my knuckles and I felt very, very beautiful.

You don't make something like mimosas just for a one-night stand.

Right then I knew—he was the one.

Lupe's Beauty House

You can tell when a good man comes into a town by the women. Once word gets around even the dried-out grandmas and the wedding-ring-bound married ladies, not to mention the high-breasted single girls, all take to wearing a brighter shade of lipstick and checking their faces in every storefront window they pass by. Because señoras are like anybody else—they like strange. A new man in the neighborhood makes them feel dangerous, sets them to fussing and primping, dreaming about different hands. Sets them to talking, too. Put them together in a room and they'll gossip so hard the air will turn blue. When Billy showed up in town I'd just started working at Lupe's Beauty House down on Chávez Avenue, and it's there I found out firsthand that no matter how high-minded these Divine Drive lady types pretended to be, inside most every single one of them battle-axes was a cockteasing Jezebel just dying to get out and shake her bootie.

"Oh my God, girls, did you see that sweet piece of man?" Señora Mirande was saying this one wickedly busy Saturday afternoon when I had to help get ten women done up for a wedding. Mirande was sitting in a chair with her feet up and air-drying the purple manicure and pedicure I'd just gave her.

In the last three weeks Billy had won almost two thousand dollars on Rabbit Street and the word had spread all over the neighborhood. "Orale, I checked him out the other day and he wasn't wearing no shirt, and hoosh! He's got these muscles in his belly so tight you could bounce a quarter off them, baby, and he's got one of them behinds, too, you know, not like these skinnybuns fools where they got the jeans all hanging down and you're like, Pendejo, who stole your ass? Nah, nah, not this boy, he's got one of them manly kind of asses, where they fill out all their back pockets just so and you know, damn! It was like, Let me take a bite outta one of your peaches, honey! Hoo-hoo!"

All the ladies were screaming and slapping their thighs while me and Lupe ran around and put the finishing touches on the mani-peds, wash-and-styles, makeup jobs, and mustache waxes, not even taking the time to sweep up the candy wrappers and cig stubs these chicas littered the floor with. We'd do the cleaning later, and besides, Lupe's wasn't much to look at, anyways. Lupe Salinas herself is a big-hipped abuelita with bark-colored eyes fringed with fake eyelashes and hair piled as high as a country singer's, and getting done up at her place was more like having your cousin work you over in your kitchen than being pampered in a real fancified salon. Lupe made do with two dryers, one sink, and three rose-pink barbershop chairs with cracked vinyl seats, and almost everybody walked out of there tarted up exactly the same way since she got her Mexican-red hair dye in quantity and could only give one kind of curly perm.

But then she hired me, see. I'm a good beautician. I got a talent for doing nails. I can do porcelains, French tips, silk-wraps, put a rose decal on your pinkie, glue tiny rhinestones on your thumb in the shape of a heart. But I didn't like working there, and not because it was hard work! Though that woman did give me plenty of overtime—Lupe's was the only room in town where a lady could pay ten dollars to get painted up brighter than a Catholic Christmas *and* put up her feet for as long as she wanted, and so we had wall-to-wall women every day. But the reason I didn't like it there was because those mujeres, both the mamas and their daughters, they gave me nothing but attitude. Holier-than-thou heifers judging me! Thinking they're better than me! It showed in the way they snickered at each other when I doodled their hair or how they squinted at me while I filed their claws, but there was something else made it even worse: I could have took the humiliation except for the diamonds glinting on their hands. Most the neighborhood girls who'd graduated from jailbait were starting to get engagement rings, and at Lupe's we had to do at least one bridal a week, which meant styling, painting, and giving matching manicures to six or more of them lucky bitches at a time.

Today we were doing Veronica Hernandez's bridal and so all the worst Divine Drive churchies and daughters were there to get turned into bridesmaids and ladies-in-waiting. Veronica had gone against her mama La Rica Hernandez and said yes to Juan "Snoopy" Cruz, a streetsweeper with a future about as bright as a smog alert. He was a bum! And her wedding colors? They could have been picked out by a blind man—purple and seafoam!—and there was enough baby's breath in her hair to choke a rhino. And still, I was jealous. It was those glittering solitaires that bothered me so bad. My own hand was naked except for my two-inch acrylics, and every time I'd pass by one of those diamonds it'd shoot off lasers that burned my eyes. I wanted to do a little burning back! I say fair's fair. If I didn't get the respect, I should at least get myself a ring. But that's the day things started changing for me a little: not the ring part; the respect part. That day, right there in Lupe's Beauty House, some of the ladies woke up to the fact that Rita Zapata don't eat dirt.

"So which one of you girls gets Mister Muscles?" Lupe asked. She was trying to give Gloria a chignon but that girl had a head like a broom and her hair poked funky out the bobby pins instead of sweeping up elegant.

"I do! I got it all planned out!" Gloria said, and then everybody was screaming and laughing out after her, "Nah, honey, that'd be me!" and "I already got dibs on him!"

"Ay, I swear that man is the finest thing I seen my whole life," Frida said. "If I wasn't gonna marry Tommy I'd be chasing after him myself."

Veronica smiled. "Frida, if Billy Navarro gave you one look you'd dump Tommy in a minute. And you know why? Because that man is got potential. Snoopy told me he never saw nobody fight as good as him. Snoopy says he's sure to go pro, and you know how much a professional fighter makes?"

"Ay, don't say that boy's name in front of me!" La Rica Hernandez said, covering up her ears. "What kind of name is that anyway? That's a dog's name."

"Mama! Don't you be like that! I'm marrying him today!"

"Well you're marrying a dog."

"Hoosh, them boxers make millions!" Señora Mirande cut in. She was another Divine Drive churchie who was good enough friends with La Rica to be in the bridal party, but she wasn't as well off as the others. Her husband had left her for his secretary five years back and these days she made the mortgage by taking in boarders.

"Man, millions." Frida sighed. "And they make even more than that if they get the endorsement contracts."

"This all you muchachas think about?" the Widow Muñoz started in. "Well guess what. You wasting your own potential. More than that, you wasting your time. First of all, here you are worrying who's gonna marry you, then you worry about how big his paycheck is. Next thing, you're worrying about if you can have a baby, then you have the babies and you worry how much they're gonna make and who's gonna marry them. Then they all die and go away and there you are alone in your house watching the telenovelas and one day you wake up and think, Wait a minute! Where is my life? This isn't my life! But you know what? It *is* your life. This is what you get! *Maria de Nadie* on Channel Twenty-eight every day at two o'clock, and that's it. Forget about the men. You should worry about school school school, and making the career number one. Okay? Listen to me! Wake up!"

Everybody sat there staring at the Widow Muñoz with their mouths open. Nobody said nothing. Frida fiddled with her bra. Veronica got busy checking out her manicure. Lupe mashed down Gloria's head some more and Gloria slapped her off then stared out the window.

"Besides, all them boxers are stupids anyways," La Rica said after a minute. "Their brains get all beat up and they can't think right. I mean, just lookit who they're running after! Did you ever see a boxer with a good woman? No. Boxers like las putanas and they spend their millions on the hookers and the parties and the cocaine and everything. So don't you go near them. All boxers want is a bad dirty girl sitting on their lap."

"Like Ruben Lopez and Cherry Salazar," Señora Mirande said.

Everybody took in their breath when they heard that name. Especially La Rica, who sat there crossing herself and cussing at the same time. The way I'd heard it, twenty-five years ago it was none other than La Rica Hernandez who'd been shaking her caboose all over town trying to get Ruben Lopez's attention, and he'd taken her out just one time before dumping her quick for Señora Mirande. Now both ladies hissed together at the thought of Cherry Salazar with her baby-blond hair and her skintight pedal pushers spending a bank account ten times bigger than theirs.

"Bitch," La Rica said.

"Slut," Veronica agreed, nodding her head. But then she looked over at Frida. "You see Cherry Salazar's new car?"

"A red '97 Cadillac!" Frida said.

"Ooh yes! A red Caddy convertible with white hubcaps and all-red leather interior and white piping!"

Now the candy-asses were hooting about Cherry's Caddy and her white mink and her hundred-dollar hairdo and how she'd caught the big cash cow when she trapped Ruben between her tits, and in the middle of that Gloria stood up and snapped her fingers in the air.

"Okay, babies, I say if Cherry bagged herself the big one, then I can too," she said, and with that freaky hair sticking up straight out her head the chica looked half human, half tumbleweed. "Don't you think? What do girls like her got over girls like us, eh? Nothing. It's just they know how to make the men blind with their slutty dresses and how they stick up their big asses like free watermelon. But I am going to go out and get that Billy Navarro and open his eyes. I got it all planned. I am going to invite him as my date to Frida's wedding and then he will see how a nice, good, honest, family-minded muchacha like me is a dream come true."

Them women were all screaming You go, girl! and pounding their feet on the floor so they couldn't hear me clearing my throat at first. When they did, though, they turned around, still smiling and wiping their eyes.

"That's a nice plan, Gloria," I said. "But sorry to tell you, I've been dating Billy for these three weeks and you know I can make a man real happy. He makes me happy, too. And you're right about him being special, Veronica. He's got talent, everybody says so. He's going places. But I'm the woman who's going there with him."

"Oooh, she's una putana just like her mama," La Rica hissed.

"Ay, hija, let her have him," the Widow Muñoz said. "She probably already gave him the vee dees."

I picked up a pair of scissors and snipped them in the air. "Be careful, señora, or I'll give you a makeover."

"Put those down, Rita," Lupe said, very calm, "or you're fired." I put the scissors down.

Gloria was still staring at me. "He'll see I'm better for him than you," she whispered. I just sucked my teeth at her, and her eyes fired. "I'll bet you're lying! I'll bet you're not seeing him! Everybody knows you're dirty, Rita! No man here will touch you!"

"Nah, she's not lying," Frida said. "I saw them two together last week and she was working her nasty over him so rough I thought the poor pendejo was going to have a heart attack."

"Why didn't you tell me that?"

"Because I knew you liked him."

"WHAT? You're letting me go on like that and the whole time you're knowing this hoochie is moving in on—"

"Okay honies, okay," Lupe started in, saying how there were enough men for everybody and that today was Veronica's big day and didn't she look nice in that color eye shadow? Gloria slumped down in her seat and picked at her cuticles while Lupe made the best of her hair. The other chicas were shut-mouthed too, except for Veronica, who started fighting with La Rica about Snoopy again. It was too quiet in there. I knew I'd just rolled the dice. Would they hate me worse now? I went from mujer to mujer, painting on clear topcoats, checking out lipliner, and nobody said nothing, but they didn't stick out their tongues or try to trip me like usual, either. And when I had to help the bridesmaids step inside their seafoam-colored dresses, Frida smiled at me weird and bashful when she put her hand on my shoulder to balance. But I didn't know I'd won something for sure until Señora Mirande winked at me and slipped me a tip, which I held tight in my fist.

"Damn, girl! You made them so jealous!" she whispered.

I should have been smiling at that, I was so hard against them. Just look at them! Veronica's dress was a white taffeta and seed-pearl snowball and the others looked like shaved baboons. They all stood there wobbling on their dyed-to-match satin heels, flicking lint off each other, holding hands, turning away from me. La Rica and Señora Mirande and the Widow Muñoz were already crying about the beautiful bride and blinking careful to keep the mascara from smearing. Veronica had the hiccups; Frida rubbed her back, whispered into her ear. Gloria put her hands to smooth down her dress and when she took them off there were two sweat prints staining the skirt, and right then I remembered the time she'd stood up for me in her bus seat all those years ago, how she smoked Lucky Strikes in secret, and the hard thing in my heart turned to water. I couldn't help it. I wanted to be girls with them. I wanted us all to laugh about Billy's back pockets, I wanted to tell them about what he was like in bed while they whooped and slapped their thighs. But they just hated me with respect now, and they were leaving me. It was time to go. In a whirl, they picked up the veil and lifted their hems and clacked out the door.

To the wedding.

It was empty in there with them gone. Lupe was already cleaning up, and I kept staring out the glass door at the street so she wouldn't see me biting my lip, but then she stopped sweeping and told me to sit down. She opened up a pack of cigs and handed me a lit one, then sat down and started smoking herself.

Now that the ladies were gone and she could roll her hose down, the woman eased up and didn't so much look like a chicana Loretta Lynn no more as a high-haired version of Garbo. That woman could smoke, is what I'm saying. She fiddled the filter with her arrow-sharp nails, took in a drag, then blew out a curl pretty as a black feather boa.

Lupe was kind, too. She knew when a girl was hurting.

"Rita, listen to me," she said, flicking her cig around. "I want to tell you about something. I have not been young for years and years. But you never forget about being young. I will tell you something I remember from a long time ago. When I was a baby niña, my mama used to tell me bedtime stories. The best stories! The most scary! My favorite stories were about las brujas. Now, these brujas, they could do anything, like fly on their brooms and make spells and turn into animals, owls and snakes. But most of them were evil. They would cut up little boys and boil them in a pot, or they would make the rain dry up so all the crops would die. But then they would always be killed by a hero, in the most terrible ways. Burned by fire, or drowned in tar, or crushed by huge stones, while the town stood around and cheered. Sssst! Can you imagine? Such things to tell a child! My mama would whisper these stories to me, and make her eyes go so big and tell me I better be good or else the bruja would come and get me, eat me up. I would shake and cry! But I loved it, too."

Lupe blew out a smoke ring, looked at me through it.

"But then one night my mama told me a story about a good bruja. This bruja had the power to make the weather anything she wanted. She could make it snow, or rain, or bring out the sun. She could make it hail. One day she came to a town after walking many, many miles, and she was so tired and hungry. Her feet were bleeding. She asked the town people for help but when they saw she was a bruja, they refused. They banished her from the town, and she went to live on a mountain, where she was lonely and afraid, and all she could think of was revenge.

"And then came the drought. A terrible drought, a killing drought. All the crops died, and the rivers dried up, and there was no food to eat, no water. The people were starving. Up on the mountain, the bruja was glad. They should suffer for what they did to me! she thought. They should pay! But one day she looked out the window, and below her she saw the people dying, and the children crying, and she let pity into her heart. She came down the mountain, stood in the fields, and made it rain. For the first time, the people understood. She was an angel, not a bruja! But they were still afraid. They cried and hid their faces and begged for forgiveness, and so the bruja left them, she went back to her mountain. But now she had no more hate in her heart. Every time she looked out her window and saw the people alive and laughing, she knew it was because of her. And so she loved them."

I stubbed out my cig in the ashtray, lit up another. "What kind of ending is that? She don't even get to live with them! The bruja still winds up alone."

"A bruja must be lonely. A bruja can't live among people. But this one did a good thing, and so she made peace."

Lupe got back up to clean some more, but I stayed sitting, smoking. My mood was changed now. I was hard-hearted again, and dry-eyed. I sat there thinking about the bruja with the peaceful heart staring out her window at her fat neighbors. I didn't like the story too much. I knew Lupe hadn't told me the real ending. I knew that someday the neighbors would get brave again, then light their torches and stampede the mountain, screaming for the bruja's blood. They'd forget about the weather. And they'd forget about her favor. Because it don't matter if she's good witch or bad; in the end they all get burned at the stake.

Besides, a girl's got to make do with what she's got. Maybe I didn't have any girlfriends, but I had my sister. I had Dolores holding my hand when it was dark. I had Billy in my bed, too. And I had these chicas quiet and wondering, I had them wishing they were me. I had Frida's shy smile. I had Gloria's nervous hands spreading on the skirt. I had Señora Mirande's money here in my hand.

I opened my hand.

I never did too good with the tips. Because I had that bad reputation, these women didn't think they were obligated. They left me high and dry all the time. Señora Mirande herself would walk by my empty jelly jar every week and never once did she throw in even fifty cents, a quarter. But now, here in my hand was her ten dollars. Mirande's manicure-pedicure had cost eighteen and change, plus tax it came to twenty, which made this a 50 percent tip.

I almost laughed. The witch in the fields! The bitch in the beauty parlor! I held that money tight in my fist and I thought, maybe it wouldn't be me who'd have to make it rain.

Maybe it would be them.

Neighborhood

There's a few beautiful things in the world, a few brave things—like music and marching armies and such. And every which one of them things has got its own special, sacred place. God's got church, and opera singers got Carnegie Hall. Baseball players got Dodger Stadium. The President of the United States lives in the White House. Movie stars stick close to Hollywood, and so on.

Around here, the brave and beautiful thing to be is a boxer; it is the brown man's dream. And in East L.A., for fighters—and I don't mean the dime-a-dozen slice-and-dice street tuffs, I mean the real deals, the ones who *want* it—there was just one place to spar and showdown and strut.

That's Ruben's Superbox, down on Chávez Ave.

I'd never been to Ruben's before. I've walked past it plenty of times, though. I've looked inside the window and seen hombres in shorts and red gloves whaling on each other; I've seen them lifting weights and flexing and skipping so quick the rope was a long white blur. There were no girls in there, hardly ever. Once I spotted Cherry sitting on a stool, flicking her hair while she waited for Ruben, but that's it. Ruben's was No Ladies Allowed. Women were known to ruin fighters, he said, because our hormones bamboozle a man's head and weak up his legs. But one day I got the chance to disprove that old fool's tale.

"I'm going to go on over to Ruben's," Billy said when he'd been here a few months. "Everybody says he's the best trainer there is."

I told him it was a good idea. It was time for him to meet Ruben. Billy had already made a big streetfighting name for himself in the neighborhood. Boys were walking around with black eyes, split lips, and borrowing rent money from each other because they'd bet on themselves. But what's the point of being Mister Man if you can't make yourself rich? Billy was so good there was real money to be made. Like the women at the Beauty House said, multimillions. But he'd need Ruben's help to get it. So Billy asked Chuco to make the introductions, and one Friday they went down to Chávez together.

I tagged along. I was quiet the whole way, which must be why Chuco forgot about Ruben's rule. He didn't say I couldn't come. Then he opened the door for me so I walked in, just like that. I stood in that place where girls couldn't go.

And inside that place, I saw paradise.

Everywhere I looked there were boxers punching, jumping, drinking water, stretching their long brown arms, taping their beautiful hands. Sure, I knew all of them. But they were better in here. They weren't part-time cashiers and minimum-wage busboys with bad attitudes no more, they were flyweight sluggers, southpaw bruisers! It was that gym that made them, it was magic. It was fully equipped with shadowboxing mirrors, speed bags and long punching bags, jumping ropes curled up like snakes on the floor, a set of white wood bleachers, and there were two blue-roped rings in the middle of the room. The crazy-making thing about Ruben's, though, was this wicked smell. If you've been around the block you'd know it's 100 percent hombre

—sharp and wet, like burned leaves and lemons. Ruben's smelled so bad because it was packed with all the scrappy dudes who thought they'd done good enough out on Rabbit Street to make a play for the bigs, and they moved around hooking and jabbing, ducking their heads and landing punches, then yelling out chingados when they got knocked down to the ground.

Those boys were trying to be just like old Ruben was, and there's no forgetting what the champ used to look like, neither. All over the walls were framed pictures of a young lightweight with a sharp-boned face straight off the fields of Jalisco, and the boy had two dead-center eyes burning out of his face and a chest so tight you could make out the cut of his muscles and the push of his bones. Right over the front door were a couple of big color shots showing him after he'd beat this Nicaraguan called Chachi Tamayo at the Olympic semifinals, and there was this crowd of wild Mexicans behind him screaming like crazy bugshits and waving their flags, but the best one was where he's raising his glove to the camera and looking straight at you, because even though his face was beat raw and his lip hung down, you could see how he's still cracking this little smile.

That's Ruben in '76, when he was the second local fighter, after Carlos the Bull, to make it to the bigs. He came out from the pachuco street wars where he'd learned the Mexican slugger style, but he'd hooked up with some Italians when the rest of the homeboys were still cutting each other up for pride or spare change. After a couple years of taking falls and fighting bums, he started knocking out favorites like Benny Huertas, Bubba Busceme, and Jack Brennan, and pretty soon he was driving down Pico Avenue in his first snow-white Caddy with one or more long-legged trophy girls sitting right next to him. Man was a legend, even if he didn't never get a title. When Ruben got to Vegas to take on that old Panamanian Roberto Duran, the people around here went way more loco than when we got ourselves Chávez Ave. Ruben wound up getting his ass knocked flat after fifteen minutes but he won himself a nice loser's purse, and when he came home with his shiners and his cut-up chin the ladies crushed around him and whispered their numbers in his ear, and the men all slapped his back like he was a hero home from the war.

Those days were long gone now. In these past fifteen years Ruben had grown a jelly roll around his washboard belly and his famous biceps were shrunk and withered, but he'd grown old graceful. He made plenty of money training the neighborhood hopefuls and has-beens for sixty bucks a month. It was highway robbery! And they all paid it anyways, just so they could step out of their security guard uniforms or take off their short-order chef hats and slip into a pair of red gloves and satin shorts and work on their uppercuts inside a real ring.

Like right now, Ruben was training Tommy Saenz and Jose, and just from their faces you could tell how much they loved it.

"I don't want to see you smiling, Jose!" Ruben barked at them from the corner. "Tommy, you think this is a joke? You GOT TO MOVE, MAN. Feel him out. Feel him out, right there on his right. Sssst. Weak. Oh, and I mean weak. What you think this is? You trying to hurt me, Tommy? I'll beat you myself."

Jose looked good. He'd swing some body blows and lowball jabs, and when Tommy started getting red-skinned and sore Jose'd dance back so he had to run after him and get worn down. Pound pound pound, man. That's what they were doing, Jose sticking and punching at the side of the head and Tommy curling into a clinch, and I heard BAM from the fists slamming and the feet stomping and there's the yelling coming from Ruben and the rest of the boys who crushed up to the ring and hollered through the ropes.

"Yo, don't let him fuck wit you, 'mano!" Pedro laughed.

"Use your right, Tommy!" Felipe yelled. "Guard your left, guard your left!"

Tommy had a raw piece of skin next to one eye and there was a minute where Jose could have opened it up and sent him to the canvas, but he didn't do that. Instead, he eased off by soft-ducking Tommy on the shoulder and backpedaling around the ring. Then he called it quits.

"Nah, nah, let's go," Tommy said. He took a swing.

Jose shook his head. "I'm tired, man. You too much for me." Then everybody started throwing gloves into the ring and booing. He shrugged. "Hey, what you want me to do? I got to treat my bitches gentle."

"Shut up. I could beat you right now!" Tommy was laughing and running after Jose, but Jose blew him kisses and crawled out under the ropes.

After that, it was time for the introductions. The three of us worked up to Ruben, and the two men traded names. Ruben took off his sunglasses and gave Billy and me the up and down.

"Get that girl out of here. Women are poison for fighting. Where'd you say you trained?"

"I didn't train nowhere. But let me up there, man. Let me up there. I can beat anybody you got in here." Billy started punching at the air around Ruben's head.

"Oh you can, can you? Cut that shit out."

Chuco papped Ruben on the shoulder. "It's true, boss. He's got a good punch."

"Fine! Fine! Keep your fuckin' hands off me, pendejos. And I said get that girl out of here. Okay. We got any takers?" Ruben looked around. "Who wants to fight this piece of shit?"

I was worried I'd get kicked out so I hid behind this guy from Fourth Street, Zookie Chamayo, and the rest of the boxers were all shuffling their feet and coughing into their hands. Nobody wanted to fight Billy in front of Ruben.

"Come on, ladies. Who's it gonna be? Hey there, Jose. You still tired from playing footsie with Tommy? Get your ass up here."

Jose did like Ruben told him to. He crawled back up between the ropes and stood in the corner, sweating and bouncing steady on his toes. He wasn't joking around like before and he didn't show nothing on his face. Billy laced up a pair of boxing shoes somebody had handed him then taped his hands and pulled the gloves on with his teeth. He swung up into the ring and stood in the other corner. He thumped on his chest twice.

"Hey, what about the headgear, boss?" Martinez said. "They should fight with some kind of protection."

Nobody paid him attention. Everybody crowded around. Billy and Jose stared at each other.

"Bell!" Ruben said.

They came out of their corners and Jose stuck out his arms to touch gloves but Billy took a shot at him right away, a sharp stick that landed on the jaw. Usually these boys feel each other out for a minute, but Billy didn't take the time. He got busy quick by hunting the head. He threw two right crosses and a hook that left a red patch on the whole side of Jose's face but Jose was a fast learner because the next two landed off the glove. Jose covered up and thought about it. Billy had it over him, you could see it in the first fifteen seconds. His arms were longer and he had the speed and every punch that landed was like buckshot. Jose bounced a little and slipped another hook. Then he moved inside. He punched at the ribs and tied Billy up and went upstairs. He landed two lefts on the head and one of them was lucky because it split the skin over the right eye, and the cut was deep. The blood came down fast over Billy's face, and everybody started yelling. Martinez was pounding the edge of the canvas and laughing. This is where Jose backed off. He knocked his gloves together and made like he was going back to his corner.

"Okay," Ruben said. "That's enough. Bell! Tommy! Get some cotton over here."

But Billy stayed where he was. You could see he needed painkillers and a needle. His eye was shutting and the blood had gone down his chin and smeared on his chest and his shorts. In a real match this would have been enough for a technical knock-out. A lot of the fighters who'd got pummeled by Billy on Rabbit Street yelled and pounded on the ring alongside Martinez. Billy didn't seem to notice any of them. He was getting a weird Kabuki look on his face that I'd never seen before, and I didn't like it. He looked like he wanted to kill somebody. He went after Jose and punched him on his back. Not a dirty punch. Just a punch to tell them it wasn't over.

"Bell," Ruben said, slapping the canvas. "This is sparring, cabrones. Bell!"

"Come on," Billy said, touching his face. "Hit me."

"You deaf, stupid?" Ruben yelled.

Jose turned around and Billy sent an uppercut straight to his chin. Billy didn't protect his eye. He raised his arms to the side and let Jose stick him there four, five times without so much as cocking a glove. It was weird, like he wanted to get hurt, and pretty soon that eye was worse, it was meat. But Jose couldn't hurt him bad enough I guess because after that Billy was punching all the time and yelling COME ON. He was so good you couldn't see the shots coming until they'd landed, and Jose was having a time covering up. He crouched with his gloves over his head, and when he'd try to shoot at the eye he'd just get one in the face. Billy looked mean. He looked scary. His teeth were showing and his blood was all over both of them so you couldn't tell at first that Jose was cut up too. Billy had opened up Jose's eye with the heel of his glove and was trying to split it bigger with combinations; the punches thwacked so loud you could probably hear them downtown. Jose had his hands low. He should have uncled but that part of his brain never did work so good so he kept standing and let his face get pulped.

Ruben collared Martinez and Felipe. "Break them up! Break them up!"

Martinez and Felipe ran up there but Billy was already going to his corner. He slipped between the ropes and started pulling his gloves off with his teeth. Jose was down on the canvas, with his arms covering up his face.

Pedro went into the ring too and bent over Jose. "How is he? Hey, man, you okay?"

Martinez pulled Jose's arms away. "Look at me, buddy. Aw, shit! That's got to hurt." He looked up at Pedro. "He'll live. He needs a doctor, though."

"This is bullshit," Felipe said. "This dude don't know when to quit. Like, Chuco, man. Chuco! Remember when he kicked the shit outta you?"

"He did not kick the shit outta me," Chuco said. "He just got a lucky punch on me is all."

"Oh, now, that's some bullshit."

"What the fuck is your problem?" Pedro pointed at Billy.

Billy was cupping his eye with one hand, but he said, "Come here and I'll show you."

"No, I'll show *you*, chingado! I'll show you!"

Ruben clapped his hands. "Okay, that's it. Shut up."

I'd been standing behind Zookie Chamayo so Ruben wouldn't see me. But now he turned around and gave me a look. "Boss! What's she doing here? No women allowed, remember?"

I gave him a good hard pinch for that.

"Ow, shit!"

"That girl still here?" Ruben said. "Somebody throw her out."

"Well then it better be Billy throwing her out," Chuco said. "She came here with him."

Now they were all looking at me.

"She came with who?" Pedro said.

"With Billy. You know old Rita. She's working over the new blood."

"'Course! She already sucked all us dry," Felipe said.

"Shut up!" I shouted that.

"That's right, shut up," Pedro said. He was waving me over. "Rita, come here, girl."

I stayed where I was, behind Zookie, who was trying to inch away from me. Ruben was going to kick me out and I wouldn't get to see nothing.

"Rita," Pedro went on. "Rita! Come here. Listen to me. You don't want in with this man. I been watching him, and he just ain't neighborhood, okay? He's from like out of nowhere. Who are his people? He don't got no people. He ain't made no friends. He don't hang around. He's too busy beating the shit out of everybody and taking their paychecks. But you, girl, you belong over here. I mean, just—what?—a month ago you and me and Dolores were going over to bail out Jose, and it was you who got all that money together, am I right? You were all going door-to-door and everything? Wasn't that nice? Now that's neighborhood. But this guy, he don't care about that. Just look at what he did to Jose here."

I looked. Jose was still flat out on the canvas. I could just make out his face, and there was blood coming from the eye and the nose. I wondered if he could hear what we were saying.

"Rita, come here," Pedro said. He waved me over again. "You don't want in with that. Come here."

They were all staring at me. Not Ruben. Ruben was looking at Billy. But the rest of them had their eyes on me, and a lot of them were nodding at what Pedro said. I stared back at each and every one of them, then stepped out from behind Zookie and smiled. They were waiting on me! They were waiting to see what I'd do! I fluffed my hair out some and smoothed down my dress. I thought about it. I sure was looking at some history. I'd done the deed with 99 percent of the bums in there, all except for Jose and this eighty-pound small fry with a pimple problem, and did I have the dirt on them. Like I'd caught that dude over there trying on my panties. This fool over here once called me his little sister's name right in the middle of the mambo. And did they know they all used the same kiss-off lines? "I'll call you later, baby." "It's not *you,* linda, it's *me.*" Then I remembered them all manhandling me nasty on Rabbit Street, and how they called me the freak to my face. Shoot! What did they think? I'm going to be running over there for the neighborhood? Did they think I was crazy?

"Rita!" Now Martinez and Felipe were waving at me too and telling me to get over there. Even Largo and Lucky were winking at me.

There was a bad second when I saw Dolores's twisted face, how she would look when she saw what kind of shape Jose was in, but I shook it off and walked into Billy's arms. Not his arms, exactly, because he was still holding on to his eye. But I walked over to him and put my hand on his shoulder.

"Hi." I smiled at Billy. He wasn't too much in the smiling mood, though. He was still looking at Pedro with his good eye.

Pedro shook his head and turned away. He bent back down and said something to the others about going to a doctor. Then Ruben went into the ring and started poking at Jose's cuts.

The rest of the fighters got fidgety. They weren't looking at me so much anymore, except for the small fry, who was staring at my skirt and rubbing his fingers together. The rest of them shook out their arms and cracked their necks while they tried to figure out what to do.

"Well, we should show this dude some a our own business," Largo Ortiz finally said. "Like the four of us, hey? Take him outside and give him a little payback for Jose here?"

"It would take four, too," Freddie said. "I never seen nobody fight like him before. Except for that part where he stopped punching back. But still, man. The rest of it? You ever seen fighting like that?"

"I seen Sugar Ray Robinson fight like that," Zookie said.

"Yeah, Sugar Ray, sure. You ever seen anybody else fight like that?"

"Maybe Julio César Chávez," Chuco said.

"No way, son. Chávez don't got the footwork."

"Damn! Did you see them hooks? He's a hooker."

"I caught one of them hooks myself out on Rabbit. Thought he'd took my eye out."

"Hey!" Largo said. "Pendejos! What about Jose?"

"Yeah right, man. Is he okay?"

Jose wasn't so okay. He was saying he could get up just fine by himself but Felipe and Martinez lifted him up from under the armpits while Pedro told them to be careful. They were taking him to County to get him patched.

"How many fingers you see?" Pedro said. He was holding up two in front of Jose's face, which was swole up blue.

"I can't see nothing," Jose said. "I smell your breath though. Ooof! Buy a toothbrush, cabron."

While they were dragging him out, Ruben walked up to me and Billy. I felt good when I saw him coming over. I felt proud. I knew what I'd just done. Neighborhood! I'd made Billy neighborhood, right there, right then. They all saw it. I deserved thanks and congratulations. So when Ruben stuck out his arm, I half thought it was my hand he was looking to shake.

It wasn't, of course, and I put it right back down.

"So, Billy Navarro," Ruben says. He was grinning. "The man who never trained nowhere before. You do got a punch, son!"

"Yeah, I got a punch," Billy says. He's letting Ruben pump his hand all the hell up and down.

"You can save that bloodbath business for the ring, though. The real ring, the matches. I got the point good enough. You don't cut up boys in sparring practice, it ain't friendly. And we got to work on your defense because it's for shit. You a right-hander, right? You got to bring your left up like this." Ruben cocked his fist in front of his eye. "But I'll teach you all that."

Then Ruben put his fist down and looked at me. I'd never seen him up close before. He'd gone to fat but his bones still showed in his face, and he had a little goatee. It was clear enough he wanted me out of there so I wouldn't thin these boys' blood with my girl hormones. But he didn't say get lost. Instead, he worked up all his manners and nodded at me, then said to Billy, "Come on to the back, I'll stitch that eye for you myself." The two of them went to Ruben's back office, and Ruben shut the door.

I turned around. The boys hadn't started up their training again. Most of them stood around in clumps and mumbled to each other, or stared at Ruben's closed door. A couple of them still looked at me, and they were in a bad mood. And that small fry with the pimples was like a pain on my nerves now.

I made my big exit. I walked across that gym to the front door, and I had to pass through all them. I was nervous. I didn't want them messing with me, and my heart beat too hard and my legs felt weird. So I worked it. I took out my Jane Russell and played that baby to the hilt. I was all hips banging and boobs bouncing and arms swinging and hair flicking and my head was held up high, and whoosh! Wáchale, honies! They stepped back and made way for me. There wasn't any of that old ass-slapping or dirty talk. Nobody pinched me or tried to kiss me. I was Moses strutting through the Red Sea and you would have burned your fingers if you so much as touched me right then, I was that hot.

The bell buzzed when I opened the door, and then I was outside Ruben's. I felt good. I laughed at them through the window and they waved me off and started up with their rope-skipping and sit-ups. I felt great. I walked back and forth on the sidewalk. I wanted to tell somebody. I wanted to tell Dolores about how none of them had laid a hand on me, and then I saw her face again and I stopped smiling. I thought of how she'd been that morning, humming while she washed the dishes. She would cry something terrible when she saw Jose's bloody mug tonight.

I must have looked like a crazy out there with my hands on the window. I focused my eyes and saw my shadow on the glass, a skinny girl with big hair. To take my mind off Dolores, I looked up at the storefront and thought about all the boys who'd come in and out of this door. The gym itself wasn't much. White, with red steps. There was a painted sign. But this place was big anyways. They all wanted in here. Even after they'd stopped coming, the old-timers would still talk about it on their porches, waving their beer bottles around.

I looked up at the sign. It was made of wood and smaller than you'd think for a place so famous, but it didn't have to be wide or tall or glittered up because nobody read it anyways. Everybody knew the white building with the red steps down on Chávez was Ruben's, the place for real fighters. That sign, too, it wasn't just small, it was old and I think Ruben had painted it himself. Painted it and repainted it, maybe three times from what I could see. He'd just painted it over in bright blue, but if you looked close you could make out the shadows of red on the edges, and then a little light peeling yellow peeking from under the red. Sort of shabby, you ask me; I say you either get a new sign or stick with one color. But like I said, he could have put big neon lights up there and it wouldn't have made one bit of difference because everyone knew Ruben's by the red steps and by the reputation. Folks just walked back and forth past this sign every day and I'll bet it'd been years since anybody really read it. But I did. For some reason I looked up at those blue letters and I read them out loud.

They just said what you'd expect: Ruben's Superbox.

A few hours later I was at Billy's place, a month-to-month apartment over on Sixth Street. We were both in his little bathroom. His eye had a deep cut, about half an inch long, that Ruben had already stitched. I was trying to clean it up with iodine that stained my fingers and his skin dark red.

Billy batted at me. "Ow! Keep your claws off me, woman!"

"Ay, pipe down and hold still, you big baby. Ruben says as soon as this thing heals you can go pro. But how's it going to heal if I don't patch it up?"

"Jesus!"

"Hold still." I swabbed it twice. "You are some boxer. I couldn't believe you out there. Nobody could."

"You know what? I don't feel so good right now; I don't want to talk about it."

"Sure you don't, beat up like this. And you know, it didn't have to be so bad. Why didn't you guard your eye?"

He reached over and fiddled with the iodine bottle. "I did guard the eye."

"No you didn't. You just stood there with your hands down and let him crack on you before you went and busted his head open."

"This is boxing, Rita, it ain't knitting. You box, you get hit in the face."

"No, this was sparring, not boxing. In sparring you don't cream the guy!"

He didn't have anything to say to that.

"Dolores sure won't be happy when she sees Jose's eye," I went on. "Pedro's going to tell her I went over to your side and then she's going to blame me."

"Nah, you girls are tight. She'll get over it."

"Oh no she won't, I swear to God I know she won't."

I kept after him but Billy didn't say anything else for a while. He rested his elbows on his knees and shook his head. Then he said: "You know, I really just don't feel so good. I must look as bad as you do in the morning."

"Oh, thanks."

"Aw, just playing." He took one of my hands and kissed it. He kissed each one of my knuckles. Then he looked up at me and touched my face and started rambling a little. "You know you look good. In fact, right now you remind me of my mama. You kind of got her mouth or something. I wonder where she is now, huh? I think the last time I checked she was back there in Tijuana."

I remembered then how he'd told me both his parents were dead. I got scared he might have a concussion and I forgot to be mad. "What'd you say? Billy, are you all right?"

"Or, I don't know, maybe you got her eyes." He reached up and started stroking my hair. "Man, beautiful women are something else. You know, whole cities been burned to the ground for beautiful women. Men get in wars and everything, kill each other. It must be wild to look so pretty and know that you're driving the hombres crazy."

I couldn't help but laugh at that. I grabbed his hand. "You're saying I'm like your mama, but I thought you said I looked like Angelina, that singer you knew back home."

He stopped touching my hair then. "Yeah, I forgot I told you that. Angelina." He looked at his feet, and opened and shut his mouth. I thought maybe he'd started feeling dizzy or sick. I got up to get a bandage, ripped it open, but when I crouched back down in front of him he was staring at me.

I sat back on my heels. "Billy, really though, I want to know. Why'd you beat up Jose so much?"

He didn't blink. "I was hoping he'd hurt me."

"What?!"

He shrugged. "Nah, nah, I'm just playing with you again." But he didn't look right. His nose and lips twitched, then he put his face in his hands and got quiet. I sat back on my heels and patted him on the knee, but it wasn't until I saw his shoulders shaking that I knew he really was crying. He cried hard, like somebody'd died. He bit his fist but he still made an awful sound, and he rocked back and forth, knocking over the iodine bottle so that it spilled on him and the floor.

I was took aback. I didn't know what to do. I put my arms around him and felt him shake. He cried like that for a long time, about an hour. After the sobs died down and he was breathing more normal he lifted his head up and wiped his face.

"I'm sorry." I saw that he'd bit his lip. "I just miss being back home." He was quiet again for a little while, and then he said, "But I don't want to talk about it."

I was kneeling in a red pool, holding on to him and thinking. I saw I had red handprints on my blouse, and my skirt was stained too. It was one of those things that could go two ways. It would have been easy to think he belonged in the boobyhatch. He didn't have any reason to cry: Everything was going great. He'd just got Ruben to back him! And plus, I'd never seen a man crying before. It wasn't the most macho. Maybe two years ago, I would have broke up with him, but it wasn't like that now. Not after the beautiful things he'd told me on Mulholland and the mimosas. So it went the other way with me.

I put my hands on his arms and tucked my knees around his legs and I felt him hold on to me, almost too tight. I stayed there with him and tried to figure this out. I thought about how hard it must have been to have so much nothing for so long. Wandering all over, rootless, trying to be brand-new for these last five years. And plus he was an orphan. The more I pondered on it, the more regular it seemed. I thought I understood it. I'd sure felt it myself, how hard it was to change your life around. And I'd felt, too, how sometimes the heart rises unexpected and splits you in half.

When I thought about that, the love rushed through me, so quick and hard it hurt. I could feel then how love can make a person lose their control because they'd want to keep it so bad. It could make you lose your sense of direction and wind up anyplace, like here, bawling in a bathroom for no reason. It shook me for a second. When that passed I sat up and kissed him on the hair.

"We don't have to talk about it, baby," I said.

We never did talk about it either, but I didn't forget it. The blouse and skirt I'd been wearing were ruined totally by the iodine, with permanent red stains. I made them into cleaning clothes, and whenever I put them on to scrub the floor or wash the windows I remembered that day in the bathroom. Most of the time I'd feel good, I'd feel that quick rush again, and think about how Billy had showed me his secret heart. Sometimes I didn't, though. Sometimes I looked at the stains and they seemed weird and bloody. I'd try and make myself feel a heart-flutter, but I could never fake it. Those times I'd take them clothes off and just put on something else.

The Raid

I didn't see Dolores until two days after Billy beat up Jose at Superbox but as soon as I laid eyes on her I knew he was wrong about her getting over what he'd done to Jose. She had been crying so much she'd worn her face out. There is a word in Spanish for her face then. Her face was afligida. In English this means, I think, to be afflicted. She was so sad and angry that she was sick with it, and this showed in her yellow skin, her red eyes.

Those red eyes were looking at me right now. We were in our bedroom, which we'd decorated together with old rag dolls, handmade curtains put together out of pink rayon, and a fuzzy pink rug. We were getting dressed. I'd already put on my blue dress and low heels for Lupe's Beauty House. Dolores was supposed to be zipping up the polyester uniform that she had to wear for her new job as a cashier at the Payless. What she was mostly doing, though, was yelling at me.

"Jose needed twenty stitches, Rita!" she said. She went on about how he'd had to wait for an hour and a half for the doctor and how it was a miracle he hadn't lost the eye. She said how there would be permanent scarring, then hollered about the emergency room bill, which was two hundred and thirty-five dollars.

"And he told me how you went off with that what's-his-name. After that guy beat him up you went right up to him and hung all over him, with Jose lying there in front of you!"

So Pedro did tell her, I thought. I'd wondered about that.

"His name's Billy Navarro," I said.

"I don't care what his name is!"

Dolores cried some more, which made her look worse. She finished zipping up her uniform and looked at me. "So, you're going to break up with him, right? You're not going to see that what's-his-name anymore." She crossed her arms and waited.

"Don't you do this, okay?" I said. "This is my boyfriend now."

"No, I'm serious, Rita. This guy could have made Jose blind. You got to do this for me."

I started feeling sick. Dolores and me didn't really fight much, it didn't come natural to us. She was my girl. But I couldn't do what she wanted. Not now, when everything was happening to me.

From outside, the morning light shuddered red and gold through the window, and it flickered over both our faces, burned white circles onto the wood floor. I walked across the room through the beams and circles of light. I went to my bureau and opened up the top drawer. I couldn't do what she wanted, but I could do this. I took out the rhinestone star pin I'd stole from Cherry all those years before, the one Dolores always had an eye on.

"Here," I said. I handed it to her.

She threw it down. "I don't want that!"

I went up to her and tried to hug her and kiss her. "Come on, please please take it. Don't be mad at me!" I put it back in her hand.

Dolores walked backwards and sat down on her bed. She looked at the pin glitter in her hands. I thought she would say something, or smile at me from remembering. We always made up, it was easy, but this time she grabbed some extra shoes and an after-work outfit and slammed out the door without so much as saying good-bye. I stood there sort of shocked. I kept on expecting her to come back and hug me. She didn't, but by the time I figured that she'd really gone it was too late to run after her and I got worried. I went over to her bed and looked. I ran my hand over the spread to make sure and then laid down on the bed and let out a big breath. It was going to be all right—it wasn't there. She'd forgave me at least enough to take the pin.

After that, I tried not to worry so hard about it. That is, I didn't mention it to Billy. I thought Dolores taking the pin was a good sign. But really, I didn't mention the fight to Billy because I didn't want to ruin my good luck with bad feelings and vibrations. Things were going too good.

I was crazy in love. I had all the stars in my eyes. Sex was like a brand-new thing. When he'd cried in the bathroom I'd known he had a tender heart, but Billy was also a real romantic. Like he always liked me to have a lot of orgasms. He thought it was great that I could have so many. Even when I was tired he knew how to start me up, and he would. Later, he would count them up and we'd laugh.

To me, him caring so much about me being happy in the sex department was a big deal. Sex had always come to me easy—that is, feeling my pleasure. I could be okay whether the guy cared or didn't. But now it was better. Afterward, I would stretch out and feel my heart beating through my whole body. And then sometimes when he'd gone to sleep, I'd put my cheek on his chest and try to match our heartbeats up. It was this game I never told him about. I'd concentrate and try to make mine as slow and steady as his.

Still, if only I hadn't been fighting with Dolores it all would have been perfect. There I was, just turned twenty-one, in love, but it was hard to be superhappy when we weren't getting along, even though there were a million reasons for me to celebrate. Everything else, not just the sex, was beautiful. Ever since I'd got with Billy my life had been going up, up, up. For one, I was doing great at the Beauty House. I was learning how to straighten hair and how to do the new airbrush manicures, and now that some of the customers thought better of me I could talk them into buying all kinds of commission products like the organic hair mousse or Nefertiti facial masks made from genuine Egyptian clay. For two, there was Ruben's Superbox. In honor of Billy, Ruben had forgot his no-woman rule just where I was concerned. These days I had my own special spot on the bleachers, where I could watch the boxers anytime I wanted. But the only time I wanted to watch, of course, was when Billy was training. This was because I never forgot where my good luck was coming from.

And I never took it for granted, either. In fact, I was living up to that hombre just as much as I could. I was making myself over with the classy minimalism look, which isn't as easy as you'd think, or as cheap. I scrubbed off my temporary rose-and-thorns tattoo and bought dresses went down to mid-thigh, and baby sweaters that hugged every inch but didn't show off so much of the cleavage. I bought matte lipstick and got rid of my glitter gloss, too, and stopped drawing on star-shaped beauty marks and gluing on the extra eyelashes. I even splurged on a real bottle of Shalimar cologne, which I'd spray on my wrists, belly, and behind both knees.

So I was on my way to being a bona fide señorita. I was giving the churchies a run for their money. My one problem, though, was my walk. I guess that swivel-hipped way of stepping I got is deep in the Zapata blood, because I couldn't tame my wiggling bootie down no more than I could grow an extra nose.

Three weeks after the fight at Ruben's, I was out by Chávez Ave working on that walk of mine. Me and my sister hadn't spoke more than a few hellos or good mornings since then, and I was getting ready to sit her down and have a good weepy make-up talk. But like I said, at that minute I wasn't worrying about nothing except for my outlaw behind, and as I strolled down Chávez I tried hard as I could to slink instead of strut, glide instead of pop; I wanted something in between Natalie Wood's waltz in *West Side Story* and Miss America as she was doing her thing down the catwalk.

By the time I'd gone a few blocks, though, I gave up and looked around me, then took in a good breath. Poor old Chávez was changing fast, and it was all for the worse.

It had just turned five o'clock, but none of the regulars were out. I didn't see Señora Olmos race-walking to Rudy's Super for some last-minute dinner shopping, and the new mamacitas Celina Medina and Susanna Díaz weren't in front of Payless hitching their red-faced babies on their hips and gossiping like usual, either. And where were the those eighth-graders Lalo Perez and Danny Sanchez, who spent every afternoon posing like gangsters on the curb? Or Carlito Ruiz, a construction worker, who had a habit of hanging in front of Carnival Liquors with his buddies after work?

Most of them were nowhere to be found. Last week la migra had raided the downtown garment district and hauled off almost one hundred Mexicanos for illegal sewing and cutting and sweeping and stitching. The ones with the rap sheets got thrown in the pen and the ones with no papers were put in a Tijuana-bound van and the legals all came home telling stories about the gringo devils who'd busted into the factories with holstered guns and asked them for ID in perfect Spanish.

It was the biggest sting in INS history, the paper said, and I believed it from the looks of things. If the neighbors hadn't got deported then they were just staying home. So here it was five o'clock and instead of color and commotion Chávez was nothing but a long black-and-white stretch of quiet, except for one or two churchies picking up roasts from the meat man and leaving off their broke high heels with the shoe man, and a couple Fifth Streeters wearing leather jackets and red bandannas and smoking their home-rolleds under a streetlamp.

The sun was still burning gold at the end of the sky but the air was darking up enough so I could make out that a few of the shops didn't have their lights on, and when I passed by the windows I either saw shadows or cashiers flipping through magazines. I went two blocks farther and I didn't pass anybody except for a poodle-permed abuela who was real careful to step out of my way and one gradeschool girl who wasn't. The girl was coming out of Carnival chewing on a stick of gum, and when she saw me she stopped, and stared, and swallowed.

She couldn't have been more than thirteen because her skin shone like a new penny and her sweater hung flat, but she was going to be something else in a year or two. She had eyes the cool color of a wave before it breaks, and long red hair that glinted gold in the dusk. The thing that made her special, though, was a real Marilyn Monroe mole she had right by one eye, not penciled-in and not a tattoo, and it gave her baby face a natural old-style Hollywood glamour that most girls have got to spend hours faking in front of the mirror.

She'd be something someday, but not just yet. Now she was a fuzzy-brained eighth-grader who'd just swallowed her gum and was staring at me starstruck, and I remembered that day a long time ago when I was a little girl in a Salvation Army dress and had got struck stupid by Cherry Salazar rolling on the sidewalk, because she'd looked to me more like Queen Cleopatra tumbled straight from heaven than a mortal woman who'd tripped over my foot. So I was nice to this girl. She was sure to be intimidated by my silky dress, my pressed-straight hair, not to mention my glittery reputation, and I smiled at her wide and friendly, like Cherry had smiled at me.

That's when I saw that this little thing wasn't starstruck. She was staring at me, and not nice. More studying me than anything, and now I was the one struck stupid all over again while I watched this niña with the manners of a billy goat raise up one eyebrow and give me the up and down, checking out my clothes, my shoes, and my face the same as a hard-bargaining vieja will squint at a cut of cloth before deciding if it's worth the price. But I couldn't tell what I was worth because those eyes of hers didn't give anything away, and when she'd had her fill of me she shrugged, flipped her hair over a shoulder, and then walked off.

The dusk was turning thick and I stepped quick so the air could hit my hot face. That little bitch! I was angry, but there was something sorrowful creeping into my bones too. The sound of the billy-goat girl's shoes clipping away from me, the black-shadow windows of the shut stores, and the lonely streetlamps throwing pale light off the black tar road reminded me of a ghost town, and I didn't feel better till I made out a group of chicas down the next block. They were all huddled in front of Carlita's Fashions and peering into its dark window glass.

When I got closer, I saw who they were. It was the Divine Drive types: Gloria, Veronica, Frida, and some other girl behind them who I couldn't make out. They were knocking on Carlita's Fashions' front door but Carlita had closed up shop and gone home. I saw that they were all dressed up for one of their ladies-only days, with done-up hair and full makeup, new manicures, the works. I knew they did this about once a month—they talked about it enough at Lupe's Beauty House. They called themselves the Latina League, and it was no joke. As regular as a religion, these women would get together at least once a month for lunch, coffee, maybe a matinee. I figured they'd probably been shopping all day and were going out to dinner, too. I looked at Gloria, who was fancied up in a good dress and a star-sparkly brooch and shined-up shoes. She said something I couldn't hear and the rest of them threw back their heads laughing and hung on each other's arms and I felt that old snake sting that usually came whenever I passed by girlfriends giggling together or doing each other's hair. But I kept walking up to them; I wasn't going to turn around. I banged out my hips for all they were worth so my flirty hem swung around and I tapped up the sidewalk so as to show off my new fancy-strap high heels, and still laughing, they turned around and faced me, and that's when I saw who the fourth girl was.

It was Dolores.

She was wearing her best dress, the blue Butterick she'd sewn for her first date with Jose, and had on a pair of white sandals I'd bought her for her birthday last year. I still didn't understand, though. She was smiling and they were smiling and Veronica's arm was draped casual over her shoulder, but my sister and my old blood enemies couldn't mix together in my mind.

"Dolores?" I said. I was smiling back at her, but her face was serious now. I saw somebody had done her hair—it was flat on her head and pressed into tiny waves.

It wasn't till I looked back at Gloria that the shock hit me, and I knew that Dolores wasn't here on accident or weird coincidence, but that she was one of las girlfriends, too. I stared at Gloria's brooch. It wasn't just any brooch picked up at a garage sale, this was the star-shaped rhinestone pin I'd stole five years ago from Cherry Salazar. I remembered being sixteen years old and untying the red satin ribbon and opening up that white box. I remembered holding it under the lamp and watching the rainbows shoot out from the stones. Now Gloria turned and the star caught the falling sun just right and a ray of burning blue light hit me straight in the eye, and then I wasn't just struck dumb, but was now blind, too.

Jose and Dolores got married on December 15, 1993, in the backyard. I'd done her bridal myself. Dolores was wrapped in white lace and a five-foot veil. Her hair was pressed back and teased on the bangs and her manicure-pedicure was the same pink as the seashell in her seashell-and-lemon color scheme. Jose had a glossy comb-back and was wearing a classic black-and-white tux, with a lemon cummerbund and matching socks. I was so caught up in the fashion details of the wedding that when they actually got up in front of the padre to take their vows, I was almost surprised. Jose's voice cracked when he repeated after the padre's promises to honor and love, and Dolores cried so hard her veil shook, but they finally got through it and slipped on the wedding rings, which were plain gold bands.

Afterwards it was lunch for forty. There was a mess of plastic plates and forks and borrowed picnic tables, red and white paper roses, macaroni salad, pork and jalapeño chili rellenos, and the white-sheet and raspberry-filling wedding cake that Mama had baked and frosted the morning before. The Divine Drive types had all been made into bridesmaids along with me, now that Dolores and them were such good friends. Veronica, Frida, and Gloria sat at one of the front tables, screaming giggles and shoveling seconds and showing off their own wedding rings. Even Gloria had one by this time, because she'd gone and snagged Chuco in her beak one night when he was good and drunk at a barbecue, and never let him go. Now the poor old man, along with Pedro and Snoopy and Tommy and Martinez, was getting skunked on sneaked whiskey and singing bad love songs on a karaoke machine. Jose's family had come too. There was Victor looking like a Tijuana hit man in black tie, and Patrice Hernandez with the shaved eyebrows and the teardrop tattoo picking at her food. They were sitting uncomfortable next to La Rica and Mr. Hernandez, who had showed up to celebrate the wedding of his nephew. It was clear enough that Mr. Hernandez had forced La Rica here. She had a face like a bull before it charges at the red cape, and she was holding her knife in her fist like she wanted to stab it in somebody's heart.

I sat next to Billy and Mama. Billy wasn't having too good a time because the bride, groom, and best man had already told him in so many words how much they hated his guts. Mama wasn't doing that great either. She tried to smile at me and Dolores as she cut dainty into her chili rellenos, but she couldn't help but look wistful at Mr. Hernandez.

Every ten minutes the Divine Drive girls would start chiming their spoons on their glasses and yell out "Besos! Besos!" And Jose and Dolores would do it, pressing their frosted faces together, kissing and giggling. After the party'd thrown back a pickup full of champagne and beer, the girls' mascara started running and they were banging their fists on the table and kicking up their bare feet and throwing the cake around, and asking to see more than just regular besos.

"Hey, ding ding ding! Let's see a French kiss, baby! Slip your man a little tongue!"

"Who-wee. I remember the first time a man slipped me some tongue. I was like, Get that slug outta my mouth, pendejo. What kind of kinkies do you think I'm into?"

"But you liked it later, am I right?"

"Oh hell, did she? I remember seeing you work your nasty all the hell over Tommy there. I thought you were gonna eat that poor sucka alive, girl!"

"Hey now, Dolores! Your turn now, girl! Show us some skin!"

"Oh damn they gonna have sex tonight!"

"Girl, you married now! Nothing like being married. You get all the sex you want all day all night, hoo-hoo. No more keeping them virgin knees together, hija!"

"You get yours, girl!"

"Gonna do it in the bedroom in the kitchen in the hallway in the bathroom . . . "

"In the shower! You babies got to do it in the shower!"

"Show us some leg, honey! Oh hot damn, Jose, you got yourself a freak on your hands!"

The rowdier those girls got, the quieter I got. I hunched down and sweated and sliced my food into tiny, perfectly square bites until a big-busted hussy dressed in pastel hot pants sat next to Billy and put her hand on his knee.

"Hi, you good-looking man!" she said. This was Ki Ki Muñoz, Frida's slutty fifteen-year-old cousin who lived in Monrovia and already had a reputation that stretched clear from San Diego to Bakersfield.

He grinned at her way too wide. "Hi back."

"Get away from him, Ki Ki," I said. "Or I'll rip that fake hair right out of your head."

"Ay, don't get your tubes all tied up."

"I mean it." I grabbed one of her acrylic cornrows and yanked.

"Ow!"

"She's just a kid playing around," Billy said, waving to her when she trotted off.

"Yeah, well, I know about girls like that. Her idea of playing around is screwing on a jungle gym."

He watched her walk away, then ate the rest of his cake while I stared miserable out at the party. Dolores was laughing and showing off her garter belt and Jose snapped it on her thigh while everybody whooped. Frida and Veronica were shimmying their shoulders, and Gloria was putting paper roses in her hair. I felt so mean and sad. I wanted to holler and clap my hands, I wanted roses in my hair, but I also wanted to slap every bridesmaid I laid my eyes on.

Except then the spoons chimed on the glasses again and Dolores looked straight at me, and all that went away. She came over, smiling and crying, and kissed me and I loved her so thick and hot then, I loved her more than anybody. I wanted to tell her that the blue light from Cherry's rhinestone pin was still burning and blinding my eyes, but today was her wedding and so not the right time. Which is why, instead of saying anything, I just reached up and held on to her tight as I could. I buried my face in her veil, then gripped on to her skirt like I was falling through space.

I guess I held on to her too long. The party got quiet and nobody was laughing anymore, nobody was singing along to the karaoke machine. I knew they were staring but I didn't care. I could have stayed there for a long, long time, hugging Dolores. After a while I felt her stir under me, and I heard the Divine Drive types whispering nasties and Billy coughing into his fist. Mama put her hand on my shoulder and said my name, then said it again. But it was only when she called me the third time that I finally let go.

The Closeout Sale

*C*arlita's Fashions used to be what you'd call an institution in this town. It was *the* place for the high-fashion clothes, tiny perfect pieces of French costume jewelry, panty hose that matched the color of a Mexican woman's skin. Every mujer in the neighborhood would make a trip at least once in a while to Carlita's, even if it was expensive. This was because of the hard work of one woman, Carlita Moreno. A skinny ex-model from Mexico City, she'd moved to the States thirty-five years ago and set up this shop. She'd made it her business to add style to the neighborhood. She swung around town in fake fur and satin shoes, wove Italian words into her Spanglish, dropped comments about the trip she'd took to Paris. But the best part about Carlita was she always had what you wanted. Needed a new skirt for a neighbor's quinceañera? A black third-date dress? Something in violet or pale pink for a second wedding? You'd find not only that but a pretty pair of two-tone high heels, a bra made of sheer spiderweb lace, or a bracelet made of tiny crystal beads, each one like a pure drop of water.

That shop was a place where the dollars flew out of your wallet. Ladies had been known to spend their end-of-the-month money there. Families had washed in freezing cold water because of a satin blouse, or ate dinner in the dark because of the price of a Spanish shawl, which is why Carlita's had survived the Vietnam War, the El Niño flood of 1975, a pack of silk-eating rats in '87, and the '92 riots.

But Carlita's Fashions had come to the end of its long rope now. It couldn't live through this last disaster—the downtown raids of '93.

Those raids killed a lot of Chávez shops. The people without papers had always done their shopping on this street for their flowers, shoes, boom boxes, makeup, and groceries, and their rubbed and wrinkled money had whispered back and forth between hands over and over, so that everybody always had a little something to pay the bills. Now they were gone, either shipped off or scared off, because la migra could come anytime, anyplace—not just to the factory, but to the street corner, the hospital, the park, the stores, even the schools—and handcuff you, pull you into a van, then drive you to the border and dump you over the line if you didn't have a green card. So the people stayed away from Chávez Ave and the stores were empty, and then one by one they started closing.

The first one to go was Las Floras, the little flower shop owned by Mister Valdes, where you could buy Mother's Day bouquets for $11.99 or Valentine's Day roses for two dollars each. Months later, there went Paco's CDs, which must have had the largest collection of Menudo in the nation. Next was SuperCandy, the place for pan dulce, and Yo Yo's Taqueria, where they had the best carne asada burritos. Then bam bam! In the space of one week Chávez Dog Grooming was dead and so was Econo Auto Glass, and when you looked down the road now you saw plenty of for-lease signs hung in dark front windows, and homeless were starting to sleep in the doorways.

And then Carlita's turn came too, here at the end of '94. In the middle of one month she had a 10 percent day, and then we saw half-off signs in the window. She tried to hang on as long as she could. She had a two-for-one day, and a Free Beauty Consultation day. She made the most beautiful displays, and once even gave out free champagne. But the ladies didn't come, legal or illegal. If they weren't scared of the INS or of the homeless then their husbands had lost their jobs so there wasn't enough money for silk scarves *or* the heating bill. Carlita was left with piles of overstock and unpaid IOUs, and she finally had to give up her shop. Today was her closeout sale and the place was mobbed for the first time in a year with every chica in the neighborhood. Me and Dolores were there, too, picking over the dresses and skirts.

"Two thirds off on the lingerie," Carlita yelled out from behind her counter. "Three-for-one silk scarves this day only."

I could tell this was a closeout that was going to get ugly quick. Some of the slit-eyed bargain hunters stuck out their asses or pushed out their elbows so you couldn't reach the bins they were digging through, and a couple penny-pinchers were already catfighting over a pair of panties. "No, I got it first," one of them was saying. "Get your hand *off* that, gorda. Okay? You don't let go a these undies I'm gonna kick you in the head."

"Half off on Italian leather shoes," Carlita was bawling.

I beat Cha Cha Rodriguez out of a rose-print halter top and Dolores got a red-and-gold sweater, perfect for Christmas parties. We shoved through the hot bodies and stood behind La Rica Hernandez, who was getting a dress rung up. The Widow Muñoz, a couple number street chicas, and Gloria lined up after us.

"Fifty dollars for real silk," Carlita said to La Rica, shaking her head. Carlita had been at this for hours by now and was starting to lose it. Her red hair was sticking up funky and her roots were showing black, and her lower lip started quivering. "Why don't you just put a gun to my head?"

La Rica raised an eyebrow and puckered her upper lip till it touched her nostrils so that she looked as mean and ugly as a jack-o'-lantern about a week after Halloween. "What are you talking about?" She was getting older, fatter, and her new ash-blond Doris Day 'do didn't hide the wrinkles. She turned around and looked at the Widow Muñoz. "What's she talking about?"

"It's the menopause," the Widow Muñoz whispered.

Carlita shook the green silk in the air. "I'm talking about this goddam dress!" Her face gave a couple tugs, then it crumpled up. "You coming in here with your new leather bag and your new Cadillac parked across the street, just so I can sell you a two-hundred-dollar dress for fifty? Where were you last month, eh? Where you been for the last six months? Well you're here now all right. You robbing me." She covered her eyes with her hands.

All of the ladies looked at La Rica. She was the one who decided who deserved charity in the town, and she could do this because she was usually good at choosing who to hate and who to help. The others went along. But La Rica was getting too old. Her temper had turned rough and stubborn. She was losing her grip. I could see this now, because she made a mistake with Carlita. She took offense, and when she turned back to the counter, she rapped her nails on the Formica and didn't let her face go soft with pity.

"You say I'm robbing you? Andale, show some dignity. Do you think I really need another one of your stinking dresses? Well, let me tell you something, let me tell you the truth."

Carlita looked up, then saw everybody staring at her. "No, wait," she said. "Ay Dios, I lost my head. I didn't mean nothing."

"Lay off her, you old donkey!" I called out, but La Rica didn't so much as flick me a look.

"No, *you* wait, Carlita," she went on. "Let me tell you this. I don't need your clothes, okay? They always fall apart, buttons come off. And they don't got any style. I could get this in Tijuana, you know that? For pennies. I just came in here to do you a favor, but now I see you in worse shape than I thought. Hoosh, yes, no wonder you lost this place, Carlita! Look at this hair of yours! And what happened to your pretty face? Why I even come in here? I see I'm not wanted. So you go and keep your dress. Green don't look good on me anyway."

Carlita wiped her face up and started shoving the dress at La Rica. "I'm sorry, I'm just crazy right now, don't listen to me." She was trying to smile again, but her face was horrible with her big teeth and the black ringing her eyes. "Here, just take it. Take it. It's free. I'm sorry."

"I told you, I don't want your garage sale trash! I come in here to help you out, you treat me like this!" La Rica shoved the dress back, waved her hand in the air.

The ladies in the shop were froze in their shoes. I saw a few of them were making mouths and shooting eyes at each other. They hadn't minded when La Rica had once turned her back on Señora Molina, who'd lost all her money to drink, or when she'd written off Cecilia Cardenas because she would never bring food to the padre's potlucks, or even when she'd run my mama out of the church. But with Carlita it was different.

I guess that's when Gloria saw her big chance. She coughed and then lifted her chin.

"Don't you talk to her like that no more, Señora Hernandez," she said. "Yelling at her and making her cry! Don't you got a heart? Can't you see the woman is hurting? Buy the dress and leave her alone."

La Rica turned around again, very slow, and locked her eyes on Gloria. "Oh no, hija, you wouldn't be showing me disrespect too, would you?"

"I don't mean to, Señora. I'm just saying—"

"Because you would be making bad blood between us if you were showing me the *disrespect.* Now why would you want to do that?"

"Señora Hernandez, I don't want bad blood between us. But Carlita don't need to get told how her clothes are ugly and her hair's a mess. What the woman needs now is us to help her, and love her, and treat her good. She got the whole world beating the hell out of her and now you too!"

"Gloria! Shut up!" Veronica yelled out. She was in a corner trying on a skirt.

"And what are we all supposed to do?" Gloria went on. "Stand around and not say nothing because we're all scared of you? Well, not today, no way. I'm gonna say something about it."

The women in the shop were all big eyes and open mouths.

"Oh yes, you are saying something, aren't you?" La Rica laughed. "You say we should love Carlita?"

"Yes I do."

"And that we should help her out?"

"That's right."

"Well, hija. That is something. Because didn't I love you and help you out?"

"No, you wait a minute—"

"Didn't I let you into my house, even though your mama was nothing but a loca whore who sold herself for cigarettes? Didn't I tell every mujer in here, Give this poor girl Gloria a chance, because she can't help who her mama is? She can't help that her mama fucks other women's husbands, now can she? She can't help that her mama walks the street without no shoes on because she's a crazy, right? No she can't. I said, Forget all that. I said, This Gloria, she's not proud, or loose, or nasty. I told everybody here to give you a job baby-sitting their babies and to invite you over to dinner. So, I was the one loving you and helping you, wasn't I, hija? But the question I got now is, Did I make a mistake?"

It got eerie in there, it was so quiet in the shop; even I'd been holding my breath. But right then, looking at those two, I was reminded of something. Billy was a fan of shoot-'em-ups, and made me watch at least one a week, so I'd seen *Pat Garrett and Billy the Kid* and *The Searchers* and *Fort Apache*. Watching La Rica and Gloria was like seeing one of those Westerns that got made in the seventies, where a gray-haired skin-and-bones Henry Fonda or John Wayne has a showdown with a muscley young buck of an Indian, and you think it's lights-out for the old cowboy, but then he pulls out his six-shooter and blows the tomahawk right out of the Indian's hand. It was like that, because with a few words La Rica had left the younger, stronger, and maybe even meaner Gloria good and defenseless. I almost felt sorry for the girl. There were tears jumping out of her eyes. She was opening and shutting her mouth like a fish.

But then something even stranger happened, something I didn't see coming. It was like we were still watching that movie and then all of a sudden the squaw comes strolling across the screen, but instead of throwing her arms around the cowboy or wailing over the hurt Indian, she takes out her rifle and shoots them both dead.

"No offense, Señora Hernandez, or you neither, Gloria," Dolores said in a strong voice. "But I don't think that today is about fighting with each other. It's not even about buying dresses. You know what I think it's about?"

Now everybody was looking at her.

"I'll tell you what I think it's about," Dolores went on. "Sisterhood, okay? So wake up! We're here to help our hermana, who has helped us out so many times. Carlita's Fashions was the *one* place we could go in this town when we needed the perfect thing to wear. Because Carlita, she wasn't in it to just make money. The mujer always took the time out to say hola and give you the gossip. And she'd help you out. Like when I got married, I didn't have too much to spend, but she gave me a discount on my wedding dress. And I know she did the same for Cha Cha here, right? Girl, I remember when you were all crying because you had to get married in some old secondhand piece of trash but then you came here and she gave you a deal on that superbeautiful strapless thing. And Frida also—honey, remember that poufy number you got for so cheap? Then Señora Muñoz always bought her clothes here, which is why she's got so much class. So did Señora Cardenas, and you too, Señora Hernandez. And Carlita gave Gloria here a makeover before her first date with Chuco, for free, and see what happened? They got married.

"So when you think about it like that, shoot. Don't it kind of break your heart to think about this old place going out of business? No more Carlita's Fashions! And nobody's going to care about it but us, because this was *our* little place. And this is *our* good friend, who's flat broke. So that's why this sale is about more than getting a good deal. It's about all of us coming together and, you know, *giving our sister a hand.*"

By now Carlita was bawling loud enough to bust my eardrum, and so were a lot of the customers. Dolores pushed past La Rica and put her sweater down on the counter. Carlita rung her up for eighteen dollars and thirty-three cents. Dolores paid with a twenty, but while Carlita was tearing off the receipt she kept digging into her purse and pulled out all the rest of the money she had in there. She put each bill down very slow on the counter, smiled at Carlita, and then got out of line with her sweater.

I copied Dolores. My halter top was just over eleven dollars, but I took out thirty bucks, and laid it out. The Widow Muñoz did the same, making a big deal of waving a whole hundred-dollar bill in the air before she handed it over, and then the number street chicas were dumping their pockets out, too. When Gloria got up to the register she looked nervy as a Chihuahua, but she was no dummy. She turned her purse inside out and made sure they all saw she was handing over every single penny she had.

"Thank you. Thank you," Carlita kept crying. She was really raking it in.

Now everybody was doing it. There was a long line of ladies wiping their eyes and bellyaching about how beautiful Carlita's Fashions was, and then dumping wads of cash out of their wallets. A lot of them hugged Carlita and let her cry on their necks, and if they couldn't get to Carlita then they hugged each other, or else they just stood alone and howled into their hankies.

And one thing more: When they were finished with their business at the register they walked right around La Rica, who from the color on her face looked like she was fighting back a heart attack. None of them talked to her or even gave her a glance, but they did go up to Dolores. My sister was circled by a ring of smiling women, and a few of them who'd never bothered to learn her name before went over and made official introductions.

I walked across the room and stood by Gloria. She was gripping her shopping bag tight to her chest.

"Guess that didn't work out too good for you, did it?" I said.

Gloria didn't look at me. She started biting on her thumb knuckle.

"'Sisterhood,'" she said finally. "My ass."

"Your ass is right!" I went on. "You really did get your bootie burned there, Minnie Mouse." I bent around and looked at her behind. "Ho! Honey, but it *is* burned. Thing's so big and red you looking half baboon."

"Shut up. Who you think you're talking to?"

"Girl with a big red monkey butt."

"Well at least me and my big butt are married. Too bad you can't say the same, hoochie!"

"You sure are married. Married to Mister Minimum Wage himself, baby. Now where'd I see Chuco working last? He ain't still flipping them burgers, is he? Or is he on to french fries now?"

"Oh, you're making like Ms. Thing just 'cause you honking some pendejo's horn. That's pathetic."

"Gloria, damn! You so jealous! You just wish you had half the man I have."

"Wrong there. Maybe Chuco's working burgers these days but at least I know where he is at nights—he's right in my bed. Too bad you can't say the same."

I got in Gloria's face now. "What you mouthing off about?"

"Aw, nothing." Gloria looked at her nails, lifted up her eyebrows. "I just hear plenty of stories, Rita. Seems like your daddy's got himself a sweet tooth, but he don't just want the candies with the cream centers or the peanut clusters. He likes the variety, know what I'm saying?"

I felt a little sweat starting up on my neck. Gloria was trying to turn the tables, so I took a slow breath and glanced around the room. La Rica was gone now, and Dolores was still surrounded by the ladies. Carlita rung up Cha Cha for a couple dresses and dabbed her eyes with Kleenex.

"Okay," I said. "If you're trying to tell me something, why don't you just say it straight."

Gloria flashed me a beautiful smile. "Okay, Rita, if you and Billy are so in love, where was he last night, eh? And where was he the night before? Way I see it is a woman don't really got herself a man unless number one, she got herself a ring, and number two, she knows every minute where that man is. But not you, right? I don't see nothing on your finger. And you just let Billy call you whenever he wants, and then you come running. Pobrecita. But where is he when you ain't with him? Huh? You ever wonder about that? Well, sorry to break you the bad news, but I hear he's been keeping himself good and busy when you're not around."

She was still smiling at me, but I drew on my strongness of character and instead of buckling I smiled back at her.

"Well don't believe everything you hear," I said. "Because I know just fine where my man is. So you don't got to worry about me."

"Whoosh!" Gloria laughed. Her sparkling eyes looked right in mine. "What a relief!"

That girl was mocking me and she did deserve a good thrashing. Any other time I would have loved to rip off the arms of one of these mannequins and use it to beat her senseless. But I didn't today. Because there was my good name to think of. There was Dolores's, too. And plus I had a bad feeling that Gloria was right.

What I'm saying is, I got eyes. I don't got my head stuck in a hole. I had my suspicions. He was beautiful, after all, and his boxing career was starting to take off, and I'd seen all these girls begging him to pick their peaches right in front of my face. He flirted back a lot, and I'd even seen him goose a girl once when he didn't think I was looking. Which is why when Gloria stood there saying that Billy was a player with the ladies, it struck me so hard and painful that I just felt like lying down. Even if she was laughing at me I couldn't get in the mood to take a mannequin to her.

I wanted to run out then but I couldn't leave yet because Dolores was still jawboning with everybody. I walked away from Gloria and sat down on a chair, but I didn't know what to do with my face and hands and I could feel them twitching. So I concentrated very hard on the face of my sister. Her hair bushed out in a big halo and her dress didn't fit her that good. She still looked nice, though. Her eyes were bright and happy and her lipstick was right for her skin tone, and I was glad those ladies were showing her some respect. But it still seemed like a long time before she was finally ready to go.

What His Name Was

*T*wo Sundays after Carlita's closeout sale, I was in the bathroom getting ready for a date with Billy. I hadn't seen him in six days. I'd talked a lot to his answering machine, though. Bottom line, I knew for sure he was cheating now. I'd seen a scratch mark on his back the weekend before, and I'm more of a biter than a scratcher, and I sure as hell didn't wear that stinking cheapie perfume he had all over his clothes. So I didn't need to catch him red-handed. A woman knows.

While I was thinking about this, I put on my lipstick very careful. I'm like an artist with the makeup. You dust on the baby powder so the color holds, then put on lipliner, two shades of lipstick, lipgloss. Then you blot and gloss again. I blotted and wondered what Mrs. Jack Dempsey or Mrs. Julio César Chávez would do in my place. They could spend a hundred dollars an hour on a marriage counselor who'd shrink his head back down to size. Or they could hire a lawyer and get a divorce and retire in the tropics. But of course, those girls were married. They had the marriage license and the rights. I didn't have none of that yet. It was him who had everything.

Billy was quickly turning into our town's Big Brown Hope. In the past year he'd fought in four pro matches and won every time with two kayos and two technicals. His name had been in the Sports once, and I cut the article out and framed it and hung it on his wall. He was booked for three more fights in the next six months, too, and not with bums. He was fighting up-and-comers, real contenders. It was only a matter of time before he got to Vegas and won the lightweight title; everybody knew it. He was a hero in the neighborhood, already a legend. Hombres yelled out Billy the Kid when they saw him on the street and he got free beer at Carnival Liquors, and once me and him had got a free dinner at Bob's Big Boy. Even I was starting to get treated with more respect. Two weeks back Frida Muñoz had waved at me from across the street, and last Thursday Cha Cha Rodriguez had let me cut in front of her in the supermarket line. Even one or two of the churchies were starting to crack me some smiles.

But still, every time I thought about him with another girl I felt full of craziness. I wondered if he counted their orgasms too. I wondered if he made them mimosas. Even now I was having trouble keeping my mascara from running. I stepped back and looked at myself in the mirror and saw how I'd have to do the eyes over again.

"Girl," I said out loud, "go get yourself some dignity."

But then, thank God, the bell rang! I cleaned up and tried not to run to the door, and there he was, carrying a wrapped present for me.

"Come here, my baby!" he said. He kissed me, then put the present in my hand. "Open it up."

I looked up at him. *Where have you been?* I wanted to ask him. *You're late. You can't treat me like this.* But I didn't say any of it. He'd combed his hair back for me and he was wearing that spice cologne I liked.

I unwrapped the present. It was a little gold-plate locket with our picture inside, one we'd took months and months ago in a photo booth. It showed us kissing. Billy put the locket on me, then threw his arms around my shoulders.

"Honey, when I saw that I knew it belonged on my prettiest girl. You know what I thought of? I thought about how when I fight my first title match you'd be sitting there in the front row wearing this necklace and I'd look at you and you'd be my good-luck charm, and then I'd go out and win. Doesn't that sound nice? You want to be my lucky charm?"

I couldn't help it. I crumbled when he gave me that piece of junk. When I turned back around I didn't yell out, *What do you mean your* prettiest *girl? This necklace is gold-plate, I could get this downtown for twenty-five dollars, who you think you're fooling?* No, I pressed close to him and said I did want to be his lucky charm. I had to, because I loved him so terrible; I'd been caught by his secret heart. Also because, for all my suffering, I was not so stupid. Clinging vines get cut off. I knew that if I was going to get any more beautiful tours of my Empire State Building, special treatment at Ruben's Superbox, and 50 percent tips at Lupe's Beauty House, I'd have to make like his other girls were ghosts, invisible and silent.

But that's not to say I'd lay my body down defenseless. I've got powers in me, earned way back when I was just a girl. I was still full of fire, see, and while I pressed my face to his chest I planned on burning my name into him, down to the bones. With my heat I'd scar him on the tender parts so that they ached and throbbed, and only I could cure him, only I'd be able to cool him with my breath. And then I'd be safe because he wouldn't want to leave me.

*L*ater there was a wine sky, and his body reflected in the twilight.

Don't turn it on, I told him. I said, We don't need that now. I took his hand from the lamp and let the blue shadows cover us, I put his hand in the dark place where it was round and it was moving. We listened to the sheets rustle under our thighs. There was no white moon and no gold streetlamp peeking through the window, and his fingers reached blind until I leaned back and let him see me, until I showed him how I made my own light.

Come on, touch it, I said. Grab it hard. I gripped on to his shoulder and his collarbone and my hair swung over my face. I rubbed my knee on his ribs while his hands twisted and the cock struck the hot spot. That's when I felt it, how my skin turned into moonstone and red coal, and I must have glowed like a blaze at midnight, and I kept going till we were both soaked and weak as water.

Then, right in the middle, I made us stop. I told him to wait there, went to the kitchen and then brought him presents, two white summer peaches with the thinnest skin and sweet perfume, and I peeled them, slow, letting the juice run down my arms. When they were naked they glistened like a girl stepping out of the sea and I broke open the flesh with my hands. I made him watch while I bit in and sucked, I made him wait. But when I was ready I was generous, I fed him piece by piece, and then tasted his mouth, his fresh lips.

*H*e was so tired afterward, but I shook him and asked him to say my name, and he did say it and kissed me on each eye. But then he fell asleep and I could already feel his handprints fading from my skin and when his breathing turned steady and slow and his face turned to the wall I thought maybe

I had burned my name into him, but I didn't know if it would last.

So I crept out of bed. I went to his desk. I looked for something to steal, something of his I could keep. But his drawers were empty except for his wallet, and his wallet didn't have nothing but money. There was paper, though, and a pen. I sat down and wrote my name.

Rita Zapata.

Rita Zapata Navarro.

Rita Navarro.

Mrs. Rita Navarro.

Señora Navarro.

And then I wrote his name, Guillermo Billy Navarro. It made me feel better. I liked how it looked so solid in black and white, and I felt like it belonged to me somehow. That no matter what happened, it would stay permanent. This is what his name was.

But then, that changed too.

I sweated through that summer and by the time fall arrived it was still hot. This one day in September the thermometer read in the 90s. I'd just got let out of work and was walking down to Ruben's Superbox because that morning Billy had told me I could stop by to watch him train for his upcoming fight with a boxer called Sugarboy Montoya. A few more of the Chávez shops had shut down in the past few weeks and they were dead dark inside when I passed them. I waved to the people I did see. There was Mr. Dennis selling booze to a down-and-out in Carnival Liquors, and Señora Gallegos burning incense in her santos shop. Then there was Mr. Cisneros in Diamond

Jeweler's, surrounded by what looked like a million dollars in engagement rings, and not one customer in the house. I'd been in there one or two times before, just browsing. But I couldn't today. I smiled at Mr. Cisneros through the window and kept walking.

Inside Ruben's the a/c was blowing but that didn't kill the heat, which sunk heavy into the skin, weaked up the muscles, and dizzied the head. Sun rays shot into the room and dust swirled in the light, boys' arms and fists and wet shoulders shifted lazy in and out of the shadows. Billy was slugging his white-taped fists in slow-mo at the mirror and the rest of the regulars were there, too, leaning up on the cool walls or stretching. When I came in Jose and a couple of the others looked up at me and raised their hands. The rest were busy listening to Pedro, who was hassling Billy. Ever since he'd beat up Jose, Pedro had hated him as fierce as he hated the police.

"Hey, man, damn! I forgot your name again," Pedro yelled out to him. "Shit, what was it? What they calling you now? Speedy Gonzalez?"

Billy didn't answer. He kept swinging at the mirror.

"Why don't you shut the hell up, leave him alone," Chuco said.

"Aw, man, I don't mean nothing," Pedro said. "Billy. Billy! You ain't taking offense, now are you, baby? All I'm saying is that shit is fucked up. A man's name is sacred, no? You can't go messing around with something like that."

Billy was practicing his jab. He shot out a good hard right. "A name ain't such a big thing."

"'Course it is! Name's all a man's got in this world." Pedro turned around and papped a 90-pounder called Tito on the shoulder. "Tito, man. Back me up here, homes."

"Nah," Tito said. "I don't get into it."

I sat on the bleachers over by the front door. I didn't know what they were all talking about until Pedro saw me and waved me over.

"Rita girl, come here," he said. "Listen to what they did to your boy."

It turned out there had been a typo on Billy's papers. La migra had got Billy's name wrong on the green card. Billy's born name was Navarro, but the INS agent must have been downing some pretty cheap tequila because he wound up writing down a screwy four-letter word instead.

"What was it they called you?" Pedro went on. "Was it Billy Bozo?"

"It's NOVO," Billy said. He glared at Pedro in the mirror. "NOVO, okay?" He shrugged and looked at me. "The INS thinks my name is Billy Novo."

"Well that is your name now, muchacho," Pedro said. "You can wave bye-bye to old Guillermo Navarro, because when the Man types your name into one of them little computers, he might as well be branding it on your ass."

Billy stopped boxing and turned around. "Okay there, César Chávez. You're always going on about the Man this and the Man that and all that racialized mambojambo. So I wanna know. Who is he? Where is he? You just go and point him out for us."

Pedro made a deep bow. "Oh, señor, I'm sorry. I forgot that you're the Man around here, Mr. Novo."

"That's more like it, cabron. Least you got that straight."

Billy stopped shadowboxing. He stood there staring at Pedro so I went up to him and rubbed his shoulder.

"Novo's not so bad," I said. "I think it's nice."

"It don't matter either way," he said. "I don't care what they call me."

"You could go down and get it changed."

"No. I don't care."

"Yeah," I said. "You know what your name is. So what if they put something else on a piece of paper?"

Billy just shrugged. He looked up at Ruben, who'd come walking out of his office. As soon as Ruben saw them all standing around he started clapping his hands and yelling.

"What the hell is this?" He looked at Billy. "What you doing? The goddammed fight's in three weeks. Three weeks!"

"I'm training," Billy said. He was doing footwork now. His shoes were shushing on the mats.

"You ain't even got a good sweat going. Go and put on your gloves. Chuco? Chuco? Go in there and work him."

Billy slipped on his gloves and got inside the ring, but Chuco didn't seem to like the idea too much. He shuffled slow over to his locker and took his time taping up his hands.

"Hey, Boss. Hey you, Boss!" That was Pedro, calling out to Ruben from across the gym.

"Hey me what?"

"What's this I hear about the INS stealing old Billy's name?"

Ruben didn't understand at first. He threw up his hands impatient. "Eh?"

Freddie stood next to Ruben. "He's asking about la migra," he muttered. "How they're calling Billy by the wrong last name."

Ruben snorted. "Oh, yeah. We got a government full of geniuses. They can put a man on the moon but they can't spell this boy's name right." He picked up a magazine that was laying on the ground, then rolled it up and started slapping it on the palm of one hand. "Chuco, what's taking you so long, son? Move it move it move it."

"You gonna start calling him that now?" Pedro went on. "He sounds like a Spaniard if you call him Novo."

Ruben nodded and slapped the magazine some more. "So what? I don't want no trouble. And what does he care? We gave him a good nickname, nobody cares about nothing but the nickname anyways."

Pedro was all teeth. "What, Billy the Kid? That's a white cowboy's name, man."

"That's all right. Just lookit him. He don't look like nothing but a Mexican; this boy's screaming Mexican. He don't care."

"Yeah, but you might mess up his head giving him a Spaniard name and a white cowboy name. You stick a Mexican fighter with a tag like that he might try and kick his *own* ass."

Chuco was in the ring by now, but Billy wasn't doing nothing but staring at the mat and sweating.

"Hello, anybody home?" Ruben yelled up at Billy. "What's wrong with you? You losing your concentration. You gonna lose the fight. I better see some action up there or else I'm calling it quits, son." Ruben looked over at me, then back up to the ring. "Like, you think Montoya's playing around with girls? He ain't. He's busy trying to get back to the top. He lost his last three fights and there is no way he's gonna lose another one, to a no-name especially. So you know what he's doing? I tell you what he's doing. He's got your picture pasted up on a bag and he is killing that bag every day. He can't wait to crack open a nobody like you. And he ain't even somebody no more. He's praying to be somebody. So you know what that makes you? That makes you a nobody times two, Billy. A double nobody." Ruben rubbed at his head and his little hairs were standing up all over his shiny skull now.

"I better go," I said.

"I'll see you later," Billy said.

Ruben put his hands together like he was praying. "Great, fantastic. Go! Maybe then this bum will start working."

Billy wiped his face with his glove. "Lay off me."

"Yeah, sure. I'll lay off you for good. You think I need this? I'll take my girlfriend on a cruise in the Bahamas. I retire from this business! Okay, boys? You hear that? Everybody get out, because I quit."

We all knew he had to be bluffing. The boys didn't like hearing that any, though. Martinez and Jose looked sideways at each other. Tito started picking nervous at his chin. Chuco twitched weird some more. Billy didn't make a move. He stayed up there sweating and staring at nothing. I could have told Ruben that pushing Billy wouldn't get him anywhere. But Ruben was a mule, too. He dug in and waited.

Pedro was leaning up on the wall with his arms crossed, and he was still grinning. After a while of listening to the quiet, he started up again, right where he'd left off.

"Yup, a man's name is a damned crazy thing," he said. "Hermanos, I got a funny story about a man and his name, and how he gave it up. I used to have this friend called Frankie Díaz, we'd been tight a long time. The brother wasn't too bright, though. Old Frankie, he had gambling trouble. That fool gambled on anything. Horses, soccer, boxing, dog races, cockfights. You know them kinds of dudes? Kind that'll bet you on the weather? That was Frankie. One day he didn't have a penny left but there was that big fight with Walcott and Duran, what, in '88? A fucking surefire, man. Everybody had it down on Duran. Frankie thought he'd just ride along even though all he could bet was his ass. Well, you know what happened. So when Duran dinged it, these heavies called the Spinelli Brothers were running all over town looking for Frankie and his money. He was scared shitless.

He hid in my house for two whole days, then started growing this mustache and wearing my clothes as a disguise. And then you know what that poor coward did?"

I made my way to the door while Pedro talked and tried to remember who Frankie Díaz was. Everybody else was looking at Pedro through thin eyes.

"He changed his name!" he said. "And you won't guess what he called himself after that. John O'Brien. You believe that? O'Brien. Like a fucking Irish! He picked it out of the phone book. I told him he didn't look like no Irish but he wouldn't change it back. 'The Brothers won't come looking after O'Brien,' he kept on saying. He was real sure of himself. But poor Frankie, man. Not only a yellowbelly, but dumb, too. He couldn't outrun them Italians. They caught up to him a couple months later when he was walking home from his girl's house and they gunned him down in cold blood, right between Fifth and Sixth. He didn't even know what hit him. We all had this big funeral and there were flowers and the girlfriend was ripping out her hair and screaming and we even had mariachis and a big party after, but it didn't make it right. Nothing could, you know? The thing that always made me feel so bad was how Frankie caught it while he was making like some Irish bum. Poor old man died with the wrong name. And that, my friends, is what happens to ignorant pendejos like him. It's a goddam shame."

The fighters waited for a second, still staring at Pedro through their slitted eyes, but then most of them started laughing.

"You fucking liar!" Freddie said.

The rest of them were holding on to each other busting up. Even Ruben was wiping his eyes. He picked up a glove and threw it at Pedro's head.

"Bullshit, son! Get the hell out of here."

Pedro ducked and then looked up at the ring. Billy and Chuco were the only ones not laughing. But Billy looked like he was ready to fight now. His eyes were fixed on Chuco and he kept hitting his gloves together. Chuco didn't look like he was feeling so good, though. He kept on twitching in his corner.

"So I still got to say," Pedro kept on. His grin was wiggling all over his face. "I believe that a man's name is a sacred thing. The *most* sacred thing. A man who don't hold on to his true name can't even call himself a real man."

Billy was grinning now too, but not friendly. He hit his gloves together some more and bounced on his toes. "Let's go."

"Shut up," Chuco yelled down. He put up his gloves. "Shut the fuck up."

I was at the door now, with my hand on the knob. Ruben started telling everybody to keep it down and get to training again. He went over to the ring and looked up and then yelled, "Bell." I opened the door and walked out, listening to the sounds of Billy's feet pounding fast on the canvas and the first solid heavy blow, and then the door shut behind me and I couldn't hear nothing more.

I stitched that new name on Billy's fight robe and jacket, which were both made out of a beautiful valentine satin, a deep heart-colored red. BILLY "THE KID" NOVO was spelled out in a pile of white satin letters, and I sewed each one on as slow and careful as I could, by hand. Everybody was going to see it. Billy's first big one was coming up. It would be his first pay-per-view match. People across the country were going to watch him fight on their television sets. But more important, all the people in the neighborhood would see him box. Him fighting Sugarboy Montoya was all anybody could talk about these days.

"I got a hundred down on Billy," Freddie told me a week before the match. "I don't care what nobody says. I got a real good feeling." The word from a bookie down in Monrovia was that the city odds were six-to-one in favor of Sugarboy, but those odds didn't matter from Eastern Ave to Divine Drive. Anybody with money was gambling on Billy, and those who were broke wished that they could put a little down on him, if just for pride's sake. Everybody from bus drivers to shop owners to the newly laid off hombres who sat wide-kneed on the curb of Chávez gave me the thumbs-up while I passed them on my way to Lupe's. The mujeres had hope too. The beauty shop queens made gentlemen's bets and asked me if he was eating right while I polished their nails or bent over cotton-stuffed toes. "Everybody says he's gonna win," they'd whisper while they handed over their tips.

And then the day came. The fight was at the Sports Arena, down on Martin Luther King Jr. Boulevard, a place big enough to hold sixteen thousand fans plus a team of ring girls who wore triple-D cups and string bikinis and seven-inch platforms that made them stumble and swing their asses perilous. When we got there the place was already one-third packed but when I walked around to look for a bathroom that didn't have a half-hour line I saw so many familiar faces it seemed like the whole neighborhood had turned out to cheer for Billy. Up in one of the nosebleed sections I spotted our neighbor Señora Montoya eating peanuts and telling her fighting hijas to shut up. These guys I recognized from Superbox, Zookie Chamayo and Chuy Gomez, were back there too, kicking their feet up and throwing trash over the heads of the middle-section folks who'd paid over eighty bucks each for their tickets. I caught La Rica and Mr. Hernandez in these eighty-buck seats, and for once they weren't the highest renters in town because the Rabbit Street boxers had traded their savings for tickets and were taking up the first two rows in one section. Down in front there was Martinez and Marco chewing on hot dogs and fighting over who was better, Duran or Chávez, while Pedro stuck his fist up and yelled out Camacho, man, Camacho. Up and to the left were Chuco and Tommy, swilling something out a paper bag and splitting their time between getting yelled at by Gloria and Frida and picking on Tito, who was trying to talk to Jose and Dolores, who sat by the aisle and didn't look at anybody but each other.

I was in the second row. I had a free ticket. I loved it even if I was smashed next to Freddie and had to listen to all those borrachos go on about who were the best fighters. Some of them were still taking last-minute wagers over the rest of the fight card. This was a big night for boxing. Billy and Sugarboy were just the first of three undercard matches before the main lightweight title fight between Koo-Koo Garcia, a Peruvian slugger who was famous for his iron jaw, and Javier "The Hammer" Zuñiga, the granddaddy power-punching champ from Compton.

"Hammer's finished, homes!" I heard Martinez bawling above me. "Koo-Koo's got it locked up. I seen him in action before and the man don't fucking bleed, see? He wiped up that Valdez last year in two. And Hammer? Fuck Hammer. He don't even got the legs now. I ain't seen him throw good since '92, remember that? When he slammed Solis down in San Diego? He's been riding on bums ever since."

Pedro was taking a pull on a beer but he spit up when Martinez said that. "No way. No way. You're talking about the Hammer, man!"

Now Martinez shook a wad of bucks in the air. "I call you fifty on Koo-Koo and you might as well hand over your money right now, fool. Hammer's down in four."

While them two were betting, this drunk dude in a sharp downtown suit got up on his feet and started hollering down at Martinez.

"Who's dissing on Hammer? Who the fuck is dissing on the Hammer? I'll take your money, you ugly motherfucker."

Martinez stood up too, then shifted his growing gut around. "Fine, baby, come on over here and I'll give it to you."

The rummy wobbled a little and was wondering what to do when one of the Arena's bouncers ran up and started barking shut up at both of them, and so they sat back down.

Then the fight started. The Arena lights flickered a little and a bald Anglo emcee ducked under the ropes and pulled down the ring microphone to mouth level.

"LADIES AND GENTLEMEN," the emcee hollered, "please join me in welcoming a lightweight from JUÁREZ, MEXICO (everybody started cheering at that), weighing in at a HUNDRED AND THIRTY-THREE POUNDS, the new hot-blooded slugger on the scene, BILLY 'THE KID' NOVO!"

"NAVARRO!" the front rows yelled and laughed out while Billy, dressed up in the red hooded robe that half hid his face, came jogging up through the crowd. Ruben followed close behind. Billy slipped between the ropes and shadowboxed the emcee as soon as he hit canvas, and when he stripped down and flexed under the lights a row of girls sitting up in the cheap seats started screaming.

Next up was Sugarboy Montoya. Sugarboy used to be a powerhouse, but you could tell by his love handles that he wouldn't go the distance with Billy. He'd come out of Downey like a rocket back in '89 and snagged the champ's belt by knocking out tough-as-nails Babyface Vasquez at Caesars Palace. He didn't stay a winner forever, though. Sugarboy liked the booze too much, and after two years of glory days a no-name knocked him out. Since then he'd lost every match he'd fought, but he made up for being a loser by showboating—like he was right then. After the emcee called his name he came running out in a purple robe with SUGARBOY spelled out in blinking electric lights on the back, and instead of listening to the ref call out the rules he danced circles around Billy and showed off the blue Virgin Mary he'd got tattooed on his chest.

Once that bell rang, though, it was a different game. Sugarboy came out of his corner thumping on his Virgin and Billy beelined straight for him, jabbing him twice in the mug so that in the first two minutes his left eye was already starting to red-up and swell. Sugarboy sobered up quick then. He stopped his grinning and swung out a couple bull's-eyes and, like usual, Billy didn't have any defense, he kept his gloves low and his feet heavy and let Sugarboy dynamite his head, but it still wasn't no match. Anytime Billy got a slug in it hit solid and pretty soon he pushed Sugarboy back on the ropes and tied him up with more headshots and hooks into the gut. The crowd loved it. All around me there was hollering. The neighborhood men were up on their feet now, bawling out HURT HIM or KILL HIM, and from behind me I could hear them cheap-seat chicas screaming their lungs out pretty good, too. Maybe loudest of all of them was Sugarboy's manager sitting in Sugarboy's corner yelling COVER UP at the top of his lungs while holding on to the ropes, but from the dingbat face Sugarboy had on I'd bet he couldn't hear nothing but whacking. He tried clinching but clinching didn't work, Billy just threw him off and kept going at the head, and after a minute or more of that kind of punishment Sugarboy broke loose, faked a stumble, and dove down to the ground.

The crowd got mean right away at that one. They all started punching their fists up and booing through their cupped hands and they got even louder when Billy stood over Sugarboy belting out COME ON COME ON while the ref ran up and held him back with his arm and did the count. Billy wouldn't take it. He kept yelling at Sugarboy to get up but Sugarboy just laid there on the canvas looking at him and shaking his head.

"TEN!" The ref waved Sugarboy out and brought Billy's glove up and the emcee blared KAYO TO KID IN TWO MINUTES THIRTY-ONE SECONDS into the microphone while the dudes behind me slammed their feet on the floor and howled cusses and one girl from the back row started screaming out Billy's name like a crazy.

Billy put his glove down and he shuffled out a victory dance without smiling, but Ruben ran around the ring laughing and holding his fists up like he'd just won himself. Then the manager slipped inside the ropes and helped Sugarboy put on his robe, and so when that clown snuck out of the ring we could still see them electric lights blinking SUGARBOY SUGARBOY SUGARBOY while he dragged his sorry ass all the way back to his ready room.

I was going to jump out of my seat and run over to Billy, but him and Ruben were already getting hurried off and waving bye to the cameras. It was time for the next fight.

"Let's go see him," Chuco said. Freddie and Tito stood up and started walking out of the arena and I got up too and went along. On our way over we had to squeeze through a whole mob of sweaty fans milling up and down the aisles, and we weren't the only ones with the idea of seeing Billy. There was already a crowd in his ready room. Lots of neighborhood boys stood around with their hands stuffed inside their pockets and stared at Billy dopey and didn't say anything. There were some girls there, too, but they weren't so shy. I spotted two as soon as I walked through the door, both of them wearing spandex ass-huggers and halter tops. One of them wasn't real hot. She was a bucktooth and kept trying to hide her teeth by puckering her mouth. The other one was a looker, though, about seventeen years old with long legs and a couple feet of cleavage she didn't mind showing off. She kept edging closer and closer to

Billy, who was leaning up by a wall and listening to Ruben brag on about the fight.

"I never seen nothing like it. This man here, he was ready to go fourteen rounds, ain't that right, Billy? Orale. What a goddam SHOW. Nobody and I mean nobody puts on a show like that no more. Dempsey did. And Robinson, way back. But now? Today? Nah. You showed them all how it's done tonight."

"Too bad it was wasted on that chump," Chuco said, giving Billy a wink.

Freddie nodded. "That fucking Sugarboy."

Just when Freddie said that Sugarboy walked past the open door of the ready room and he must have heard his name. He stuck his head in and gave Billy a wave.

"Hey, man. Good fight," Sugarboy said. His face was cut up but he didn't look too hurt.

Chuco waved him off. "Go on, go on, you bum," he told Sugarboy. "Where you get off taking a fall, eh?"

All the boys in the room were rumbling.

"You a goddam coward."

"Fight like a fucking *woman,* man."

"Hell, yes he does. Bend over, motherfucker."

Sugarboy just shrugged. "Hey," he said. "What's your problem? It's only business. I ain't getting my ass split in three." He shrugged. "Why should I? Get paid either way."

Somebody threw a beer bottle at Sugarboy's head and missed. That's when Sugarboy decided it was a good time to take off, but he didn't hurry.

"Adios, assholes," he said.

Freddie covered his eyes. "Oh shit! Man, am I depressed. I used to watch that dude on the TV. On the Friday night fights. I was always rooting for Sugarboy, you know? It was like, fucking SUGARBOY, man." Freddie looked over at Billy. "Don't that get to you? I mean, your first fight and you get old Sugarboy there chumping out in the first fucking round."

"Nah," Billy said. "I don't give a shit."

I'd made my way through the crowd of boys and was up close to Billy by then, but so was the Looker in the spandex. She'd put her hand on his shoulder.

"Get your hand off him," I said. "Get your goddam hand off him or I'll break it off." She took it off.

Billy laughed down at me. I told him congratulations, touched his black eye, then kissed him till I heard wolf whistling. I wanted the Looker to see. She was over in a corner now, drinking beer with the bucktooth and watching us. Billy let me keep kissing him but I saw him shoot his eyes over to the Looker once or twice. When he'd do that I'd grab his chin to turn his head back and he'd laugh.

Everybody was celebrating pretty hard. Ruben brought in more beer from the concession booth and they had chugging contests. With drinks in their bellies some of the boys got braver and started pushing up to Billy and telling him things.

"Fucking hero, man," slurred Zookie Chamayo. Zookie was leaning up on his friend Chuy Gomez and they both stood there grinning sloppy at Billy. "I mean, you're like . . . who's that? Who's that dude?" He elbowed Chuy. "Who's that hero dude?"

"Eh?" Chuy said. "You mean like a superhero? Like Superman?"

"No, man, not Superman."

"Like the Lone Ranger?"

"No, not like the fucking Lone Ranger!" Zookie was rubbing his face all around. "Shit, I can't remember that dude's name. But Billy, you know, hey, FUCK. I fucking love you, man! We all just love you so bad, Billy my brother!"

"Whoa," Billy said. He patted and pushed Zookie back on the shoulder. "Looks like you need another beer, man."

They all kept up their partying for a couple hours. After a while Billy started looking around for a clock. "What time is it?" he asked me. "You got a watch?"

I shook my head and tried to kiss him again, but he didn't want that now.

"Boss," he yelled. "BOSS, man. What time is it?"

Ruben was laying down on the table they had set up for massage, and the bucktooth was digging her fingers into his big back. He was good and blasted. "It's your time," he called out. He raised up one of the beers. "It's your goddam time, Billy my son."

"No, Boss. Listen to me. I wanna know the real time. Is Hammer fighting yet?"

"Ah, Jesus. I don't know. What time is it?"

The bucktooth picked up Ruben's wrist and looked at his watch.

"It's around eight."

Ruben laid there with his eyes closed. "Oh, yep," he said after a couple seconds. "Hammer'd be up by now."

Billy wanted to go and see the fight. He got dressed in his regular clothes and all of us who were still standing followed him back out to third row, then settled down to watch Hammer and Koo-Koo duke it out.

It was round seven of one of the worst slaughters I ever saw. Hammer was getting wasted. He had fresh cuts tearing up his mouth and a slash under the right eye, and from how he was lugging around heavy-footed it didn't look like he had the juice in him no more. The whole thing belonged to Koo-Koo. The Peruvian had ten years on Hammer and his form was good, too. Koo-Koo was all surprise punches and fancy footwork, and he didn't have any trouble connecting his right with Hammer's head. Hammer's problem was that he was an old-style street-fighter, just like Billy—a toe-to-toe slugger who carried his hands low and let his face get pulped without ducking. Like right now Koo-Koo was letting a flurry loose over Hammer's head and Hammer just stood there bleeding. The crowd sure did love that. Everybody was screaming. But then, right before the bell, Hammer showed what he was made of. He was a socker. He got on the inside, snapped up his skull in a head-butt, then tattooed Koo-Koo straight on the plexus.

Koo-Koo went down, and the place was crazy. Koo-Koo had the wind punched out of him and was having trouble getting to his feet. He grabbed the rope but his legs kept on giving out. Hammer stood there puffing and bleeding, and the ref pushed him back and started the ten count with the crowd chanting along, but on five Koo-Koo struggled to his feet and put up his gloves. Hammer put up his. And then the bell rung.

The fighters went back to their corners and the ring girl went out there, holding up the eighth-round card. She was almost naked in that bikini and she had this big behind that bounced around. The crowd started screaming for her bootie and she laughed and jiggled herself and they roared louder. In his corner, Koo-Koo spit water into a bucket then slumped down. Hammer sat on his stool and stared straight ahead while his cut man worked his face over with ice and Vaseline.

When the bell rung again Hammer came out of the blocks raw and shiny but he looked strong. Koo-Koo looked like he'd been punished, though. Sometimes a knockdown can mess with a fighter's head and put him on the defense, and a defense fighter is a loser. For the next three rounds he was backpedaling and blocking. Hammer stayed working the plexus with his jab. Koo-Koo tried to move a left cross to the cut eye, but by now he was slowing up and hugging. Hammer slipped him and tagged him good in the ribs, and Koo-Koo went down again, and he stayed down for eight counts. When he got back up you could see it was over. He must have been busted up bad on the inside because he could only block with one hand and he was running his ass all over the ring, and when Hammer finally caught him on the ropes the slugs went straight to the belly, and then Koo-Koo went down for good.

You never seen more crazy Mexicans in the same room in your life. A pack of fans came racing down to the ring to get a better look and when they saw Koo-Koo twitching there on the ground some of them ran around hollering and holding their heads and the rest slipped through the ropes and lifted Hammer up on their shoulders. The count wasn't even over yet. The ref bent over the loser and yelled out numbers while a few Koo-Koo diehards started booing, but the ref didn't pay them attention and when he got to ten he waved that poor bozo out.

While all that was going on I looked over at Billy. He wasn't caught up in the heat and screaming. He was staring at Hammer.

"What's up, honey?" I asked.

Billy crossed his arms. "You see that chingado? I'm gonna fight him and I'm gonna beat him," he said. In the ring Hammer was riding the shoulders of two goons. He tried to hold up the prize belt and grin at the crowd but he was roughed so bad even that was giving him trouble. He was sort of flopping all over the goons.

"And then I can be the Mrs. Lightweight Champion of the World," I said, not too subtle.

Billy opened his mouth and looked at me out of the corner of his eye but then he got saved by the groupies, a whole hump of screaming gigglers who ran up and wanted him to write his name on their program or at least goose them on the ass. Those girls were shameless. They were all hitching up their skirts to show off caramel thighs and squeezing their arms under their breasts and serving them up like mile-high pies. I'd got shoved to the side and was shoving back so as to make my way to Billy. Not that he minded. Like he was letting one of those cream puffs kiss him on the cheek right now, and another one wanted him to autograph her belly. I told myself not to get my temper up, but then I spotted the Looker trying to put her arms around Billy, so I went over, caught a soft piece of her arm between my fingers, and squeezed hard as I could. I knew it must have hurt. She tried to brush me off but I stuck on her like a crab, and when she saw I was ready to scratch her to pieces, she pulled away and ran off.

The rest of them were leaving now too, waving, smiling, winking. We walked out of the Arena. When I looked around I couldn't find Dolores or Jose anyplace, so Tito and Freddie and Billy and me piled into Chuco's van and we headed back home at eighty miles an hour with the radio turned up all the way. Through the windshield you could see thin clouds lit up by a silver moon and the air felt good and all of us were laughing. Tito picked up a bottle of tequila that was under one of the backseats and passed it around, and after some swigs Freddie started singing Santana songs and Chuco told nobody in particular about how Sugar Ray Robinson couldn't fight worth a damn, and Billy stuck his head out the window and howled at the cars we raced by.

And then I finally forgot all about those manhunters trying to steal him away from me. I leaned back drinking straight from the bottle and listened to him howling and that's when it really hit me how he'd beat Sugarboy.

This is what I sat there thinking: Billy won. He won he won he won he won he won he won.

* * *

*A*t five o'clock that morning, we were in bed, but awake. We'd been drinking steady all night long and were still high from the fight. Outside the sky was paling fast. Lights were on in the windows across the street but nobody was out yet. I leaned over and touched his bruises and cuts, which I'd washed and covered with Bactine.

He was resting on one arm, and every once in a while he'd reach up and goose me or tickle me. He was poking my belly button with one finger when I grabbed his hand with mine.

"Billy," I said. "Let's get married."

"Oh-oh. What?" he said. He stopped trying to fiddle with my belly button.

"You heard me."

He opened his eyes. "You been taking too many Midols, baby? You sure are talking funny."

"Billy, shut up. Let's get married."

He waited for a second, then he said, "Nah. Married? Nah, girl, that's not what you want."

"You tell me what I want, then."

Billy ran his hands all over his chest and belly and wiggled around, grinning. "You just want to use me for sex!"

"No I don't!"

"It's okay, baby, you don't got to deny it." He spread his arms out. "Use me just for sex. I won't tell nobody."

"Come on, Billy."

"Be gentle now. Have mercy!"

I put my hand on his cheek. "Hey, look at me. I'm serious."

He stopped wriggling and did look at me. Then he got out of bed and stood up.

"Hey, it's late. Maybe you should go home," he said.

"I am not going home. We're going to talk about this. We've been together two years now."

"It don't matter how long we been together."

"Why? It matters to me!"

He started picking up my stuff. "Go on, I'm driving you home."

"I'm not going anywhere!"

His face flinched, and this wild and sad look stuck on it. Right then I remembered the night in the bathroom when he'd cried for an hour and I'd sat in the red pool.

"You don't get that from me," he said, kind of loud.

"What? What the hell is wrong with you?"

He stood there with his hands dangling. Now that he was standing I could see he was feeling the drink. I was feeling sober enough, though. There was a bottle of red and a bottle of Cuervo on the bedstand. He picked up the red and took a couple of sips of that.

"That's not good for your training," I said.

He emptied the bottle, and as soon as he finished the last gulp he got a burst of energy. "Man, it is late! We been up all night? Listen to this. I'm gonna tell you a story. Okay? I'll tell you a story and you'll see why I don't get married."

"I'm not in the mood for your damn stories. I want you to sit your ass down here next to me and make me a commitment."

But he stayed standing and eyeballed me.

"Okay, here's my story," he started. "When I was a teenager? There was this murder in our town. A terrible bad triple murder like on the TV. It happened to these people I knew. One was this girl, and she was married to this cowboy kind of guy, name of Paco Gomez? Paco, man, he was okay in the beginning. You would never know. He was like a normal guy, except for he was just so ugly, shit you wouldn't believe. He had these scars all over his face from fighting? He had these bad teeth, too, and only one eye."

I just looked at him. "That is ugly," I said, after a couple seconds.

"And it was funny because being so nasty-looking, Paco still wound up marrying this beautiful girl. Boof! Hermosa! The most gorgeous! She was a skinny bitty thing looking like an angel. But it was too bad for Paco because that pendejo married the girl before she was ready and women are like fruit, you know? Whatever, if you're picking 'em too green they don't dig it and they got to ripe up someplace else. Anyways, so he's all married to her and one day she went and figured that no way, he was like a big fucking loser. She made one hell of a mistake. She wants to come live in the States, in the city. She wants to sing and dance and do all sorts of locuras. But what she wants to do most of all is ditch this husband she's got, so she goes and falls in love with another man. A better man. A somebody. So she leaves her ugly husband and goes and lives with the new guy.

"But Paco there, he can't take it. He goes from a normal guy to a crazy guy. He starts following them everyplace they go."

Billy stops and shows me how Paco goes crazy. I'm kind of squinting at him. Maybe I ain't winning any spelling bees anytime soon but I still got a couple beans rattling around in this head. So I sit there squinting and squinting and I even raise one of my eyebrows at him, like Spock. But Billy don't notice. His eyes are getting real red.

"She tells him," he goes on, "to leave her alone! Go away! But he won't. And then he gets himself a gun, and one night he goes up to their house, and he shoots them both dead. The beautiful girl died. And then Paco shot himself in the head and died too. Ka-bam! It was terrible. But he deserved worse than that,

I'd say. Paco's parents were glad he was dead, too, because they knew he was crazy. They hated him, and they would never say his name again, they forgot he ever lived."

He was just raving on and on.

"So do you see what I'm saying? Marriage is no good. I can't get married after seeing something like that. When that happened, I said to myself I would never ever marry nobody. I couldn't let that happen to me."

By the time he was finished he wasn't too steady on his feet.

"What was the girl's name?" I ask.

He didn't answer me. He laid down on the bed and wiped his face with a T-shirt. He looked wrung-out. "I ever tell you that story before?"

I'm still just staring at him, waiting for him to open his eyes. But after a couple minutes I guess he passed out.

"Yes you did tell me that story before," I said. "And the last time that girl was alive and making records here in Los Angeles. And her name was Angelina and the guy's name was Pancho Villa and you killed him yourself."

But he couldn't hear me now. He was snoring. Not me, I was wide awake. Outside the sky was the color of Siamese eyes. It was weird to stay up all night. But I could think okay, and what I thought was, Who did he think he was lying to get me in and out of his bed? Did he think I was a stupid? And he was carrying on like a drunk. He'd better watch it. Across the street there was already a vieja in a pink bathrobe sweeping her front steps.

I tried to lay down next to him, but there was no way I could sleep. After a while, I got up and went outside on the porch. The vieja was done sweeping now and was watering some plants with a green plastic can. And the other folks were rising too. I sat there until eight o'clock watching the other mujeres come out of their houses to sweep their steps and peek out their kitchen windows while they made breakfast. After that I washed and dressed and was ready to go to work, and he was still in bed. On that one morning, I didn't kiss him good-bye.

So all right, he wouldn't marry me yet, but I still got my engagement ring. I knew where he kept his wallet. It was in the top drawer of his desk. A few days after he told me the story about Paco Gomez, the one-eyed killer cowboy, I looked through the wallet and found his new MasterCard. It was sky blue, with his brand-new name spelled out in tiny silver letters, and hell, yes, I took that puppy out and put it in my pocket. Except I should say this also: I did it because I was mad at him for lying, but I also did it because I loved him and wanted him and I knew he loved me too, and so even after his cheating and lying I was going to go and buy what I deserved and what he was someday going to get me once he came to his senses.

Anyways, I went to Diamond Jeweler's.

Diamond Jeweler's was owned by Mr. Cisneros, who in our town was more like Aladdin's genie than a regular hombre because his store sold every girl's wished-for prize—genuine top-quality jewelry. If you'd passed by it in those days, odds were you'd see hand and nose prints on the window glass from all the niñas who tried to get a good look at the magic inside. The shop was stocked with gold chains and pocket watches for the misters, hoop earrings and anklets for the ladies, but the reason the store was still kicking was that most of the local Romeos—no matter how poor, no matter how much they hated begging for construction jobs in front of the Home Depot or even, Dios mío, selling black market food stamps or picking a pocket or two—most of these men were willing to pay the price for true love no matter what it cost, and Diamond Jeweler's had what they were looking for. There was every kind of engagement and wedding rings you could imagine in there: plain bands, fancy carved bands, hunks of gold studded with diamond flakes or heaving a chunky rock—real or cubic, whatever you liked—that sparkled under the lights.

With Billy's credit card in my hot hand I went inside Diamond Jeweler's and looked down through the glass at the rows of rings. Some were yellow gold and some were white gold. One had round diamonds shaped into a heart. One had a blood-colored ruby. My favorite was the biggest, a Liberace-sized monster that needed its own bodyguard.

Mr. Cisneros came over. He was shorter than me and as small-boned as a bird. Not too much hair, but a dresser. He liked pinstripes and suspenders and he wore a pinkie ring, which was rose gold with a quarter-carat diamond in the middle. He kept a nice shop, too. The carpet was mushroom-colored and there was classy music in the background. You wouldn't barely even know that the Eastern Ave borrachos were stumbling around just outside the door.

"How can I help you?"

"Let me see that one," I said. I pointed at the monster.

He took a key out of his pocket and bent down to unlock the case. He told me about the ring while he got it out. It was a two-carat brilliant-cut, set in fourteen-karat yellow, four prongs, used to belong to Señora Araiza, did I know her? Passed away, poor thing, but this was good quality, good good quality. Mr. Cisneros's cologne smelled like pine needles and he smiled all the time when he talked.

The ring was on a piece of black velvet, staring up at me. Mr. Cisneros took out a little magnifying glass and I looked right into the rock. It had some nasty black scratches on the inside, you wouldn't even know it. Mr. Cisneros called them inclusions. But when I just looked at it plain again it was still pretty. I put it on my finger and worked my hand under the light so the rainbow glowed and glittered. I didn't care about no inclusions.

"And this is for the engagement?" Mr. Cisneros asked.

"Oh no, me and my husband got married two years ago," I told him. "But we didn't have money back then, we were flat broke. Just starting out. But now there's enough so he said I can finally get my diamond. My husband, he's a boxer. You know boxing?"

Mr. Cisneros shook his head. He said he didn't follow the sports.

"Well, that's okay. Anyways, he brings in plenty now and this morning he said, 'Honey, you go and get yourself that ring you been driving me crazy about.' So here I am. And it's about time, too, don't you think? A girl shouldn't have to wait forever to get her engagement ring."

"Oh no, of course not! Every woman must have a diamond. You are doing the right thing, absolutely!" Mr. Cisneros started taking out more trays of rings and showing them to me. There were square-shaped diamonds, pear diamonds, yellow diamonds, snowflake diamonds, diamond chips bunched together like a bouquet of white roses.

And then he said, "Oh, I'm sorry. I have not introduced myself. I am Jimmy Cisneros, at your service. And you are?"

I shook his hand, very gentle, so he'd know I was a lady. "Rita. Rita Novo."

"Ah, the beautiful Señora Novo. It is a pleasure. Would you like to try on any of these other rings?"

I looked at my diamond. It had stars and snowdrifts and white fire inside it.

"No," I said. "I'll take this one."

* * *

I didn't have to give the ring back. Billy was mad at first, and told me that I better take it back. But I yammered and bawled and just wouldn't stop crying. I cried for six hours—while eating dinner and washing dishes, while I took my bath. Finally he gave in. He'd won a ten-thousand-dollar purse from his fight with Sugarboy, what could it hurt? He told me that the ring didn't mean we were getting married and I said okay. So I got to keep it.

That piece of ice sparkled cold and beautiful on my hand. And I figured it was practical, too. I knew someday he'd finally come around and when he did, I'd already have the ring. For now it was just safekeeping. I loved it. All that year I never took it off except for cleaning, and I checked it all the time to make sure it was still on my finger. Later, though, it was lost. But it wasn't my fault. They robbed that ring off my hand, at point-blank. That's how they got it from me, but they couldn't any other way. I wouldn't never have gave up something so precious of my own free will.

You Go Get Yours

A neighborhood can ride through a slump for a while, so as you can hardly tell how hard folks have been hit in the pocket. Women will complain about the high prices but still put something nice on the table and even keep buying the name-brand baby food, and the men can shrug off their lost jobs and still have just enough loose cash to spot a buddy, buy a drink, or keep their place at the gym.

Those days were over now. Half the shops on Chávez were shut down, and the leftover cash had dried up a long time ago. Cashiers and stockboys who'd got their pinkslips were looking for work in Downey, Rancho Cucamonga, Burbank, Pacoima, but most of them came off the bus at the end of the day ready for a stiff drink, and if they didn't have a spare two bucks for a tequila then they'd settle for a fistfight. We were seeing plenty of brawls then, the blurry-faced hombres hunched over and slugging, the screaming wives rushing out into the street to try and hold them back.

There was no denying that the town was tanking. The wear-and-tear signs were starting to show up everyplace you looked. I think they showed up worst, though, at Ruben's Superbox.

Almost all the Rabbit Street boys were busted flat and couldn't pay Ruben's membership fee anymore. They tried everything they could think of to hang on. Chuco promised to clean out the buckets. Tommy wrote out a mess of IOUs. Martinez made jokes about the lottery and Jose tried to sneak in and out of the gym without getting caught. And what's more, a new crop of sharpshooters were starting to come in. Ruben was getting a name because of Billy, and Mexican ringers from as far off as Fullerton and Ventura were asking him for training. They'd show up at the gym, hooking their thumbs in their shorts and checking out the scene with hooded eyes, and then start blasting the heavy bag, or working the speedbag so fast it disappeared. So it got to be different around there. The gym was too quiet and the Rabbit Streeters slunk around and made way for Billy. They knew they'd be out soon, but he'd stay on.

And then it happened, about a year after I bought my diamond. Martinez was the first one to go.

It was a cold spring then. The sun gleamed through the gym windows clear and pale, and the smog had been scared off by the chill. The gym was crowded that day with boys in red sweatshirts and shorts, and they hung around talking, doing sit-ups, rope-skipping, and working the medicine ball. Billy shadowboxed by the mirror, and a couple of Ruben's new sharpshooters were there too. One of them was from Fullerton, and the other guy was a dude from Pomona with a big shiny pompadour that kept getting whacked out of place. Both of them were sparring in the ring, their flashing red gloves bright as blood spots, the sweat flying off their heads when they got hit. Chuco walked around picking up towels, a metal spit bucket banging against his knees. Jose was there too, doing push-ups a yard away from me and grunting out a number every time his nose touched the mat.

I looked up to see Pedro coming out of the locker room. He walked up to Jose and touched him on the shoulder.

"Martinez is out, man," he said.

Jose sat up, pushed his hair from his eyes. "What? What do you mean, out?"

"Ruben just kicked him out the gym."

"Nah, nah, man. There's got to be some mistake."

"What you boys talking about?" I asked. Pedro wouldn't look at me.

"I don't think so," he said to Jose. "Ruben just cleared his locker out and packed his bag. He even asked for his key back."

We could hear something now, a crashing and thumping coming from the lockers.

"You can't KICK ME OUTTA HERE," Martinez hollered.

Jose stood up. "Oh shit," he said. "What's he doing in there? He busting the lockers up?"

More crashing. "I AIN'T FUCKING GOING NO-WHERES, RUBEN!"

Ruben's low voice answered, mumbling something I couldn't make out.

"I told you, man," Pedro said. "Didn't I tell you?"

There was some more banging for a while and now Ruben was yelling out filthy chingados loud and clear and Martinez started screaming even dirtier cusses back and slugging the lockers with a big THUNK and THUMP and then it got quiet again.

"Does he got a gun?" one of the sharpshooters said.

Pedro looked at him and smiled. "A big, big gun, baby, just the right size to blow off your fat Fullerton head." His bad eye was twitching terrible.

The sharpshooter with the pompadour smacked his friend on the shoulder. "Don't listen to Mr. Magoo here, man. Sucka's trying to psych you out."

"I'll psych you out, Ricky Ricardo!"

The Fullerton dude started laughing and Pedro lunged for Ricky Ricardo just slow enough so Jose could hold him back, and that's when Martinez came out of the locker room. He was wearing a RUBEN'S SUPERBOX boxing shorts and T-shirt set and holding his ripped-up duffel bag, stuffed full of gear. He just stared at everybody. We stared back at him. Then Ruben came out, his last few hairs sticking straight up out of his head.

"Come on, buddy," Ruben said. "Don't make it like this."

Martinez shook his head. "I ain't making it like nothing. You're the pendejo who's making it into something. You're the asshole bringing in a bunch of fucking nobodies and ditching the brothers who been loyal to you, Ruben."

"Okay, that's it, I heard enough," Ruben said. "You're finished. Get the hell out of here."

Martinez put his duffel bag down. He stayed put.

Ruben yelled at him, waving his arms. "You heard me. Get lost."

Martinez still didn't move.

"You get out or I'm calling the cops," Ruben said. But he didn't go over to the phone, he stayed put where he was.

"You some kind a genius, Ruben, what they gonna arrest me for, eh? They gonna arrest me for being thirty-six fucking years old?"

And then Martinez started laughing. Except he was laughing too much. His body shook helpless and his face was wet and stretched.

"No, cabron," Billy said. "They gonna arrest you for impersonating a man." He turned around and started shadow-boxing again.

"Martinez!" Pedro yelled. "Cut that shit out!"

Martinez nodded and took in a deep breath. "Okay, right," he said. "Right."

When he was okay again he looked up. "Sure, no problem, you assholes. Guess what, Ruben. I was through with fighting anyways. And you know what? I'm goddam happy to be out of this business. I really am. I mean, hell, man, what the fuck kind of living is this, anyways? Any of you ever think of that? Getting the shit beat outta you or beating it outta somebody else ain't no kind of life. So I am—I *am* glad. You get that, Ruben? Hey, Ruben, my man"—Martinez was really hollering now and the Rabbit Streeters started whooping—"Ruben, my old hermano, listen up, 'cause I do thank you. I think maybe you set me free, you motherfucker."

He bent down and dug through his duffel bag, then started throwing his gear all around. His jock, his socks, his extra shirts and boxing shorts, his gloves and headgear—all of it went sailing through the air. One of the T-shirts draped over Ricky Ricardo's head. The gloves just missed Billy's face by a couple inches. Pedro was standing on the bleachers and cheering through his cupped hands. Jose and Tommy were giving standing ovations.

When the bag was empty Martinez stood back up and pointed at Ruben. "Man, I been training with you since I was seventeen years old. NINETEEN YEARS I been coming here. So you ain't kicking me out, I'm the one who's quitting you, see? I'M the one who's fucking quitting YOU."

"Yeah, great." Ruben spread out his arms. "So quit me, already."

"Oh no, just one more thing, my friend. I still got to give you back all your shit."

"Keep it!"

But Martinez was already stripping. He bent down and slipped off his Superbox shorts and threw them across the room. The Rabbit Streeters clapped and catcalled; Tommy jumped up and caught the shorts in one hand. Then Martinez peeled off his Superbox T-shirt and flung it over his head. There was all kinds of racket—high-fiving and war-whooping and fists pounding on the heavybags. The number street flyweights zoomed around the room laughing, and Pedro and Jose saluted Martinez and started singing the Mexican anthem.

They stopped their cheering, though, when they saw what kind of shape Martinez was in.

A few years ago Martinez had stopped taking his shirt off when he fought. Now we knew why. His body had took some bad beatings, and it told the tale. The belly hung loose; scars cut up his shoulders and chest. Broke blood vessels stained up his ribs, and his muscles had shrunk. It was like pulling back the wings of a lamed hawk and seeing the thin cracked bones, the fragile heart thumping under the ripped feathers.

A lot of the boys shot their eyes away. Martinez was still their hero. He'd been to Vegas. His shoulders used to be like bowling balls and time was you could hurt your hand if you punched him in the stomach. But that was all done now and Martinez didn't hide none of it. He let us see, and when he figured we'd had enough he picked up his duffel bag and swung it over his shoulder. Then he walked out the door just like that, in his underwear.

Billy and the sharpshooters started training again and Ruben went to his office and slammed the door. The rest of the fighters looked at each other but I couldn't even meet eyes with them. It was bad. Everybody knew they were looking at their futures and none of the Rabbit Streeters so much as moved until Ruben finally came back out and told Chuco to clean up the mess.

After that day, Ruben cleaned house. More and more of those sharpshooters were coming in, and there just wasn't room for no-talents. So Freddie was canned next, and a few weeks later Chuco got made water boy. Another month passed and then Tommy was out too, slamming his locker shut and wiping his eyes with the back of his hand. The last of the Rabbit Streeters to go was Jose. He saw it coming, though. After Martinez got the boot he gave up on his boxing dream. Dolores told me he was thinking about getting into pro wrestling. Word was, a slugger could make some real money there if he didn't mind faking punches and getting dressed up like a fool.

So he was ready to get kicked out, but I still think he took it hard. That day Jose came whistling in like usual and went back to the lockers, but when he came back out he was still full dressed. Billy wouldn't look at him and neither would the sharpshooters. Ruben finally came up to him and said something and they shook hands, and when Ruben turned back around I saw Jose wipe his hand on his pants. He was coming up my way now. I still remembered that time he'd gripped on to my legs, and the time Billy beat him up and I didn't make a move, and those memories accused me. I felt sick.

"I'm sorry, Jose," I said to him before he went out the door. "I don't know why Ruben's got to do this."

Jose didn't say anything at first. He hitched up his bag and looked close at my moving face.

"You know, you still can box," I went on. "This isn't the only gym. You could go someplace else and train there."

He tried a smile. "Nah, girl, this was the only place for me. It's finished up. I got to take it. But it's not so bad, you know? Did you hear? I'm getting into pro wrestling. I got try-outs tomorrow."

Then he said, "Hey, don't look so bad! It's gonna be all right."

Something hot flickered in my mind when he touched my arm, and he was quiet, and not smiling anymore. We'd locked in a stare and my ears went deaf to the world then. All I could hear was the quick drumbeating, and the weather turned warm and green and wet, like it does before a storm. But I was the first one to look away. I remembered Dolores laughing in her wedding dress, and then I heard Billy talking to one of the sharpshooters.

"Go on, go on," I said. I waved Jose off. I shrugged like it was nothing. "Go home, and I'll see you and Dolores later."

Jose turned away from me. He looked out at the gym for a long time, gripping on to his bag. I could see him working his jaw muscles. Then he hitched up his bag again, pushed through the door, and left Ruben's Superbox for good.

*W*hen all those out-of-work boys got booted from Ruben's, there wasn't anyplace else for them to kick it but out on the streets. Not that the streets were such a great place to be by then. Folks didn't have cash for car repairs and so there were lemons left for dead on the side of the roads; cracked windows stayed that way; screen doors broke off their hinges kept swinging. There was more trash, too, week-old newspapers and fast-food Styrofoam rolling in the gutters, and the sight of all that dirt and ruination made our men mad. They'd roam around the avenue with nothing to do except stew in their own hot juice about the run-down town and the bets they'd lost on boxing and fútbol, so it was just a matter of time before they wanted to steal, fight, and get high.

That's where Victor Mendoza came in.

*I*t was that Victor who brought in the drugs. It was him who put it out on the same streets where clunky-shoed viejas used to shop for Sunday dinner and gradeschoolers used to shoot marbles and play double Dutch. And when he did that, he helped start a killing fire that burned higher and steadier all that year, till it caught a breeze and took over the whole town.

Victor's Fifth Streeter gang was fifty strong by this time, most of them castaways who wanted to be pirates. You'd see them staked out on corners, standing there slumpy, rapping, laughing, pulling saran-wrapped packages of pills out their pockets and slapping them into the hands of the wide-grinning fools who paid or promised them a twenty.

All of them just loved to party. Once I took the long way home from work and I passed by the Mendoza house. The Fifth Streeters were having a barbecue there, and the whole front lawn was full of cholos and bimbos and number street joes and even some ex-boxers. Like Zookie Chamayo was there. That chump! That poser! He was trying to be badass flashy in his perfect-pressed Kmart baggies and wrong-way baseball cap, but he might as well still have had that two-dollar price tag stuck on them knockoff Nikes he was wearing. Zook was hanging around with Victor, eating a burger and chuckling stony, trying to slap Victor some skin but missing, then laughing even harder. Victor didn't seem to mind. He laughed along, then grabbed at a girl. The two of them started tickling her, and she giggled shrieky so they'd do it some more.

Zookie made a mistake getting in with those gangsters, though. Zookie the meth freak. He was speeding all the time from what I hear, but speeding's expensive. He couldn't pay his bill and so he lost his good buddy Victor.

A few weeks after that barbecue, Victor shot Zookie in the shoulder, trying to rough the money out of him. Zook holed up in the hospital for close to a week with busted tendons. After that he could only raise his right arm so high. And then you just couldn't shut him up, he was always going on about how I almost got killed and look at my scar, and this old war wound cost me my boxing career. He liked it.

Victor was a wanted man now. He hid out from the police, who sent over extra black-and-whites to cruise the neighborhood. He was still on the run from the time he'd stuck up that liquor store, and what with the drugs and the shooting he'd be looking at three strikes if they ever caught up to him. But Victor was a natural fugitive and was a genius at being invisible.

So he stayed disappeared. Nobody seemed to know where he was—nobody admitted to it, that is. I figured somebody had to be helping him, but at that point it was a mystery even to me.

*W*ith Victor hid out these boys turned rowdy fast. The next month this is what happened: two more liquor store robberies, three knife fights, one overdose, another shooting.

* * *

We never even thought about getting a gun to ward off the outlaws. That was Mr. Hernandez's idea.

In the past year Mama had broke up with a construction worker, a car salesman, and a sharp-dressed bum who made his living off the black market food stamps. All of them were borrachos she'd met at the bars, cigar-chomping bastards who always cleaned out the fridge and never learned my name. But now she was seeing Mr. Hernandez again, two or three times a week. I didn't have it out for Hernandez. He was a cheater but he was clean, and even though the sight of him on the porch steps spelled the depression later on, Mama was always happy while it lasted. He was her number two true love.

One night I came home late and saw him right before he left to go back home to La Rica. They were in the living room, drinking martinis out of water glasses. The air smelled thick of cigarette smoke, Shalimar, and the gin bottle, and there was music playing, something with horns and a sorrowful woman singing. Mama was wearing a present he'd gave her, a red robe made of Chinese silk and stitched with flame-yellow dragons. Mr. Hernandez said good-bye to me on his way out, and I almost laughed at his tousled hair, his funny short man's strut. On the couch, Mama had rubbed-pale lips, and her smoky hair was over one shoulder. When he was gone she lifted up her arms into red wings and asked me to dance.

I put my head on her chest and breathed in the cologne. I could feel her pulse in my skin. Mama stroked my hair and hummed in my ear along with the sorrowful woman while the dragon on her thigh swayed and curled its tail, and I closed my eyes. When I opened them again, I saw the box on the sofa. What was it? Another present? Jewelry?

"Let me show you," she said. She opened the box and inside was the gun. It was silver nickel with thin bronze bullets, and when I picked it up it was heavy.

"He says we need it for protection, but I don't know," she went on. "I don't like guns. And what I'm going to do? If somebody breaks in here I'm going to shoot them? If they want to kill me, they kill me."

I aimed it at the TV. "I think it's a good idea. This must have cost a lot of money."

"Put that down! Just looking at it makes me shaky." She put the gun back in the box and closed it.

"What, he buys you this and you're not going to keep it?"

"I don't know. At least it shows that he loves me." She touched her lip. "I'll have to think about it. I'll just put it some-place safe now."

We went to her closet and put the gun way at the back. We covered it up with towels, and then blankets, and a quilt. We packed it all down, shut the door, and left the room. It was like the closet was full of exploding danger.

For the next few weeks, she talked about that gun a lot. She couldn't make up her mind what to do with it. Throw it away? Sell it? She was halfway decided on giving it back to Mr. Hernandez, but then he died. And when that happened she couldn't part with it, neither that or the red Chinese robe or a pair of high-heeled shoes he'd once gave her. She kept those things the same as a church keeps the hair and teeth and bones of saints, because out of all those years with him, that was all she had left.

*M*r. Hernandez died of a heart attack in the middle of the night, in his wife's bed. We heard about it the next day, thirdhand, from Señora Serros, our next-door neighbor, who said he'd never had a chance: When La Rica woke up he'd al-ready been cold and his skin was turning silver.

Mama wasn't the same after that. Her body bent down and seemed so heavy it was like Mr. Hernandez's ghost had wrapped itself around her neck and her foot dragged with every step from the terrible weight. She stopped wearing lipstick and the color red. Her hair hung flat and she let the white show in it, so that when she shook her head there was a tumble of shadows and snow flurries. She would still come home late and stumble over the furniture but she didn't touch the men again for a long, long time. They seemed scared of her dark dresses that weren't fancy or slick and chic, but more like the sad clothes that widows wear.

But Mama didn't stay cold forever. We come from a long line of needful women and that need doesn't die just because a man does. She took it slow, but she learned how to curl her lip up again, and ask for a cigarette just so. She never did paint herself up pretty anymore or laugh with her head thrown back, but she could still snag a man by brushing her hand on his, or by lifting her naked face to the light and smiling. I don't think it was good with the strangers anymore, though. I'd grown up hearing the hot sounds of love talk and the hopeless yelping. Now she was quiet with the men, she whispered. And she kicked them out quick the next morning.

No matter how much Mama hurt from Mr. Hernandez's heart attack, I still think La Rica took it worse. She didn't have the survival in her like Mama. She was destructed. Word was that when she woke up next to a husband as cold and gray as a shark, she screamed so loud neighbors from six blocks down jumped out of their beds. But she didn't open her mouth again after that. She took her mourning so serious she wouldn't say a word, not even to her own daughter, who she talked to now in signs.

This is something I don't think any of us could have predicted. Some women gather their power when they become widows. They thick up and broaden, and their backs straighten up once they can forget about cooking dinner and bending over ironing boards. These are women to be afraid of. They yell like sergeants and bend folks to their will like warlocks. This is what La Rica had been marked for; we all thought she would grow even stronger and crush the whole town in her fist. But she didn't. She let go of her grip without a fight. She shrunk down and withered and didn't like to go out anymore. She pulled the curtains closed in her house and wouldn't answer the phone.

Who would have thought it? Mr. Hernandez had never seemed like nothing to me. He'd had a face like a mouse. His bones were thin and delicate as a greyhound's. Somewhere, though, deep in his skinny chest, he had a burning love magic that could break women down. It had rubbed my beautiful mama down until she was thin as a sliver of soap. And it took the appetite from power-hungry La Rica, so now the neighborhood was left without a leader.

For a while, anyway. It was Dolores who took La Rica's place.

Dolores got pregnant around the same time that Martinez was kicked out of Superbox, but instead of becoming more womanish and delicate, she became more political. After her first trimester she was all Chicana Power and grass roots and Mahatma Gandhi. I think it was because of the OD. A thirteen-year-old Fifth Streeter wanna-be named Chong Montalvo had snorted a handful of cocaine and his dying chilled the heart of every mama in town. Mujeres tried to keep their children close and they went through their pockets for any sign of the drugs. Dolores didn't have her baby yet, but she looked around at the dirty streets and the gangsters with their fake Rolexes and the blocks and blocks of double-bolted doors, and she put her hands protective over her growing belly. It's around then she started talking to Pedro.

Pedro was still big into the politics. He'd found part-time work at a Taco Bell downtown, but his full-time job was being a radical mofo with a mission. He sure did dress the part, with his camouflage pants and his brown berets and his T-shirts made out of the Mexican flag. He had his own group now, too. It was called the Chicano Warriors except he spelled Chicano in this Aztecan way, Xicano. The Xicano Warriors. It didn't have too many members. There was Sammy Peña, a jumpy *Star Trek* fan who believed in space aliens and collected comics; Sancho Porras, a ninth-grade pyro fresh from juvie; Jumbo Gomez, a fat boy who wore Black Sabbath concert shirts and walked with his head down; and Rafa Serros, a big-brained math freak who talked nothing but computers and slung tacos alongside Pedro. Every now and then Tito and Martinez and Jose would pound Coronas with Pedro and his new dudes, but they weren't offi-cial Xicanos because they didn't put on the Army Surplus clothes and call everybody hermano and go to the meetings in the park where Pedro speechified about socialism. So when you boiled it down the Warriors were just Pedro and his four fruit-loop Mexican commies, but that didn't get in his way. He held tiny voting registration rallies. He told us to write letters to senators. He was burning for us all to jump in our pickups and go march on Washington to protest la migra. And him and his boys would picket in front of Rudy's Super, where they'd hold up antigrape signs and tell everybody not to buy strawberries.

It was after Dolores and me had gone grocery-shopping and caught Pedro jumping up and down on top of a fruit crate that she went to go see him. He gave her some books and she started talking in them ten-syllable words. She read Gandhi and Martin Luther King and Malcolm X and put up César Chávez's picture next to her Virgin and crucifix. Then she started her own group. It was called the Latina League, after the lunch club the Divine Drive types used to have, except this Latina League was open to anybody. Dolores made posters and called every woman she could think of, knocked on doors, cornered shoppers and checkout girls at the super, hassled chicas strolling their babies in the park, anything to get them to show up. And they did, too. It turned out to be a real success.

The Latina League met every Thursday afternoon at Lupe's Beauty House because that was the only place big enough, and plus Lupe had offered the salon as a way to drum up more business. Right away it had mucho more members than the Xicano Warriors. All the ladies joined, not just the hard-ups from Eastern Ave looking for free food. When I walked into the first meeting that October I saw how practically every mama in town had come. There was Lupe, the Divine Drive types, the churchies, the number street chicas, and the cleaning women I always saw getting off the bus. Most of them flocked around the card tables set up with enchiladas and rice salad and flautas and Jell-O parfait and flan; the rest sat at the manicure stations and barber chairs and were already eating.

Dolores was up by the dryers, rapping her hand on one of the plastic hoods. She was looking different these days. The baby was pushing out from under her dress and he'd put a gold glow in her skin. Her hair was different, too. I'd done it myself that week, in a style more chic and powerful. It was short and burned back, and sleek as a seal. But even with that hair, Dolores was still having trouble getting the meeting started.

"All right, come on now," she kept saying. "Let's go, señoras."

It was no use. Those women wouldn't get going on the political mumbo jumbo till they were good and finished complaining about their men or crying after them. They shoveled the chili-spiced meat in their mouths and blatted about their no-good husbands. They dug into the red Jell-O and whispered true confessions about their druggie sons. I picked up a paper plate and wondered why I'd come. I wanted to get away from those twittering hens. But then Veronica and Frida came up, both of them holding their huge-headed newborns like they were econo-sized sacks of masa and grinning at me so hard I could see their gums.

"HI! How's it going?" Frida said.

"How you doing, Rita?" Veronica said at the same time.

"Fine."

They kept grinning at me and balanced their babies onto their hips. Some of the other mujeres came up then, too, Mimi and Rosario and Cha Cha and Connie, all of them giggling and pointing at my diamond ring. Then I saw how even the Widow Muñoz was looking at me almost friendly over her high-piled plate. Only Gloria turned her back to me, but I still saw her biting her lip and squeezing her kid too tight.

Frida's baby started fussing and she put her pinkie in its mouth. "Well you must be doing better than fine! You must be doing super! Billy is just going up and up and up. We couldn't believe it when we saw him in the paper, and then, hoosh! On the TV!"

"Oh my God when I saw him on the TV I just screamed!" Rosario said, standing up on her toes.

I smiled back at them. They were right about Billy going up in the world. He was getting to be like a star now. A few weeks ago he'd fought a sure bet called Mickey Crockett, this New Jersey 40-and-0 ringer with the biggest arms I'd ever seen on a lightweight. Crockett had been going someplace. He drove a Porsche Carrera and had three sons by three different girls and word was that he trained by fighting two middleweights at the same time. Billy was just supposed to be Crockett's ESPN warm-up before he took a stab at the Hammer on pay-per-view, but it didn't work out that way. Billy had been studying his tapes and knew that Crockett's weak spots were his legs and his body defense, so when he got in there he ran him dead around the ring and blackjacked him in the ribs and then knocked him out easy in the fourth with a crack to the nose. When the count was over Billy had got up on Ruben's shoulders, and he was handsome, laughing through his mouthpiece, raising up a glove. The glove-raising shot got ran on page three of the Sports the next day, a black-and-white close-up with a headline that said UNDERDOG KAYOS CROCKETT IN FOUR.

I grinned at the memory and shrugged at the Latina Leaguers still huddling around me.

"Man! I wish Eddie would do something like that," Mimi said. She was married to Eduardo Vasquez, an ex–security guard.

Cha Cha laughed raspy about her husband, Lucky Díaz. "Don't we know it, girls? Damn! What I'd pay for a good man!" Her and Connie high-fived.

"Your man's not so bad," Rosario said.

"Not if you don't mind a beer-sucking TV-watching monkey who don't do nothing but sit on your couch and complain how he can't get a job!"

"Hoosh yes!" Veronica said. "I got all that and plus Snoopy and me haven't had sex in six months, girl!"

"Oh honey I heard that."

"You know they get depressed when they can't find work," Rosario said.

"Work nothing!" Frida said. "Marco told me I got too fat after the baby and he won't touch me till I get back in a size ten."

"Like they ain't getting fat! Like they ain't getting fat! I got Mr. Pop-n-Fresh himself sleeping in my bed."

"Ay, give it up. It's got so bad I'm putting ketchup over Slim-Fast and telling him it's home-cooked meat loaf!"

The chicas heaved up their babies and laughed till they wiped their eyes, even Gloria who was standing behind them, her mouth turning up like a kinked wire.

"Nah, nah," Mimi said, "just kidding. Eddie's my man. I wouldn't give that chump up for the world."

Cha Cha nodded. "Don't I know it. They pains in the bootie but you can't help but loving the men."

They all started talking at the same time about how their husbands were really angels, but that's when Dolores started making her racket again. "Let's go, mujeres! This meeting's started!" She'd got a curling iron and was rapping it on the dryer.

We went to sit down. The stools were all taken but some of the folding chairs were still empty. Frida and Mimi sat on either side of me. Veronica touched me on the shoulder, passed me a sign-up sheet. Dolores stood in the front, her fresh-burned hair gleaming, and told us Welcome. I peered around casual, caught Señora Mirande snapping at her girdle. Connie cradled her hija and kissed her head. The Widow Muñoz settled in a barber chair. Cha Cha and Rosario smiled at me when I met their eyes, and Gloria didn't look at me at all. Nothing was like usual. Nobody tsked or looked at me cross-eyed or made like they were better than I was. Dolores started going on about Neighborhood Watch and Project Jobs and day-care pools and I sat there, feeling good sitting knee-to-knee with the other ladies and listening. I know that except for Dolores, I shouldn't have cared one straw about any of those women, but I couldn't help it. Seeing and feeling their little smiles and shoulder and knee touches was like finding buried treasure to me. I was happy. I had Billy's ring on my finger and I didn't care nothing about the past. I was finally one of las girlfriends. And Dolores was our leader.

Pro wrestling is like a circus, a streetfight, and a magic show all wrapped up together and then drug through the dirt. A pro wrestler is not even good enough to stand in the same room as a boxer. He is a con-artist clown with the heart of a coward and the fashion sense of a brain-damaged superhero. In comparison to the sport of boxing the pro wrestler is shameful, something to hide your eyes from. There is no bravery or skill in it. No pride, and no guts, neither. Pro wrestling is full of never-beens and wash-ups and steroid-pumping cheating bums. It is the graveyard of boxing.

So know this: I did not want to go see Jose wrestle. I did not want to see him be humiliated. But Dolores invited me to his first match, and I love her too much to tell her the truth. This is why I went.

Dolores was eight months pregnant and as big around as a redwood when Jose had his first bout. It was at the Olympic Auditorium downtown, where they usually hold the fights, but as soon as we walked inside I could see this crowd wasn't anything like the fight fans. I made only one or two cowboys and just a handful of cholos but there was lots of kids, tired-looking women wearing extra-large T-shirts, and bald Anglo daddies with red noses. There was a good number of freaks, too, like the three dummies with red-painted faces buying beer at the snack stand, the fool in the hot-dog line wearing a silver cape and a matching Mohawk, and the two-hundred-pound lady squeezed inside a hot-pink cat suit who was holding hands with a midget dressed like Uncle Sam.

Dolores looked around and put her hands under her belly. "Oof, he's kicking me terrible. Let's go sit down."

Our seats were in the fifth row, where all the hard-core koo-koos were. It was hot and crowded, and I tried to keep my elbows in so I wouldn't touch any crackpots. We were sitting in the middle of a family of wrestling nuts: a mama, a daddy, and four screaming boys, every single one of them wearing bright blue wigs and shirts that said NEW WORLD ORDER and holding signs that, when put together, spelled out

N-I-T-R-O!

And it didn't get any better. There was seventies funk blaring over the speakers and a whole mess of blue-haired and red-faced folks were disco-dancing around the ring. Shirtless kids ran wild through the stands. Skinheads were doing the wave. Two ladies done up in black vinyl stood and did the bump. I looked over at Dolores to see what she thought but she had her hands over her stomach and had closed her eyes.

"Ugh, he's kicking so hard. I'm just going to sit here; tell me when it's time," she said.

I shook her on the shoulder after about half an hour when the announcer got inside the ring with two wrestlers and started hollering into the mike.

"LADIES AND GENTS! WELCOME TO THE WORLD WRESTLING CHAMPIONSHIP!"

Everybody stomped their feet and cheered.

The announcer pointed to one of the wrestlers, a dude the size of a side of beef who was wearing gold chains and eight inches of spandex and had this wild neon-blue hairdo. "In the BLUE," he yelled, "is the CHAMPION MASTER OF DISASTER, the one and only SUPERSONIC, DEATH-DEFYING KING of PAIN—NITRO!"

There was a whole lot of hissing and shrieking while Nitro ran around the ring and flexed. The blue-wigged Nitro-lovers sitting around me jumped up and down in their seats and waved their signs.

"And in the RED," the announcer went on, "is the CHALLENGER, the PRINCE OF PUNISHMENT, the RED-HOT BARD OF BLOOD HIMSELF, BLAZE!"

Now the other wrestler, a thick-bellied monster with a blood-colored mug and cannonball-sized biceps, was bawling out threats and beating on his chest, and the Nitro freaks stood up and booed.

Dolores tugged on my sleeve. "Jose told me about these guys. See that Blaze? He's an ex-druggie who's heavy into Jesus. He's trying to get a pro-wrestling ministry started but is having trouble raising the money. And that Nitro there, he's a gay. He lives with his boyfriend and two sons in Pacoima."

I looked back at Nitro and Blaze, who were wrestling now. I'd never seen such cheating chicken-fighting in all my life. They banged around the ring with their hair flying and their fists pumping, twirling each other up in the air, bouncing graceful off the ropes, all the while pulling punches and kicks and snapping their heads back when they pretended to get hit. But the crowd loved it. They clapped and screamed and kept on doing the wave up and down. The Nitro fans were having the best time of it. Nitro had Blaze by the head and was faking slugs to the face and Blaze was flapping his arms helpless. That went on for a while, until Nitro finally knocked Blaze to the mat and pinned him while everybody chanted ONE TWO THREE and then the match was over.

"Okay, here we go!" Dolores said. She started cheering and whistling and the announcer ran back into the ring with two more wrestlers. One was an Army general done up in a white beard and stars-and-stripes skivvies smiling under his belly, and the other one was an Indian with red war paint and a feather headdress and a leather loincloth. When I got a good look at his face I think I started yelling along with the crowd because that Indian was Jose. He stamped around and shook his feathers at the crowd and hollered out Ay Ay Ay Ay like a spaghetti Western Apache, and then he grinned horrible and showed his teeth. The general worked it too. He jumped around and threw his head back and roared. He pounded his chest and flexed his tanned muscles so they shone and rippled under the lights. The announcer was yelling into the mike this whole time, going on about vicious bone-crunching Crazy Custer and that cold-blooded scalp-stealer Tommy Tomahawk, while the crowd kept up with the booing and the cheering.

"Jose doesn't like that Crazy Custer," Dolores said. "Them two don't get along."

Jose took off his headdress and ran skull-first at Crazy Custer, who stuck out his arm and clotheslined him. Jose spilled on the mat and wiggled his arms and legs in the air the same as a flipped-over beetle. Then Custer picked him up above his head and propellered him around and around and when he was finished with that he dropped him on his knee, like to break his back. Custer bounced him up and down a couple more times while Jose spinned his arms and screamed and made phony faces. Then Jose got up and Custer threw him into the ropes and Jose boomeranged back and got him into a bogus choke-hold, but when Custer broke loose he socked Jose square in the eye so hard it started bleeding, and then he hit him again so he fell down.

"Jose's hurt," I said.

"He's not supposed to do that!" Dolores yelled. "They're supposed to pull their punches!"

She was saying something else about how wrestlers got demerits if they broke the rules but I could barely hear her with all that hollering and commotion. In the back of us there were ladies screeching out TOMMY and the circus sideshow with the silver Mohawk was doing the twist in the front row. Now Jose got back up to his feet and started swinging at Custer for real, and here it was—real bare-knuckle fighting, not the comic-book sucker-punching they'd been playing at before. Jose got in a good full round of right hooks and jabs and one or two upper-cuts and Custer didn't have any defense except for some clinching, so soon he was bleeding from the nose and had a red rose blooming under his left eye.

"Stop it! Stop it!" Dolores yelled. Then she looked down and touched her stomach and said, "Oh, wait."

"No, he's not waiting for nothing, he's going for it right now!" I laughed. Custer had his fists down, and Jose kept working the head so it papped back on the spine. Then Custer reeled and fell on the mat, and the crowd was on its feet, screaming. They cheered on Jose, who was dancing wild and barefoot, with the blood and paint streaming down his face and his arms raised. I was on my feet too. I was yelling out his true name. But when I looked down I saw that Dolores was still squashed in her seat and breathing quick and shallow as an animal, and she reached up and pulled me close.

"He wasn't kicking," she said. She looked concentrated, serious. "I'm having contractions."

"What? What'd you say?"

She grabbed my hand hard and breathed into my face, and that's when I saw how the pain was jerking her back and forth. "Rita, I need you to help me," she said. "I'm going to have this baby now."

*J*ose Miguel Jr. was born on October 12, 1996, at eight pounds, six ounces, just small enough to fit in the curve of an elbow. His head was made of eggshell and bent in strange directions. He had fists the size and shape of flower buds and punky hair like a blackbird's wing. When he sucked on Delores's nipple it stretched wide as a silver dollar and his eyes shut tight, but I didn't need to see them to know what color they would turn—shadow black and deep, and when he'd grow older and women would look into them they'd feel like they were falling down a manhole, or swimming a river in the dark dead of night.

The hospital white was a shock—I didn't like it. It wasn't kind to Mama, who had a face like a cracked china plate. It glared unfriendly on Delores's face, and Jose's, too, and it shone cold over the baby's, but they didn't seem to notice. Jose's skin was still red from the war paint and he looked bloodstained and dangerous. He bent down and touched the blackbird hair very gentle and held on to Delores's hand.

Just for one moment, one breath, did the jade-green jealous flow through me. She was holding him and before that I'd always known she'd loved me best. And I wanted what she had, too, I would have snatched it in my grabbing hands if I was able. But then she looked up, the tiredest woman I ever saw—sweat-stained, ash-colored, blood dots broke around her eyes—and held him out to me.

I took him from her and as soon as I touched him I loved him speechless, and when I held him I was shaking and gripping so tight that his eyes flew open and he cried, and she took him back.

I didn't know it could be like that. I didn't know it could stretch you out so much. I loved Dolores and that baby with an animal heart, and it came leaping out my mouth so that I choked and sobbed.

Mama and Jose were very quiet. They looked at the floor uncomfortable. But Dolores was smiling up at me. She laced her fingers in mine.

"It's your turn now," she said. "You go get yours, girl."

What It Takes to Get to Vegas

A month after Jose Jr. was born, Billy won his next fight. It was in the Downtown Sports Arena again, and I was in the thirty-fifth row this time, next to Freddie and Chuco, who'd both come stag.

Billy was the second match, up against Bobby "Boo-Boo" Larue. Boo-Boo was a half-Indian from Tarzana who'd won a bronze in the Olympics and had beat every contender he'd come up against. The Sports was calling him the Big Red Hope but you wouldn't know he was Indian from how white his skin was, except he had his hair tweaked out in a Mohawk and his eyes tilted up, so you knew he had to be something.

As soon as the bell rung, Boo-Boo was moving all the time. He went for the body right away. Billy was more holding back, taking hits, holding his gloves low. I was chewing on my knuckles and there were all these Tarzana punks shouting and Freddie and Chuco jumped out of their seats. Ruben was in Billy's corner, screaming out pointers with his mouth wide open. But Billy didn't look excited. He stared close at Boo-Boo while Boo-Boo hit him, and while he was sightseeing he took a round of hooks right in the plexus. He started weaving around a little more, still watching, but Boo-Boo kept on landing. You could really hear those hooks going into the ribs and all of a sudden I wondered if this was quits. But then, two minutes into the third round, Billy got the inspiration. He switched to southpaw and started slugging at the face.

Later some said it was dumb luck how Billy won, and maybe it was. Who'd know Boo-Boo was an egghead? See, the jawbone's a delicate operation; some of these ironmen who can take it forever in the gut got a weak jaw and a good punch will crack it in two. That's what happened to Boo-Boo. Billy took aim and let one fly on the side of the face, and it only looked like a regular journeyman head jab, but right away it was sayonara for Boo-Boo. Afterward we found out it was a clean jaw break and Boo-Boo had to get his cabeza wired up and he'd be out the business for a good six months to a whole year, but even not knowing that yet you could tell it hurt. The boy dropped to the canvas on both knees, grabbing at his head with his gloves, and smiled gruesome. Then Billy started prancing and yelling NUMBER ONE and all the Eastelayers including me got up on our feet and cheered out the ten count and then cheered some more when the ref announced KID WINS BY KAYO, and Ruben ran out waving his arms and carried Billy on his shoulders while the ring girls shook their goodies at the crowd.

Ruben sure was happy. He tried to lug Billy all the way back to the ready room except he couldn't make it for more than ten feet. And then inside the ready room he was swinging back tequilas and whooping up a storm and holding on tight to Cherry Salazar, who was making a guest appearance here in a snazzy silver lamé cocktail dress with plenty of cleavage.

"That was beautiful, that was beautiful," Ruben kept saying. "Another one-rounder, and that sonofabitch got hurt bad too! And goddam me if I didn't see them reporters scribbling!

You bet they starting to notice you, you just try and bet me you're not in the Sports tomorrow."

Billy nodded and rolled his shoulders and head around to loosen up. He wasn't much of a talker after a fight. He took off his satin jacket and threw it on a chair, and then Freddie picked it up and put it on.

"Cool jacket!" Freddie started posing for everybody and cocked his head at Billy. "Man, can I have one of these? I want one of these. Come on."

"Leave him alone," Ruben said. "And take off that jacket. That's a two-hundred-and-fifty-dollar piece of clothes there."

Freddie begged after Billy some more but Billy was more keeping to himself, staring off. It didn't even seem like he noticed anybody else in the room. The place was full of folks again, even more crowded than after the Sugarboy match. There was a pile of drunk dummies crushing up against each other and a circle of spiky-haired groupies staring at Billy like cockatoos begging for birdseed. I saw that Looker there, too, the one who'd first made a play for Billy after he'd beat Sugarboy, and she was slutted all the hell up in three inches of Lycra over a Dolly Parton wonderbra and was flirting with anything still sober enough to stand. But Billy didn't check out her or any of the other girls. He was all deep inside himself, thinking.

"That wasn't no real fight," he said finally.

"That sure was a real goddam fight!" Ruben told him. "You went and broke Boo-Boo's head!" Right now Ruben had one hand over Cherry's behind and she was smoking and looking around bored.

"Nah, he was nothing. I want somebody good. I want Hammer."

Ruben poured himself another drink with his free hand. "Well, you gonna have to wait on that one—I'm afraid I ain't no miracle worker. Six-and-oh won't get you in with a champion, and besides, we got you all busy enough anyways, don't we? You booked up till March with Cheech Martinez, Butterbean Montoya, Montezuma Jones, all of them serious, good fighters, genuine fire-eaters." Ruben raised up his glass in a toast. "But Billy, seriously, son, I'll get you whatever else you want. Like hey, you want a car? How 'bout a car, you earned a car. A nice black Buick, what you say?"

I shrugged my shoulders, hoping Billy would see. Cherry drove that white Caddy convertible with the custom hubs and the vanity plate. I wanted one of them. But Billy wasn't paying me attention. He stared at Ruben.

"Or an El Dorado?" Ruben went on. "A Lincoln? Or what about a Mustang? Some nice muscle car? Something in red?"

"Hey, Boss," Chuco said. He'd shuffled over to Ruben and had his hands in his pockets. "Boss."

"Or anything else, too, Billy," Ruben said. "Like how about some clothes, you want some clothes? You want a TV, a wide-screen? Or what about some nice R and R? How 'bout I go and set you up with some fun? Have a change of scenery, meet nice new people, get a little steam blown off, ride away all them tensions. . . . " Ruben was eyeballing some of the groupies then winking at Billy, while the Looker started jiggling and waving her hands over people's heads to try and get noticed.

"Honey, you so much as touch him I swear I'll bust your implants," I yelled out at her.

The Looker stopped her jiggling and looked at the men around her. "These ain't implants."

Cherry gave Ruben a good hard smack. "Shut up, stupid," she said.

"These are real!" the Looker was saying.

Billy shook his head at Ruben. "Boss, listen up, okay? I'm going to tell you something here. I'm done with these bums. If you don't get me with Hammer in my next fight, I'm finding another manager."

"WHAT?"

Cherry broke free and walked over to me when Ruben started sweating.

"Ah, naw, don't do that," he said. "Don't even talk that way, man! You know we're a team!"

"I'm the team, Ruben," Billy said.

"Of course you are, baby, of course you are. But you know, you and me together are the ones making it happen. Still, I bet I can rig something up, all right? Okay? I got a couple connections. So you don't have to get all fucking prima donna on me, because you know I'll set you up good."

"Well," Billy said, "I'll be waiting for that."

Cherry leaned on the wall next to me and fired up another cig. I hadn't been this close to la famous Cherry since that time I'd seen her shopping at Carlita's, years ago. She always had been some kind of dresser. That silver lamé thing she had on now was three hundred, easy, and she was showing as much skin as a stripper, but she had buckets of class, too.

"So he's your boyfriend, right?" she asked me after a minute.

I nodded, proud. "Yeah."

"Hmmm, then honey, it looks like you got your work cut out for you. That boy there's gotta be a fucking full-time job. Shoot, I'll bet he's just like Ruben, just like all these boxers, all of them christalmighty goddam pains in the ass, let me tell you."

I put my hands together and squeezed them. "I don't have any complaints." I tried not to show surprise. Cherry was nice and classy in that dress all right but when she talked she seemed tougher and way more inner city than I'd remembered.

The party was starting to ramp up now. One of the groupies was already bawling in a corner and a shaved-head cruiserweight was testing out the Looker's bazooms and a mess of drunks were circling Billy and lifting up their shirts to show him their scars.

"I told you to take off that fucking JACKET," Ruben yelled out.

Cherry picked at her nails a little and let her cig burn down. "He'll do it, too, Ruben will."

"He'll do what?" My eyes were following Freddie, who ran by both of us still wearing the jacket.

"He'll find a way to set up a fight with Hammer if that's what Billy wants. Ruben knows where he gets his bread buttered. And I'll bet he's gonna set your man up some R and R, too, just like he said. He'd do it in a second. Hell, he *has* done it. I remember this one time in Atlantic City he hooked up some of his business buddies with a couple Ecuadorian cleaning ladies and when I walked into the hotel room there they all were, naked and fucking on the carpet. You imagine? Jesus, it was ugly. Them assholes were all shrunk up and still wearing their black socks, with the lipstick everywhere. I had to chase them all out by hitting them with my hairbrush, and then I screamed at Ruben for two days straight and charged up three thousand on his card. I made him pay good for that one. But yeah, he'd drag a hundred whores in here to keep Billy happy if he thought he could get away with it." Cherry started to smoke her whole cigarette in two seconds flat. "Fucking men."

My mouth opened and shut. I looked at her. She was still smoking, down to the nub. The cig paper was burning black and gold and the tobacco smell reminded me of Carlos the Bull.

"Can I have one of those?"

"He's all I hear about every goddam day," she said, tapping two sticks out her pack and handing one over. "Billy this, Billy that. This is it, this is the one, he keeps saying, and no offense but holy shit, I am going crazy with it. Ruben would do anything for him, anything! Not like with the rest of these small fries"—she started pointing around the room, using her cig like a finger—"here, you see what I mean?"

Cherry was looking at Chuco, who was still standing in front of Ruben and shuffling his feet.

"Boss, hey there, Boss," Chuco started again.

Ruben raised up his eyebrows. "What."

"How about me, Boss? What you say, you know, about setting me up with some fights too, eh? I'm real ready for it—I been training too."

Ruben shook his head. "Nah, son, I don't think so."

Chuco's face turned a burning red and his eyes started blinking too fast.

"That's the breaks," Cherry said, talking low enough so only I could hear. "Still, that poor damn bastard."

I felt sorry for Chuco too. He'd been shaming himself awful as the water boy. Ruben stood up then, belly-first, so Chuco had to take a step back. "Freddie, you pinche cabron, I swear to Christ this is the last time I tell you."

"Man, I was just messing around." Freddie hung his head and started drawing circles on the ground with the toe of his boot. Then he unzipped the satin jacket slow and put it on the back of the chair next to me. "I wasn't going to take it or nothing."

I reached on down and picked it right up. I could because I was the girlfriend. The satin was thick and shiny, good quality, and there were the letters that I'd sewed perfect across the back. I put it on. The sleeves hung long off my arms and the pockets were deep. I felt small inside it, and good. I wanted Billy to look over and see me wearing it, but he was busy checking out the bullet scar on Zookie Chamayo's naked chest.

Cherry touched the satin. "Nice. You can't beat boxing for jackets."

I smiled and took another one of her smokes and she lit it for me, with a gold and mother-of-pearl lighter that looked like something you'd pull off a mobster, then we both kicked back and watched everybody partying. It wasn't as good a shindig as the others. Most of the dudes there had been between jobs for close to a year by then, and even though they were guzzling cerveza and snapping their fingers to the funkadelic Mexican rap that was playing on the blaster you could tell they were down-and-out. Nobody was partying like usual. Instead, the boys had slumpy shoulders and puffy pale faces and they swung their fists around like they were looking to pick a fight. The girls were different, too. Not so easy and flirty and prancing. They hung back, leaning on the walls, drinking beers and whispering to each other while they checked out the Looker, who was practically screwing the cruiserweight on the massage table while little Tito watched from the doorway, his bangs hanging in his eyes like a mutt's.

"Chill out, potato head," I heard Billy say. He was lifting a barbell now and talking to Zookie. Zookie had stopped showing off his scars and started banging around, slit-eyed and making fists.

"I could be a fighter too, you motherfuckers," he started howling.

"No you couldn't." That was Freddie, trying to dance with one of the groupies, his hair and T-shirt soaked through with beer. "First generations can't fight worth shit. Gotta be from the homeland like Billy here. Billy, where you born again?"

"What? Mazatlán."

Chuco stepped in too, swaggering and stumbling. "I'll show you who could be the fighter, cabron asshole. I won the fuckin' Goldens in '90, I beat Robby Moreno in four fuckin' rounds."

"Robby Moreno? So the fuck what?" That was Chuy Gomez, sitting on the ground, drunk off two six-packs and playing the bongos on his belly. "You ever seen him fight? He's just a chump, man. My old abuelita could beat Robby fucking Moreno."

Those fools started to tango then. They puffed up their chests, grabbed at their balls, jabbed their fingers in each other, and swore about who was better than who. Billy just sat there on his chair, finishing a bottle and looking more and more moody. The groupies were getting nervous, though. They walked up to the boys and touched their backs, pulled on their shirts, talked to them in soft voices.

"Hey, honey, why don't you just have another beer."

"Baby, come on, come on and dance with me."

But the boys wouldn't listen, they kept staring down each other and taking deep breaths and pretty soon somebody or another pushed somebody else and we had ourselves a brawl on our hands. Freddie started whaling on Zookie and Chuy got Tito by the head and punched him in the face. The Looker jumped off the table and ran off screaming with her skirt hiked up around her belly button when Chuco clipped the cruiserweight on the chin.

"Aw jeez," Cherry said, while we pressed ourselves close to the wall. "Here we go."

Soon most everybody was into it, the groupies hanging on to boys' elbows and screeching, fifteen-year-old baby spider-weights tussling with each other on the ground, Ruben, fast on his feet with his belly bouncing, ripping boys off each other and smacking them on the heads, all except for me and Cherry and Billy, who was still sitting in his chair and drinking until Chuco came lumbering up to him, red-eyed and dripping wet, cocking his fists and slurring out something about him getting up off his ass and fighting like a man.

Billy waved him off and finished up another bottle.

"I said why don't you fight me, you bitch," Chuco hollered out again.

Billy got up out of his chair and looked at Chuco for a second. Then he started laughing. "Man, you couldn't beat me if both my arms were broke. It wouldn't even be interesting."

Chuco was swinging blind but he eventually connected one on the shoulder. "Come on, come on, I'll get you interested."

"See? Now I couldn't even feel that. If you want to fight me, you're going to need some help."

Chuco stood there blinking and swaying back and forth and swinging more random punches that didn't land.

Ruben was breaking up a scuffle but he started yelling over at Chuco. "Hey, José Feliciano. Sit the fuck down!"

"Nah, man, you don't even got a chance," Billy said. He picked up that barbell and put it in Chuco's cocked fist. "Here. That'll even up the odds." Then he put his hands behind his back. "Take a shot, champ," he says.

I didn't get what was happening at first. I yelled out, "What are you doing?" Then I saw it was a fifty-pound weight Chuco was holding on to, heavy enough to split Billy's skull.

Ruben had a couple spiderweights by the collar now but he dropped them back on the ground. "What I tell you, Chuco!"

Everybody else stopped fighting to check out the stand-off. Me and a couple of the groupies started yelling at Chuco to put the barbell down.

"Well?" Billy says. He stuck out his chin. "Come on, champ."

"Stop calling me champ," Chuco tells him, in this tight voice. He was holding the barbell out in front of him. Billy raised out his arms so Chuco had a clear shot anywhere, and I ran up and started shrieking and Ruben was hustling over, and I thought something terrible was going to happen, but then nothing did. Billy stopped, and waited, then turned away. He put his hands back down to his sides.

Once you looked over at Chuco you could see why. Chuco was crying. Tears slid helpless down his cheeks and chin and dripped off the tip of his nose, and he didn't wipe them off. Ruben took the barbell away from him and pushed him into a chair. The boys in the crowd started mumbling.

"What kind of fighting is that?" somebody said.

"Bunch of fuckin' yo-yos, man."

"Maybe those two took too many punches to the head. Maybe they got Alzheimer's."

Freddie went over to Chuco and shook his shoulder. "Hey, hey, buddy boy, it ain't so bad. You gonna get in there. Right, Boss? Old Chuco's gonna get in the ring soon enough, ain't that so?"

"Huh? Hmmmmmph." Ruben grabbed the spiderweights again, and he looked like he wanted to knock their heads together.

The rest of the boys in the room kicked at invisible stones and coughed and cleared their throats and the girls raised their eyebrows at each other. Billy stood there sweating. He shook his head, then spit.

Next to me Cherry rubbed her neck and whispered to me through a haze of smoke. "Girl, I am so glad I am a woman. I'd never ever want to be a man, you know what I'm saying? Being a man's a fucking heartbreaker."

Over on the other side of the room Chuco was still crying while Freddie tugged on his arm. Then there was a clicking
sound and the tape on the blaster shut off. Now all you could
hear were boys still hacking uncomfortable and Chuco's ragged
breathing.

I watched Chuco sit down on a stool and rub his face.
Billy was staring weird at nothing. I looked at the other boys
too, the ones with the red bruises and split lips. I thought about
what Cherry said. She sure did seem to have a point.

I nodded at her and wrapped his jacket around me
tighter.

*B*y February of '97, Ruben had bought Billy a leather
jacket, a two-hundred-dollar pair of Nikes, and season tickets
to the Lakers, but the best bribe of all was the brand-new black
Ford Bronco that he'd parked out in front of his apartment. It
was the Bronco that told me Billy was home that Saturday I went
there. His phone had been off the hook all afternoon and I was
worried so I walked over and saw the car. It was beautiful, fresh
off the lot. The paint job was high-gloss and it gleamed like
still black water, but when I looked closer I saw it'd already been
keyed. There were long white scratches scarring the driver's door
and then by the bumper somebody had carved out the word
bitch.

I went into the building. I knew where the manager kept
the spare skeleton key, under a flowerpot. I walked down the
hall and when I got to his door I heard the noises. There was
long high crying and lower huffy breathing, bedsprings creak-
ing. Then it stopped. I didn't have nothing in my hands. Later
I thought about what I could have brought from home: a steak
knife, Mr. Hernandez's revolver, an ice pick, a cleaver. But I went

in there defenseless, and not only could I hear evil now, but I could see it, too.

He was with the Looker. She was hunched down over him, shiny-skinned, dark hair waving over her back. His mouth was wet; he had his hands on her. We were all looking at each other. Their faces were too clear. Every hair on Billy's arm was bright black. The soles of her feet were cut with wrinkles. Her belly hung loose over his. There was an empty champagne bottle on the bedstand, the glass clear green as pond water. My legs were doing something, not so much shaking as jumping around, and I got embarrassed. But then the Looker moved off him and put up her hand, and said "Wait," and that's when the jealous flowed quick and free through my bones and made me strong.

I went over to the bed and got her by the hair. I pulled her off with one tug and she screamed like a trapped cat and I kept tugging. Her fat butt blubbed around and her breasts swung like bags and her feet with their Aztec red toenails gripped the floor. I wanted to smash her head into the wall, and I would have done it except for Billy getting behind me with his wet penis nudging me and his arms locking around my shoulders.

"Okay, stop it," he said.

She got loose and backed off from me but my legs were free and I kicked at her with my heels and she sat down, hard, holding her thigh. I was still bucking but he had a tight grip and I wasn't going no place. While we stood there jerking she put on her clothes in a hurry and slipped inside her clogs. She touched her head delicate, looking at him. I could feel them making eyes at each other and I told her if she looked at him like that again I'd go get a gun and kill her, and then she grabbed her purse and limped out the door.

Billy stayed behind me, his arms still locked.

"You done now, Bruce Lee?" he said.

"No. You fucking PIG."

"Fine. I'll wait." He kept on holding on. I pushed my arms out against his, screamed filthies. I kicked my legs some more, but it was no use. Finally I gave up and felt my face go to pieces.

Billy turned me around. He had both hands on my shoulders. I could smell him. The hairs on his belly were still wet. There were red sucker marks on his neck.

"Rita," he said. "I told you there wasn't going to be any marrying. What'd you think that means? I never promised you nothing."

I stared at his lips. I thought if I could kiss him he'd see how he didn't need anybody else. But my mouth wasn't working right. It was open and wet from crying.

"Yes you did," I yawled. "You did promise me."

"No I didn't. Wait, sit down. I'm telling you something. Sometimes I'm just gonna see other girls. If you don't like that we can break up then. I mean you just ain't been around lately. You're with your sister, with her baby. I mean, who do you really think you are? A princess or something? You think I'm going to wait around for you? I never promised you nothing and so I'm going to find somebody else if I feel like it."

I closed my eyes. I knew all this already. I was making a mistake and he would leave me. But I couldn't help it. I thought about how I'd been busy helping out Dolores by rocking Jose Jr. and feeding him his bottle and giving him baths while she went shopping or slept.

"I'll be here more now," I told him. "I won't go off."

He let go of my shoulders. "Stop crying." He picked up a towel from off the bed and started rubbing his belly with it. "You shouldn't be with me. You go with somebody else."

"I won't go off no more."

He threw the towel down and pulled on his boxers and his pants. He straightened up the room around me while I kept crying. After a long time he looked at me again and I could tell he was starting to feel sorry. He came over and sat down next to me.

"Rita."

I didn't say anything.

He started playing with my locket. Then he stroked my head and tried a smile. "All right, okay. Guess what. This'll make you feel better. Remember when I gave you this locket? Remember what I told you?"

"You said I was your lucky charm." I started crying hard again.

"Yeah, okay, but remember how I told you when I was going to fight a title fight you'd be sitting in the front row wearing this locket?"

I gulped like a fish.

"What I'm saying is I got good news today," he went on. "I got the call last night. From Hammer's people. You get that? I'm gonna fight Hammer. In VEGAS. For the title! It's a fifty-thousand purse even if I lose!"

So here it was. This was it, what we'd been waiting for. I made my mouth spread up and felt my face flatten out, but I still had to grip my hands together so I wouldn't scratch his skin off with my nails.

He touched my hands, gentle. "So what you say? You know you're my best girl. Try and forget about all this. You want to go with me to Vegas and watch me win the belt?"

I sat on the dirty bed and felt the blood whirring in my head and looked down at my white fists. He should have his hands only on me, I thought. I thought he should love me better because I loved him so hard. And then I thought of something else too. I knew that if I left, there wouldn't be anyplace else to go but back here anyways because without him I would be dead in the neighborhood. I would be a nothing. And so, even then, sitting on those filthy sheets, I kept my head together. Because I could see it now, right in front of me. I did. On the one hand I saw me, the nobody putana talking to answering machines. And on the other, I saw a long gold road leading me out of this life. I saw myself sitting in a big room eating room service, and making long-distance phone calls. I saw my one-second close-up on HBO. I saw me in Vegas, dressed beautiful and laughing, so happy I looked like a stranger.

I knew then that there was no choice. I would have to take it. I would take it. I had to take the good with the bad.

"Yes, I'll go," I said.

Vegas

Vegas.

I was born to be in Vegas. Everything there is make-believe. In the velvet-dark casinos with their sparkling slot machines and big-breasted bar girls and red-medallion carpets and chip-piled craps poker blackjack roulette tables it's two o'clock in the morning twenty-four hours a day.

I loved everything about it except for the getting there. You'd think the pay-per-view moneymen would have sprung for first class when it came to a title-hunter like Billy, but all of us—Billy, me, Ruben, and Cherry—flew *cucaracha* coach on Southwest Air, jammed tight into midget-sized seats and sweating through our matching satin jackets and buying up four-dollar beers to go with our stinking honey-roasted peanuts. Chuco and Tommy, who Ruben had brought along as corner boys, spent the flight complaining and sticking their legs all out in the aisles. But once we landed and I felt the mind-bending July desert heat and saw the nickel slots right in the airport, that didn't matter anymore. I picked up my bags and wanted to get wherever we were going, fast.

Where we were going was Caesars Palace. It's el más best hotel you ever saw. When you drive up in your cab you see marble

Roman sculptures greeting you outside the front, ladies missing toes and noses and dressed in togas and a warrior man wearing a pointy helmet shaped like the paper hats fast-food servers
wear, all of them blinding white under a burning Vegas sun that
stretches wide over the sky. And once you get inside to the air
conditioner, you can't see nothing at all except for shadows until
your eyes get used to the dark, and then slowly you can make
out the fast-walking figures of miniskirted waitresses balancing
trays of martinis and red-suited bellboys lugging thousand-dollar
leather bags, and the hump-backed gamblers digging quarters
out of plastic cups or staring dead-serious at the whizzing flicking hands of card dealers.

I got my very own suite, on the eighth floor. I went up
the elevator with the bellboy, a pug-faced geezer with hairy hands
and a name tag that said FREDERICK and the best manners
I'd ever seen in my life. Frederick opened the door with a plastic
card and let me go inside, and when he came walking in after
me and the door shut behind him I got twitchy and almost told
him to fuck off but he just put my bag on the bed and told me
about the minibar and the cable TV and where the ice machine
was down the hall and called me ma'am twenty times. When he
was through with that he stood there just for a second rubbing
his collar and I remembered about the tipping so I gave him five
dollars and wondered if it was okay but he palmed it without
looking, smiled me a thank-you, and then split.

I turned around, looking at the room, and hugged myself. The bed was as big as our kitchen back home. It had a spread
with a pastel floral pattern and the sheets underneath were pearl
white, ironed, perfect. I jumped on top and rolled around, laughing, then got back up and turned on the TV to a cable station,
ran into the bathroom and looked at the extradeep tub (no Jacuzzi
jets) and the complimentary shampoo-conditioner that smelled

like peaches and the white terry towels stacked over the toilet. Inside the closet I found a triple-thick hotel robe, so I stripped off my clothes and put it on, then cracked open a baby champagne from the minibar and settled down to watch a shoot-out scene in a four-year-old movie starring Don Johnson.

I was on my third champagne and chowing Pringles when somebody knocked on the door.

"Rita? You in there?"

It was Cherry. Her and me hadn't spoke since the Boo-Boo Larue fight and on the plane over here she'd kept to herself, reading a Danielle Steel with a sulky look on. But now here she was, tricked out in a silky kimono and plastic see-through sandals and taking swigs out a three-ounce scotch bottle.

She swung around the room, her skirt dancing. "So, what you think? Isn't this great?" In the window behind her there was a view of shiny high-rises cutting into a cornflower blue sky.

"Oh I LOVE it, I just love it so REALLY much. HEY, CHERRY, Cherry, listen, you got a camera? 'Cause if you got a camera I wan' you to take a picture a me sitting here in my room at CAESARS 'cause I never been in a hotel before and they got everything, they got, you know, shampoo and room service and a fitness center and just, like, LOOKIT THIS ROBE."

Cherry finished up her scotch and started laughing. "Man, you are green."

"Hey, you on this floor too? You and Ruben got a suite, I bet. I wanna see it. Let's go to your room."

"My room is just like your room. But all right, come on."

She was ten doors over and I ran down the soft-carpeted halls, giggling, the robe flapping around my knees.

"See?" she said when we got inside. "No different than yours."

It was the same, except for what she'd done to it herself. Cherry'd already decorated the room with candles and tiny teddy bears and framed pictures propped up on the bureau. The pictures were the soft-focus Glamour Shots kind. One was of her and Ruben, smiling cheek-to-cheek. The other one was just of her done up in a low-cut tube-top dress and frosty lips, with her hair blowing all over from a wind machine.

"Pretty," I said, staring at it real close. "That's just so damn pretty."

Cherry petted one of the teddy bears like it was alive. "Whenever me and Ruben go someplace new I like to make it homey right away. Otherwise I get to feeling lonely."

"Where's he?"

"Who, Ruben? Hell, could be anyplace. Off doing the business with your boy or busy partying. We probably won't see them all of today, or tonight, neither." She pulled out another scotch from the minibar, screwed it open, then drank it in two.

"Hoosh, don't I *know*. Billy won't never have nothing to do with me before a fight." I sat down on the bed, bounced a little, then laid down and slapped my knees together. "Well, what we going to do till then? Oh man let's do something really really good. We're here a whole day early!"

Cherry laid down on the bed too and her mouth rolled up into this grin that made her eyes shut tight and then she didn't say nothing for a long time. She was getting as high as I was on that scotch. I almost fell asleep waiting for her to say something. Finally she opened her eyes back up, still grinning weird, and leaned up on her elbows. "Oh shit and goddam, there won't be no problem finding things to do. Who-wee. Them men can go yanking on their weenies all day long fer what I care. And don't think I don't need to blow off some steam, neither, honey! Caramba! We a couple wild girls out on the town now. Just git your mister to give you some a tha cashola and you and me gonna go gambling."

The gamble I loved best was blackjack. Roulette was too James Bond, poker was for seniors chomping stogies, and nobody but bowlegged grandmas with pastel hairdos played the slots. But blackjack, now there's a girl's game. Simple, quick, and it's a tease, too, the dealers with the gold vests and perfect-manicured nails shuffling kings and queens and diamonds while you wait for the number, your heart clipping, your mouth dry, your fingers clicking red and blue chips together.

And I had plenty of chips to play with. I'd gone up to my man's suite on the tenth so as to get some cash, but Billy, watching tapes with Ruben and talking in grunts, only gave me two hundred. I was good and brave on four of them baby champagnes by that time, though, and even if he'd hid the credit cards from me I still knew he kept spare checks in his inside coat pocket, so on my way out I stole one, then forged myself a cool five grand.

And now here I was, a real high roller.

"Hit me," I said to the dealer. I'd learned to say that from Cherry, who was teaching me how to play.

"Oh yeah, honey, you go!" Cherry was sitting next to me on a stool in front of four thou worth of her own chips that'd been snuck from Ruben's AmEx. Now it was her turn. She looked close at her cards, her thick mascara lashes blinking sticky, then wiggled her fingers at the dealer. "What the hell. Hit me too, sweetie."

The dealer slapped us another card. It was a woman with blond Farrah hair, the gold vest, tuxedo pants, little patent leather shoes, bored eyes like blue buttons in a quiet counting face. Name tag said PAM.

"Fuck-all," somebody whooped, me or Cherry. She had twenty-three and I had twenty-six.

Pam reshuffled the stack, then tapped it together. "Another game?"

That gave me and Cherry a case of the giggles. It was past midnight by then and I'd lost over two thousand already and she'd burned even more. I pounded my fist on the felt-covered table. "Hell yes, woman! But I first got to get us some more drinks. You wan' another drink, Cherry baby?"

"Oh yes I do wan' a drink."

I waved down a bar girl, ordered two of something.

"We are partying so hard, honey!" I had my arm around Cherry and was squeezing her and squeezing her. "You ever party so hard in your goddam life?"

"Oh sure, yes I have. That's what girls like you and me do best. We all's doing the party."

"Whatchoo mean girls like you and me?" I looked at Pam. "Pam, what she mean girls like her and me?"

"I don't know, ma'am. Would you like another game?"

Cherry was squeezing me back. "I mean girls like you and me, girl, you know, tha slutty girls."

That struck me funny and I laughed so hard I peed a little bit. "Yeah! Oh, hoosh. Yeah! You and me the sluts! Oh, gawd, that's too good. You and me the bitches!" I slammed my glass down. "Pam, oh Pam baby, did you know you are talking to the easiest women in East L.A.? Ah, Jesus, this girl over here that I got my arm around, she's just one big skank."

Cherry pointed at me, laughing out a streaky black face. "Whoo! She's a skank too."

Pam didn't say nothing. She was looking over our shoulders and making a tight mouth.

"Pam! Hoo-hoo! 'Nother game for us two hoochie mamas, please."

"What'll you bet, ladies?" The cards flicked and rippled in her hands.

"Where's them drinks?" Cherry turned in her stool and almost fell over. "I am thirsty for my DRINK, for fuck's sake."

But she didn't see how the barmaid was already next to us setting down two martinis. I tapped Cherry on the shoulder and she turned back around, started chewing on an olive. "I love these Beefeaters so bad," she said. She raised her glass. "Cheers."

I clinked mine to hers. "To lonely women."

"Nah, fuck that. I ain't drinking to that bullshit." The martini was slopping some out our glasses. "Here's to being a bitch."

I liked that. It was tough. "Yeah, cool. Here's to us bitches." We clinked again.

Pam had slapped cards down already and was standing there looking at us. Her face was sort of moving around like it was underwater. "What's your bet?"

I couldn't see what my card said. But I felt good. That last martini made my brain warm and I couldn't feel my lips or fingers. Cherry was leaning up on my shoulder and sticking her olive pick into the felt.

"Hey, Cherry. Let's ride the whole thing."

I heard her heels banging against the brass legs of the stool. Then she said, "Yeah, good." She started shoving all the chips at Pam and giggling helpless. "Here ya go, old Pam, you little pendejita."

Pam slapped down some more cards, then we both said Hit me and then she stopped. I looked at my draw but I still couldn't make out the numbers. I got her by the wrist.

"What they say? Read 'em."

"They say twenty-two and twenty-four. Ow! Let go of my arm!"

Cherry started howling. "Hoooooo! Hoooooo! We busted, honey! How much was that?" She knocked her glass over.

Pam pulled away from me and then I felt my face on the felt. I was hugging the whole table. "You and me together makes ten thousand."

"Ten thousand! Ten gees. Pam, you hear that? Pam. Pam-e-la. Damn, girl, you must be like the whitest thing I ever saw. Where you from, Mississippi? Pam, where you going with all my chips? Don't leave! Come on, I'm just kidding. Have a drink with us, honey. Let's have us all some more a these delicious drinks.

"I wan' another drink." I looked up, but Pam was gone. I looked back down at the felt table. Then I fell asleep.

One second later, somebody was pulling on my hair and I woke up again. It was Ruben.

"Ow!"

"I said get up!"

"Where's Cherry?" I made my eyes focus. First thing I saw were the curly hairs poking out the collar of Ruben's shirt. Then I made her out, hanging on to his tie and trying to give him kisses.

He got me by the shoulder. "Fucking blackjack. You ain't saying one word of this to him till after the fight. Get up. Get up or I'll beat you right here, I don't care. Five thousand. Five fucking thousand dollars. Rita, you're a woman who don't got no respect for money."

I felt wide awake all of a sudden. I shook him off me and tried to stand, but then I was on the floor and my ass hurt. I had to look up at them.

"Well you're just plain wrong, Ruben honey. I do got plenty a respect for *my own* money, see."

Cherry waved hello down at me and then we made eyes at each other and started giggling again.

*7*he next morning was fight day and I was hungover ugly. I puked nothing into the toilet; there was booze stink rising off my skin. My head split wide with pain. I swore to God and la Virgen I'd never touch that devil's stuff again, and meant it. I was damn sick about the five grand, too.

Around two-thirty I could get on my feet without heaving and I rattled through the room, showering, digging around to find my clothes. And then in the elevator I tried not to look at the mirrored walls but saw anyways that I hadn't done the beauty routine good enough. Mascara still flaked under my eyes, and there was a long scratch across my nose from falling somewhere I couldn't remember. My bangs had dried wrong and stuck up like a broom.

At Billy's door I could hear the TV turned on high and it took a minute before Chuco let me in. Tommy was on the couch flipping between Mexican and American channels and Ruben was parked next to him, chewing on an unlit cigarette and talking in Spanish to a lady and a man sitting on a love seat. Right off I could tell these two were real Mexicans, not the U.S. kind. The lady had an Indian-hooked nose and didn't wear jewelry, just a homemade dress and cloth shoes, and the man had on a polyester shirt and a stiff leather face that scowled.

Billy was over by the wall window, scowling just exactly the same way, so it was almost spooky. He looked up once when I came in and squinted at my black-and-red mug, then his eyes went back to the woman. She was talking excited to Ruben, something about money. I saw how he had some of her in him, too. The mouth, and also the jaw a little bit.

Sure enough, I knew these were his parents. These were the folks he'd always told me were dead.

"All these years, all these years," the woman said to Ruben. "And not one word. He doesn't send us one dollar. We've been suffering! There's no work; we don't have anything! He knows how it is. But he forgets us."

She was crying and pulling on her hands and the man sat there grumbling. Tommy started jiggling a knee and put on the mute button. Chuco sat in an easy chair and watched the picture. Billy stared out the window.

Ruben saw me by the door, then put his hands on his thighs and stood up. He opened up his briefcase, pulled out a checkbook, and started writing.

I went over to him. "Who are they? They his parents?"

"This ain't a good time, Rita," he said. He wrote so hard on the check he almost ripped it. "I could still take a swing at you for last night. Hell, I'd swing at anybody right now. The fight's in four and a half hours. This is it. This is the countdown. And do you know what Hammer's doing? He's getting a massage. He's doing the meditation, the visualizing. Eating a little protein. Warming up. He's not having no fucking family reunion." He pointed at Billy. "Just lookit this one. That look cool to you? That look ready to fight?"

"Don't you worry about me," Billy said. "I could beat Hammer right now."

Ruben tore off the check. "Don't me worry! Good, okay. Now I don't worry."

Tommy looked up at me for the first time. "Christ, do you look like shit!"

"Shut up." I pointed to the man and lady. "These are his parents, right?"

"Yeah, that's them." Tommy flipped the channels some more. "Old Mom and Dad. Saw him in the papers and bused all the way from Tijuana just to see him fight. Something, ain't it?"

Chuco grinned at Tommy. "Really something."

Ruben went over to the parents and waved the check at them. The leather-faced daddy didn't look too happy.

"I don't want none of your money," he said. He had rough knuckly hands that he ran over his face.

But the mama didn't seem to mind. She cried even louder and gripped her hands together. She called out his name, Guillermo! Guillermo! She went on about how proud she was, how much she'd missed him, how he was so different. Billy was still staring out the window, but then he looked at her and changed. His heart gave. His eyes started softing, crinkling. The sky behind him turned a slow blood-colored fire and when he put his hand on the glass to steady himself he seemed to touch it. She reached up and took Ruben's check.

I walked closer to the parents and smiled. They stiffed up, shot looks at each other. I guess I was still pretty ripe. Ruben turned to Tommy. "Ah, Jesus. Get her out of here."

The mother started saying something to Billy, too fast for me to translate. He ran his fingers over his eyelids. I tried to get their attention. "Did you tell them about me? Do they know about us?" I wiggled my hand so they'd see the ring, but Tommy was already behind me, pushing me out.

"Hey, there. Bride of Frankenstein. Why don't you go and get your toenails painted or something?"

"Hands off. I want to talk to Billy."

Tommy had already got me outside the door, though. He waved at me, then shut it in my face. Inside I could hear Ruben trying to kick the parents out, too, promising them good seats at the fight.

I pounded some, but they didn't let me back in and it only made my raw head hurt worse. I got into the elevator, stared

at my shoes, and went back to the eighth floor to catch up with
Cherry, but when she cracked open her door I saw a yellow kisser
and gummy eyes, smelled the same reeky day-old gin that was
floating around me.

"Be there tonight," she croaked. "Hangover's a killer."

So I went down to the lobby by myself. I sat at a table
and ordered coffee and dry toast from the Mexican waiter, who
tried to flirt with me. "What'd you like in that coffee, señora?
Anything special?" he said meaningful, hunching over my shoulder and touching his mustache, until he got a good look at my
face; then he stood up straight again.

When he set the food in front of me I felt better. The
coffee was burning dark in a white porcelain cup and the cream
was cold in its silver pitcher. The toast was fine white bread with
no crusts. I drank the coffee in little sips and ate the toast slow
so as to keep it all down. When that was done I started looking
around. Caesars was really something. There were ficus trees
planted between the tables but when I peered close I saw they
were made of plastic. And in front of me there was a marble
sculpture of what I guessed was Julius Caesar but I could tell it
wasn't a genuine Roman doodad, looked like a hunk of plaster
of paris that'd been carved in Hong Kong that morning. The
best thing, though, was a phony waterfall over to my side, a
tumble of lava rocks piled high by the wall with a sheet of sparkling electric-blue water shooting out the top then diving down
to a mossy deep green pool waiting at the bottom.

I liked that waterfall a lot. I thought about how work-
men must have put it together, with a pump and a hose and bogus
lava bought from a store and the plastic moss plants that sure
enough were from a factory somewhere. It made me think of
Billy, sitting upstairs with his newfound family, leaning up on
the picture window while his left-for-dead mama sat there big
as life begging for money. It made me think of my own self, too.

I started remembering how on Mulholland Billy'd said he'd been working hard at being brand-new for five years, moving from Cuernavaca or Mazatlán or Juárez, or whatever the hell, Tijuana, to Arizona, the Bronx, and L.A., and I knew that if anybody was going to understand what that means it would be me because when I was fifteen I'd shed my damn skin like a snake. And I thought, too, how when you're trying to build up your new self you'll reach for anything that's glitzy, like a heart-broke viejo named Pancho Villa and a one-eyed killer cowboy, or a pair of fuchsia heels and foot-long hair extensions, and that sometimes when you step back and take a good hard look at what you made it'll just seem like a cheap sham, but other times, when you get lucky and the light hits it just so, you might see that out of all that shiny trash you went and built yourself something almost better than nature, something that sparkles and bubbles up like an oasis right in the middle of the desert.

I sat there thinking this while I drank my decaf refills and listened to that water falling. I finished my toast and ordered some eggs and started feeling such a sense of the optimism that it numbed me even to my hangover. It was funny, but me finding out for sure that Billy was a fake triggered a quick flood of love again, the kind that can make you lose your direction. Except now I didn't feel like it was making me lost. Because even if he was a cheater and a liar and a ladykiller and a man, Billy and me had everything in common; really, I thought he was my heart's twin.

When the check finally came I tipped the waiter extra.

At seven o'clock Cherry and me went down to the fight together and when we got to the auditorium it was a wild scene. The fight crowd here was way slicker than in L.A.—no competition. Alongside the regular T-shirt-and-Reebok-wearing Chicanos and grubby-fingered underage scalpers, I made out fancy cowpokes flashing alligator boots, manicured Mexico City dudes sporting diamond Rolexes, and platinum-haired Barbies hanging on to Italians in double-breasted suits.

We crushed inside, got to our seats. It was just like the Coliseum with the stands, the sixteen-foot TV screens, the ring under white spotlights. The undercard fights had already started. A Texican with toothpick legs and a bushy-headed Salvadoran were deep into their fifth round. The Texican had one puffed-shut eye but he was winning with a sledgehammer of a right hook. He kept hooking into the head and the Salvadoran was teetering on his feet and shooting blanks. Pretty soon the Salvadoran fell down and blinked up at the ref, who called it a kayo. The Texican tried to do a victory dance but he was bleeding too bad, and his manager came rushing into the ring and squeezed his nose shut to stop the running mud.

Cherry was still sick some from the hangover. She was quiet for a while, watching the fights. She drank her beer and lit a cig, then drank another beer and started perking up.

"Jesus what a night! Did you and me do some damage at the blackjack or what? Ruben almost killed me, I swear to God." She finished up the beer and started to look around. "But boy oh boy, here we are. Las Vegas. They don't call it Sin City for nothing, whoosh. These men sure do got the money. Place is full of richies." She crossed her legs when she thought she caught the eye of one of the Barbie-wearing Italians and then leaned into me, stinky and mysterious behind her sunglasses.

"Check out that one. He's looking right at me, right? Bet he'd take me to bed, dump that chickadee in a second flat. Lookit that watch, them cuff links. Hundred percent gold. He would, wouldn't he? I ain't past my prime. How do I look? You know, I am so sick of this business. This is some life. I don't even like boxing! Never did, ever. Fighting's for a buncha assholes who want to see two half-naked boys wrassling around. Woo-woo! Just think about it. Pretty soon they won't even need us women no more." She'd forgot about the Italian, then eyeballed him again. "Aww, hey. You see how he's smiling at me? He's smiling at me, ain't he? Will you look?"

But I didn't answer her, I was too busy screaming at the TV screens because Billy was up there. Between the undercard matches they showed live footage of him and Hammer warming up in their ready rooms and then getting weighed in. Billy shadowboxed and grunted into a microphone. His face was as big as a billboard, each tooth the size of a refrigerator, and then he was gone.

Now the screen showed the next pair of boxers who were crawling into the ring. But these weren't just regular boxers, these were lady fighters, one in pink and one in baby blue. Both of them were thick-legged Anglo girls with lumberjack arms and sandy hair pulled back in ponytails, white plastic breastplates peeking up from their U-necked tank tops. They slipped off their robes and jogged in place, then punched the air and posed for the TV men shooting them with steady-cams.

I elbowed Cherry. "Oh man, I heard about this. Check this out. It's girls fighting."

Cherry didn't look at them, though. She was still staring ahead at the Italian, but he'd turned back around by now and had his arm locked tight around the Barbie.

"Girls fighting," she said, her mouth hooking down. "What else is new?"

The announcer bounded up to the ring, bellowed into the mike that the blue one was Frankie "The Queen of Mean" O'Malley and the pink one was called Rosebud McKenna, but it was hard to hear him over the cockeyed fans who started jeering and the crash of beer bottles catapulted from the balcony.

"STRIP, BABIES!" I heard somebody hooting out.

Tank-shaped bouncers skedaddled up the rows, but the booing and bottle-tossing didn't quit till the ladies started throwing down. It was some of the roughest fighting I ever saw. Neither of the girls knew squat about defense and it was just round after round of toe-to-toe mashing. The Queen of Mean threw a lot of slugs to the body but couldn't connect with the head. Rosebud was better, a skull-crusher. She shot bull's-eyes to the face and cut the eye in the first two minutes, then worked the wound for the next three rounds so by the sixth bell la Queen was streaked with blood and punch-drunk.

The audience loved it. Even the balcony drunks were cheering now. They were all for Rosebud, and they chanted her name while she turned Queen into a cow-eyed stumbling goon who hung her gloves low, her head jerking with every punch, until the technical knockout was called three minutes into the fourth. Queen slumped onto her stool, red-toothed as a cannibal. Rosebud jumped up on a man's shoulders and threw kisses to the crowd, laughing through her mouthpiece.

"You see that?" I yelled. "They were fantastic!"

"Freaks a nature is what I'd call them girls," Cherry said, pointing the hollow bottle at Rosebud. "Besides, they ain't so tough. I'll tell you who's a million times tougher than that, Rita, is women like us. I mean, ain't we tougher than any of these battle-axes here?"

"Nuh-uh. No way I'm as tough as them," I said.

"You're wrong there, honey. We sure are, and we got to be too. Like when I go through our neighborhood nobody says one word to me, you know that? Not one smile or a hello, or a wave or anything. They wouldn't be caught dead talking to dirty

Salazar, right? But they do talk plenty behind my back. La Rica Hernandez used to tell people I was a hooker and a junkie on the heroin. Hell, once I even heard that old Muñoz was saying that I was one of them transenvestites, them men who dress like the women and get their cocks cut off? But so what. I knew they were just mad they didn't land him themselves. They tried to hurt me but I didn't care. And then, get this, they got to thinking that maybe 'cause I had Ruben's money I was respectable enough after all, so they started asking me to their parties. I said, No way, fuck off! I ain't going to none a your stinking parties. I mean, can you believe that? What balls!"

"That *is* something," I agreed. I didn't want to tell her that I was a member of the Latina League, or that last week I'd been invited to dinner by the Widow Muñoz, so I tried to change the subject. "Where'd you say you're from again?"

"By San Diego, little place called Encinitas. I never belonged there, though! I was gonna be a star—you know, the whole thing: came up hitchhiking, wound up waitressing, met Ruben at the restaurant. I knew he was the real deal first thing. Stayed here for him. And that's what I'm saying, see: These girls got nothing on women like us. It takes a toughie to stick it out in the big city where nobody talks to you, being so lonely. Takes a tough tough cookie."

Cherry wasn't crying yet but her cheeks flickered when she took off her sunglasses. I tried not to show my surprise. This was la Cherry! She had that Cadillac, the fur; she had enough power to make the neighborhood ladies sick with jealousy. But now I saw that all these years of being special had wore her out, because she looked tired, she slumped. Seeing her so broke up made my eyes burn and I put my arm around her shoulders in case she came apart. But she didn't need me to. Cherry was right—she was tough. She was just like her name, soft and red on the outside, but with a tough little pit in the middle. In a minute she ran her thumbs under her lashes and then said, "Oh, forget it. Ugh!" She sat up straighter and shook her hair out, then pointed. "Look, never mind. Forget about that. Here's your boy."

I looked up and everything went ba-boom. It was already time for the main event. The announcer was chattering Billy's name into the mike and mariachi music came screaming from the speakers. This was Billy's fight song. A pack of girls behind us started hooting. Hammer diehards booed through cupped hands. And that's when Billy came jogging out, his eyes hid by his red hood. He was circled by Ruben and the gym boys wearing matching jackets. They ran up to the ring and got inside. Billy took off his robe slow and his face showed up on the two huge screens over his head. He was beautiful. Black eyes, copper skin, deep-groove muscles throwing shadows under the spotlights. I screamed his name so loud that Cherry jumped and clutched her heart.

After that Hammer came running out in a black robe to the tune of blasting salsa, surrounded by ten black-jacketed groupies waving their arms. The announcer was yelling his name. The crowd stood up, howling even louder now so I was deaf except for the roaring. Women tried to stampede him, wound up hugging bodyguards. Folks held up signs that said COMPTON LOVES U HAMMER and HAMMER'S NUMBER ONE. Mexican flags were waving everywhere. Hammer and his crew got to the ring, climbed up through between the ropes. One of his groupies helped him off with his robe, and then he turned around to the cameras.

I wiped my eyes so I could see him. Hammer looked good. Older, with a flattened nose and a thicker middle, but still strong, chunky with muscle. And he sure did know how to work the crowd. Billy stood there staring into space but Hammer put his gloves together and shook them, first one side of the ring, then the other, the whole time grinning like he'd already won. He was getting a great hand. He knew it, too, that he was the favorite. He flexed and gave the thumbs-up and threw the screaming girls kisses. He was a real pro. Billy was too, but in a different way, standing there tough and sweating with this mean underdog mug on, even when the singers came up and started belting out the Mexican and American national anthems.

After that it was time for the rules. The ref was a pink-faced fat boy getting choked by his own bow tie. He told them both to come to the middle of the ring so he could give them the line about the ten count and about how three knockdowns add up to a TKO. They stood there pretending to listen. Billy was the taller one. He glared down and made muscles, but Hammer was friendly, a Mister Popularity. He egged Billy on by grinning at him, then he wanted to touch gloves.

They went back to their corners. Billy was bouncing on his toes but Hammer made a big deal of crossing himself and praying, and then the bell rang and they both went out. Billy rushed Hammer and started jabbing the head right away. He jumped two punches into the left eye and slugged one into the mouth with a fancy loop. Hammer must have had a lot of scar tissue because he bled fast from the eyebrow, but he didn't hide in a clinch or backpedal. He took the punishment with barely no defense. For the next two rounds Billy got in more slugs to the ribs, shoulders, one more on the face, and Hammer stayed put, watching him, shuffling his feet a little. Billy got his head hid behind one hand and he started hooking. He gets some more in. Then he got cocky and let the other hand down, like Ali used to do. Hammer's fast. He saw the hole and coldcocked Billy with a right to the chin and a follow-up tattoo between the eyes and then I'm holding on to Cherry tight and screaming because there's Billy twisting funny from the blow and tripping over his feet and falling in slow motion while he flaps his gloves and goes sprawling.

Ears ringing. A thousand fists are up. There goes the title. There goes the money. Then he's up on his knees. A red glove reaches for a rope.

The ref came running over and Billy's already staggering to his feet but fat boy flagged his hands and started the ten count. Billy's baring his teeth, yelling and swinging, because a knockdown means he lost the round. Hammer's standing on the ropes shouting. The newsmen gobbled into mikes or hunched over scribbling; the steady-cam dudes raced to focus in on both their close-ups. When the count's done the bell rings. Round's over.

The Caesars ring girl comes out dressed like a harem slave and does a belly dance while holding the number card over her head.

The next round went the same way. Billy chipped away at Hammer with flurries and combinations and slipped punches with his zippy footwork and peekaboo defense. Hammer was cut up pretty bad, got a split lip and muddy nose on top of the gash over the eye, but he stayed on his feet while his skull snapped back. He was waiting for an open shot. Every once in a while Billy would go stupid and forget to cover up and that's when Hammer would brain him, and Billy had to work hard to keep standing because two more spills would lose him the fight.

Rounds three to five Billy got into a rhythm. He did two things: work on the cut over the eye and tease Hammer with shamming play-punches. The eye cut was getting bad, but every time the ref looked like he was getting close to calling a TKO Hammer would pick up the pace and start swinging harder. I think it was the teasing that got to him worse. Billy gripped on to Hammer's head and jiggled it around, then ran away so the champ got dizzy and winded. After Billy clowned like that four or five times Hammer started slowing down. His footwork was dead and he was wasting his juice on dumb slugs that didn't land. His chest pumped wide when he tried to catch his breath. The steady-cam zoom lens caught his cracked face, broadcast it on the wide screen while Billy busted the cut open even wider and the blood sprinkled Hammer's shorts. Billy was really doing it. He was winning. He brought the glove up to wangle Hammer's head again, and he was reaching, his arm stretched out.

Then Hammer put his fist through the empty air and hit Billy hard in the eye. Billy's knees buckled and all at once he was falling. There's yelling and yelling, I'm flying out my seat and running down the aisle, still watching the screen. Billy's sitting up and shaking his head and Hammer walks up, then hits him again, a sap straight on the top of the skull. The ref jumping between them. Billy lands face-first on canvas and holds his head. Ruben is halfway inside the ring when security pulls him back.

The clock's stopped. A doctor crawls under the ropes and bends over Billy, who grabs his hand and gets up. They come back to the corner. I'm yelling out Billy's name but nobody pays me attention, not even security, who's too busy with Ruben and the drunk thugs rushing the ring. I can't see too much. There's the back of Billy's dark head, his glove on his knee. The doc's brown walnut face, red tie, the tiny flashlight shining into Billy's eyes. Ruben squatting on fat haunches and holding an ice pack. Chuco and Tommy peeking worried through the ropes.

Doc flicks off the flashlight. "Well, I don't know. You got a slow eye there. I should call this off right now."

Billy doesn't say anything. Sweat's streaming down his body.

"Hammer knows he can't win," Ruben says. "He's trying to get outta this by disqualification."

The ref nods. "This'll go on a D.Q."

Doc peers close at Billy again, chews on something. "Okay, that's it. He doesn't look right. I'm calling this one."

But Billy stands up, spits blood into the pail. "No, I'm going back out."

"Sit down!" Ruben yells. "If he D.Q.'s you win!"

"I'm going back out."

"Billy, you have a slow eye," the doc says. "You have to go to the hospital to get it checked."

"I feel good. Let me go out there, man! I won't take the D.Q.!"

Ruben grabs his glove. "Sit down! Sit down!"

But Billy looks at the ref and the doc and shakes his head. "I'm going."

"Okay, have it your way," the doc says.

The ref shrugs. "All right by me. It's your life."

The ref gives Hammer a one-point penalty. And then Billy and Hammer come back out of their corners and start boxing again.

The fight's different now. The crowd wasn't chanting HAMMER anymore and the Compton signs are down. Billy's fans were booing, too. From where I was standing I could see the richies in the front rows watching the match as calm as corpses and then farther up the Eastelayer types throwing trash and howling. CHEATER, they're hollering. PENDEJO. BASTARD. Hammer hears it. Knows he made a mistake. He tries to swagger off the shame by yelling back at them and beating on his chest, but it doesn't work. His fire was going out. The face was swelled so bad I don't think he could see. His shoulders hunched protective and he swung clumsy, not even landing solid when Billy left open a hole. But Billy was connecting with every shot.

After the eighth round Billy says, "His legs are going."

It got uglier then. Hammer was finished but he wouldn't go down. He stayed and stayed, bleeding all over everything. Billy had to be careful. He stopped slamming the head so it wouldn't bleed so bad and he could still win by knockout. He beat the body instead, inside on the plexus and ribs. He socked the gut and sternum hard enough that they could hear it in the back rows. Hammer jabbed and missed, jabbed and missed, his feet glued to the ground. The ref hopped around close and kept his eyes on Hammer's cuts, yelling YOU OKAY, HAMMER? but Hammer didn't answer. He had one more trick. He tried to hide in a clinch and moved in for a head-butt, but Billy took the butt tough then got back on the inside, brought up his elbows, and uppercutted a rat-ta-ta-tat onto the chest and chin.

And that was that.

Hammer fell backwards. Knees stiff as wire, arms floating by his sides. His red head landed first and then went the rest of him, gloves and heels drumming on the canvas.

Billy's arms up, face up, his bending legs hurling him to the ropes. Ref counting FIVE SIX SEVEN. The crowd boiling and screaming while the flags whip and billow. Hammer pawing and kicking. Ref's hands cutting up and down. EIGHT NINE TEN.

He was out. We all ran in. Ruben threw Billy on his shoulders and paraded. Chuco was yelling number one. Tommy grabbed the gold belt from the announcer, waved it at Billy. Then the parents showed up. The daddy was sweating circles under his arms; the mama gripped on to one of Billy's shoes and started crying.

I reached up and tried to touch Billy so I could tell him I love him but all I got was the wet hair on his shin. He was laughing over me and reaching to the ceiling. I looked around. The crowd was crazy! The Eastelayer types had stampeded over the front-row richies and were cheering and scuffling outside the ropes. Dudes with mashed faces and soaked shirts did spazzy dances and girls cried and pulled on their hair. Some of them were bawling at Hammer, too. Hammer was wasted. They'd got him to his corner by then and he was slumped back on his stool while the cut man worked him over with ice and thrombin. His face was hurt bad but it was the dead look on it that was worse. He stared at the spotlights without blinking or squinting. Just blank. Then the cut man started to sew him up and he closed his eyes.

Billy finally bent down and got the waving belt from Tommy and then stretched it out over his head. He was saying something but I couldn't hear it with all the yelling.

The belt was pretty. Bright gold with spangly miniflags from all over the world, and the words WORLD CHAMPION done in green-and-red sparkled letters.

He held it up there for a long time.

After the fight, Caesars threw Billy a congrats party back in his suite. It took a while for us to get back there, what with the jabbering sportscasters crowding around him and the girls jumping at him to get a kiss or rip off some of his hair, but all of us along with three blond cupcakes that Ruben had handpicked finally got into a couple of limos and drove to the hotel.

Me and Billy were in separate limos, not my choice. I went with Cherry and we got caught in a traffic jam that was all red lights and honking. I bit my nails the whole way, thinking about him stuffed in the backseat with them pawing gigglers.

In the suite, the party was already started. Some setup. First thing, we got greeted by a full bar with a girl bartender. Lounge lizard music came warbling out of an invisible stereo-system. Barhops with scoopy cleavage offered us tiny food on trays. One of them was feeding Billy grapes by hand like he was a hurt bird while Ruben tried to get her friend to stuff him with shrimp. Cherry watched Ruben goose the friend on the ass then got herself a martini and stared moody out the twinkling window. I stayed by her sucking in my cheeks and thought about socking the girl with the grapes, but instead of that I ordered a mai tai and tried caviar for the first time.

"Champion of the world!" Ruben kept saying, between shrimp and slugs of bubbly. The parents, who were eating chicken skewers on the couch, squinted up at him. Chuco and Tommy yelled hurrays and gripped on to the blondes.

Billy tried a grin too, but couldn't cut it. More gritted his teeth and stretched his lips while he tried to eat the grapes. He didn't seem like his regular self. His face had puffed out lop-sided and he was moving slow and I knew he needed me, not that girl, so I barreled past the sexpots and the heavy-lidded borrachos groping boobs to the sleepy beat of Sinatra and got between him and the barhop.

Up close, though, I could see he wasn't really right.

"Hey, Rita," he said, sort of muffled. "Fuck am I tired."

I believed it. He'd took a bad pounding. His left eye wiggled and the one side of his mouth bent down. The welts kinked his face. Except he still looked so good to me. I shoved the girl back with my behind and tried to figure out how to tell him the beautiful things I'd figured out when I saw the blue water fountain at the hotel.

"Hey, Champ!" Ruben yelled then. "Champ, how's it feel?"

Billy turned away from me to look at the boss but stopped halfway.

"How's it feel to be the greatest in the world?"

Billy didn't say anything to Ruben, or to me either. He'd caught his eye on the couches, where the parents were working on their shish kebabs. Between bites of chicken the daddy was bugging at a couple of groupies doing a slow grind. Billy didn't mind him—he was looking at the mama. His mouth twisted while he took in her fifty-cent dress and her big eyes rolling at the trays of lobster tails, the fizzy champagne in crystal.

"Billy," I said. "I want to tell you something, honey." But he didn't care. Only me and the barhop looked at each other. She sure was a smooth one. Red hair, green eyes, and I could practically hear the cash register clanging in her head. I grabbed the grapes from her but she wouldn't let them go. They rained down on the carpet and split under Billy's shoe.

He was walking to the couches. Slow as a sleeper, his shoulders bent, then shaking. He was sobbing. He went straight to his mama and when she saw him coming she put her plate down and opened her arms. They didn't say any words. He bent down onto his knees and cried into her legs, a long low wailing, while she smoothed his shirt over his shoulders and petted his hair.

Everybody stopped talking.

"Cheer up there, man!" Tommy finally said. "It ain't so goddam bad to be the champ!" But his joke fell dead and Ruben told him to shut up, mumbling something about postfight blues. No one knew what to do. Girls shot looks at each other, snapped their underwear, and then Tom Jones came crooning into the room and the drunkest blonde started dancing. Soon Tommy was whispering to the bartender and Chuco made a move on the redhead. Cherry, blasted off martinis again, talked to the view outside the window.

I stayed where I was, watching the mama hush and pet, the daddy squeeze his black cracked hands together. Billy had his mama's skirt curled into his fists. I couldn't go over to them. I was on the outside. I sat down on one of the chairs and poured a drink, spilled it.

Cherry rested her forehead on the window glass and breathed out.

"Vegas gets old fast," I heard her say.

Wanted

*B*illy slept on the plane ride back. His mouth was wide open and he wheezed. Pink bandages were thick on his split lip and head cuts. I sat next to him holding his hot hand and wishing he'd wake up and look at me. Two rows up I could see Cherry's frizzed head leaning on Ruben. Right in front of us were the parents, crackling the peanut wrappers and drinking cola. They were coming to live in the States now.

For some reason I thought about the plane crashing, a red killing fire, how I would tell him I loved him on the way down.

I whispered his name in his ear and watched his lids flicker strange. Wake up! But he kept his eyes closed till we landed.

*T*he first thing we saw out of the airline gate was flags. A screaming and woofing crowd of neighborhood fans had showed up to welcome us home with red-green-and-white Mexican banners. Gamblers getting off with us slowed, craned their heads around, and stared. The mob chanted BILLY, held up signs that said NOVO'S # 1 and EAST L.A. 4—EVER, and made such a racket that soon a police lady in some not-so-flattering polyester pants hustled over and told us to hold it down.

Dolores hadn't shown, but Gloria, Frida, and Veronica were there, heaving babies on their big hips and shouting, permed curls like Slinkys jumping away from their faces. They gave quick hello kisses to Chuco and Tommy, then pressed over to Billy, oohing over his Band-Aids and telling me congratulations. Tito was next, then whooping Freddie with his fat cousins from Norwalk, then a clump of screechy knock-knees who crashed down on us, pulling on Billy's shirt, shoving paper in his face, and begging for an autograph. Billy, his red-and-blue bruises hid behind black sunglasses, took the papers and somebody's pen and wrote his name slow, in shaky letters.

"That's enough, that's enough," Ruben said, putting his arm around Billy, pushing ahead. "He's tired. He's got to rest."

All of us walked together to the dark echoing parking lot, looking for our cars. There was chattering and laughing, cardboard signs clapping on legs, a baby crying. The knock-knees made eyes at me, some touched me on the elbow and shoulder, a skinny red-nosed one asked What's Vegas like? Frida winked at me while Gloria stared thin-eyed. Oh, it's beautiful, beautiful, I said. All they got there is lights and money. The women wear the silk chiffon and drink champagne. There's waitresses built like Playboy bunnies. They got mafiosos with gold chains and gold teeth blowing thousands on roulette.

Their mouths dropped open, eyes like pinwheels. They gripped on my arms, saying Tell us.

But when we got to Ruben's Caddy, he wouldn't let me inside. "I meant it when I said this boy's got to rest," he grumbled, first letting the parents into the backseat, then pushing in Cherry, who shot me a good-bye look. Billy stood there, teetering a little. He let me grab on to his hand but he didn't say nothing about me coming along. He was still sick from the beating and didn't look like he cared one way or the other.

"You go on with one a these," Ruben went on, pointing at the crowd. "Who wants to take this girl home?"

Veronica and Frida smiled at me friendly as sisters. The fat cousins elbowed each other, the knock-knees gawked and gabbled. Then ten hands shot up.

*W*hen the car got a block inside the neighborhood I saw how it had changed in the three days I'd been gone.

The town looked like a flamenco dancer who'd just laid down after a hard night of partying. There was confetti, paper flags and flowers, Mexican streamers everywhere. On Sixth Street I saw a busted pig piñata laying in the street, candy spilling out of its gut. On Eastern we went by a homeless wrapped elegant in streamers and wearing a party hat. Down on Chávez there were Hammer's and Billy's bloodlusting eyes staring out at me because somebody had taped up fight posters to all the dusty storefronts.

"We celebrated after the fight," Tito said. "Man, Rita, you should have seen the slam! Even the viejas were dancing! And Martinez got so blasted he had to go to the hospital."

Tito was driving me home in his rattletrap Dodge. Chuco was in the front seat, Frida and Veronica and Gloria were in the back, with me stuck in the middle. It seemed like everybody was holding a baby.

"Tell us about the fight," Frida said. She smiled at me with her lips closed.

I looked back out the window and saw Billy hanging off a streetlamp. There was another poster under him, showing a face I couldn't make out. The same poster was on the next streetlamp, too, and the next. Faces blurred by.

"It was great!" My voice sounded loud in the car. I told them how it was a bloody ten-rounder, and how Hammer had fought dirty. I went on about how the doc wanted to call it but Billy wouldn't let him. They leaned forward, oohing.

"And then they went back out and the crowd was booing!" I talked with my hands, bragging. "And Billy started punching and punching!"

We were stopped at a light. I looked outside again. I saw another one of those posters stuck on a streetlamp. It was a WANTED poster. And this time I made the mug shot on it. Wide cheeks, buzzed-up hair, black eyes. For a second my heart stopped because I thought those were Jose's eyes, but I was wrong.

It was Victor.

"Oh yeah! Didn't you hear?" Frida asked me over her baby's head. "Victor is in trouble. Since he went after Zookie he's been laying low for what, a year? Two days ago I guess he just got fed up. He walked into a 7-Eleven, shot the clerk and a customer dead, and made off with three hundred dollars. It's been all over the TV, the newspapers. So now we got two boys who's famous."

Veronica nodded, rubbed a baby belly. "Dolores says Victor's Public Enemy Number One. She wants us to help the police catch him."

"I still say it's a waste of time," Gloria said. "He's probably in Mexico by now."

Then the light went green again and everybody was talking at the same time and Victor sped by. But now that I knew it was him I saw his twins everywhere, hurling at my head, passing, then showing up again. He was rushing me on every corner, streetlamp after streetlamp after streetlamp.

*   *   *

I should have took Victor's twins as a sign of strange danger, but of course I couldn't know that then. I wish I still didn't know. I wish I wasn't as smart as I am now.

I haven't been to church since the Sunday Mama saw our grandma's ghost and La Rica ran us out of there for good, but I still remember the Bible story the padre had been telling that day. It was the one about Abraham, where God tells him to slit his son Isaac's throat, and then He stops him just in time. I've thought on that story through the years, mostly about Abraham's wife, Sarah. What if she'd found out? Wouldn't she have been mad? What if she'd hid her son from Abraham's killing knife, would God have punished her with His holy fire, or is loving your own blood so bad really a sin?

I think I know the answer now. I know that being holy don't come natural to folks, that it don't make sense, and that heaven can hand out a mean and bloody piece of judgment. I think Sarah would have been judged a criminal, love or no love, and then she would have been punished. I say she would have been the next one put under the knife, and this time there would be no mercy.

*A*s president of the Latina League, Dolores's main mission in life now was to go after Victor. She said he was an embarrassment to La Raza, that he had brought the drugs into our neighborhood, and that he had committed the worse sin imaginable: brown-on-brown violence. She was in cahoots now with the police to try and catch him. The Latina Leaguers had put together a Neighborhood Watch program. They're the ones who had tacked up the WANTED posters on the streetlamps. The rule was, if anyone spotted Victor, they were supposed to call the police right away on 911.

This didn't make Jose too happy, of course. He loved Victor. They were still brothers. So Jose's heart was divided, and this caused trouble at home. The day after I got back from Vegas I went over to their place and found them fighting, but I tried to stay out of it. I took Jose Jr. from my sister, then sat down at the kitchen table and started feeding him applesauce.

"I want you to call your dogs off," Jose was saying. "The police'll handle it. They'll find him soon enough."

Dolores laughed. "Police! Hoosh, they don't know where to start looking."

"Well you got no business nosing into this," Jose yelled.

Dolores crossed her arms and looked at me. "I got no business, he says. Heh!" She looked back at him. "Oh yes I do, mister. I'm doing this for the family. I'm doing this for your son."

"But Victor *is* family!" Jose paced around, then put both hands on the table. He was even huger now from the pro wrestling, iron-pumped and bulky under his black button-down, but he didn't look good. His face was sharp with worry.

"It ain't like you even know what happened that night," he went on. "Victor made a mistake. He never meant to kill nobody! Rita"—he was waving at me now—"help me out here. Talk some sense into this woman."

I shook my head and told him I'd learned good enough by now that there wasn't any convincing Dolores when she had her mind made. But that just made Jose even more mad, and he yelled and banged his fist on the table.

The noise got Jose Jr. worked up. His face turned purple, his tiny hands grabbed at his sides, spit bubbled on his lower lip. Then he pitched a wail right into my eardrum and applesauce splatted back onto my blouse.

Dolores didn't even look at the baby. She put her fingertips together and breathed in slow through her mouth.

"What do you mean he made a mistake? Did you talk to him?"

Jose didn't say nothing.

"You did—you talked to him. You're helping him hide."

He pointed at her. "Don't you turn this around now."

"Did you see him or not?"

Jose stared straight at her, then opened up his shirt to show her his chest. "No! But I wish I had. If I did I'd hide him right here, right in this house. Under the roof that I pay for!"

Dolores laced her fingers together and stared back at him until he gave in and looked down at Jose Jr., who was honking and screeching terrible.

"I got to get out of here." Jose buttoned his shirt back up and picked up his black jacket off the wall hook. "I'm going to work."

"It's three o'clock," Dolores said. Jose didn't wrestle until seven at night.

"Yeah, well, then I'm going for a walk. I'll see you tonight." He stomped to the back door, but closed it gentle behind him. Then he stomped down the porch stairs and made sure to slam the van door. The engine rattled and roared and the wheels squealed when he drove away.

Jose Jr. was howling. I had him up on my neck and cooed a lullaby. I wished he would turn soft under my hands, but instead he jerked back and his strong legs kicked.

Dolores took him from me and went over to the window. Outside there were green leaves and hot sun. A helicopter motored over the house. She tucked him inside her arms and started rocking until his face went from red to pink and he hiccuped himself to sleep.

She was looking out the window but she didn't seem to
see anything.

"You better not be lying," she said.

*T*he next night Dolores had another meeting at Lupe's
Beauty House, the last Latina League meeting I ever went to.
The agenda just had one thing on it, which was Victor. Dolores
was going to hear a report from Cha Cha and Connie, who made
up the Neighborhood Watch subcommittee, and Frida, who was
the LAPD liaison. So far, the search for Victor had got nowhere.
He was good as disappeared, and Dolores was worried that the
Latina Leaguers were running out of interest. All that afternoon
she wrote up to-do lists and plans for a new antigang hot line
and fought with Jose on the phone, and by the end of the day
she'd worked herself up into a knot.

Which is why I didn't tell her, but I had my own agenda
for that meeting. There was no mistaking who I was now. That
mujer they had all laughed at or pitied was gone for good. I
had come back from Vegas on the arm of the Champion of
the World. After all these years of waiting, I would finally put
my foot in the glass slipper.

The ladies showed up at the Beauty House around
seven. There were thirty of them, forty, every which one mis-
sile-breasted, roly-assed, wearing flower prints and Sunday
shoes, smelling tangy of Aqua Net and perfume. Half of them
were packing babies. Most of them went for me before the food.
I sat at my manicure station and organized my orange sticks
and cuticle clippers and smiled at them when they all crowded
around. My diamond glittered light rays onto their faces and
nobody said Rita, I heard you bought that engagement ring
your own self, who you think you're fooling? Or, Only a loca

would take on the name of a man who won't marry her. Or, Why ain't you had a baby yet? They didn't, because they weren't in any position to. Who'd got as close to the real deal as me? Nobody. Who'd soul-kissed Famous and got squeezed in its strong arms? I had. I was the one who'd got flown first class (as far as they knew) and slept in fresh-pressed Caesars Palace sheets and smiled at tuxedo-wearing doormen and ate caviar and lost five thousand dollars of a rich man's money at blackjack, and I started telling them all about it, every last true detail and then a truckload of made-up ones. They pressed close and held their breath while I flicked my hair back and went on about pillow mints, pink champagne, complimentary conditioning shampoo, and front-row seats, serenading violins, lobster dinners, sweaty sex on a white bear rug, the after-fight party with the movie stars and trillionaires. . . .

"Rita, come here for a second."

That was Dolores, bothering me right in the middle of my glory. She was standing by the dryers and staring ahead zombie-eyed like she'd lost her marbles and was searching for them desperate, but I waved her off and started bragging some more, saying, "And then he bought me a new designer dress, and I got a facial and a manicure and he gave me his gold card and said Baby why don't you go and do some shopping? And hoo-hoo, Honies! you know I ain't the kind of chica who says no to that!"

"Rita!"

I did stop talking when she yelled at me. And then the mujeres crushing close to me all turned at the same time and looked where Dolores was staring, and then I looked over there too, and that was the end of my million-dollar minute.

It was la Looker. She was slutty-seeming, sluttier than I knew I ever could have looked in my whole life. Hand on her hip, ass jutting out, wearing a red satin jacket and a micro-mini, with tumbled hair, black-lined Cleopatra eyes, a cherry-colored whorehouse mouth.

The Latina Leaguers, who'd been kissing distance before, now inched away from me, slow, until there was a cold space between us. Cha Cha and Connie dropped their heads and snuck pity looks at me. The Widow Muñoz was tsking. Frida smiled wicked so her broke teeth showed; Veronica's mouth popped open and flared pink. Over their shoulders I saw Gloria cheering. What was going on? Why weren't they hushed and pawing me no more? My head was buzzing and nothing made sense, but when I turned back to the door I saw what my problem was.

That red satin jacket on the Looker wasn't just any old jacket. It was a fight jacket, and not just any old fight jacket—it was Billy's. Red was his color and there was his name stitched over the breast pocket, loud as a woman screaming, and everybody in there, me included, knew for certain there were only two ways she could have took hold of it: She'd either got close enough to him to steal it, or he'd gave it to her himself.

"Rita Zapata," the Looker said now, rubbing his jacket and folding up the collar in case any nitwit had chanced to miss it, "I came here to tell you that me and Billy are together, and that you better forget him. I just was with him the last two days, and he asked me to marry him. Okay? Him and me are getting married. So hands off. He don't belong to you no more."

"That's Flora Gomez," somebody whispered. "That bitch from Downey I was telling you about? The one who fucked my brothers?"

"Poor, poor thing."

"It's the battle of the gold diggers!"

"Ay, Jesus, aw ha-ha-ha."

Things turned bright and quick then. I heard Dolores behind me calling my name again and the gasping and cackling of the ladies and the sound of my own feet stamping, and then I saw the streak of all their gaping faces and my sister leaping fast and reaching. Dolores held on to my shoulders but she couldn't anchor me, because I felt something in my hand like a weapon, and then I was flying fast as a witch at the Looker called Flora Gomez with her red satin and bad mouth and black eyes and hair still wild from Billy's gripping fingers and when I brought it down, I saw that what I was holding wasn't a bat or a cleaver or a gun, the damn thing wasn't a real weapon at all, just the same pair of clippers that I'd used to clip the cuticles of every woman in this room, but I thought that maybe if I angled them right and tried hard enough, they could almost work as good as a knife.

The Waiting Woman,
the Crying Woman

*B*illy was sick. His face was a stained mask stretched tight over his skull except for the left eye, which drooped heavy as a sleeper's. He sat up in bed, the red in his skin already turning to a leaf green and queen's purple and a shiny dark eyeshadow shade of blue. His forehead scar was a slice of white moon. He looked at me when I came in, not smiling.

"I heard what you did," he said.

I didn't understand. How could he know? From looking at me? My hair was messed and maybe my eyes were a little wild, but I didn't have no blood on me, and just a few scratches. I hadn't had good luck with the clippers, they were too small and not sharp enough and besides, all the Latina Leaguers had come pouncing down and took it away before I could do that squirming girl any real damage, and then I'd run straight here, straight to him.

He brushed my hands off, I was reaching out without knowing it. "Ruben told me this morning. I know you stole my money."

My mind was so jumbled it took me a while to figure out that Billy wasn't talking about Flora Gomez at all but that he was mad about me forging one of his checks in Vegas and blowing his money on blackjack.

"Aw no, baby," I told him, laughing. "I can explain that."

He did hold my hand gentle then. "It's a good thing, I think. This is a good place to end it."

"Nah, nah, look here, listen to me." I gripped on to him while I talked. "I got these things to tell you. Listen. When I was little, see? When I was little, did you know I met my dad once and I hated him? I ever tell you that? I ever tell you I had to wear these hand-me-downs that were so ugly and me and Dolores would walk to school and get made fun of? And then when I got older, I made some mistakes and nobody but nobody liked me, nobody would talk to me nice, and I was waiting for you to come, I knew you'd come before you even got here, and then you did. But I didn't even know who you were, see what I mean? I just knew you'd save me, but then, when your mama showed up, then I understood, Billy, I saw how much you and me were like the same person."

I could tell he wasn't hearing me right. He squinted out his window.

I pulled on his shirt. "Listen to what I'm telling you."

"It isn't just the stealing," he said. "Okay? I'm sorry. I just don't want to hear any of it. Don't tell me all that."

"Why? Why not? Because of Flora?"

"No." He did look at me then, for a long minute.

"Remember I told you once there was this girl from my town who cheated on her boyfriend and he went crazy?"

I sat back in the chair. But I was still gripping on to his shirt.

"Well, I loved her. Angelina. She didn't love me back. She was with some other guy and she cheated on him, and he shot her and she died. You reminded me of her, okay? Hustling around in them sexy clothes, both of you wanting the city and money and all that. But the thing is, you were different then. And now a lot of other girls are reminding me of her."

He breathed in. "Look, I can help you out. You need some cash or something, I can do that for you. But get this. We're broken up now. I'm not dating you. You go with somebody else."

"No," I said.

He turned away from me again. "Please. Shit! Go away."

I sat there begging him until he got disgusted. I couldn't help it. All along I'd been competing with a dead seventeen-year-old girl and I sure as hell wasn't seventeen no more, I was twenty-four. How could I beat her? Right then I saw myself sitting at a bar cadging umbrella drinks from married men and getting run off Chávez Ave by barking churchies, while girl after girl after girl walked in and out of his bedroom, and I felt the love and fear and jealous flood up in me and spill over and all at once I knew I was in danger. I could feel it. I was in trouble. And then, coming from out of nowhere, I remembered two other mujeres who were famous for their own brand of man-troubles—ladies I hadn't thought about in years, ever since that day I'd seen them painted on Jose's van.

I thought about the crying woman and the waiting woman, those two hermanas who got caught on the same sharp blade as me. The crying woman's the dark-minded bitch who killed her own babies for love, drowning them in the river just so she could see the same wilderness that was eating her alive blazing inside her husband's eyes too. The other chica is the patient heavy-heart who died on a mountain, waiting for her lover to come home from war.

Watching him look out the window I felt at that minute that if I so much as blinked I could turn into either one.

"Okay, you loved that girl Angelina. But are you going to marry Flora Gomez? She's telling everybody you are."

He shook his head. "No, I told you. I'm not marrying nobody."

I looked down at him and decided. I hadn't scratched all the way up here to get turned back now by a girl who was kicking at the dirt. Maybe a dead woman's your worst competition, but one day he'd want a living sweetheart to take her place, and I swore on my bones it would not be that liar Flora Gomez. I belonged in that blank place anyways, by right. I'd been betting my life on it for four years and couldn't quit now.

That's what I thought, anyhow, smiling down at him in a dark and cooling dusk while he told me to go. And I would go now that I'd made up my mind. Even if it hurt me I'd try hard as I could and be like the waiting woman, good and kind, watchful. I would have patience. I'd wait for him to come back around.

Then the shuttered room, a hot sheet over me. My eyes closed. Trying not to hear the street sounds outside, they hurt my ears.

The waiting woman's got a round heart, deep as a canyon, like a cup you can fill and fill and it won't ever spill over.

After a while I was sure that she's nothing but a man's made-up story. No brown woman could have ever been like that for real.

I'd been ditched by boys before but I'd never really had a broke heart. Once, years back, I'd sat in a bathroom with Billy while he cried because he was homesick and I'd got a glimpse on how loving somebody so much can make you lose your control. And then I guess I'd forgot that I had that feeling waiting in me. That wildness and confusion. I'd grown dumb and prideful because I only half pitied lovesick women. I thought that they were a little loca. But now I remembered the wildness and I understood them, every dead-eyed widow and ash-faced jilted girl and used-up bride, every mujer I'd ever seen who'd lost her sense over a man.

I understood Mama, stumbling drunk in the dark.

Because who wouldn't get drunk? Or use drugs or see ghosts or fuck any man that asked? Can't see good anyways, can't walk a straight line, can't hear or feel nothing except your own raspy breathing. All you can do is cry and sleep and wait and wait in your shut-up room, hid tight under the bedcovers. And that's what I did. I shut my eyes and slept for a while, which is why I was blind at first to what was going on.

I'd been working so hard to build myself respect. When I was little and I saw La Rica Hernandez walking around rich with it, that respect seemed like it was made of something hard and stiff, tough as brick. You couldn't knock it down. But later I figured out that respect is something softer, made up of words and air, of folks' ideas about you, and that is a tougher thing to build with than bricks. It still didn't stop me, though. Here, to have a famous man will give you that good reputation, and that's what I did. I got myself one, and then built my own brand-new self out of those light-as-a-feather see-through things, and she bought me smiles, knee touches, a ride in the backseat, a place to sit down, and the chance to get in on the joke.

But since I was hid in my room I couldn't know that my house was crumbling. What built it undid it. When I got strong enough to crawl back out from under my warm dark covers, I walked out the door into a strange changed place, full of whispers. The neighborhood ladies were saying I'd had a nervous break-down and belonged in the loony bin with Panchita Sanchez, the Lucky Strikes junkie.

I heard this from chicas who called themselves my friends.

"They're talking up a storm about you," Frida told me. "The girls are saying you're not right in the head."

Or Connie: "How you been, muchacha? I been hearing some wicked business about you lately."

Or Veronica: "Most of them just worried about you, Rita. But some of them are happy. They say you're getting what's due."

I wondered. While they all were telling me about these gossips, I thought I saw something sneaking in their own eyes, like a black-masked bandit slipping around a corner, which made me worried that maybe *they* were the ones saying those things about me, or if they didn't say them then maybe they smiled, and nodded, and ribbed each other with their elbows when they heard them. Maybe now all that jealous they'd kept trapped under their tongues had come flowing back out and it painted me worse than before, so I wasn't just nasty now, but foolish too, plumb cleaned out of what every Mexican woman's supposed to own no matter how dirty or poor she is: a nice healthy slice of the Virgin Mary's self-control.

It wasn't too long before my suspicions got the confir-mation. A week or so after I'd finally pulled myself out of bed and wandered back into the world, moving delicate as a just-hatched bird, I walked down to Lupe's. It was mid-August by then, '97, and I hadn't worked steady since the title fight but I wanted to see if I still had my job with Lupe, never thinking that with my jumping hair and raggy bit hands I didn't have the right look for a beauty salon.

The Divine Drive types were in front of the Beauty House—Frida, Veronica, Gloria—shaking their huge freshly permed heads and jiggling their runts on their hips. Gloria was in the middle of them, curls tight as phone cords, laughing. For a flash I saw us young again, twelve years old and waiting at the bus stop. Except this time it was worse because I didn't have any fire-making magic in my hands, no dangerous man thrilling me.

When I got closer they hushed. It was an ear-burning quiet, and while I stood there listening to it, the bandits they'd been hiding in their eyes came rushing out and shook hands with each other. Gloria winked at the others and smiled.

"My my my. Look at what we got here, chicas."

"Ah, Señora Novo!" Frida laughed. "So nice to see you again!"

Veronica patted Gloria. "Didn't I tell you? Don't she look like a dead cat?"

I took a breath right then and looked good and hard at Veronica when she said that and really, I wasn't in no position to disagree, because I knew I did look as stiff and hairy as anything you'd expect to find between the jaws of a happy dog. I felt worse than dead, too. My knees were buckling and my heart was beating irregular, but the one thing that has never failed me is my mouth.

What I'm saying is, if you went back to the cavemen's time and looked up my relatives, you'd probably find a rat-haired knuckle-dragging girl yelling ooga-ooga-ooga at a tribe of other knuckle-draggers, my bitch instinct is so strong.

So I looked at Veronica and even though I was ready to pass out I pulled up my posture and said to her, "Well, at least I wasn't stupid enough to get one of those perms."

And of course, that didn't go over too good with those girls.

"Right, Mrs. High and Mighty," Gloria started up. "Always holding it over our heads!"

"Why don't you go back to Vegas, bitch?"

"Yeah, they got everything there, don't they?"

"Ooh! They got complimentary shampoo!"

"They got room service!"

I tried to slip through them and yelled at them to get out of my way. Frida, with her baby, wouldn't budge.

"Why, so you can fix yourself up then go after my Tommy?"

"Damn, you found me out, girl," I said. "I always did want an unemployed man with a one-year-old brat and a two-hundred-pound pet moose."

"Slut!"

Gloria shook her head. "Nah, she would go after our men. She don't have nothing left." And that's when she looked around to see if anybody was watching, handed her baby to Veronica, then gave me a push.

In the past few years she had turned broad and thick. Her hands were tough hams. But I was thin as a fishing line and she didn't have any trouble throwing me to the ground. I got hurt; one of my knees was bleeding.

"Get out of here now," she said. "Or I swear I'll do you worse than that."

"Well hoosh, just don't sit on me Gloria cause you'll kill me for sure."

I did get up and leave then. I could razz them all I wanted but in the end I knew it was no use. I was back where I started, worse than where I started. The only place for me to go was home. I turned around and went back down Chávez and walked past the faded peeling posters that showed Billy's eyes following me, and past the reflecting shop windows that showed that mujer who was me, skinny as a shotgun with a mess of tangled undone hair, shuffling slow and weird down the sidewalk.

"You got to snap out of this," Dolores was saying. It was a few weeks after I'd got beat up by Gloria Sanchez. I'd never told my sister about that, and I was glad I hadn't now. She had on one of her flower-print dresses with roses that looked like mouths, fancy-strapped shoes, her burned-back hair gleaming. Jose Jr. hung off her hip, his hand on her breast. The girl was looking great. She'd grown into her face so it didn't look crooked anymore so much as interesting, high-boned as an Olmec's. Her passion for the politics was taking her places, too. Two days before she'd gave a speech to the city council on getting more police to patrol East L.A. And her antigang hot line was doing really good. That is, she'd told me that arrests were up.

Right now it was late afternoon on a Thursday, an hour or so before Jose had to go off to work, and she had me in their bathroom and was trying to fix me up. Jose was getting ready for wrestling by stretching on the living room rug and warming up his war whoop. Every time he whooped she winced. They still weren't getting along that great because of Victor. They didn't touch when they passed in the hall and they spoke short to each other. I could see from the way he looked at her under his eyelashes that he was starting to break down, but Dolores wouldn't budge an inch. She hated the gangs more than ever and in the last couple weeks had been saying she didn't just blame them for violence and drugs but also for all the lost jobs. She said they were bad for the Chicano reputation in the national media, or something like that, and it was because of gangs that brown men couldn't get good work these days. She also said that Latinas should get ourselves self-reliance because we'd all been taught from day one to depend on a man for everything but those days were over and we needed to get in touch with our feminisms and our brown female power.

I thought that she sounded like she was on Fantasy Island but she just kept right on lecturing me about it anyways. "Honey, you've got to forget this man and get on with your life," she told me. She'd put blush on me and now was covering up my busted capillaries with concealer. She said I had a whole mess of them right around my eyes because of my crying. When she bent over me her neckline dropped open and I could see her big breasts in her pink bra and her belly fold. She smelled nice, clean, like Tide and lemons, and her fingernails were short, right up to the finger. "You don't need a man anyways. It is time for you to find your independence."

I said that sounded like a good idea. I didn't tell her the truth. I didn't tell her that one night I'd sat on the edge of the tub and looked at a razor blade. I didn't tell her that on another night I'd called him fifty times until he pulled the phone out of the wall and then I'd sat in front of Mama's closet door, thinking about the gun Mr. Hernandez had gave her. What I'm saying is, independence was a big word you used if you already had yourself your perfect *amor*. I didn't. I'd already lost more than twenty pounds.

Dolores put some more concealer on my capillaries, then stopped. "Do you think the city council's going to do it? Hire more police, I mean?"

I just looked up at her. Her eyebrows were unplucked and pretty and they stitched together. I couldn't even picture what she was talking about.

She waited for me to say something and then smiled at me when I didn't. She put the baby in my lap and took my face in her hands.

"You're my hermana, okay?" she said. She kissed me twice on the face. "I love you!"

"I love you, too," I said. I leaned my head up on her belly and looked at Jose Jr. His eyes were wide and surprised and night black already and I wanted to kiss them, but then I thought of how, when I found Billy with Flora Gomez, he'd blamed it on me spending too much time with Dolores and the baby. So I didn't. I listened to Dolores's belly make squealing noises and Jose's sneakers padding back and forth out in the hall. He was pacing.

Dolores tilted up my chin. "I think you need the black liner. With the black liner your eyes will come out better. Where is it?" She started going through the makeup we'd piled into the sink and tested out a navy pencil on her hand.

Then Jose popped his head in.

"What, you girls got a hot date?" he laughed. You could see how he wanted to make up. When neither of us answered him he said, "How you two beauties doing?"

Dolores shrugged, then gave him the baby. "I think the black's in my bag. I'll be right back." She went to go find her purse.

Jose stayed in the doorway and bounced Jose Jr. It felt like Dolores was gone for a long time. Jose was looking at me over the baby's furry head.

"You're a beautiful woman, Rita," he said. "I know you don't feel like that, but you are. You shouldn't let that punk mess you up."

He said this without any flirting or smirking. He said it totally serious, like a friend. I remembered when he'd held on to my legs years ago and Dolores saw us. For a long time I'd wanted him to do that again but I didn't anymore, and I could see he didn't either. But I did feel like crawling into his lap and hugging him. If I could have done it without it being took wrong I would have. But I just told him thanks.

Dolores came back with the black then and did my eyes.

"Dolores," Jose said.

"See?" she said. "Doesn't that make a difference?"

"Dolores."

"What?"

"Come out here. I want to talk to you."

She sprayed my hair and teased it a little. "No."

I gave her a spank and told her to go and talk to her husband, and then Jose dragged her out.

I looked at myself then. I'd been running away from mirrors for a while by that time, but I didn't know it was really so bad. Jose was wrong. I wasn't a beautiful woman. I was an ugly now, a bowwow. The capillaries and the eyeliner made me look like I'd been punched in both eyes. My head looked shrunk and there were red cry lines around my mouth. And then all of a sudden it scared me because I thought about how I'd never get Billy back looking like this. What was I thinking? I could wait all I wanted but he would want a pretty girl. He'd get over the dead girl and go off with a good-looking live one. He wouldn't want me back until I was glamorized again. The shock gave me a burst of energy and I picked up one of the powder puffs while Jose and Dolores talked in the next room.

"I swear I don't know where he is," Jose said. She told him that he sure as hell better not know because he'd be sleeping in the car if he was lying to her, but he promised, and said he didn't want to fight, and then I could hear him trying to kiss her. After a while of that I guess she bought it because she quieted down. I could just hear them murmuring while I kept putting on powder and blush. I uncapped Dark Rose lipliner and put it on very careful, right on the edge of my lips, then I filled it in with Hot Burgundy, and dabbed on a little gloss. I put on three coats of mascara and some white highlighter and tweezed my brows under the arch. When I was done I still looked bad. Painted, but bad. The broke capillaries still showed, and worst of all I was a bone. But at least I knew what I was going to do.

I went into the kitchen and opened their fridge. By the time Dolores came back out with Jose Jr. I'd had two glasses of whole milk, a brownie, a banana, and was working on a slice of a chocolate chip ice-cream cake frosted with whipped cream that she'd bought from Baskin-Robbins.

"What are you doing?" she said. Her hair was a mess.

I didn't say anything. I was busy.

"Look at you go, baby!" she laughed. She seemed happier and her cheeks were colored up now. But I didn't pay her too much attention. I should have. I should have asked her about the increased police and about Jose and about Victor. But I didn't because I was a crazy-brain and all I thought about were my own problems. I kept scooping up the ice-cream cake into my mouth without tasting it. Dolores would never do that. She loved food, even when she was sad or tired, but especially when she was in a good mood. Now she sat down and kissed Jose Jr.'s head, then reached behind her and pulled on the drawer and got out a little spoon. She fed Jose Jr. some whipped cream. After a couple minutes we heard Jose yell out "Adiós, sweeties!" and the door slam. Then Dolores slapped her thigh.

"Well, if anybody can eat like a caballo it's you, but I'll join in anyway."

We wound up eating the whole entire thing.

I was almost back in business by the end of September. Like me, summer was still hanging on. The sidewalk trees bloomed red berries and tiny white flowers, the morning light stretched peach and gold into the kitchen. The weather was a hot breath on your shoulder, and women were showing a little skin. Viejas rolled down their knee-high hose around their ankles; Catholic gradeschool girls going to the bus hiked up their blue-plaid skirts; and older chicas took out their see-through dresses and painted their toenails frosty pink to show off in sandals, making the men on the street walk backwards and catcall at them.

I noticed all this because I was finally coming back to my senses.

Since I'd scared myself back into a beauty regimen, I'd put myself on a high-calorie diet and had been eating everything in sight. If I hadn't been in such a hurry to get my butt back I would have done it smart, eating only the steak and full-fat milk and protein shakes like they tell you to. But I didn't have the time so I ate pan dulce coated with pink crystals, tamales filled with red fire, caramel flan made with canned sugar milk, fast-food burgers and fries, pumpkin candies wrapped in wax paper, and if food didn't taste as good as before it still made me stronger and gave me a little something to put in my bra. I set to work on my hair, too, dyeing it, oiling it down, and wrapping it in rags so it turned softer and curled into blue-dark waves that caught the light, and then I manicured my nails into points and painted them a beautiful blood color. After that, I wasn't afraid to be seen in the neighborhood again.

The mujeres were watching me. That's the first thing I noticed when my clear head came back. When I was with Dolores they kept it civilized, giving me looks like I'd just farted loud as a firecracker, while my sister squeezed on my hand and kept them back with friendly hellos. But when I was alone they were wicked. This one evil Saturday afternoon I was taking a walk from Eastern Ave to the tip end of Chávez and saw them tracking me like they were scared I'd go cannibal. They squeezed their babies tight between their breasts and whispered to each other about the next man-killing move I'd make. But that didn't bother me too much. It reminded me of old times and told me I was getting back into good shape, so I hitched my behind out a little more, smiled mysterious to myself, and tossed my new hair over my shoulders, all the time reminding my unsteady feet to take step after step after step.

It was hard to walk smooth, though, because of the second thing that caught my eye, which was the high school chiquitas with the glittering toes doing their after-school shopping and flirting. When had the knock-knees got so big? They had long pony legs now and their bite-sized candies had grown into C cups, and their brand-new blond hair swung over the tops of their bottoms while they teetered sexy and helpless on six-inch spike heels. Those show-offs set me back, whether they were number street girls or chicas from Divine Drive. They all had nectarine skin and they moved light as butterflies and their laughs, while they held a boy's hand or huddled together on corners, floated up like bubbles. And they dressed different than the flirts had in my day, too. There was una moda that was all the rage on the streets now, and instead of ass-grabbing skirts and V necks and hot pants, every teenaged girl I saw was wearing the same thing—a whisper-thin baby doll dress that showed eight inches of thigh, clung tight or billowed depending on the wind, and was held on by teasing spaghetti straps that just begged to be untied.

I tramped past them in my platforms and my old black Band-Aid dress and tried not to trip over my own feet. I knew I looked a whole lot better next to the huge-assed Latina Leaguers than these long-stemmed roses, and whereas I'd liked my second-skin clothes this morning, now they just seemed cheap. What about this body, anyways? The baby dolls were tight as green fruit but with every step my breasts jittered and when I reached around like to fix my skirt I felt my flat pancake behind. And what about my laugh? In the middle of Chávez I put my hands on my hips and let out a loud one, but it didn't float up like bubbles; instead my guffaw was dark as molasses and it made a couple of scruffy hermanos sharing whiskey lift up their bottle and toast me like I was one of their own.

I went on walking past the shadowy parts of Chávez and told myself a whole mess of things. That any man would still want me better than those tadpoles because I had the sex-experience that could leave him tongue-tied and breathless, and because I knew how to cup my chin with my hand and listen dewy-eyed while he talked and talked and talked. I kept marching and went by Ruben's, where three more candy-colored chicas posed by the door and tried to rope the fighters going inside. If I kept eating red meat my ass was sure to round out and if I practiced my laugh it could grow feathers and fly. I passed Arizona, then Ford, until Sancho's Coffee Shop was in sight. I figured that maybe I'd even buy a baby doll dress and put streaks in my hair. And maybe I'd give up cussing, teach myself how to walk helpless, chew gum and bite my lips and play stupid so shameless that folks would think I'd been dropped on my head. Just in case.

Now I was in front of Sancho's, with its big paned windows and flower boxes on the ledges. I looked into the window glass to check out my hairdo and saw a dark shape on a bright-lit background, but once I finished patting down my hair that black-and-white picture gave way to a full-color shot of the people inside, and what I saw in there told me that no end of meat-eating or hair-streaking or stumble-walking or lip-biting or, most of all, waiting for a man to get over the memory of a teenager six feet under was going to win me back the one and only thing I ever wanted.

There was Billy, sitting in the red-brown leather booth across from the most beautiful baby doll I'd come across that whole day. She was a hot-rollered redhead with peach cheeks, ocean eyes, and a genuine Marilyn Monroe mole that wasn't tattooed or penciled in. But even if she was full-grown now I still recognized her. This was the billy goat. This was the girl I'd run into years ago who'd gave me the up and down, the one who'd looked at me like I was a cheap Hong Kong knockoff and then flipped her hair disrespectful over her shoulders. I looked down at the same shoulders now—they were decorated by the pink bow-tied spaghetti straps of her dress. Billy was tugging on one of the strings and laughing. She was laughing too, and slapping him off. I stopped watching her then, though, because I was staring at my baby's smiling face, and then he glanced up and saw me there with my nose and hands pressed to the window and my hot breath and mascara smudging the glass, and shut his mouth. But his brain didn't talk to his hand, I guess, because his fingers kept tugging on the string, and while him and me were locking eyes the baby doll's shoulder strap came untied and one of her tits came popping out, all creamy bronze with a big rose-colored nipple, showing that she was either so devilish-clever or so brainless that she didn't even bother to wear no bra.

I flew home like a bird or a sheet of paper being flung and snapped by the wind, and I don't even remember my feet touching the ground, I rode the air so fast. When I hit my street, though, I took a fall. Face first, knees second, arms out, skidding on the concrete, so I broke open the old scars on my knees and skinned my feet and left cheek.

A neighbor tried to help me up but I said Get away and stood up by myself. I wasn't hurt too bad, but it slowed me down, and I walked the rest of the way home holding my face.

*I*n the kitchen Mama was sitting at the table, wrapping her hands around a cup of coffee. I came stumbling in with my streaked face and dripping chin, my scuffed knees and bleeding feet. She told me to sit down and gave me her cup so I could have a sip. Then she cleaned me up with a wet towel and extra-large Band-Aids and looked at me in a waiting kind of way while I rubbed the mess off my nose.

"He's not coming back to me," I told her.

Mama took another sip of her coffee and stared into the cup with the look that she gets when she goes through her shoebox. It's the same kind of hard, dazy look that fighters get a lot at the end of the tenth or eleventh round, when they know they don't got enough points and they wish so bad that their manager would throw in the towel. "Of course he's not, m'hija."

"But it hurts. What am I going to do?"

"Well now, you know, baby, I ain't the right person to be asking *that* question."

She sipped some more from the cup and let me cry for a while. When she finished her drink she took my hand.

"Rita, mi preciosa, you got your heart broke and you are like a crazy right now but you keep quiet for a minute while I tell you something. I never had no favorites between you and your sister. I always loved both you equal. But you, my baby, you and me are like the same, and so I got a special place for you in mi corazón. I said this to you before but you didn't listen and I want you to hear me now because I'm going to show you why.

"You and me, we come from a long line of lonely women. Tu abuela, tu tía, their mamas and abuelas and tías, every single one of them. Las Zapatas never had no luck in love. And this is because we got a curse on us. For years we been cursed with bad man luck! Generations! A long time back, there was your great-great-great-abuela, named Lourdes Pura. She was so pretty, a real mestiza, and with some figure. But Lourdes Pura fell in love with the wrong man, a married man who lived in Oaxaca. I don't know his name because nobody in this family would ever say it out loud but I do know that he was the big love of her life. Now this married man, his wife was a dangerous mujer. She was una bruja, the kind who talks to the devil. And hoosh! Was she jealous of Lourdes Pura! You can just guess. She told your abuela she better stop messing with her husband or else. But Lourdes couldn't do it. Her love was too strong, so she acts stupid. She stayed with the man.

"One day, her and the man ran away from Oaxaca to Calexico. They got a house, she gets pregnant, everything's beautiful. They think they're free of the bruja. The months go by and they have your great-great-abuela Conchita Pura, the one with the blond hair? But then the day finally comes and the bruja shows up at their door. She's found them. And she is pissed off. The way I always heard it told is that she made two curses, one for the man, and one for Lourdes. They say that the bruja turned the man into a Chihuahua, with a teeny-weeny penis, and that he slept on Lourdes's pillow for the rest of his little dog life and ate Alpo and all that.

"Now I don't believe that, but I know the other part of the story is true. The bruja put a curse on Lourdes Pura and all her hijas, that they would be the kind of women who need love but never get it. That we would run from one baby-making man

to the next to the next till we were loca or just plain worn out.
And that is just what happened. When Conchita grew up she
went after every dog in pants that came her way and then she
had three hijas who did the same, and so on and so on till there
was your great-tía Dora with the six sons and a set of fake teeth
because a jealous wife knocked out her real choppers with a lead
pipe, and your abuela Chita, who should have charged all the
losers she shacked up with because we at least would have been
rich, and then there was me, who ran away from home hoping
to ditch this goddam curse but anybody can see I couldn't because
here I am with two girls, no man, no money, and even so, even
though I'm hitting fifty and got nothing but bills and this one
pot to piss in, I still love sex so bad that I got to keep screwing
these losers just so I can get some sleep at night!

"And now here's you, too. Okay, your sister? She's different. It looks like maybe she got lucky and will go on living
like a regular woman and for that I say thanks to God, but Rita,
mi linda, you are like the rest of las Zapatas. So what I'm telling
you is to forget Billy for keeps because that manlove is a killer.
And you don't got no choice, anyways. Because you are cursed,
the same as me."

I'd stopped crying by now. I didn't like this fairy tale.
She was trying to bring me down with her but I wouldn't let
that happen. I was getting mad, and that was good, because when
my temper fired up I let the white-hot angry bitch who'd started
knocking on my heart as soon as I saw Billy and his baby doll
come on in and make herself at home, and she was a hell of a lot
better than the weeping softie who'd just been nesting there.

"Mama, maybe you screwed up your life, but that don't
mean that I'm going to mess up mine. I do got a choice."

"No such thing as choices when there's a curse on your
tail."

"No such thing as curses!"

"You're looking at living proof of one."

I could hear the blood in my ears. She was making me crazy, and I almost knocked the table over, but that's when Dolores came bustling through the door wearing a white-on-white silk jacquard businesslady suit that showed off her grapefruit knees and a matching pillbox stuck jaunty on her head, yelling What the hell happened to your face? and me and Mama didn't finish our fight. I fell on my ass, I said, and Dolores laughed with her eyebrows stitched together. Mama, like to switch the subject, grabbed up Jose Jr. and set to baby-talking and chucking him under his chin, and after that we took out a defrosted chicken and veggies and the pots and went about making one of our family dinners.

Dolores took off her jacket and pulled the bobby pins out of her hat, then started cutting up the potatoes with quick jabby slices. She was heated up with the politics again because she'd just got out of another one of her city council meetings. "You remember that speech I gave on gangs and how we need more police in the neighborhood? They just approved a twenty percent emergency increase in foot patrolmen in East L.A.! They took a vote and it was unanimous! And then they said that until they do the hiring they're going to encourage overtime." While she was going on she handed me a pile of carrots so I'd wash them. "Afterward they all came up and shook my hand and a photographer was there and he took my picture with them and Councilman Lefkowitz told a newspaper reporter that gangs were a national emergency and the solution was increased law enforcement and that I was the lady that lit the fire under their behinds to get them moving on the issue. And then the reporter started interviewing me and he asked if I was interested in running for office and damn! Just hearing that made me start sweating but I said Why not? I'm as good as anybody else. . . . "

I was having trouble listening to whatever Dolores was saying. All I could think of was the sting on my knees and Chihuahua dogs and the baby doll's chi-chi popping out of her dress and the hot bitch who was stamping around my heart in her high-heeled shoes. So what I did was concentrate on washing the carrots. I scrubbed and scrubbed them until they squeaked and Dolores took them away from me and chopped them into circles. Next thing I knew we were eating dinner, and then dinner was done and we were drinking coffee. Had I ate anything? My plate was a mess, with ripped-up chicken. Everything was blurry except for the shape of my temper, which was sharp and shiny as a blade sticking me. Right then one of them asked me something and I must have answered because the other one said You sure? and I said Yes, and then they were laughing and I laughed too and after that we all got up to wash the dishes and the baby started up with crying and Dolores said: "Well then, can you do it now? He needs it pretty bad. I smell something on him." And then I knew they wanted me to clean up Jose Jr.

I took him into the bathroom and ran the water. It rushed white out the pipes and sounded like a storm and I sat on the toilet with Jose Jr. on my lap and watched it fill up the tub a green-river color. The baby pulled hard on my hair but I let him because I barely felt it. Then I took his clothes off and rubbed his *cola* with a baby wipe and set him in the tub and he splashed around and showed me his gums while I started sudsing him up.

Now I want it known that I loved that little boy because he was my own blood but my mentality wasn't working right that very minute. I washed him gentle enough at first, his fat arms and bowed legs and puppy belly, and I dribbled water down his tiny chest so he laughed. But in my head I heard Billy whispering hot songs in my ear and they turned into the whispers of neighborhood ladies that sounded like wasps in a jar, and then it seemed like every piece of hurt I'd ever suffered was coming home to settle under my skin—the churchies staring at me with their evil-packed eyes, the fighters shoving me around Rabbit Street, the Divine Drive girls giving me black-bandit looks, Billy saying he'd help me out for a little while—and that's when my heart changed color. I wondered if Mama *was* right, that I was cursed the same as her, and then I was having trouble breathing because the bitch rattling my ribs reached up to my lungs and strangled them, then crawled into my arms, the tips of my fingers, and tried to move me like a puppet. I worked hard to keep my hands still and soft on the baby, but when I looked down I saw his penis floating up in the water and it struck me that maybe it wasn't no bruja's curse that was hurting me after all, but just this natural one, manhood, which had gave las Zapatas our heartache, and I guess by that time the bitch had worked herself up into my brain because then I thought maybe it would be better if no man had ever been born on this earth.

That idea put such a spell on me. After it flew into my head my strong arms worked by their own selves, and I didn't hear or see nothing but clear green silence for a long time.

Then the world came crashing back in like a car accident outside your bedroom window in the dead black of night and you sit up straight, eyes blind, mouth open. There was the sound of a rushing river and a woman howling and the scuffle of shoes, and somebody pulled on my shoulder and tore my hands out the wet and slapped me, but it still took me a while before I broke out of my trance. Later I wondered if a devil had visited me and entered my body, or if my free will which had been trapped by the curse had been straining wild against its chains. Either way, when I woke I saw Jose Jr.'s bruised face coughing and my sister's red mouth and white teeth shrieking and Mama hitting and pushing me away from the baby that I'd just tried to drown by holding his head under the water while the air bubbles came boiling up and his little hands scratched at me helpless.

But he was all right. He was all right. He was crying, and that meant he was breathing. I fell back and watched Dolores hold him upside down, and the water streamed out his choking mouth. Mama held her eyes on me, and her hands together, praying loud enough for heaven to hear, but it was too late because I'd already sunk into hell and burning damnation. Sitting there in the splashed-over water that soaked my skin, with my crusted cuts splitting fresh and the hot lava woman in my head laughing wild, I was being killed by shame. And listening to them screaming and accusing, I knew I'd took a wrong turn, because I shouldn't be hunting after no baby boys; instead it was my own self I should go and murder.

I stood up and walked into Mama's bedroom. I opened up the closet and started digging under the neat piles of extra blankets like a prisoner claws at mud under a barbed-wire fence, and I kept going until I hit bottom and found Mr. Hernandez's gun, the one he'd gave her to keep us safe.

It was bigger than I remembered and even covered up under the wool it was still cold to the touch. Already I could hear the bang and smell the blood and it scared me, and I had to tell myself to be brave. But out in the light of the room I looked down and smiled at the glinting silver, the thin curved trigger and the dark eye staring, and that's when my tangled mind loosed and untied so I could understand my salvation.

See, it didn't have to be me I was killing. It could be him. Because this was his doing, you could track it all back to his leaving me. He was the one putting me in danger.

What it was, was self-defense.

Confession

I was strong, then, with that gun in my hand. I ran faster to his house than I'd flown home, even, and I didn't fall this time.

Billy had moved apartments but I'd heard where he lived. This new place was bigger and with a better address, at the tip of Divine Drive. The front door was locked and I didn't know where he kept the spare keys, but I didn't need them. He'd got himself a gardener and that gardener had put in decorator river rocks in the front yard and they worked good enough. I put one through the windows by the door, then reached around and grabbed hold of the knob, cutting my hand with the glass. The door sprung open for me, and I walked inside.

"What's that?" I heard him calling from the bedroom. "You break something?" Billy's mama and the daddy weren't anywhere in sight, but his brand-new baby doll had been doing the dishes in the kitchen and now she was turning around, and facing me, and soon as she saw me floating over the floor holding that silver killer and bleeding red from the hands and feet like Jesus she dropped her dishes and scatted out the house, so scared her open mouth couldn't scream.

I let her go. I knew by now that she'd get hers, and I'd smile when that day came. But I wasn't here for her. I was here for Billy.

Who was in the bedroom. I heard him rustling the sheets and I stayed put, crooking my head to one side while I wondered where I should do it. In the love nest where he was waiting for his new chica? Or right here by the stove and the sink because it's the only real place in a house that belongs to a woman? I liked the feeling I could choose. I could have stayed there for an hour picking out the perfect spot, the perfect painful way to make him dead, except then I heard him walking towards me and so it was decided that this would be a kitchen killing.

I stopped feeling so brave when I saw him in the flesh, though. He was so handsome it hurt me. Even now I could see signs of the beating Hammer gave him from how his mouth still hooked down and how his right eye hung wrong, but those weak parts just made me love and hate him harder, like a war vet who wants to both kiss and slap away the scarred face of his old enemy. Besides all that, too, I would have had second thoughts anyways because dead-eyed or not, that hombre was just pretty as a snapdragon. He was shirtless and in this light his skin didn't look like it had a color so much as it had a flavor and it made me remember the times he'd lifted my hair, the one finger stroking, the soft lips on my neck shooting sparks down my spine.

Him being so weirdly calm didn't help my state of mind, either. When he came into the kitchen fear flickered over his face but then it passed and he just sort of looked interested.

"Well look at this," he said, leaning up on the sink. "Rita got herself a gun."

I was crying and shaking terrible and holding that heavy thing up so it pointed straight at his heart.

"So, what. You trying to get back together?"

"I love you," I said.

"You want to shoot me, huh? You want to kill me?"

"I love you so much," I sobbed out. "Why don't you love me?"

"Give me that," he said. He took the gun from me and looked at it. He looked straight into the barrel. Then he popped it open and looked at the bullets before snapping it shut again.

"You only got two bullets," he went on. "You need a little luck to kill a man with two bullets." Then he started doing this horrible thing, he started pounding the gun on the sink. He pounded it six or seven times with the barrel pointing up at his head. "See?" he yelled. He stopped pounding it. "If you had a full round it would have gone off."

He gave the gun back to me. I stood there holding it and bawling.

"I don't love you," he said. "I liked you, though." Then he looked at me for a minute. "Rita, you know why I'm such a good boxer?"

I couldn't say nothing. For a second I saw Jose Jr.'s blue face again and I thought I might fall down.

"Because I'm fearless!" He spread his arms out, then covered his face with his hands, and his body started shaking.

"Rita," he said after a minute. "Rita, listen."

I was still holding the gun. He put his hands down and I saw he was crying.

"You remember I told you about Angelina? Well, it was me. I killed her. Her boyfriend took a knife to my head and cut me up but I shot them both and then I ran away."

My mind wouldn't let me see him doing that, but I looked up at the proof in front of my face. His scar was blood red now. I looked at his red drooping eye, too, and his sagging mouth, and it hit me right then that he might be dying already.

"I suffer so bad" was all he said next. Then he rushed right at me with his arms raised and grabbed at my neck so that even if I should have been the one dead I did it. I reared back and pulled the trigger twice and killed him.

My eyes punished me by not going blind then. He landed elbow first, then hip, on the linoleum and his heart came flooding out the stomach wound while he opened and closed his hands and drummed his heels on the ground like he was running away from the shadow that took the shine from his face. He blinked three times and then stared out the window surprised. His mouth opened, but that was me screaming, wasn't it? I was screaming and bending over him and there was red everywhere and my mind was a flock of crows after the bad boy throws his rock, scattered to pieces and fluttering while I grabbed the hands that wouldn't hold, and shouted to the eyes that wouldn't see, and then my screams didn't sound the same, they pitched higher, and sang for a long time, until they sounded too high to be human, and I knew that it wasn't me.

I heard the sirens, and then I woke up.

The men in the suits ran through the door with their red-and-blue light and their lifesaver machines, and the police came right after. When they asked me what happened (the paramedic on the ground pumping and buzzing over Billy, another one yelling into a phone), the truth was a bulky thing in my mouth but I could not say it out loud. I could not hand my story over to those strangers. So I showed them my scraped face, my cut hand, my raw knees and feet.

"He hurt me," I said. "He was trying to kill me."

Haunted

I know what a ghost looks like now. Because if I wasn't cursed before like Mama said all us Zapatas were, I sure enough was cursed by this time, and worse than cursed, even, I was haunted. A spirit started spying on me and making himself known when I least expected it, but instead of walking around in a white sheet or biting me with his fangs, this one made faces, or punched at the air, or simply smiled at me lonely-looking and rubbed his red gloves together.

It was in the reflecting lens of the policeman's Polaroid that I first saw Billy, back from the grave. Those police had their suspicions about me, I guess. Down at the station they asked me a million questions about How many times had he beat you ma'am? and Why didn't you leave him? and shook their heads at my cuts, and when I started up giggling and crying they gave each other the eye and started reading me my rights. It was after that my mugshot got took. They put me by the wall and when I looked into the camera I didn't see my own face reflecting back from the lens, but instead there Billy was, small and alive and screaming silent at me from that glass circle, and then came the click and the flash.

That was just the beginning. Once they got me into County I saw him all the time. I was there for a few days before I got set free on bail but because of my haunting it seemed like dogs' years. I had this Anglo cellmate whose name and crime I never learned because every time she tried to talk to me her eyes would go from blue to Indian brown and her voice would sound like a man's, and I couldn't listen to a word she said. It was like that with everything. I couldn't eat the prison food because if I cleaned my plate I'd see Billy at the bottom, showing me his red gloves. When we got to go outside for exercise he'd be there already, shuffling his feet in the dirt and trying out his upper-cut, and I wouldn't take another step. At night he'd squeeze through the bars and sit on my bed, dripping blood from head to toe and wrapping his hands with white tape, and I'd never get a wink of sleep. And it got so bad I couldn't even talk straight to my lawyer because of how Billy's face could show up in the glossy parts of her teeth, earrings, fingernails, and the shined uppers of her shoes without warning.

It was that lawyer of mine, though, who got me out of that place. She was free but good, one of them save-the-whale types. First time I met her she took one look at my red skin and started scribbling quick onto her yellow pad.

"I think we have a good case, Rita," she said. "There's a definite claim here for self-defense. So how long have you been a battered woman? How exactly did he give you these injuries?"

I tried to tell her tales about the emotional abuse and the battered this and that along with the true story of how he came barreling at me and would have shot my head off with that gun if I hadn't done the work myself, but my voice dimmed down to a whisper and my words blew apart like dead dandelion heads when I saw Billy in one of her gold blazer buttons, giving me a wink. The lawyer didn't mind my weird way of talking, though.

She just scratched on her pad faster and said something about me trying not to worry while Billy reared his head back, ripped at his hair, and disappeared.

Then the next day was my bail hearing.

Dangerous cons got to wear chains on their way to the courtroom, so I rattled into that place slow and clanky as a spook, with a guard at each elbow. My lawyer was thumbing through papers at her table. The D.A. was doing the same at his. Mama was there too, sitting on the benches with a heap of other losers waiting to hear on their jailed folks. The place was packed. Besides the black hump of a judge sitting up high and the rice-colored lawyers sticking their faces in files, there was mostly women, the older fiftyish ladies sucking in their breath and gripping their handbags, the younger girlfriends holding wobbly-headed babies and hissing at their rowdy toddlers to sit down. A couple of seniors were in the back, one of them with his eyes closed, the other one nibbling his lips. But even though it was so full in there, it still seemed too empty to me. Dolores and Jose Jr. weren't sitting next to Mama like they should be. No Latina Leaguers were there, either. No Rabbit Street men. I made eyes at Mama but when she saw my chains she started crying and I had to look away, up into the closed face of the guard, who took out his key and unlocked me.

All the law-and-order types started talking. The D.A. got up first and went on about how I was a menace to society and the judge put his fingers together, making a little pagoda, and looked down at me. Then my lawyer got up and started jawing about the self-defense and the battered things and I looked back over at Mama to see if she was getting mad, except then I saw Billy running through the rows of people, laughing and pointing at me.

I crossed myself right away even though I'd gave up on the church. I didn't like how he was laughing at me. There was something evil in it besides pure haunting, with that pointing finger blaming me for something. I started shivering like a hairless dog and my teeth chattered so hard I bit my lip.

I must have looked meek then, though, because that's when the judge gave me bail. He said he supposed I didn't pose a great danger to the community. The D.A. puffed and bluffed some more, but the gavel came down. I was free on a bail bondsman's ten thousand. My lawyer squeezed my hand and said something friendly. The next shysters came up and shuffled around their papers like they were playing cards. Then the guards came to get me so I could get processed back at the jail, but at least I didn't have to wear the chains anymore.

On my way out I passed Mama. Her face was wrecked, rubbed red under the eyes. I reached out for her. "Where's Dolores? Why didn't she come?"

"Something happened," she said.

"What? Is it the baby?" The guard had his hand on me, and was pulling.

Mama wouldn't look at me. "The police shot Jose and he's dead."

That's when the hand on my shoulder jerked me around, but I didn't come face-to-face with the guard. It was Billy, dressed in blue, with a gun and a club, carrying my chains. Except he wasn't shouting and laughing now. He was crying.

How I Saved My Own Life

*W*hen we got to the jail's parking lot I saw the witch with the streaming blue hair, howling mouth, and hell-dark eyes pointing at me with her red-clawed hand. Mama had brought Jose's old custom-painted van to take me home in. She said that hoodlums stole her car yesterday and this was the only ride left, so I shrugged, opened the door, and climbed up.

"You know all the police Dolores wanted to get in the neighborhood?" she said, pulling out the lot, pushing the gas too hard, jerking on the brakes. "Well, we got them, sure enough. Whole mess of them roaming around past few days. And they caught up with Jose and that brother of his, that Victor. The one on the posters. Police ran into them by that alley, the one where that boy got shot few years ago. You used to go there all the time. What was that again? What's it called?"

"Rabbit Street," I whispered. The van speeded onto the freeway, the engine whacking.

"Yes, there. The police got their guns out, and the brother had a gun too. So they were all shooting, but it's that brother who gets away. And Jose's the one who's dead. Right there, in the same place as that other boy. Your sister, we had to get a doctor in to give her some medicine because she was screaming so much. I think maybe she wants to kill herself. And hey, how's this: Maybe I'll kill myself too. Shoot my own self in the head, how you like that? It sounds like a damn good idea right now. What with this and that. Okay? Because really, when I heard you killed Billy? Rita? Well now I'm just dead inside." Mama was quiet for a minute, trying to keep her jumping hands on the wheel. Then, "What I'm even supposed to say to you?"

I stared at the road and tried to blank out my mind.

She went on. "I never thought we'd all be coming to this. Only thing I can tell is that you and the rest of this whole world is gone upside down." Mama pointed at the newspaper in the backseat. I didn't want to look at it but she told me to twice and so I picked it up and read it. It said:

POLICE SHOOT-OUT IN EAST L.A. GANG LEADER DEAD

Under the headline was a picture of Jose, an old high school yearbook one, took right before he dropped out. He was about fifteen years old there, all bangs and too big teeth but, like always, looking spookily too much like his big brother. And it did hurt me seeing that. This was a dirty case of mistaken identity. They were saying Jose was Victor, and going on about how he'd done terrible things like shooting folks and selling drugs.

Mama rubbed at her face. "Somebody made a big kind of screwup when they did that. People are too mad at this one. Ever since that news came out we've been having trouble in the neighborhood, and I never, ever seen nothing like it. We got violence in the streets now. I don't even want to go back home; I'm scared to."

Something started coming up in me that second and then I was yawling. "You should be scared of me, Mama. You should be scared of me, I'm the one who's bad."

"No, Rita," she said. "Try and listen to what I'm telling you. We don't got time for all that now, we got to be calm and smart. Because there's an emergency at home, see? There's been riots."

*T*he first sign of trouble was a mile before our exit, when we saw the black smoke blending in with the bruised sundown sky. Not long after that came the burning palm tree, lit up orange with a flashing red heart, the flamed leaves jerking up to the falling sun like a praying man's hands.

Then we got off the freeway and the neighborhood was on fire, blood clouds floating over buildings. Eastern Ave was ash already. Trees had got torched till they were black sticks. The old homeless dumps with their sleeping blankets and paper bags were scorched and trashed, spread over the ground. That was a ghost street, empty except for the one loco homeless I saw running, bleeding from his head and banging two garbage can lids together.

It was the other streets that were still alive—the number streets, Fourth Street in particular, the one lined with unrepaired houses. Men I knew all my life—Marco, Felipe Peña, blue-eyed Francisco, the Sancho's Coffee Shop cash register boy—they were there, standing in the twilight shadows that were brightened by hot yellow flowers, but mind you, not the kind of flowers a man would send to his ladylove wrapped in heart-stamped paper, but instead more like sizzling roses bubbling from volcanos, because those were match fires the boys were starting in the bushes surrounding the flophouses, and the tenants, the mamacitas holding their babies and the slipper-wearing viejos, they stood outside on the sidewalk and watched silent, or screamed at their husbands and sons to stop, while the flowers bloomed and faded, bloomed and faded. Bushes were burning here and there while the men hunkered around, fanning the flames with their hands and blowing them stronger with their breath, but the real burning-down fire hadn't caught just yet.

Two boys ran through the middle of the road, carrying baseball bats and yelling over the far-off sirens.

A beefy cholo in a knit cap raced by us, hammered the van's hood with his fist, then flew off.

Right then a mujer came out of the flophouse holding a shotgun and blasted it in the air, and Mama pressed on the gas, speeding past the rest of the number streets, which were lit up red with more flame-dancing trees.

The quickest way home was through Chávez, but that turned out to be a mistake because most of the fire-minded men were there already, spilling off the sidewalks, thick in the street, and one look at them butting shoulders and raising hands that were either empty and squeezed into fists or holding more baseball bats, or a .22, or a yellow-burning piece of newspaper, told you this was an evil patch of trouble that had broke the minds of not just our criminal boys, but some of the regular joes too. Over by the for-lease flower shop there was Madball Medina, a drug-selling Fifth Streeter, and he was smashing through the plate glass with the help of Sonny Zuñiga, a laid-off garment worker and daddy of four. By the old Payless where Dolores and Cha Cha once worked little Tito was kindling fire with Shy Boy Zepeda, a dude so wicked he'd once stuck up a schoolteacher to feed his needle habit. Pedro was screaming Jose's name over and over in front of the dead bakery while Chuy Gomez splashed gas on the vacant Pic-N-Sav. Zookie Chamayo threw window-

crashing rocks at Diamond Jeweler's and Freddie rattled its burglar bars.

The rest mostly stood by, and cheered, and shot their
guns into the sky, or ran inside the empty shops to see if there
was any good looting to be done. Some of them, though, turned
and saw me and Mama shivering in Jose's van, and we must have
looked better than any kind of cheap loot stole from a shut-down
store because that's when their faces lit up the same as the bon-
fire palms: Now they were running with their arms out, and
laughing.

Didn't they see who I was? Because those weren't stranger
boys rushing at me, I knew those men good. Here was Freddie,
rattling on my locked door, and Chuco running behind him
raising a hammer. A bowlegged thug whose name I didn't remember but who I once flirted with shameless was pounding
over too, and then I even made out Martinez and his black jacket
who was my first time in the backseat, and then there's Tommy
holding steel chains. I figured maybe they didn't recognize me
because of my still-scarred face so I yelled out to them my name
RITA NOVO RITA NOVO but that just made them worse
because they started banging on the car like I was not me, not
the me they knew and had stroked with their own hands, kissed
with their own mouths, whispered to and once wanted so bad
they would have crawled on their bellies for just one touch, but
instead like I was that strange bitch who'd strangled me and
moved me like a puppet, a somebody else who was dirty, who
needed a good scare, or a good bloody beating. They wouldn't
do that though, would they? Reach through this rolled-up window glass and hit us? Hurt us? But I was scared because their
laughs told me they would, and Mama must have known it too
because she was screaming something and blowing the horn.
There was the sound of more plate glass crashing, burglar alarms.

But even with that booming, smashing, screaming, loud scared heart beating, there was a second where I could still see out that moving muscle wall of men, and I made out Pedro, not rushing or busting shit up, but standing six feet tall on a soapbox, and I could hear, faint through the window glass and the rest of it, some of what he was preaching. He said:

"HERMANOS! You got a RIGHT to be mad. Hear me? A RIGHT. We should feel ANGRY, CRAZY at what they done to our boy! Don't you want to burn this place down? Well, you should! Be mad, be crazy. That's right, burn it down then, motherfuckers! Burn it down! Burn down the stores that can't give you work. Smash down the houses that charge you too much rent. Kill the man who murders your brother. Kill it all, hombres. Hear me? Kill all of it!"

And then I couldn't hear another word because now the men closed up around us and all I could see were plaid shirts and pressed hands on the window glass, and two boys up here on the windshield with red stretched faces, and the rest of them were drumming their fists and bats and chains on the crushing steel body and still laughing, and Mama was fumbling the key in the stalled van but would we be able to get anywhere with all them weighing on us? and shaking us? because now we were shaking, they'd got ahold of the bumper and were bouncing the van and when my head hit the ceiling that's when two things happened: The burning-down fire caught in a whoosh that sounded through the windows like a sigh, and the ignition reared back and roared.

We were driving. Slow, through bodies of boys. The monsters on the windshield peeled off, mouths opened into round shadows, hands gripping glass. The others backed away and went after other loot or good trashing, except for a stray hanging on to the rear bumper, and another boy jogging along and jiggling at a door handle. Through the smeared windows we could see the fire. It was a red dragon with a sun-stained tongue crawling up the shoe store and taking out big bites. Then it was twelve red dancing ladies with orange tap shoes dancing feverish on the roof, hard enough to cave it in. Now there were devils inside the store, banging their gold fists on plate glass still plastered with posters showing Billy's peeling, burning face, and black ghosts rising from the cracked places and spinning with their arms stretched out.

It was hell-hot but we were passing it, until the black-and-blood-colored shoe store circus was in the rear window, and then we were stopped by another solid block of riot boys who got busy with banging on the hood. Now we were right by Pedro. Tall on his soapbox. He'd quit the speechifying and was back to screaming out JOSE MENDOZA JOSE MENDOZA JOSE MENDOZA JOSE MENDOZA, ringing them words over the heads of the locos breaking down doors and busting holes in plaster walls and ripping up floorboards and setting a dozen more baby fires up and down the street so they'd know they were trashing this place as payback for a brother's blood when it came spilling out him on Rabbit Street and for the lie that was told in the paper the next day. And Pedro, he was different up there. His bad eye wasn't jiggling anymore, and he wasn't stooping. He looked fierce and righteous as Moses carrying the law down the hill and like he'd lost any speck of mercy, and when he stared down at me I started shaking because I had a brotherman's blood on my hands, too, and so what would he have all these hombres do to me?

But he didn't evil his face up at me, or spit, or throw stones. Pedro stopped his chanting, then did the strangest thing. In all that crazy helling (now the fire up on the shoe store was a crackling red witch rising from the ashes) that old strange Pedro looked down on me and smiled. Smiled. Friendlier than ever, like I was a hero in this parade. Like this was a Fourth of July party and those sparks were from fireworks, not a mix of matches and gas or Jack Daniel's. And then I did something strange too, because I smiled back, my cheek hurting from the scabs and my lip cut from where I must of bit it while Mama's yelling What the fuck you doing? but I only smiled bigger and then my face wobbled and leaked when Pedro said HEY, RITA GIRL, and then told the killers to get off our car and let us go.

And they did. We drove, still slow to keep from hitting the cheering, drinking, dancing boys in the road, but free all the way down Chávez. Here the milagro store was catching fire. Here Carnival Liquors was screaming a siren. Two blocks down we saw the black-and-white cop cars coming, and the blue men inside them barking at their radios. At Ruben's Superbox, Ruben wasn't waiting for the police to help him, though. Because there he was outside his front door holding a shotgun at the boys he'd kicked out before and who wanted back in now, and a couple of them were teasing him with newspaper torches or heaving bricks at the windows. But we didn't stop to help him. Kept going. Past the wig store that used to sell curly rugs to balding viejas and one-foot hair extensions to me and now had one boy in there cracking the glass counters with a pipe. Past the old ice-cream shop where the knock-knees once sucked sodas and flirted with bumpy-faced Romeos, and now was scarred up with red graffiti saying FUCK YOU four times on the door. There was Carlita's Fashions, with its sign ripped off and laying in the street. Rudy's Super, dark as midnight inside with women streaming out the open doors holding cans in their skirts, whole hams under their armpits, eyes squinting at the whoop whoop of the alarm loud enough to break an eardrum. Then Sancho's Coffee Shop, joining the song with a long solid siren howl, while burglars broke open the cash register and looted pie, their glossy heads lit white by buzzing fluorescent.

And then it was gone. We were turning the corner, off Chávez and on our way home, and Mama was smiling like a castaway who sees the rescue plane come floating out the storm clouds. "We made it. We made it," she kept saying, and she was breathing easier, but I wasn't. Because on top of the snow-cold sad of everything else—Billy being dead, Jose robbed of his life *and* his name—there I was mourning that street, those stores, like they were a person dead and gone just the same. Even though I hadn't cared about the place for a long time—those shops where folks looked at me funny when I came in through the door, the street where boys had pawed and shoved at me and chicas whispered nasties when I walked by—I did now that it was burned, because I remembered giggling in that diner with Dolores, shopping for dinner with Dolores in the super, eating vanilla cones with her in that ice-cream shop, looking with her in the windows at dresses and shoes we couldn't buy. Who can figure a thing like that, me feeling that way right then? But I did feel it. I always made like I was only renting space here, wasting time, and never thought once that this neighborhood belonged to me, but that's the minute I knew that me and my baby sister, who'd laughed till we were weak-bellied on this corner, played hopscotch on this block, fought screaming under that tree, had owned this place as free and clear as anybody else, that it'd been ours too.

Dolores. Where was she?

*N*ot in the house. Girl, you in here? Answer me! Me and Mama searched feverish, mud-eyed, clawing the covers from the bed, calling her name inside the closet, until one of us thought of checking for a note and there it was, stuck on the fridge with the pineapple magnet. Gone to Gloria's was all it said and when we tried the phone, it was dead.

We couldn't go out and find her, though. This wasn't no weather for two women to go walking in. Sitting in the kitchen with all the doors and windows locked and bolted and chairs stuck under the doorknobs, we held our heads in our hands and listened to the world heat up worse while night fell darker, deeper, going from dusky blue cut with sundown rose to black shot through with lamplight. Nobody burned the houses on our block but there was a rat-tatting outside from guns. More sirens. Men laughing. A lady screaming awful for minutes, then sobbing. Sounds of feet running and brakes screeching and the slurry shouting of a borracho going on about how he was gonna kill somebody, then the thumpy heeching sound of that somebody getting mugged, and stabbed too? "What if they try and come in here?" Mama asked. "Gun's gone now." So her and me grabbed steak knives, talked about how we'd use them anybody so much as tried. I thought about one of the burglars cracking open the back door and me sticking that bright knife in his splitting wet neck, killing him. But then I remembered Billy with his eyes rolled back and I knew I couldn't do murder now, no matter what. Anybody broke in the house, it'd have to be her.

The night crept by slow. We passed some of it watching the town burn on the TV. Already after midnight and half the channels showed Rudy's Super, not even a store anymore but a black cave full of lightning-white rattlers flicking red tongues. The other half had speed-talking blondes yabbering about powder kegs and community violence and they kept rolling clips of National Guard guys spilling onto Chávez out a black van. Round two in the morning Channel 5 showed the mouth of Rabbit Street, done up with red roses and blue Marys and the lit santos candles throwing gold on the bloody brick and the taped-up pictures of Jose.

But Mama hadn't seen Jose's altar. Her head was back and her eyelids flitting. Her sleeping face was lit silver by the TV screen.

"Mama?" I said. No answer. I got up and went to the bathroom and checked out my ugly face in the mirror, the black scabs on the cheek, blue eye bruise mixing in mascara. Then the dirty neck, stained shirt, my cut hand swelling up. I barely recognized that beat-up thing winking back at me. A wash and I'd look more like my old self, except I didn't have the energy for it. What I did do was crawl into the dry tub and sit there with my knees up, eyes closed, feeling the cold with my hands and legs and trying not to think of anything, but that didn't work either because soon I heard the water splashing again and Jose Jr. coughing, and saw the green color that had dizzied me into evil.

It was Billy who woke me. When I opened my eyes there he was, sitting on the floor, faint as smoke. He wasn't a powerful ghost now. He was fading in and out, his face made of raindrops, his body made of cold breath. The only thing bright about him were his star-brilliant eyes that stared at me terrible and full of sad. Who would have thought dead could be so lonely? But I did know then that it was. Because he was looking hungry at me, not vicious now. He didn't show his teeth or make himself bleed to scare me. He just blinked his eyelids up and down so the stars twinkled out the fog. And shot me a sad smile, too, just a frosty whisper of lip. But yes, he was hungry. Starving, even—for what? The feel of a human hand on his? Or the ground under his floating feet? I thought about reaching out to try and touch him but I worried about mixing him into mist, so I didn't.

After a while he looked down at his gloves and started rubbing them together again. His bright eyes were gone now.

And he was fading faster, becoming lighter, thinner, until all that was left was a curl of smoke hanging in the air; then that was gone too.

And that's when I remembered something. A long time ago Mama had told me the story that spirits will only haunt you if they have business to finish with you. I guess he was finished with me now. But him showing me what a lonely hell I'd put him in was the worst punishment he'd gave me yet.

Sign of a crazy mind? These are the things you keep secret, when the fairy tales come true and cold hard facts look like lies.

But those bedtime stories were real, weren't they? I saw them with my own two wide-open eyes.

I mean, I think I did.

Because now my eyes were opening again and there weren't ghosts anywhere in sight, just sunlight slanting through the bathroom window. My crooked back hurt from the cold tub and it was already morning.

*T*he city was smoking and glittering ice when I stepped into that early sunlight. Devil's winter. From the porch steps I saw thunderclouds coming off the tops of Chávez shops charred coal black and crumbling, and the winking ice caps of broke glass spread out over my street. Here was somebody's coat in the middle of the road, tore up in places, stained dark with something, I wouldn't look to see what. Here was a white T-shirt dipped in blood and ripped to shreds, scattered like snowflakes on the sidewalk. The city was silent like winter, too. Quiet as a held breath. All the neighbors were hid in their houses, probably crouching behind their jammed doors speed-dialing 911 on their dead phones or jerking under the bedcovers still dreaming of the night before. But I couldn't wait for the power line to come back up or a policeman to drive over and tell me it was all right. I went straight out into that wilderness to go and get Dolores.

The van wouldn't start, probably because of the wrecking hands of the rioters, so I had to walk to the number streets where Gloria and Chuco lived. The town felt ghostly but peaceful because of the quiet; the only things loud were the dark pieces of red streaked on a wall or spilled cold and harmless on the sidewalk. More than that, there wasn't an hombre in sight. I walked up Eagle then turned the corner down to Rockport, and the only folks I saw were neighborhood ladies. One by one I saw them peeking out their windows then unbolting the bolts and staring stony at the rubble with their hands on their hips. Nobody said nothing much. I heard a sigh here and a cuss and tooth-suck there over the sound of my own shoes shuffling. Then more and more they came out, until there was a woman on every porch. Now phones started ringing. A few babies were crying. One or two of them called out "You okay?" while others answered "Shit, what you think?" Some of them went into the street, kicked at the tinkling glass, stepped back tsking. Then one of them spit at me and the rest of them slitted their eyes, and I kept walking. It took a minute until I figured out that a couple of them were walking down the street too, following after me.

Well, not following exactly. More just going the same direction. I felt them on my heels and when I looked over my shoulder I saw I was being trailed by two Latina Leaguers, old Señora Orozco and this newlywed Rubi De la Torre. They were saying Dolores's name and talking about holding a meeting, then whispering something about me and Billy. I didn't mind them.

Or the others, either. The next street down I saw five more Latina Leaguers walk out their front doors, join each other in a group and go ahead of me, all of them surefooted, empty-handed, stepping a little quicker than normal while we went through the steaming road past smashed TVs, a huddle of cops standing around like stoplights, a wild barking dog, two crashed cars, busted fences, ripped-up lawns. When I looked behind me more mujeres were there, too, getting drawn into the crowd. Walking, whispering, shooting me evil eyes. I was alone. Nobody said hello or sorry or smiled and I would have run past all of them if I could, but I was too tired. All I wanted was to backtrack through Chávez and hoof it down to Sixth to see if the building my sister'd slept in last night was still standing.

But I don't make it to Sixth Street. When I get to Chávez the first thing I see isn't the cindered shops, or the ash falling from the sky. I don't even notice the police crawling under yellow tape and poking at a dead man lying facedown on the sidewalk. I'd remember that later, after. What I see right then is a world of women. Thick in the street. Spilling off the sidewalks. Standing shoulder to shoulder or bending hip to hip in front of Lupe's Beauty House, their faces shut tight as triple-locked doors while they clear out the shop. All of them were Latina Leaguers—number-streeters, churchies, Divine Drivers—some bending up and down to pick up the crushed hair dryers and the cracked nail polish bottles spilling flower colors and the broke hair dye cans bleeding Monterrey Red, others lugging the three barber chairs that'd got pulled from the ground and thrown into the road, or sweeping up the broke glass if they'd thought clear enough to bring brooms, and they're all working around Lupe, who's standing very still and covering her mouth with her hands.

I can't see Dolores for all these mujeres milling around. The women I'd walked here with brush past me and join the rest. Rubi De la Torre is pointing at me and I hear her say bitch and that's when the others look up and their locked-shut faces open wide. There's Cha Cha and Rosario with their hands stained murder red from hair dye looking at me with eyes full of knives. The Widow Muñoz and even La Rica stooping down sweeping then standing straight and mumbling a spell. Veronica making hitting fists. Frida baring her broke teeth and saying Billy's name. All them liked me once, didn't they? They liked me fine when he was alive and would put his hands on me so people could see but now that their hero was dead from my gun I guess they wanted me that way too. I didn't care. Is Dolores here? Now I am calling for her. Is Jose Jr. with her? Had the building burned down when she was sleeping? Had the bad men come to hurt her? Dolores? Dolores? I scream it out and now the women part and she is there dead-eyed with the baby and they are all in one piece. Jose Jr. is bruised, though, blue and green on the face and neck from where I'd tried to drown him. And Dolores is different. Her blank face opens hot and mean and hateful at me so she doesn't even look like my own sister no more, she looks like the rest of them; like they are all sisters and I am the stranger but I keep calling her hoping her eyes'll change back to the color I remember.

But they don't. Gloria is beside her moving her mouth and I hear Billy's name again. What's she saying? The mujeres are pressing together around Dolores and the baby tight as packed bricks and they are spitting their lowest words at me now, killer puta bitch whore pendeja. But what hurts is I can't touch my sister through them. I only see her stranger face behind their shoulders and hear her saying I don't know. The baby's crying. Gloria's got her mask off now and there's hellfire burning inside each eye the same as the time I caught her smoking that Lucky Strike cigarette. She hates me so bad. She is saying something nasty inside my sister's ear again and then she's yelling at me. Get out Get out, she says. The other ladies nod their heads, they got eyes like pointing fingers. They got things in their hands, too, the hair dye cans and hair-cutting scissors, needle tweezers, teeny death-sharp razors.

"What the hell you think you're going to do with all that?" I say. "Dolores. Honey, come here."

Dolores shuts her eyes. "Stop it stop it."

"She don't belong here," Gloria says.

"Dolores, please come here."

"She killed Billy! And look at what she did to Jose Jr. You don't got nothing left but that baby."

Jose Jr. is hurt worse than I thought, with those green thumbprints on his throat. I want to tell Dolores I didn't do that I'd never do that somebody else made me except I can't say it, all I can do is keep begging her. "Dolores. Let's go home. Let's go home."

But she opens her eyes and sees the blue bruised skin, the hit baby face that looks like Jose's and it is too much for her to take.

"Get out of here," she says, not looking at nobody. They are listening to her. All of us, waiting for her words. Then she says, straight to them: "Get her out of here."

And that's when the women come at me. They push tight together first, some of them shouting gutter Spanish, others mumble-cussing broke and ugly English and Gloria's talking all the time, saying, Go on! Go on! Go on! Her hellfire eyes are happy now. She's smiling. Now the women roar louder in no language at all, building up a boil till something breaks in the air and their feet lift off the ground like a storm wind's blowing them from the back. Somebody throws hair dye on my shirt so I look shot dead through the chest and belly and then I am bleeding for real, they're trying to pull the hair out my head and scratch the skin off my bones with their knife nails and scissors and even though I beat them off one of them tears my locket from around my neck. I try to run away but something's got me and then I see it's Frida, holding on to my ring finger and laughing. That's my engagement ring, the one he gave me. She can't have the one last thing that's mine! I curl my fingers into a fist and pull back, but shit them women are tough, they're going to bust my bones for kindling and set me on fire with gas and matches if I don't run, and I see I lost it all anyways. So I do it. I open my hand and the ring slides free and I do it: I run.

Through the steaming street. Past the yelling blue men. Past the dead man lying behind the yellow ribbon who I see now, he's face-up and staring at the raining ash and heaven clouds. Past the dead burned buildings and the gleaming cut glass, past the street signs blinking white one after the other, me so fast my feet don't touch. Later the mujeres would talk tall tales about me, tell their bedtime babies that sometimes a girl will grow so bad and evil-hearted she can turn herself right into a broom-flying bruja, why they saw it themselves, a bitch so wicked she could grow invisible wings and ride the air like a crow, like a stinging bee, light enough to slip out of law's reach.

It's a mystery even to me how I did it, how I saved my own life. I don't think none of us ever will know what happened that day. What I remember is I felt the wind and heard the sound of my sister calling me, and I was fast. Faster than a girl like me should be, faster than a tough-muscled boy, even, or a man. Because that's what I was, I was made of air, and so witch-quick I could slip the sharp hands of them furious and righteous and blood-hungry women chasing me out of town.

Garden of Eden

*I*f you take a map and spread it out and look at the pink and blue and yellow Southern California towns, you'll see a neighborhood they call Gardena, about six inches—that's thirty whole miles—west of East L.A. Gardena. Say it. Sounds like Eden, even like freedom, I think. I guess it's no different than eastside; there's a poor part and a rich part, dirty-kneed kids playing in the streets, women walking in their high heels to market, men coming home from work tired-looking as bloodhounds, sidewalks lined with brown palm trees and boxwood bushes and the roses pink as ladylips that come up in the spring. Gardena seems better to me, though. It doesn't got the same heat as inland east, the same molasses nights that make you snap your fingers and listen for the lovers whooping next door, that make you want to throw your head back and do some love-crying yourself. But there's still something sweet about it. Dolores doesn't believe me but I say the light's different here, you get kind of a lemony shine in the morning that brights the wings of the power-line-sitting sparrows and a quieter cool-colored dusk without all that red in the sky come sundown. A body can stretch her arms out in all that shade. You can hide in the shadows and come out into the lemon-light brand-new, too. I can, anyways. Nobody in Gardena knows my real name.

I live here now. I like it.

Not at first, after I got run out the eastside. Right then I was nowhere, I was nobody. I was a scuffed-up girl trying to fly through burned-down streets and when I landed there wasn't nothing anywhere for me but bushy-headed confusion. Nowhere to go but a hiding place; lock the door and pull the curtain lest those women find and get me, clip my wings. I wound up in Tarzana living in a motel room rented with Mama's money, watching black-and-white TV with the radio on and waiting for the mob to come knocking. The one thing for certain was court, the long marble halls with the navy suits and the talking mouths and that hump of a judge sitting on high in his black robe, holding on to his gavel. At first they said I'd committed murder, then they said I'd gone and slaughtered a man, which I thought was worse but my lawyer said was better. My lawyer told me, Say you're guilty, and so I did. In a long skirt, in a button-down blouse, in her low-heeled hand-me-down shoes. I stood in front of all them in the court and said Guilty and I thought, Now, God's hand's gonna strike me dead, but nothing like that happened. I said it and they wrote it down, then my lawyer pointed to my faded bruises and speeched about the self-defense, and that judge gave me five years probation.

Go on, click your tongue then. I'm sure enough used to it. After all this time I know the neighborhood women still like to sit on their porch steps drinking their ice tea in the thick of the middle-day heat and slap their knees while they go on and on about how I slipped the law. But I don't know, did I?

Nah, I didn't. If anybody slipped between the jail bars it wasn't me, it was a bruja whose skin I shed a while back and then buried in the yard. Maybe I still see her eyes in the mirror but I don't got her name anymore, and Dolores has gone and forgot about her, too, or at least forgave her.

Dolores.

*O*nce when Dolores and me were just chiquitas my hair caught orange fire and she saved me. The cigarette flame flickered hot and big over my head and it would have burned scars into my face or worse if she hadn't beat the killing thing off my skull. For days, weeks after, though, we could still smell it, the smoke on our skin, right up inside our noses. After a while it faded but it could come back sometimes even years later—the heat, the screaming, the smell and sound of hair sizzling. Who could forget something like that?

Well, not me. Not her either; not forever, anyway. I know there's families out there who run clean out of love. Mothers and daughters and sisters and brothers and daddies who hurt each other so bad there's nothing left to stitch up, put in a pocket, or rub gentle with a thumb. But me and Dolores got something different. See, a person doesn't save a swimmer from the sharks, then feed her to the lions. No sir! No, you love who you save more than anybody else in the world because they remind you of your best part, the beautiful fighter that's boxing behind your ribs. So I didn't worry about being like them families who chill too cold to ever say hello again never mind I love you. Even though those folks got thick blood tying them together, that's just not red-hot enough. But me and Dolores got more than blood. We got fire between us.

My job was to remind her.

The first thing I tried was words over the phone but every time she picked up and heard me breathing or saying Hey or Wait! she'd slam the receiver down before I could string two of them together. The next thing I did was write long letters but they came back fast bleeding all over with red stamps that said return to sender. She sent my postcards back too, and my tapes, and one night when I walked up to her door and yelled I'M SORRY I'M SORRY her lighted windows shut their eyes and the house went to sleep.

"Hush yourself," Mama said in my motel room, banging on the TV to get the color on. "She needs some time."

So I took the advice. I stopped my talking. I learned how to wait for her quiet, but I didn't do it invisible. I hitched my nerve up and crawled back into the neighborhood during daylight then watched for her outside her front door, and whenever she'd come out I'd wave. I worked at my penance hard. I sat on her front lawn or stood with one foot on the other right there on the sidewalk hoping it would rain on my head, but the weather never did me the favor. I got shamed other ways, though. The first few times the mujeres ran me off with kitchen knives and scratching claws, but I always came back. And after a while they left me alone more or less. They'd walk by me staring, whispering, laughing, crossing, cussing, maybe giving me a little push or pulling on my hair, but I stayed put and pretty soon the day came when I turned into another neighborhood crazy. The loca who waits for her sister.

It was funny feeling the change. Going from the hot tamale to the bruja bitch to the psycho singing to herself on the sidewalk. Then pretty soon that name burned off too like fog in summer, and I was nothing at all. The chicos would walk by and not kick me. The ladies stopped looking into my eyes. I passed my twenty-fifth birthday out there and didn't really mind. It wasn't too lonely because Dolores was behind the door. And there was the city around me, not my city no more but good company anyhow, the folks stamping their shoes and stray dogs

sniffing at the bushes, the birds flying and the bird-cats leaping, the sound of the freeway floating over the tops of the houses.
There was me, too, not the waiting crazy or the sex girl or old
maid but the me living inside my own skin.

One day standing in that good sunshine weather for the
sixth month in a row my brain stretched and expanded and I let
the world come inside it, and I could think thoughts wide as the
sky itself. I thought about God. I knew then that I was smaller
than that pebble there next to my shoe, and that the girl I used
to be was gone for good. And that's when it hit me: Who was
she? Who was me? What was her real name?

And then I forgot to answer those questions because
that's when Dolores opened her door.

"Hi," she said, then let me in, just like that, handing me
the baby and snapping her tongue about the mess she'd made of
dinner, a chicken dish that hadn't come out right. I told her don't
worry and went straight into the kitchen, added some bay leaf
and peppers and a splash of Tabasco and wine to the bubbling
pot then set it to a simmer and stirred slow while Jose Jr. tried
to talk his first words in his high chair. When we sat down to
eat we must have been a sight. Her smooth-headed, dressed in
pressed pastels and thirty-dollar shoes; me as bug-eyed as a street
preacher, clattering the shaking spoon on my teeth when I tried
to take a bite.

I couldn't taste anything again. The clock ticked and the
baby fussed over our small talk. I wondered if we'd go on like
this, faking like nothing happened, but then she reached over
to touch me.

"It's my fault he died, Rita," she said. "He'd be alive if
I'd kept him away from Victor. He'd be alive if I hadn't been
asking for all the police. Why can't I do it over? I wouldn't never
never say nothing about no police. Why can't I take it back?"

I reached out and held on, and if any old ghosts were peeking through the windows or floating up between the floorboards they left us alone right then. We stayed there rocking for a long time, not talking, but I'd swear we could both smell the smoke and hear the kindling crackle when the fire started again. And it wasn't the killing kind of fire, mind you, the kind that lighted the riots and made the trees dance. No, we weren't afraid of the flames because this was the kind of fire you can walk into and hold in your hands. It's the kind of fire you can live through.

*W*hen Eve got run out of Eden and saw all the lonely miles of dry brown grass, the rib-thin animals that needed killing, the tall trees that needed chopping, and felt the cold wind blowing over her naked skin, she must have trembled. I imagine she got on her knees and held up her shaking hands and prayed to the silent sky and said I'm sorry a thousand times while she tried to forget the sweet taste of the apple.

But that's justice for you. Justice is a pretty, shamed woman running for cover. Right?

Well, I say no. Not always. Me and Eve are the same in most ways but one. Where she got run out of Eden, I got run out of my home and straight into the garden, where the cool sundown colors calm me and the bright-winged sparrows sing me awake. That's why the Latina Leaguers like to go on about how I jumped away from the snapping jaws of the law, because I wound up here in Gardena free as the nighttime breeze that blows through town. But they're wrong about all that. Because the woman I used to be doesn't live here anymore, so there's nothing left to trap behind bars. She can't come if you call. Won't play nice in the backseat if you ask her to. And her ears don't burn if you start telling them old lies.

Where is she? Disappeared. I'm the one who took her place.

I changed my name from Rita Zapata Novo to Maria Pura Gonzalez so nobody here would know who I was. Maria Pura's nice, you think? Sounds regular and clean to me. Everybody here calls me that, even Dolores and Jose Jr. and Mama who I live with on a street whose name I won't tell you, just in case. I got another job, too, doing nails at a salon from nine to three six days a week, but down here I don't do many of the fancy manicures—these Gardena girls want a standard silk wrap or French tip instead of Day-Glo two-inch acrylic jobs and such. But I like it anyways. I go sssst at the gossip and grin at the tips and when I get off I watch the sun slide down through the sky from my porch, see the pale colors gather up in my glass. We're dancing into the year 2000 but I've got plenty of time now, plenty, and I don't rush at the future no more. I watch Jose Jr. grow up. Rub Dolores's shoulders when she comes home from her Rape Crisis Center or her Immigrant Clinic. Listen to Mama going on about this or that. And I sit here on this porch drinking my twilight wine and think about the questions I started asking outside of Dolores's front door.

So those neighborhood women shouldn't worry so bad; there's nobody left here that needs chaining up or whipping or even a talking to. That bad chica can't be found because a steady-minded manicurist named Maria Pura bought her sensible shoes and is busy walking around on her feet. Who can know what went through that old girl's wild mind, anyhow? How'd she get drove to such wickedness in the first place? Nobody can tell, not even me, really. I can barely remember her electric heart and hot mouth, how she laughed too loud and banged out her hips and turned every man's head and ran so fast she rode the air. Who was that girl, anyways? She wasn't me, was she? No, I don't think so. I don't remember any such thing.

Not usually, that is. Sometimes Dolores's bad memory gives way and she forgets to call me my new name.

"Rita," she'll say. "Hey, Rita?"

And I can't help it when she says that. I smile.